# THE COSMIC KNOT PARADOX

## BY JOHN HOWARD

The ISBN record for this series is available from Nielsen BookData
www.nielsenbook.co.uk/isbn-agency
Tel: +44 (0) 1483 712 215

Paperback ISBN: 978 1 0686668 0 3
Hardback ISBN: 978 1 0686668 1 0

Wesh Corporation Ltd
c/o Unit 114A, Business Design Centre
52 Upper Street, London, N1 0QH
www.cosmicknotparadox.com

# Warning!

This book is extremely blasphemous and contains significant and gratuitous profanity, as well as multiple descriptions of excessive alcohol consumption and drug abuse. Oh, and there's also quite a lot of violence, some bestiality, and several murders.

Do not read this book if you are religiously sensitive or easily offended.

You have been warned.

This book is generally dedicated to each and every one of the millions of people who, throughout human history, have been killed, tortured, manipulated, terrorised, coerced, or denied the right to freely express their beliefs and opinions by bigoted, theist zealots, determined to impose their delusional beliefs on the rest of humanity. More specifically, the dedication is to the twelve people barbarically murdered in Paris on 7th January, 2015.

In memory of:

Georges Wolinski
Bernard Maris
Mustapha Ourrad
Bernard Verlhac
Philippe Honoré
Stéphane Charbonnier
Jean Cabut
Elsa Cayat
Frédéric Boisseau
Franck Brinsolaro
Ahmed Merabet
Michel Renaud

**Je suis Charlie**

"To travel is better than to arrive."
**Robert M. Pirsig.**

# Contents

# Chapter 1
# Alien

Charlie awoke with a terrible hangover. He didn't usually suffer from hangovers, but this particular morning, his head banged and throbbed with every heartbeat and an intense nausea had invaded and overwhelmed what felt like every cell of his body. He imagined an army of tiny psychotic goblins armed with club hammers running amok inside his head.

The night before, Charlie and his partner, Lucia, had hosted a dinner for their close friends, Flore and Sylvain, who had invited another couple, Tom and Marion. Charlie and Lucia hadn't met Tom and Marion before, and with this particular evening marking something of a watershed moment in their history with Flore and Sylvain, the hosts had been worried that the presence of newcomers might result in a somewhat stifled evening; perhaps neutered and muted by trivial, polite small talk, rather than the fluid, uninhibited ambience they were used to. The reality had ended up being very different.

Early in the evening, a simple question had stimulated a conversation that continued throughout dinner and into the small hours. It had been one of those conversations that had very quickly taken on a life of its own; a pivotal, seminal discussion that captivated the imaginations of its participants to the extent that everybody present knew that their lives would take radically different courses.

Eventually, sometime after midnight, with a catastrophe of empty bottles already present, the conversation had finally given way to dancing, laughing and more drinking, which had continued until around four-thirty.

Charlie remembered the scene of devastation as he had stumbled to bed. There were full ashtrays, dirty dinner plates and glasses strewn throughout their usually well-ordered home, whilst a forest of empty bottles seemed to have colonised every surface, proudly proclaiming their roles as both accomplices and witnesses to the excesses of the night.

But the intemperance hadn't been confined solely to alcohol. Tom had distributed some sort of psychoactive substance that he'd called 'Placido';

part of a clinical trial he'd said, which everyone had trustingly accepted and, without question or diligence, enthusiastically swallowed like naïve, thrill-seeking teenagers.

'I'm too old to be doing this sort of thing,' Charlie thought to himself, wondering how many years he might have aged during the previous few hours – a full decade at least, he supposed, probably more.

The goblins attacking Charlie's head had now been joined by what felt like an alien serpent, writhing and twisting inside his abdomen, simultaneously gnawing at and constricting his internal organs. The sensation brought to mind a scene he'd seen in a film, and he imagined that at any moment some hideous creature might burst from his stomach and scurry away to a dark corner.

With the nausea rising in intensity and thinking that he might feel better if he got out of bed, Charlie took a deep breath and prepared himself for movement.

Slowly, mentally bracing himself for the pain that he knew would come with the light, Charlie cautiously opened his eyes. What he saw next would, for somebody in a normal physical and mental state, induce abject fear and near heart-stopping panic, followed by either sudden explosive violence or a scramble for the door; but Charlie's dreadfully debilitated state rendered him incapable of any fight or flight response.

There, standing silently at the foot of the bed, staring at him intently, was a creature that looked like an alien from a science fiction film. Charlie thought he must be dreaming or, more likely, was the first of Tom's test subjects to experience hallucinations from the experimental Placido that had been dispensed the night before.

"You're not real. Go away and let me sleep," Charlie said out loud.

Lucia stirred at the sound of Charlie's voice but didn't wake.

Charlie closed his eyes, hoping that when he opened them again the hallucination would be over.

# THE COSMIC KNOT PARADOX

# Chapter 2
# The Party

"So, here's one of those big, hypothetical questions for you. Imagine you found a deserted island and colonised it; made it habitable and self-sufficient. How would you want to run it?" asked Charlie.

"Wow, what a question! To properly deal with a topic like that would mean breaking all the rules about not discussing politics whenever alcohol has been consumed," Flore said with a smile as she topped up everyone's glasses.

"Yes, I know. That's why I asked it. We'll probably also end up discussing religion and a whole load of other topics that are meant to be taboo whenever booze is involved," Charlie replied.

"Yes, we'd end up covering absolutely everything," added Sylvain. "We'd get into themes like philosophy, economics, politics, and criminal justice. Then there are the broader questions about the values of the society you want to create, meaning you'd need to define morality, and, as you said, that would probably drag you into a debate about religion."

"Exactly. There would be so much to discuss," said Charlie. "Things like the sort of culture you would want to create; would you run the island as a sort of autocracy, or would you allow collective decision-making involving the people you bring to the island? What you might call a democracy.

"So then, would you have any sort of constitution and if so, what would be the principles and ethos to underpin that? And if you're going to have a constitution, you'd need to have some rules or what I suppose you'd call laws."

"And who's going to make those laws, and by what process? Then, of course, there's the question of what you do if someone breaks your laws. Are you going to have punishments? Fines? Prison?" added Sylvain.

"And how would you populate your island? Would you only invite people you know and like to come and live there, or would you accept applications from people you don't know, or maybe even just let anyone come and join you there?" said Flore.

4

"Then, there are all the tricky issues about finance. You'd need money to run your island and maintain whatever infrastructure you've built, so would you have taxes?" asked Charlie.

Flore and her husband Sylvain, both in their early thirties, were around twenty years younger than Charlie and Lucia. They were what people would describe as a 'handsome couple', almost like living examples of the bride and groom figurines typically found on the top of a wedding cake; or perhaps, a couple you might expect to see in a TV soap opera or advert. Flore, slim, blonde and pretty, and Sylvain, dark and handsome with piercing blue eyes. Their faces radiated both intelligence and pathos, to the extent that even from a distance, the casual observer would know that they were looking at bright, kind people.

Lucia, in her early fifties, looked ten or more years younger and regularly turned the heads of both male and female thirty-somethings with her striking good looks. Curvaceous but slim, a genetic heritage including Spain, Peru, Paraguay, Russia and Italy, had bestowed upon her the gift of a blend of high cheekbones, a lipstick model's mouth, light olive skin and long chestnut-coloured hair. If she'd been out somewhere, Charlie would often jokingly ask her things like, 'How many road accidents have you caused today, my love?' or 'Any cyclists crash into skips or parked cars today?'

Charlie, now mid-fifties had gone grey at the temples but otherwise had a full head of thick, blonde hair which he now wore almost shoulder length. He didn't see himself as good-looking, but Lucia always insisted to him that he was handsome, to which he'd reply, 'You're just saying that because you love me.'

The generational gap between the two couples was highlighted by the fact that Flore's parents were the same age as Charlie and Lucia and further emphasized by Charlie and Lucia's eldest children being only a few years younger than their friends. In addition to the age gap, there were cultural differences too. Charlie was the only English member of the group. Flore and Sylvain were both from France and Lucia from Spain.

Despite the disparities of generation and culture, conversation between the four was always stimulating, yet relaxed and easy, even when potentially divisive and polemic subjects, like tonight's, were raised. The two couples had become the best of friends, regularly enjoying evenings together at each other's houses; eating, drinking and talking, usually into the early hours of the morning. Two or three years before, Sylvain had given the group the name 'The Tipsy Dinner Society', and the name had stuck.

This particular Tipsy Dinner Society soiree, 16th October 2021, was much like many of the others that the two couples had shared. Charlie and Lucia had prepared a meal, and a large container had been filled with bottles of beer, champagne, white wine and lots of ice, and three bottles of red had been opened to give the wine time to breathe before being served with the main course.

However, tonight's dinner would be different because both couples knew it would be the last for some time. Instead of the usual early morning farewells of 'See you in the pub on Wednesday' or 'See you at our place in a couple of weeks', tonight's goodbyes would be more like 'See you in a few months', or 'Let us know when you can get time off work to come and see us', because the following day, after several years in London, Flore and Sylvain were returning to their native France to start a new life in Marseille. Although not the end of the story of their friendship, it was certainly the end of a chapter.

Additionally, with it being their last night in London and having struggled to be able to find time to meet up with all of their London friends during the preceding fortnight's flurry of farewell drinks and dinners, Flore and Sylvain had asked if they could invite their friends, Tom and Marion, to the dinner. "Tom's a bit crazy, but nice crazy; Marion's easy going and really good company. You'll like them both," Flore had said.

So, it was going to be an evening of six rather than four; three couples rather than two. Charlie and Lucia privately wondered whether the addition of two new people to the group might change the comfortable and relaxed dynamic they always enjoyed with their friends, but they both liked meeting new people and trusted Flore and Sylvain's judgement.

# THE COSMIC KNOT PARADOX

# Chapter 3
# Alien 2

With his eyes still closed, Charlie took a deep breath and then exhaled slowly and gently to steady his thoughts. Despite his throbbing head and the battle royal still raging in his stomach, he at least felt rational and lucid. For the second time that morning, he slowly opened his eyes, hoping that having taken the time to carefully settle himself, the hallucination would be over. To his horror, Charlie discovered that not only was it not over, but the alien now seemed even more real.

Despite its extra-terrestrial appearance, there was something oddly familiar about the strange creature standing at the foot of the bed, although Charlie couldn't recall of exactly what or whom. Most likely, he thought, his mind had colluded with Tom's Placido to recreate something he'd seen in a film, which seemed to be becoming something of a theme that morning. He was now deeply regretting the folly of accepting and taking an experimental drug from someone who, in essence, was a complete stranger. What had Tom really given them, Charlie wondered.

Screwing up his eyes, again hoping that this might make the hallucination stop, Charlie implored again, "You're not real. Go away!"

To his astonishment, the alien started to speak, and to his further incredulity, it sounded almost exactly like Boris Johnson.

In perfect English, the alien said, "I, err, am real, and I come in peace and mean you no harm. I wish only to, err, show you the future that you will create, so you can, err, learn from your mistakes before you make them".

This time, startled from her slumber by the strange voice in the sanctuary of the bedroom, Lucia did wake up, immediately screamed a scream of abject terror and, without a moment's hesitation, launched the glass from her bedside table at the alien with all the force she could muster. The glass struck the creature's face, shattering into a thousand pieces.

# THE COSMIC KNOT PARADOX

# Chapter 4
# Tom Sawyer

Charlie and Lucia's faith in Flore and Sylvain's judgement in inviting new people was entirely vindicated almost as soon as Tom and Marion arrived. With humility and empathy, the newcomers immediately offered their apologies for gate-crashing the dinner and expressed their gratitude for the opportunity of seeing Flore and Sylvain on their last night in London.

It very quickly became apparent that rather than detracting from the evening's dynamic, Tom and Marion very much added to it. They were interesting people, both scientists; Tom researching the causes of dementia, and Marion working in pharmaceutical research and development. Conversation quickly revealed that outside of work, both had a very diverse set of interests and a busy social life.

They were another handsome and unusual looking couple about the same age as Flore and Sylvain, and also French. Marion, tall, with the majestic elegance of a North African queen, and Tom, fit and slim – wiry, like a welterweight boxer. Charlie and Lucia remarked that Tom seemed quite familiar; it felt like they had met him somewhere before, they said.

Marion told them, "Oh, everyone says that about Tom. We even had that in the taxi on the way over here. The driver, who was about the same age as Tom, kept looking in his mirror, saying things like, 'I'm sure I know you from somewhere. Where did you go to school?' and, 'Did I take you to Heathrow last week?' I think Tom's just got one of those faces. It's a small world, so you may have met him before; only, if it was more than eight years ago, he wouldn't remember."

"Well, eight years is a long time. I struggle to remember people I've met the same day," said Charlie.

"No, it's not just that. Eight years ago, Tom had some sort of accident and doesn't remember anything about his life before that," Marion explained.

"What? You really don't remember anything from before eight years ago? Nothing about your childhood? Surely, your friends and family have been able to help you piece together memories," said Charlie, looking at Tom with a quizzical expression.

"I don't know who my friends and family are. I was found floating unconscious in the sea off the coast of France, near Monaco, with two gunshot wounds in my back. I woke up in a hospital bed in Nice and remembered absolutely nothing about being shot, why I was in the sea, or anything about my life before that. To the astonishment of the doctors, within a couple of days, physically, I was completely recovered, so the hospital had no option but to discharge me. Knowing my circumstances and that I had nowhere to go, one of the nurses took pity on me and said that I could stay at her flat for a few days. She'd said that amnesia after major trauma is quite common, but usually only temporary, and that my memory would probably return within a short time.

"That nurse was Marion's cousin and Marion was staying with her at the time. When I met her, it was pretty much love at first sight, and we've been inseparable ever since."

"Wow! What an incredible story. But how do you know you're called Tom if you don't remember anything?" asked Lucia.

"Marion named me Tom after the character Tom Sawyer, from one of her favourite books when she was growing up," Tom explained.

"I would have named you Jason. But how do you…" Charlie started to ask, but Tom interrupted.

"Please don't think me rude, but I don't really want to talk about this, and normally we never do," said Tom, casting a slightly reproachful glance at Marion, "I don't blame you for asking, and I understand your curiosity, because you've probably never met anyone like me, but I have this idea that talking about it and speculating about what happened, might create false memories and put the recovery of my memory even further out of reach. I'll just tell you that the only memory I have is a very vague recollection of an old lady, who I assume must be my grandmother, but absolutely nothing else. So, that's about all there is to say. You now know as much about my past as I do." Tom concluded.

Picking up a bottle of Cava from the ice bucket, Lucia broke the silence that had descended on the group.

"Who'd like a top-up?" she said.

# Chapter 5
# Alien 3

Despite the considerable force of the impact of the glass that Lucia had thrown at the alien, the creature appeared to be completely unharmed. With a small, almost imperceptible shake of the head to dislodge the shards of glass from its face, the alien suddenly reached out and firmly grasped Charlie's hand with its two long, bony fingers, that might better be described as claws. Calmly, but still sounding like Boris Johnson, the alien said, "Now I will take you to the future. Hold Lucia's hand and, err, try not to be afraid."

Instantly, the couple were transported through a swirling mass of fragments of light and flashing images. Moments later they found themselves in a clearing at the top of a hill on a small island surrounded by a turquoise sea. The clearing was a scene of devastation. It was immediately obvious that something terribly violent had happened there very recently. In the centre of the clearing were the remains of a small house; mostly just rubble, apart from what was once a chimney that rose perhaps two metres from the still smouldering ruins. On one side of the chimney, a carved stone fireplace, still complete with its mantlepiece, remained miraculously intact. A stone bust in the centre sat majestically, as if surveying the carnage and looking out towards the forest of trees and plants beyond the wreckage.

Now fully awake and looking dishevelled and angry rather than scared, Lucia said, "Donde esta mi café?" The alien ignored Lucia's demand for coffee. A moment later, Flore and Sylvain were suddenly and inexplicably both by the alien's side, Sylvain haphazardly clutching the creature's claws with one hand and Flore's hand with the other. Both looked completely dishevelled and disorientated and had very clearly woken only moments before.

"What just happened? Where are we?" said Flore.

# Chapter 6
# Wesh

Within fifteen minutes of Tom and Marion arriving and the formalities of introductions, apologies and thanks out of the way, the three couples were chatting and laughing together as if they had all known each other for years.

Sylvain told Tom and Marion, "Charlie's had this idea of finding an uninhabited island and colonising it." He then spent the next few minutes recapping what had been discussed before their arrival.

"So, what are you going to call this Island?" asked Tom.

"I've no idea, I've only just come up with the idea, so haven't given any thought to a name. Any suggestions?" replied Charlie.

"You could call it Wesh," Tom suggested.

"Wesh? What kind of a name is that? It sounds like a mix of West and Wish," said Lucia.

Tom explained, "Wesh is a French slang word with an Arabic origin. It got adopted by French youth, initially amongst the rap community in the poorer suburbs of Paris, called the Banlieues. It's one of those words that can be used in lots of different situations. It's sometimes used as a greeting or a farewell – a bit like the Italians use 'Ciao'; as an affirmation… 'Would you like another beer?'… 'Ah, wesh, bonne idée.'; as an exclamation of surprise… 'Wesh! I didn't know you were coming,' or as a way of describing something cool… 'Do you like my new car?'… 'Ah oui, très wesh'.

"It's a bit like how in English the word 'fuck' can be used in such a wide variety of situations to convey different meanings or add emphasis," Sylvain added, going on to give some examples, "Surprise…'What the fuck?'; insult… 'Fuck you'; annoyance or frustration…'Where are my fucking keys?'; disappointment…'Fuck my luck'."

"Yes, and John Lennon's last words… 'That's not a real fucking gun', or General Custer… 'Where the fuck did all those Indians come from'. Anyway, let's eat, I'm fucking hungry," said Charlie.

With heavy irony, Charlie explained that he and Lucia had made a special effort with the evening's menu because of Flore and Sylvain's impending move back to France.

"You'll be moving from this paragon of epicurean excellence to that barren gastronomic wasteland, where they'll make you eat unspeakable things like confit de canard, bouillabaisse, tartiflette, and a lot of dreadful cheese. So, to get you ready for the horrors of French cuisine and the shock of there being no fish and chips, all-day breakfasts, pork pies or microwaved chicken tikka masala, we've made a starter of scallops wrapped in Jambon de Bayonne, pan-fried in butter, and served with a saffron sauce with a hint of Pastis. After that we'll have a Boeuf Bourguignon, followed by a selection of those awful French cheeses, and to finish, a tarte au citron with a coulis de framboise. It probably sounds terrible, but it'll prepare you for your arrival in Marseille tomorrow."

Through the meal, the conversation returned to the idea of the island community, which was now being referred to as Wesh, L'île de Wesh and the Democratic Republic of Wesh. As the conversation progressed, the similarities and differences in the opinions amongst the group were revealed, with the biggest ideological divide being on the subjects of economics and politics, and mostly between Charlie and Flore.

If asked, Charlie would describe himself as being extremely socially liberal and a free market libertarian, often going on to explain the extent to which he believed in the ability of a truly free market, unencumbered by bureaucracy and interference, to improve and enrich people's lives. He would often qualify the 'libertarian' description, not wishing to be associated with what he would describe as 'the redneck MAGA nutcases', whom he felt had hijacked the label he had used for three decades or more. Nevertheless, he would passionately describe his scepticism of the ability of governments to do anything very well, apart from waste money. He strongly believed that the redistribution of wealth happened most efficiently outside of the tax system, and that punitive tax regimes resulted only in stifling opportunity and aspiration, making everybody poorer, and simply increasing the incentive for people to both avoid and evade paying tax.

Charlie liked asking his left-leaning friends whether they thought any government would have had the vision or ability to invent the internal combustion engine, smartphone, television, radio, MRI scanner, vacuum cleaner or even the post-it note. He'd follow up with questions like, "And do you think the government would be capable of delivering hot food from any one of a thousand different cuisines direct to your home in twenty minutes?"

Charlie would freely admit that twentieth-century capitalism had been a significant contributory factor to the ecological challenges of the twenty-first century but believed that the free market was uniquely positioned to solve those problems and that governments alone were simply too inept to be capable of doing so.

More recently, he had also taken to asking whether any government would have been able to develop and manufacture multiple Covid vaccines in less than a year without the help of those evil, profit-driven pharmaceutical firms.

What frustrated Charlie more than anything else was that the UK had failed to provide him with a political party he felt able to vote for, and for most of his adult life had been effectively disenfranchised by the awful choices British politics had offered. Whilst the Conservative Party were almost on the right side of Charlie's views on economic policy, Charlie believed that the Tories were mired in outdated, socially conservative traditional perspectives. A collection of little Englanders for whom decency could be achieved and evidenced simply by going to church on a Sunday, being a member of the right golf club, and making sure that one's shirt was always properly ironed and tucked into one's waistband.

In Charlie's opinion, a large percentage of these traditional Tories amounted to little more than parochial xenophobes, infected with a nationalistic superiority complex and the arrogant delusion of believing that they had complete moral authority and a monopoly on decency. He was revolted by the sexist, racist and homophobic views that they discretely, and often not-so-discretely carried around with them, and disgusted by their toxic mix of bigotry, hypocrisy and heartlessness.

The other political parties also fared pretty badly. Their economically leftist policies were obviously problematic, but it was their nanny-state approach to structuring society that Charlie found most abhorrent. Charlie wanted small, non-intrusive government; government that put doctors and nurses in hospitals and teachers in schools, collected the rubbish, fixed the roads, defended the nation, provided a safety net for those who genuinely couldn't provide for themselves, and not much else. More than anything, he didn't like the state meddling in his life or deciding what was good or bad for him.

His other big loathing was political correctness, or 'woke', as it had so insidiously and perniciously, in Charlie's view, morphed into. He considered himself extremely socially liberal and inclusive, and abhorred racial, gender and sexual preference discrimination, but over the previous decade or more, he had become increasingly frustrated by what he considered a hyper-sensitivity that had infected large swathes of society.

He viewed the rewriting of Roald Dahl's works as nothing short of cultural vandalism, and the persecution of the writer JK Rowling, by what Charlie branded as 'an army of disingenuous, self-promoting, virtue-hijackers' as simply disgusting. He reserved particular contempt for what he would provocatively describe as the 'actors and actresses,' who had so cynically joined the Rowling witch hunt, rather than defend the woman who had provided the platform for their fame and fortune.

Similarly, for Charlie, the demonisation of Harper Lee simply beggared belief. He considered her one of the greatest writers of the twentieth century, and that her magnificent 'Mockingbird' had set out racial injustice and inequality more poignantly and eloquently than any work of fiction before or since.

"So what if she wasn't black? Why should that disqualify her from writing about racial injustice? Doesn't that make the central message of her book all the more poignant?" he'd ask whenever the subject came up.

Charlie's favourite rhetorical question to summarise his dislike of woke was, "When did everyone become so fucking sensitive?"

In contrast, Flore regarded woke as a necessary antidote to endemic cultural and societal intolerance and prejudice, and would answer Charlie's question by stating, "We became so fucking sensitive when white people started putting black people in chains; when misogynists started burning women at the stake, and when moral bigots started beating and killing people for their sexual choices."

Flore's economic perspectives were as far to the left as Charlie's were to the right. In earlier conversations, during other dinners, Flore had described her political perspectives as, 'Very far left of centre, almost communist.'

She was certainly very politically knowledgeable and earned her living working in a senior management role for a company that provided software to help political parties analyse and engage with their audiences. The role exposed her to political parties globally, along with the dynamics of their national political ecosystems.

Earlier in her career, Flore had worked on Bernie Sanders' 2016 Presidential campaign and strongly identified with Sanders' social democratic policies, rejection of neo-liberal capitalism and his commitment to eliminating economic inequality. As such, Flore believed strongly in the redistribution of wealth through a progressive tax system and regarded capitalism as being responsible for many, if not most, of the world's bigger problems.

At the same time, she was passionate about the freedom and rights of the individual to live life however they might choose, free from discrimination, repression, or persecution.

Despite Charlie's 'unwoken' perspective, his liberalism and commitment to personal freedom was one area where his and Flore's political views were aligned. They also found themselves very much in agreement on environmental issues, although Flore's lifestyle and green credentials were far more faithful to the views she expressed than Charlie's, who still enjoyed powerful, petrol-engined cars and rarely remembered to take his 'bag for life' to the supermarket.

Despite having political labels that might be described as polar opposite, their agreement on environmental matters and personal freedom meant that were you to plot the things that they cared most about as a Venn diagram, the central ellipse where their opinions and beliefs overlapped would be quite large.

Although less forthright and vocal in casual conversation, Sylvain's work as a documentary filmmaker, often covering subjects with a social injustice theme, revealed a political and socio-economic outlook broadly similar to Flore's.

Tom and Marion were also left-leaning, very individualistic and liberal in their outlook, and rather more than a hint of anarchism was very definitely evident in Tom.

# THE COSMIC KNOT PARADOX

# Chapter 7
# La Movida Madrileña

Although Lucia didn't have much interest in politics or economics, the social outlook that very much defined her had been formed by her having arrived at adolescence at the height of a seismic cultural shift which had started in Madrid, where she had grown up, and quickly spread to other Spanish cities. Known as La Movida Madrileña, the movement emerged after Franco's death in 1975 as a hedonistic counterculture to the dictator's socially repressive thirty-six-year regime.

By the mid-1980s, La Movida Madrileña was in full swing. It was similar to London's Swinging Sixties twenty years earlier, but further fuelled and perhaps given extra edge by the anarchistic influences drawn from London's next countercultural revolution, the 1970s Punk movement.

With a significantly more socially conservative starting point than 1960s London, La Movida Madrileña represented a much more extreme swing from ultra-conservatism to ultra-liberalism. Having endured almost four decades of autocratic social repression at the brutal hands of General Franco, Madrid's young embraced and asserted their new freedoms with a passion, reinventing social and sexual politics in the process.

With Franco dead and homosexuality decriminalised, thousands of men and women burst out of the closet like corks from Cava bottles; even straight men cross-dressed just for the thrill of their freedom to do so, and for the first time in decades, writers, musicians and artists found themselves able to write, sing and paint whatever messages they wanted to convey from their hearts, without fear of torture, imprisonment, or death. It was a time characterised by an explosion of creativity and a robust reclamation of personal freedom.

Enrique Tierno Galván, Madrid's Mayor at the time, publicly told the young to go and have parties, play music and make love in the parks. The Madrileños took his message to heart and Madrid partied like no city has partied before or since. As well as the parks and city squares, they partied in the bars and clubs which between them provided round-the-clock, twenty-four-seven drinking venues. When the local bars would finally close at around three in the morning, the clubs would play host until seven, eight or nine, by which time the local bars would be open again. Madrid became the city that truly never slept.

Having witnessed, and experienced first-hand, the sudden change from the socially oppressive environment of her childhood to the anything-goes freedom of her mid- to late-teens and early twenties, Lucia's outlook was very much defined by this ultra-liberalism and an unshakeable belief in the right of the individual to make their own choices.

# Chapter 8
# Acid House

Hang on, if we're going to talk about something so potentially wide-ranging, these might help," Tom said, as he reached into his pocket and produced a small plastic bag containing little squares of paper. "I wouldn't normally do this on a first date with new people, but they might help stimulate the imagination."

"Is that what I think it is?" asked Sylvain. "Acid? Surely, you're not serious? We'll end up thinking we're all superheroes or that the lamp has turned into a dragon or something." The mood in the room had very suddenly changed.

"Yes, and we've got a flight to catch tomorrow morning, Tom. And you don't know Lucia and Charlie well enough for this sort of thing. Maybe it wasn't such a good idea to invite you tonight," said Flore, looking both angry and a little embarrassed.

"It's OK. It's not a problem, we're not offended," said Lucia, intervening to diffuse the uncomfortable moment, "But I don't think some wild acid trip is a great idea. I'm not sure that any of you are ready for what Charlie might turn into on acid. We've not done it, but you need to trust my intuition on this, it could be horrific."

"Hey, thank you for that Lucia, but you don't need to worry," said Tom reassuringly. "This is actually part of a clinical trial. We're experimenting at work with micro-doses of a combination that includes Lysergic Acid Diethylamide, LSD to you, and Psilocybin, which is the active compound in what you would call magic mushrooms. We're calling it 'Placido'. We believe that what we've created might be effective as both a prevention and cure for dementia, but first, we need to test the treatment on healthy adults below the age of sixty. Provided there are no significant side effects, we'll move on to the sixty to seventy age group.

"So far, out of more than two thousand test subjects, there have been no serious adverse effects; just one poet who wrote more than one thousand pages of near-perfect iambic pentameter verse in two weeks. Poor guy had to be put into a medically induced coma to deal with the sleep deprivation, followed by a month-long caffeine detox and several hours of surgery to remove the callouses that had developed on his writing hand," said Tom.

Charlie interrupted, "Lucky he wasn't a pornographer. The blisters and carpet burns would have taken months to heal."

"That's funny," said Tom, generously, "but the poet was the only problem case, and anyway, had lied about his use of other substances, which was probably the real cause of his manic writing. Almost all of the other test subjects not only reported an absence of any negative side effects but showed a significant improvement in memory, mental agility and problem-solving. Critically, nobody reported any hallucinations." Reaching into his bag and producing a handful of pre-printed documents, Tom continued his explanation, "So, the risks are minor, and you'll be helping us to take another step towards eradicating dementia. If you're happy to be part of the trial, I'll need you to sign these disclaimers."

"I'll take part," said Sylvain, without hesitation. Lucia nodded her agreement. Flore said, "Me too if it's going to help cure dementia," while Charlie added, "Well, I can't remember what I had for lunch, so count me in."

With that, Tom distributed four of the forms, four pens and four little squares of paper, each one printed with the Imperial College coat of arms on one side and 'Placido' on the other. All four signed their forms, returned them to Tom, and then swallowed the little squares of paper.

"Well, I'm glad we sorted that out. Sorry that I doubted you, Tom. Anyway, back to Wesh. What rules will we have?" asked Flore.

"Well, none of us seem to like other peoples' rules, so I suggest we have just two. Rule one, there are no rules, and rule two, obey the rules," ventured Charlie.

Marion was the first to speak up. "Surely that depends on how many people end up living on the island. If it's just the six of us, then Charlie's idea is probably fine, but what if it's a thousand, or even just fifty? In that case, we'd probably need to have some rules to set expectations and standards. Suppose some guy came to live on the island and started hitting on all the women, nobody would be able to complain or do anything about it if there wasn't a rule about sexual harassment."

"Yes, but unless we import a complete set of laws from say, France or

England, it would take more than our lifetimes to come up with a complete legal framework, and it seems obvious to me that one of the major reasons that this idea is interesting is because, like Charlie said, none of us particularly like living by other people's rules," said Flore.

"Well, we could import French or English law and then repeal the laws we don't like," Sylvain suggested.

Lucia suggested, "How about we just start with one main rule, which is 'do no harm'. So basically, everyone can do whatever they want, provided it doesn't harm anyone else. Then we can get together from time to time to agree on any new rules that we think are needed."

"That seems like a good idea. What else? How are we going to decide who can come and live on the island?" said Charlie.

"Hang on, we're not finished on the subject of rules. We've only talked about the things we want to prohibit, which for now we've decided is harm, but we haven't talked about the things we want to encourage and promote," said Flore.

"What do you mean?" asked Marion.

"Well, this is an opportunity for us not just to live our own ideal lives, but to create a blueprint for a social utopia for other countries to follow. "We could be a model for social liberty, tolerance and inclusivity, which I think we all feel strongly about. And we can use our collective imagination and intelligence to evolve a better, fairer and more sustainable way of living, where greed isn't part of our vocabulary. What we discover and create could be replicated elsewhere to make the world a better place," said Flore.

Charlie was quick to respond.

"How are you going to get anything done without greed? It's the secret sauce for any society that wants to motivate creativity and hard work. Greed isn't a very nice-sounding word, but societies need to offer people the opportunity of reward for their vision, creativity, and effort. Of course, as an alternative, you could do things the way they're done in communist regimes and try to motivate people through fear instead. Just look back to the twentieth-century Soviet Union to see how well that worked out. Anyway, isn't there a bit too much mission creep going on here? We started by talking about colonising an island to create a place where we could lead happy, comfortable lives and now you're talking about reinventing the Ten Commandments. If the island ever got big enough, the best thing we could do would be to evolve an alternative to the common forms of democracy and hope that it gets adopted elsewhere."

"An alternative to democracy? What are you talking about? There is no alternative. Democracy is the cornerstone of any civilised society," said Flore.

"Democracy, at least how we know it, has a lot of flaws," said Charlie, "It doesn't always work that well. Don't get me wrong, I am an advocate of it, but only because it's the least-worst option. The autocratic alternatives of dictatorships and theocracies are just terrible, but don't forget that Hitler got his big break democratically; America elected George W Bush, not once but twice, and then followed up by putting Donald Trump in the White House just eight years later and will probably do so again if the scumbag doesn't end up in prison. Vladimir Putin came to power through a democratic process, as did Robert Mugabe, Hugo Chavez, Nicolás Maduro, and Aleksandr Lukashenko. I could go on and on. History is littered with examples of dreadful individuals who won elections and then went on to subjugate, exploit and abuse the very people who gave them their mandate. Democracy, at least in the way it's been practised so far, is far from perfect."

"So, what's the alternative?" asked Flore.

"For the moment, I'm not going to say. Just think about the problems I've described and recognise that democracy isn't perfect," replied Charlie.

"You can't just toss a problem like that into the conversation without offering a solution," said Flore

"Yes, I can. I just did. And I'm not going to offer an alternative right now. I've got a few ideas which I'll share with you when we've found Wesh – but not before," Charlie said with a smile.

"Well, at least tell us the basis of your ideas and how you came up with them," Flore countered, fishing for a hook that she might be able to bait to get Charlie to elaborate.

"I'll tell you that my idea is to create a system of representative democracy without all of the problems that normally come as part of the package. But I'll leave it at that for now. The ideas only came to me this evening, just a few minutes after taking Tom's Placido. Looks like Tom and his team might be on to something," Charlie replied.

"That's interesting," said Tom, reaching into his bag for a notebook and hurriedly scribbling something on a page filled with other scrawled notes.

"Why do we need to even think about democratic systems now?" said Lucia, "Aren't we getting a long way ahead of ourselves? I mean, there are only six of us and you're thinking about a system for a nation of millions. I think we'll be able to make fairly good decisions just by having a simple show of hands, and if a decision is evenly split, we can just toss a coin."

"Agreed. Delegating decision-making to a coin is a great idea," said Tom, smiling, "We can revisit Charlie's ideas when we've found Wesh and he's actually thought of something. So, just to recap, we've decided on a 'do no harm' rule, and Charlie might have an alternative to democracy, but we don't know yet. It's beginning to sound like a great foundation for a society." Everyone laughed. "What else?"

"Well, wouldn't it be great if, as a result of solving the problems of living on an island with no infrastructure, we ended up inventing things that could improve people's lives in other parts the world," said Flore.

"Yes, we can sell our inventions. It'll cover the cost of developing the island. And with what's left over we can buy Ferraris, yachts, and private jets," said Charlie, enthusiastically.

Flore was quick to reply, "No, Charlie. We'll give the inventions to the places in the world that need them most. This is the whole point for me. If I get to the end of my life without having made a difference and a positive contribution to humanity, even if it's something small, I'll feel as if I've failed. I know that this island idea was just your way of getting us all talking about some of your favourite topics, but the more I think about it, the more plausible it seems. It would be a huge challenge, but we could do it, have a great time doing it, and the things we learn in the process could benefit the wider world. Let's say we found an island with little or no fresh water but came up with some new, clever, and more efficient way of removing salt from seawater to satisfy our need for drinking water, it would be almost criminal not to quench the thirst of the millions of people living in a state of water poverty. Imagine if an idea like that could be scaled, and not only used to create drinking water, but to irrigate land and maybe even to turn desert into forest or agricultural land."

"Wow, you think big. OK, let's add 'help the wider world wherever possible' to our list," said Tom.

"I've got something else to add," said Sylvain, "Tom's Placido stuff seems to have done its job for us tonight as a stimulus for creative thinking. None of us are seeing or doing anything weird, and in the space of an hour, we've come up with some great ideas. So, how about everyone on the island has a regular Placido dose or maybe even a monthly acid trip?"

"Are you insane?" said Charlie, "It would get completely out of control with idiotic decisions being made and all sorts of stupid accidents. Don't misunderstand my perspective on this; the libertarian in me thinks that nobody should be prohibited from doing whatever they want, just so long as, like we've said, it doesn't harm anyone else, but I struggle to see how monthly state endorsed acid trips could be a very good basis for a healthy society."

"If Sylvain is suggesting regular doses of a quantity of a psychotropic substance typically taken by recreational LSD users, then you're almost certainly right. It would be a dreadful foundation for a society and most likely have catastrophic results, both short- and long-term. But in addition to the very positive results we're seeing in our research into dementia, there's a lot of compelling data from a multitude of studies that have shown that regular micro doses of certain psychoactive substances can have all sorts of beneficial effects on creativity, cognitive function, self-understanding, and as cures for anxiety and depression. I mean, look at how quickly you came up with your ideas for alternatives to traditional democracy that you might or might not share with us at some point in the future," said Tom.

"Great. I can see the newspaper headlines. 'Drug Cult' and 'Stoner Island'. You were talking about creating a blueprint for a social utopia to serve as an example for other countries. You need credibility to achieve that, otherwise no other country, no matter how messed up, would risk copying anything you do to solve their problems. There'd be too much political risk," Charlie said with certainty.

"Maybe they would if they saw what we were able to achieve in terms of creativity, invention, wellbeing and happiness. I mean, it might take time, and we'd need to support everything we claimed with good scientific evidence, but we've got two world-class scientists amongst us already," said Flore.

"OK. Let's add it to the list," said Charlie, a little grudgingly. "So, we've got an advanced judicial and legal system underpinned by our single 'do no harm' law. Key decisions that we can't agree on through discussion will be delegated to the flip of a coin, which will probably be most of them because there are six of us. We've decided it'll be a good idea to be stoned most of the time, and we're going to reinvent democracy when I've thought of something. Oh, and last but not least, there's our 'help the wider world' initiative; or, put another way, make all of our best ideas open source instead of making any money from them. Watch out G7, Wesh is coming. Anything we've forgotten?"

"Yes, if you're going to find this island, you're going to need to buy a boat," said Tom.

"Well, fat chance of that. I spent ninety per cent of my net worth on tonight's meal. But, no worries, I'll check down the back of the sofa tomorrow morning. Maybe there'll be a few hundred thousand that I've forgotten about," said Charlie, sarcastically.

"Maybe you'll win the lottery," replied Tom.

"Hmm, that's quite unlikely." Said Charlie.

"Why? Someone has to win. It could be you," said Tom, mimicking the voice used in the lottery adverts.

"Mainly because I don't play the lottery. Always thought of it as a stupidity tax," Charlie replied.

"In that case, you're probably right, it's unlikely you'll win," said Tom.

As the evening continued and the empty bottles piled up, the Wesh discussion gradually gave way to more trivial subjects, and eventually to just dancing, drinking and laughter. Finally, at around four o'clock, Flore reminded Sylvain that they had a flight to catch in only a few hours and insisted that they had to leave.

Marion said that they would also head home, adding, "If I don't take Tom home now, he'll still be here drinking and dancing at ten or eleven in the morning, maybe even mid-afternoon. Even at thirty-something years of age, he's like a hyperactive child. God knows what it must have been like for his mother. I feel so sorry for her, whoever she might be." Everybody laughed.

As the two couples put on their coats and scarves, Flore turned to Lucia and said, "Hey, we've got what I think is a Swiss cheese plant that there wasn't room for in the removal van, and anyway wouldn't have been able to take, because of Brexit. If you'd like it, please come and get it in the morning. I'll leave it in the front garden for you. We call her 'La Monstera'. She's lovely, please look after her."

As the three couples exchanged their goodbye hugs, Sylvain said, "Come and see us in Marseilles. We'll be waiting for you."

"Come and see us in Limehouse. We've got a view over the marina. It's like St Malo on a really bad day. Anyway, sorry we have to leave so early," said Tom, laughing, as he stumbled out of the door and down the street.

# Chapter 9
# Back to the Future

"This is L'île de Wesh, and the date is 16th April 2155. The four of you colonised this island in 2025. I have brought you here to tell you about your journey here, your purpose in life, and to let you work out how you might stop this from happening, again," the alien said, casting his arm around him like a Roman emperor to indicate the devastation.

Now looking quite angry, Lucia shouted, "Coño, mi café. Ahora mismo."

Charlie spoke up, "Listen, I don't know who or what the fuck you are, or why the fuck we're here, but you're not going to get very far with anything until she gets her fucking coffee, so for fuck's sake, sort it out or fuck off."

"Just like how I said last night," Sylvain whispered to Flore, "did you notice how many different ways he was able to use 'fuck' in that sentence? What an incredible word."

The alien sighed with frustration, but the next second was holding a tray of four coffees which he offered around the group. A moment later, a paper bag containing four croissants magically appeared in his other hand.

"I couldn't eat anything. I feel like throwing up," said Flore.

With that, like a magician, the alien turned over his clawed hand to reveal four pills: two red and two blue. "It's OK, it's not like, err, in the Matrix. The red and the blue pills are the same, they're just from different batches."

"What are the pills? What do they do?" asked Flore.

"They're a hangover cure. They'll, err, get rid of your headaches and nausea," replied the alien.

Sylvain was the first to reach out and take one of the pills. Tentatively, and conscious of the fact that it was the second time in twelve hours that he would take something of unknown provenance and effect, he put the pill into his mouth and then swallowed decisively. The others watched him intently, not sure what to expect. After just a few seconds, Sylvain reached out and took a croissant. "I feel fine. The headache and nausea are completely gone," he said, immediately looking better.

Almost in perfect unison, the others all took one of the pills, which they popped into their mouths and swallowed with a gulp of coffee. Within a few seconds, one by one, each member of the group began to look markedly better. Lucia got up from where she had been huddled on the ground and drew a deep breath, then asked where she could buy the pills. The alien ignored her question. The haze cleared from Charlie's eyes, and the colour returned to Flore's previously pallid, rather sick-looking complexion. Sylvain had already finished his coffee and croissant and asked if there were any more. With another sigh, the alien magically produced another four coffees and another bag of pastries, this time pain-au-chocolat.

"OK. So now, you can tell us why we're here and what the fuck is going on. And how can it possibly be 2155? And how did you do that thing with the coffees and pastries?" asked Charlie.

"As I said, I will, err, explain everything; why you're here and what went wrong, in the hope that you might do things differently next time," replied the alien.

"What do you mean by 'what went wrong' and 'next time'?" asked Flore.

Dispassionately, the alien replied, "You all died here yesterday, 15th April 2155 at 15:44 local time. Your deaths were caused by stupidity and were, err, entirely preventable."

An array of confused expressions spread across the four human faces.

"Died yesterday? 2155? I would be over one hundred and sixty years old. How could I possibly be alive in 2155?" asked Flore, a mix of incredulity and frustration dominant in her tone.

"Be calm and listen carefully, I will err, explain everything".

"Any more coffee?" asked Lucia, hopefully.

# Chapter 10
# A Night at the Movies

Suddenly, the alien was holding a large flat-screen television in one hand and what looked like an orange in the other. Propping the television against the fireplace and plugging a cable from the television into the 'orange', the alien explained, "Normally, I would share my thoughts telepathically, but none of you have that capability yet. So instead, I shall project my thoughts onto this primitive televisual device, so that you can see what I wish to convey to you as a movie. It will be like watching a Netflix series. Are you sitting comfortably? If so, I shall begin."

Like a group of kindergarten children, the group all nodded their agreement. Moments later, images of the plants around the clearing appeared on the screen which then cut to the scene of a Mediterranean harbour full of yachts. The alien's narration played through the television's speakers, but the creature showed no sign of speaking, and instead sat cross-legged and motionless, leaning against a boulder, seemingly in a sort of trance.

Let's start at the beginning. "You all set off from a small harbour near Marseilles on Charlie's yacht, the 'Salty Box of Frogs', at just after two in the morning on 25th June 2025.

"It was a completely spontaneous and unplanned voyage that you only decided to make just an hour before, during a particularly heavy drinking session. The decision was made by tossing a coin. Heads would mean the coin had chosen to immediately start the 'Search for Wesh', that you had jokingly talked about for the previous four years, usually after many drinks, but had never actually got around to planning; tails would result in just opening another bottle."

The screen now showed Flore, Sylvain, Charlie and Lucia sitting on the stern deck of an impressive-looking yacht, chatting and laughing with drinks in their hands, and a bottle of champagne chilling in a pewter ice bucket. The yacht wasn't the gin palace type of vessel that one might see in the harbours of Monaco, Puerto Banus or Sotogrande, but was nevertheless an impressive and elegant-looking craft, probably fifty feet in length.

In a state of surreal astonishment, the group watched themselves engaged in a conversation they had never had. Every detail, unique facial expression, distinct gesture and manner of speaking was being portrayed on screen with complete authenticity. They watched Sylvain take a coin from his pocket and flick it spinning high in the air. It spun for what seemed like an eternity, appearing to defy gravity, then on its descent, the coin was caught, covered, and revealed to the group.

"Heads!" exclaimed Sylvain, "To Wesh and beyond!"

With the decision that had been delegated to the coin now resolved, and the excitement and trepidation of such a sudden and life-changing choice having been made in just moments, all four became almost instantly sober as the excitement rose and the adrenaline coursed through their veins.

Hurriedly, but with purpose and clarity, they prepared the Salty Box of Frogs to sail and then, opened another bottle. Once they'd made it out of the harbour, they set the main sail, plotted a course towards Greece, set the boat's autopilot, finished another two bottles of Champagne, and then promptly fell asleep. The screen showed the yacht moving through the Mediterranean, interspersed with scenes of the four asleep in the main cabin with empty bottles rolling around them as the Salty Box of Frogs carved its path, rising and falling through the swell.

The four awoke at just after ten the following morning to find themselves being propelled at speed by a strong north-westerly wind that had already taken them to within a few kilometres of the western coast of Corsica. Conscious of the irresponsibility of having fallen asleep drunk, Flore remarked that with the myriad of ferries, cargo ships, and other yachts that must have been at sea in perhaps the busiest part of the Mediterranean, they had been exceptionally lucky to survive the night and not crash into something. All four agreed that they would be more careful during the remainder of their voyage. Charlie asked if anyone fancied a Bloody Mary with breakfast.

The day before, hours before the decision to start the search for Wesh had been decided by the coin, Sylvain had insisted on a trip to a nearby food market where he kept finding local 'specialités de la region', telling his friends, "Ah, you have to try this," and simultaneously interacting between the group and the market traders, "This is amazing...un kilo, no deux kilos s'il vous plait....".

At a fruit stall, Sylvain explained that he was going to go and get something special but returned a few minutes later, empty handed and looking rather disappointed.

"The guy I wanted to find wasn't there. His stall was closed and one of the other market traders said something about an accident," Sylvain told the other three.

Looking perplexed, Flore asked, "What was it you were after?"

"It was going to be a surprise, but it doesn't matter – I'll find it another time," Sylvain replied.

In any case, surprise or no surprise, the galley of the Salty Box of Frogs was now very well stocked with food. So well stocked, that every cupboard and chiller cabinet was filled with fruit, vegetables, fish, and meat.

"We're going to need a bigger boat," Sylvain said, as he emptied the last bag, squeezing four shark steaks into the remaining space in the fridge.

By the following evening, the Salty Box of Frogs had passed Sardinia and by the evening, as the group tucked into their côte de boeuf dinner, was halfway to Sicily. After just five days at sea, the Salty Box of Frogs was amongst the plethora of islands of the Aegean Sea, and as if guided by a divine hand, had passed Crete on a north-east course, slipped between the Islands of Naxos and Paros and was headed towards Turkey, when on the sixth morning, Flore called excitedly from the helm, "Come and see this."

Sylvain, Charlie and Lucia rushed outside and following Flore's pointed finger, looked ahead to see an island, perhaps ten or twelve kilometres away, rising majestically from the sea. It was no more than five or six kilometres from one side to the other and appeared to be mostly green. The group looked at each other and, as if suddenly telepathically connected, said in perfect unison, "Wesh!".

An hour later, the anchor was dropped in a small cove and, too excited to lower the dinghy into the sea, all four dived into the crystalline water and swam ashore.

The rest of the day was spent exploring the island with its forest and dense vegetation. It was like a tropical paradise. A stream ran through the trees, cascading over rocks and forming pools that overflowed to more pools below, before arriving at the beach they had swum to from the boat. The jewel in the island's crown, at the centre of the island, high on a hill, was a pretty stone house shielded from view by boulders and trees.

# THE COSMIC KNOT PARADOX

# Chapter 11
# La Villa Strangiato

On one side of the house, a natural spring bubbled from the ground, the water collecting in a deep pool, big enough to swim in. The water that overflowed from the pool was what formed the little streams that ran downhill through the forest.

The house was encircled by dozens of fruit trees. Fed by the abundant water from the spring, the trees were all heavy with fruit. Oranges, apples, and peaches were plentiful. There were lemons and limes, persimmon, dates, walnuts and almonds. Walking over to an apple tree, Charlie saw that it had been shrouded in netting, presumably to protect the fruit from birds; but on one side, the netting was broken. As Charlie reached in and up towards the hanging fruit, Flore exclaimed, "Don't! Look at the sign".

There, on the trunk of the tree were the words, 'Don't Eat!', and below, 'Défense de manger', and below that 'Nicht Essen'. Then, finally in Greek, 'μην τρως'. Ignoring the warnings, Charlie picked a perfectly ripe apple and took a bite. The apple was sweet and crunchy.

"Wow! This is the most amazing apple I've ever tasted," Charlie enthused, "Anyone else want one?" But, with appetites dulled by the excitement of the discovery, and deterred by the warnings, nobody else was interested.

Further away from the house, a cluster of olive trees stood with stoic presence, their branches hanging like tired arms laden with dark green fruit. Under the trees, goats and chickens were feeding on the fallen olives. As the group approached, everyone noticed that the animals weren't scared and seemed almost oblivious to the presence of the excited visitors.

Having absorbed the spectacle of the goats and chickens, the group turned to walk towards the house. Charlie thought he heard someone shout "Arsehole!" It was a quiet shout, if such a thing exists, sounding sort of half-shouted, half-coughed; like an errant schoolboy might deliver an insult to a teacher; deftly dispensing their slur into the anonymity of a full classroom with the simple, but ingenious disguise of a cough. But, turning around, nobody was there. Just the plants, trees, goats, and chickens.

A sign next to the house's weathered front door read 'La Villa Stran-giato'. Venturing inside, a simple kitchen greeted the group. A few very old-looking copper-bottomed pans hung from a rail next to an antique wood-burning stove. On a long and wide wooden shelf above the cooker, there was a selection of simple white plates, bowls and serving dishes. Opening the rustic wooden drawers and cupboards revealed very little apart from a few knives and forks, but no food.

Beyond the kitchen, a rustic table and six chairs provided a dining area, and next to that, a sofa and armchair had been arranged facing a large fireplace. Three doors along the wall on the left of the room were presumably bedrooms. At the far end of the room, French doors opened onto a stone patio, and to one side of the doors, there was a small bathroom with a washbasin, toilet, and shower.

Lucia flopped onto the sofa and started to say, "Oh what a beautiful fireplace," but then, in a shocked tone, said "Oh!... Oh, my god!" Raising a finger, she pointed to the wall above the fireplace. There, chiselled into the stone chimney breast in bold capital letters was a single word.

# 'WESH'

The astonished group approached the chimney to look closer. Flore noticed that there on the mantlepiece, propped up against a marble bust was a white envelope, hand-written in spidery script and addressed to 'The Tipsy Dinner Society'.

"That's us!" exclaimed Flore, hurriedly opening the letter. Inside, a sheet of parchment was scrawled with the same untidy script as the envelope.

*Dear Flore, Sylvain, Lucia & Charlie,*

*Welcome to Wesh. Astonishing you arrived safely. Well, actually, not so astonishing. I'll explain when I see you.*
*Make yourselves at home. The place is full of booze and food if you can be bothered to find it.*
*Help yourselves.*
*Happy tipsy dinners.*
*Oh, and remember the proverb, "On a journey of discovery, always press ahead."*

*See you soon.*

*Your host*

*P.S. Don't eat the fruit in the garden.*

All four stood open-mouthed, staring at the letter, then the wall, then at each other again, trying to comprehend what they had just seen and read. Finally, Sylvain broke the silence.

"Anyone fancy a gin and tonic? Apparently, this place is full of booze, we just have to find it."

As the four rifled through the shelves and cupboards looking for the Gin, Lucia said, "Whose place is this? And how do they know about Wesh? And what was all that about some proverb? On a journey of discovery, always press ahead. I've never heard that proverb."

A look of clarity spread across Flore's face, "That's not a proverb. It's a coded instruction. The letter was propped against the marble bust... shoulders and head....press ahead....press a *head*!"

All four raced back to the fireplace and stared at the bust.

"He looks kind of familiar," said Sylvain.

"Nobody you know though," said Flore pointing to a chiselled inscription at the base that read, 'MLBS MD', "MD are the Roman numerals for the year fifteen hundred. MLBS must be the sculptor's initials."

"Surely not! It can't be," said Sylvain, "Those are Michelangelo's initials. I read an article about him last week. Michelangelo's full name was

Michelangelo di Lodovico Buonarroti Simoni…MLBS. Michelangelo would have been about twenty-five years old in the year 1500, just around the time he started selling his sculptures. Wow! If that really is a Michelangelo, it must be worth millions."

"That's all really interesting, but who's going to press the head?" asked Lucia. Charlie said he would do it, and with a trembling hand and much trepidation, reached out, put his hand around the elegant marble scull and pressed down. At first, nothing happened. Then, a few seconds later, accompanied by the sound of whirring metallic wheels and pulleys, the wall next to the fireplace slid back to reveal a flight of stairs leading down to a basement.

With hearts pounding, the group crept carefully and silently down the stairs, as if in fear of waking some monster or whatever other horror might be lurking in the darkness below. At the foot of the stairs, they found a huge room that looked like an industrial kitchen. Ominously, the door through which they had entered started to close with the same mechanical noise as when it had opened, finishing with a heavy and rather menacing clunk.

Most of one side of the room housed a series of large industrial-looking fridges and freezers. Gingerly opening the door of the first fridge, Sylvain discovered that the fridge was stocked with hundreds of bottles of beer. The next fridge contained bottles of Schweppes tonic at the bottom and dozens of bottles of gin at the top, now beginning to glisten as the warm sea air started to condense on the chilled glass.

The third and fourth fridges were full of food. There were meats, vegetables and more than fifty cheeses all carefully and beautifully wrapped and labelled. Next, the freezers. The first was full of ice cubes, the second was also full of ice cubes, but the last two were packed with meats and vegetables.

On the wall opposite, an array of cupboards stood floor to ceiling. Opening the doors revealed a myriad of different types of food. Rice, lentils, chickpeas, beans and other dried foods, all neatly labelled and arranged, filled the first. The next was full of preserved vegetables; then a cupboard packed with jars of preserved fruit and conserves. The last two were stocked with every type of tinned food imaginable; everything from baked beans to confit de canard, cassoulet and Japanese unagi.

At the far end of the room, a long stainless-steel worktop with an impressive range cooker to one side and a large, deep sink to the other, completed the space. A dozen or more machines and gadgets sat on the worktop and the shelves below, while pots and pans hung neatly from hooks on the racks lining the walls. This was a professional kitchen that would be the envy of many restaurants. The space in the middle of the room was dominated by a long table and twenty chairs.

"Wow! Imagine the dinner parties we could have here. Let's explore some more," said Flore.

At the other end of the kitchen, next to the staircase, were two more doorways. The door on the left led to a corridor more than fifty metres long with ten rooms along one side, each one a bedroom complete with an en-suite bathroom. On the other side of the corridor were five more doors. Behind the first was a fully equipped gym, sauna and swimming pool; the next was a lounge area with sofas and chairs, and a bookcase covering the entire ten-metre length of the room. The third room contained a fully equipped recording studio, complete with a Steinway piano, more than twenty guitars, two full drum kits and what seemed like every musical instrument that had ever been invented.

The fourth room was equipped with a lot of very sophisticated electronic equipment, most of which, none of the group had ever seen before and had no idea what purpose it might serve. Computer monitors covered one wall and a big control panel, with perhaps two hundred buttons or more, filled most of the surface of a desk at the other end of the room. The buttons were all labelled with place names which included what seemed like every one of the world's major cities. Some cities had several entries; there were at least ten 'London' buttons, including 'London, Limehouse', 'London, Mayfair' and 'London, Stoke Newington'.

At the far end of the room, a huge safe silently but unambiguously declared by its very presence and stature that only the worthy would be permitted to enter its inner sanctum. Made from highly polished stainless steel and titanium, with fingerprint and retina scanners to lock and unlock the huge door, it looked like the type of device one might find in the vaults of a Swiss bank.

To the left of the safe was another door, behind which a huge walk-in wardrobe housed a dizzying array of garments. It was like a theatre costume store. Four, ten-metre-long racks held the most eclectic collection of garments imaginable, men's on the left, women's on the right. Clothes at the beginning of the rail were quite contemporary, but as the group ventured further into the room and along the rail, the clothes became increasingly older. Labels above the rails read things like, '1960s – US – Casual', below which there were items such as flared denim jeans and flowery shirts. Further along, below '1930's – UK – Formal', a sombre pinstripe suit with a bowler hat hung from the rail.

On the women's side, the section '1920's – US – Cocktail' contained elaborate dresses, some with huge feathers attached. At the end of the room, floor-to-ceiling racks held a large selection of footwear – again, men's on the left, women's on the right, and in the middle, a long, wide desk with a mirror behind was home to a vast selection of makeup and perfumes. The fragrances were all unbranded with hand-written labels. One read, 'France – 1940 to 1960'; another, 'England - Late Victorian Era'. Removing the cork stopper released the fragrance of roses and violets.

Sylvain said, "Hey, this one says 'England – Medieval', I didn't know they wore perfume then." As soon as the top was removed, a pungent aroma of body odour, urine, excrement, and rotting straw filled the room. Sylvain quickly replaced the cork saying, "Wow, that's disgusting! Whoever lives here really likes dressing up and takes it really seriously. Maybe they're an actor or something." Flore looked pensive but said nothing.

Going back out into the corridor and along to the fifth and final door, the group found another heavily protected entrance. Just like the safe, there were fingerprint and retina scanners on the wall next to the door, but in addition, beams of red light crisscrossed in front of the door.

As Lucia reached out to touch the door's smooth titanium surface, her hand broke one of the light beams. Immediately, a loud, stern recorded voice boomed, "Warning – Do not attempt entry without first using the fingerprint and retina scanners. Further attempts at unauthorised entry will result in electrocution".

Sylvain pointed to a sign on the wall. It read:

**"WARNING!**
**DO NOT ENTER.**
**DANGER OF DEATH"**

"Wow, whoever built this place really doesn't want anyone to get in there," said Lucia.

"What could be inside?" wondered Sylvain.

"Maybe it's full of money," Charlie said.

"Perhaps there's a collection of important artworks. More things like that Michelangelo sculpture upstairs," ventured Flore.

Lucia just sighed and said, "Who cares? Let's go and explore the rest of the place."

Back in the kitchen, attention turned to the other door, behind which, was another big room, but separated by a full floor-to-ceiling glass wall. On the other side of the glass was a fully equipped laboratory. It looked like the set of a sci-fi movie. Entry to the laboratory was via a glass 'pod' at one end of the glass divide. A large green button with 'OPEN' stencilled in white suggested that it might be the way in, and a press on the button vindicated that theory as the door to the pod slid open with a Star Trek-sounding whoosh.

There was only enough room in the pod for one person at a time and Sylvain volunteered to be first to go through. With some trepidation, he stepped into the pod, and as the door whooshed shut there was a sudden flash of blue light followed by a mist of some sort of gas that descended from a vent in the ceiling. A moment later, the second door opened, and Sylvain stepped into the laboratory on the other side of the glass divide.

"I'm in and I'm OK," he called to the others.

One by one, the rest of the group followed; each individually wondering whether they would be able to get out again, but saying nothing, so as not to spoil the adventure.

Inside, there was what seemed like every possible type of laboratory machine. There were centrifuges and sterilizers, microscopes and scales, together with other more obscure devices that none of the group could name. Racks of Petrie dishes in both chilled cabinets and glass warming cabinets lined one of the walls, and what looked like an industrial freezer carried a prominent yellow triangle with the words, 'Warning! Minus 230 Degrees Centigrade' on the door.

Still in a state of shock and awe, each with a thousand questions tumbling through their minds, the group decided to leave the lab to explore back on the other side of the glass. An identical 'OPEN' button on the inside permitted their exit, and one by one, the four adventurers whooshed back through the pod to the other side.

There were three distinct areas. In one corner of the room was what looked like a very big microwave oven. Bold letters on the door read, 'FUSION 5000', and a kitchen bin containing just eggshells and banana skins stood next to the machine, together with a box of Kleenex tissues.

"Banana skins and eggshells!" exclaimed Sylvain, "In the sci-fi world, those are the two raw materials needed to make nuclear fusion work. According to the stories, when combined in the right way, trace elements in the eggshell bind with other rare compounds in the banana skin to make a substance that's ideal for nuclear fusion. Surely, it can't be. That technology is at least twenty years from being a reality."

In the middle of the side wall, a mass of thick pipes emerged from what looked like a covered well. Following the pipework, they fed into a series of big industrial-looking containers and then onto more tubes.

"This is an industrial water desalination plant," Charlie remarked. "It must be what's providing water for the house and irrigating the land outside."

The third area was again behind a glass wall with another whoosh pod to get in and out. Inside, a rack of computers occupied the wall on one side, whilst above a desk, the full width of the room was occupied by a dozen screens attached to the back wall of the room. A light touch on the computer mouse on the desk brought all of the screens to life, each displaying a myriad of charts and graphs, tables of flashing numbers, and pages of scrolling news. Astonished, Charlie quietly whispered, "This is a trading room."

All four stood momentarily speechless until Sylvain said, "This place is a bunker. It's like a very high-end panic room. It's got a power source, a water supply, and an information stream from the outside world; everything you would need to live comfortably, and with enough food for twenty people to eat well for two years or more."

"This is too much to take in," said Lucia, "Let's have that gin and tonic."

With that, she loaded a tray with a bottle of gin, some tonic, an ice bucket and a lemon and the group retraced their steps up the stairs, through the sliding door and back into the old house.

# Chapter 12
# Them, They and Their

The next day, everyone awoke, still in the living room. Flore and Lucia occupied the sofa. Sylvain was slumped in the chair, while Charlie was sprawled on the floor, having seemingly used the flagstones of the fireplace as his pillow. Empty bottles littered the floor.

Charlie complained that his chest felt uncomfortable. It was like a dull ache on both sides, he told the others. Remembering that at one point during the booze-fuelled night, having lost Sylvain's 'heads or tails' coin-toss challenge, he'd had to satisfy his side of the bet by attempting to break-dance for three minutes, and then lost three further coin-toss bets over who would drink the line of tequila shots that Sylvain kept lining up.

It didn't seem to matter which side of the coin Charlie chose, each time the coin landed and was uncovered it would be the opposite.

"I injured myself last night, perhaps slept in a strange position; or maybe, it's just alcohol poisoning from Sylvain's stupid coin-tossing drinking game. Anyway, I don't feel good. My entire body aches and my chest hurts," said Charlie, with a pained expression. Sylvain chuckled.

Having unanimously resolved not to drink for at least the remainder of the week, Charlie and Sylvain prepared breakfast, remembering not to use any of the fruit from the mysterious and enigmatic host's garden. Over croissants and coffee, the discoveries of the previous day were discussed.

There were so many questions. Who was the host? And how did he or she know they were coming? How could this place be called Wesh? Was this all something that was pre-ordained, controlled perhaps by some invisible divine hand? With so many questions and no answers to any of them, it was decided that even though the experiences were quite freaky, so far at least, they weren't 'bad freaky'. Lucia suggested it would be best to just go with the flow, enjoy the experience and at some point, the host would arrive and hopefully explain everything.

Once breakfast was finished and the cups and plates had been cleared away, the four trekked back down the path, through the magnificent forest, down to the beach. On the way, Charlie noticed that the pain in his chest felt worse and that it was now quite swollen. Perhaps a muscle strain from the break-dancing, maybe an insect bite, or possibly, he speculated, some new hangover symptom that he'd not experienced before. Still, it was a beautiful day, and arriving at the tranquil beach with the blue water gently lapping the sandy shoreline, he quickly forgot the discomfort. After a short swim to the Salty Box of Frogs, the dinghy was lowered into the water and loaded with the clothes and what was left of the food and drinks, then taken ashore.

It took three trips up and down the steep path through the forest to get everything to the house, at the end of which, everyone was hot and sweaty from the exertion. Sylvain suggested a cold beer. "Just one, to cool us down," he said. Flore and Lucia didn't want beer, so they opened a bottle of champagne. Thus, the resolution made only a couple of hours earlier was broken. And so, it continued for the remainder of the day; slightly more restrained than the day before, but another full day "à la sauce" as Sylvain had described it. Beer and champagne flowed while a lunch of barbequed souvlaki was prepared, and bottles of red wine were open when the food was ready. Lunch consumed the afternoon, then stealthily morphed into dinner, with more grilled meat, bread, salads and yet more red wine.

The big shock of the day came at just after eleven that evening. Sat around the table outside on the flagstone patio, partway through the second bottle of gin, Sylvain slurred, "Charlie, I have to tell you…you're a top guy, and…I've never noticed before, but you've got great tits. I mean, really, first-class tits. Bravo, mon ami."

A panicked and hurried check with both hands confirmed that although quite drunk, Sylvain was indeed quite right. A staggered scramble through the house to the bathroom mirror followed, knocking over chairs on the way. Tearing off his T-shirt in front of the bathroom mirror revealed the full extent of the horror, as Charlie discovered that what, only a few hours before, had been a slight swelling, perhaps an insect bite or muscle strain, was now a pair of quite large and perfectly formed breasts. They were probably a D cup, possibly even a double D. Perfect, pert nipples bounced and bobbed as if elegantly choreographed as Charlie sobbed, "What the fuck is happening to me?"

Appearing through the bathroom doorway, Lucia calmly said, "You're going to need one of these," as she held out a red bra, "Sylvain was right, you do have great tits. Wow, this is an experience I wasn't expecting."

Still in shock, with the brutal discovery making any sense of perspective or priority impossible, Charlie protested, "But, but, I don't want a red bra. I'll look like a cheap twenty-dollar hooker. Don't you have a blue one?"

Within a few minutes, Flore and Lucia had gently and sensitively persuaded Charlie that the red bra was his best and only option and were helping him to put it on, carefully adjusting the shoulder straps until it was a comfortable fit.

Sylvain had offered to help but, rather ungraciously, Charlie just told him, "Fuck off! You're not touching my tits."

Turning to the door and heading out of the bathroom, Sylvain shouted, "I was only trying to help…. fuck, why is he so moody?"

Charlie shouted after him, "Don't call me he! From now on you can refer to me as they."

# Chapter 13
# Prometheus

Back outside and sat around the table again, Charlie with the red bra now comfortably fitted, and everyone with a large Margarita that Sylvain had prepared, the sea could be heard gently lapping on the beach below, perfectly complementing the sound of crickets from the forest behind. Heavy scents of jasmine and rosemary filled the air. It was a magical night.

There was no moon, but with the new round of drinks, Sylvain had had the presence of mind to bring some candles on the tray, which now flickered hypnotically on the table. With this wonderful ambience and being with friends who now felt more like family, Charlie's mood lifted.

"I'm sorry I was so grumpy and rude Sylvain. I know you were only trying to help. It's just, this is all a bit of a shock".

Sylvain told him that he understood and not to worry.

"Well, now I've got my own buoyancy aids, I guess I won't need to wear that lifejacket while I'm out on the boat," Charlie joked. "Although will I still know how to drive a car?" Flore threw the wedge of lime from her drink at him.

"Seriously though," Charlie continued, "how has this happened? The only thing I can think of is that the day before we arrived on the island, I got up to brush my teeth and mistakenly put Lucia's HRT gel on the toothbrush instead of toothpaste. Because I was quite hungover, it took me a while to realise, so maybe…"

"That's, err, not the reason", said a voice from the edge of the patio.

Startled, all four turned towards the direction of the voice to see the strangest-looking being stepping forward from the shadows and into the candlelight. Two metres tall, with smooth delphine skin and a large, teardrop-shaped head with huge black eyes, it looked like an alien from a science fiction film. Instead of hands, the creature had just two long, bony fingers, a bit like a langoustine's claws.

Flore and Lucia screamed the loudest screams that had ever left their bodies, and Charlie fell backwards off his chair.

Calmly, Sylvain took a sip of his Margarita and said, "Evening Tom, what took you so long?"

"Tom!" screamed Flore, her voice trembling with fear, "How do you know its name, Sylvain? How?"

Lighting a cigarette and taking a sip of his Margarita, Sylain said, "I'll do my best to explain. This is going to be hard for you to understand because I barely understand it myself, but this is Tom, as in Tom and Marion. Tom from London. He…."

The other three stared back at him, incredulous expressions silently conveying their collective disbelief, to the extent that their astonished faces stopped Sylvain from speaking. Before he could gather his thoughts to continue, the creature interrupted, "Sylvain, let me, err, explain."

Taking a seat at the table next to Sylvain, the alien started to speak.

"Hard as this will be for you to comprehend with my unusual appearance and voice, I am indeed the Tom you, err, remember from London."

Looking at Flore, the creature asked, "Do you remember your last night in London in 2021 before you moved to Marseilles? We talked, laughed, drank, and danced until four in the morning".

Flore and Lucia both nodded. Charlie was still rubbing his head where it had hit the ground when he had fallen off his chair, but the others could see from an almost imperceptible nod of his head that he remembered.

"We talked about colonising an island, calling it Wesh and how we would live; whether we would have rules and laws; how we would make those laws and who we would invite to join us. I have come back from the future, from the year 2155 to be precise, to try to help you."

Flore interrupted, "Come back from the future to help us? What do you mean?"

Tom continued, "Yes, I've come back from the future, and this isn't the first time. I've visited you more than a hundred times already, both before and after now, to help you in some way. You could say I've been your guardian angel.

"The first time you left that harbour near Marseilles, you made it less than five kilometres out to sea before, at two thirty-seven in the morning, just after you had all fallen asleep, drunk, you crashed into the ferry to Algiers. The Salty Box of Frogs sank in less than a minute, and all of you drowned.

"So, when I discovered this and the timing of your accident, I visited the boat at two-thirty, seven minutes before the collision, found you all asleep inside, surrounded by empty bottles, and steered you onto a different course, so that the Salty Box of Frogs would avoid the collision with the ferry.

"You all thought that the boat's autopilot had brought you safely around the toe of Italy, into the Aegean and on a direct course straight here, but I intervened no less than seventy-four times to avert disaster during that voyage.

"And this isn't the first and only time you've arrived here," Tom continued.

"What? I've never seen this place before, not until the day before yesterday," Charlie protested, "And why have I got tits?"

"I'll explain about your tits in a moment, but about you not having been here until a couple of days ago, that's entirely true in this thread of the multiverse," Tom replied, "but there are infinite other threads that make infinite yesterdays and infinite todays. There are infinite tomorrows too."

"This is too much to understand. What are you saying?" said Charlie, still rubbing his head, and now looking very confused.

"What I'm trying to explain to you is the concept of the multiverse. Each choice you make, big or small, together with all of the external factors present at the time you make those choices, takes you off on a different journey through time, with different outcomes not just for you, but everyone and everything around you.

"I've tried to allow things to take their natural course as much as possible, but every time one or more of you have made choices with catastrophic outcomes in one multiverse thread, I have intervened to make it possible for you to continue to live on in a new thread. A new space-time continuum.

"For example, the first time you arrived here on Wesh, it was very different from how you see it now. There was no house, no forest and no stream. There was no fresh water and no fruit trees, just sand, rock, and dusty, dried earth. When I arrived, the Salty Box of Frogs was wrecked on the rocks, because you didn't secure the anchor properly.

"I found the four of you sat in a circle on the beach, staring at each other with eyes the size of dinner plates, surrounded by the booze bottles, all empty of course, that you'd managed to salvage from the boat before it sank. The four of you were completely stoned out of your minds, having also consumed, in less than a week, the twelve-month supply of LSD that Sylvain had acquired at the food market on your last day in Marseilles. You were all so stoned and so dehydrated that there was nothing I could do for you and by the following morning, all four of you were dead."

"But I didn't bring any LSD. I couldn't get any before we left," protested Sylvain.

Tom again raised a claw, "I'm coming to that, be patient. So, that thread of the space-time continuum had reached a dead end, but I was able to travel back in time three weeks, called Charlie a few days before you set sail, and casually dropped into the conversation that I'd just heard from a friend whose boat got wrecked as a result of a poorly secured anchor. "Then, having sown that seed of paranoia in Charlie's mind about boats getting wrecked on rocks, I just let events unfold and visited you again at the same point in time that I'd visited you before.

"That second time, the boat was still floating and was securely anchored about thirty metres from the rocks. Without the shock of the boat getting wrecked, you'd at least managed to build a shelter, and having finished the food on the boat, had been living off fish you'd been catching from the beach with an improvised fishing rod and barbequing on driftwood.

"But you'd still drunk all the booze, and Charlie and Sylvain were halfway through the acid, so within another week, Lucia and Flore had moved back to the boat for safety, and Charlie and Sylvain, having fried their brains with the LSD, were throwing rocks at each other from opposite ends of the beach. It was quite a scene with Charlie shouting, 'I am the King of Wesh' and Sylvain shouting back, 'Non, je suis le Roi de Wesh….submit to my authorité as your King or I shall taunt you a second time with my superieur French phallus.'

"When I tried to speak to them, they took one look at me and my 'unusual' appearance and then cried like babies for two days. That didn't seem like a very good foundation for the utopia we had talked about creating, so I travelled one month back in time so I could properly deal with the LSD problem.

"Do you remember that last day in Marseilles at the food market? Sylvain told you he was going off to get something special, a surprise, but returned empty-handed. Remember that?"

"Yes," said Sylvain, "Like I said, I didn't get any LSD, the guy who sells it on the nectarine stall wasn't there; the other traders said there'd been an accident."

Tom smiled, "Exactly. Well, almost exactly. He wasn't there that time. But he had been there in the two multiverse threads before that, so I had to deal with him."

"What do you mean, deal with him?" said Flore, looking shocked, "You didn't…"

Tom interrupted, "No, I didn't do what you're thinking, I just called Charlie's friend Pippa. She took care of it. We knew she would because we had used her before."

# THE COSMIC KNOT PARADOX

# Chapter 14
# Assassin's Creed

Tom explained to the group that they might find what he was about to explain rather shocking, but then, without pause, started to tell the story of how Pippa dealt with the problematic nectarine vendor.

"Pippa knew exactly what to do. Within twenty-four hours of my call, she had travelled to Marseilles, broke into the LSD vendor's flat, whose name by the way was Claude, and installed hidden cameras. She spent the next two nights watching his every move from her hotel room nearby.

"She discovered that every evening, about an hour before going to bed, Claude would give himself a hot water enema whilst masturbating to a video of Marine Le Pen singing La Marseillaise.

**cosmicknotparadox.com/video1**

"The following day, while Claude was working at the market, Pippa once again entered Claude's flat. She altered the plumbing to the tap that Claude used for his enemas by incorporating a temperature-triggered valve and a cylinder of compressed hydrogen that she hid in the bathroom cupboard. She then modified the 'dirty' end of the enema hose with a new, more flexible piece of rubber.

"That night, Claude returned from work at his normal time, cooked himself a dinner of andouillette and potatoes, watched some TV, and then started his bedtime routine. He got his video of Marine playing on his phone, which he propped up against the bath taps, ran some water to raise the temperature, then inserted the tube and turned on the water again, only this time, it wasn't water, it was hydrogen gas at three hundred Bar of pressure.

"Just as Pippa had intended, the modified end of the tube instantly expanded inside Claude's bowel, meaning that the tube couldn't be removed or forced out by the pressure. During the following nine seconds, Claude inflated like a balloon. His abdomen was more than triple its normal size when the laws of physics intervened, and Claude exploded. Pippa showed me the video she'd captured using a hidden camera. She was very pleased with her work. 'Rather messy, but quite quick. On balance, perhaps a bit too quick, but I'm quite happy with how things turned out. I love the bit where his liver hits the bathroom mirror,' she told me."

"All four were stunned into silence, struggling to take in what they had just heard. After a few moments, Lucia asked, "But what about the police?""

"Oh, the Police weren't interested, not at first anyway. Claud had a long history of sexual deviance," Tom explained, "The year before, he turned up at a Marseilles hospital clutching an old upright vacuum cleaner, the handle stuck out in front of him like a big erection, with the base of the machine covering his crotch. The emergency staff immediately saw that his trousers were completely soaked with blood. "Turns out, he'd read something online about how vacuum cleaners are better than girlfriends, and how they 'suck but never complain', as he'd explained to the astonished medical staff. Unfortunately for Claude, his vacuum cleaner was one of the old-style machines with the revolving brushes. It took over four hours of intricate surgery to separate Claude from his mechanical lover, and then another three lengthy operations to surgically reconstruct his shredded penis.

"The year before that, Claude had decided to expose himself whilst ascending the escalator at Notre-Dame-du-Mont metro station in Marseilles. Unfortunately, his pubic hair got caught in the moving handrail and the soft skin of his scrotum was then also dragged into the mechanism, leaving poor Claude screaming in agony for almost the entire eighty-metre ascent of the escalator, until another passenger, who by a bizarre coincidence was Marine Le Pen on a fund-raising visit to Marseilles, had the presence of mind to press the emergency stop button. That experience probably explains Claude's subsequent obsession with her.

"A catalogue of other events like these, stretching back more than fifteen years, started when Claude was a teenager and somehow managed to superglue his penis into his teacher's ear. When the Police arrived at the school, Claude was manically shouting, 'You never listen to me, so hear this.' With that background, the Police just assumed that the whole hydrogen enema thing was just one of Claude's sick perversions that had gone terribly wrong."

"You said that it wasn't the first time you had used Pippa. What else has she done for you?" asked Flore.

"I'll tell you about that a bit later," replied Tom.

# THE COSMIC KNOT PARADOX

# Chapter 15
# La Monstera

"But this is insane," said Lucia, "How can you travel through time? And sorry to ask, but why do you look like, well, an alien? And what's happened to your voice? I mean, why do you sound like Boris Johnson?"

"Those are all good questions," Tom replied, "I'll get to why I look and sound the way I do, but as far as the time travel is concerned, it's surprisingly easy when you know how. Essentially, it's where quantum mechanics intersects with biology and chemistry."

"How so?" said Flore.

"OK, so I was telling you about that last night in London, just before you left for Marseilles the following morning, which was a Sunday. We all had a great time and had plenty to drink. Charlie had said that the following day he was going to go to your flat to collect that plant that you had called 'La Monstera', but the following day he had such a bad hangover that he just spent the whole day in bed and didn't retrieve the plant.

"The day after that, I had an accident on my bike and ended up spending the afternoon in Accident and Emergency with a very deep gash on my forearm, a few centimetres above my wrist. The doctor at the hospital had told me I had been very lucky and that whatever had cut me had missed the Radial artery by just a few millimetres. She closed the wound with twelve perfect stitches, bandaged my arm and sent me home, telling me to be more careful in future.

"Anyway, somehow, I don't know how, on the Tuesday I awoke with a strong feeling that Charlie still hadn't collected the plant. It dominated my thoughts throughout the day, so straight after work, I got the bus to Stoke Newington, intending that if it was still there, I would take it to Charlie and Lucia. I thought it would be a nice surprise for them.

"The plant was indeed still there, so I picked it up and started to carry it down the street towards their flat. Almost as soon as I took La Monstera into my arms I started to feel an inexplicable sense of calm and a strange bond with the plant. At the same time, with my cycling injury from the day before, I found it quite painful carrying something so large and heavy. Feeling a little bit guilty, I stopped walking, booked an Uber and took the plant home. It just felt like the right thing to do."

"That's all great, but what does the plant have to do with time travel?" asked Charlie.

"I'm getting to that," Tom replied, "So, a few days after I took the plant home, I woke up one morning feeling terrible. I had a fever, a headache, brain fog, a terrible pain behind the eyes and a dreadful cough. A lateral flow test confirmed the obvious. I had Covid. The symptoms were quite bad, but not bad enough to need medical help, so I took a couple of Placido tabs; remember those? They helped a bit with the headache and brain fog, but I still felt terrible.

"Marion had been working away in Scotland for a few days, so I called her to tell her my news so that she could decide whether or not to end her trip early and make the five-hour journey home. She decided she would return, but knowing how easily I get bored and that I was going to be home all day with nothing to do, before setting off, she called Dan at our local shop and arranged for a stack of newspapers and magazines to be delivered to the flat.

"Less than half an hour after speaking to Marion I was flicking through National Geographic magazine and found an article about the etymology of ancient civilisations. The article had been written by a researcher who had found what he thought were hieroglyphics on the wall of a cave that had appeared after a mountain slide near the border between Peru and Ecuador.

"The researcher was convinced that some of the symbols were early iterations of some of the letters of the modern Western alphabet. There was a photo of the wall of the cave with what looked like text carved into the stone. But as soon as I saw the photo, I knew the researcher was wrong…barking up the wrong tree, as you say in English.

"It was so clear to me. The image on the cave wall wasn't text, it was an eroded drawing, and what was left of it was a bit like a child's join-the-dots picture. To prove it to myself, I took a pencil to the photo in the magazine and drew continuations of the marks on the cave wall where the stone and the cave drawing had been eroded by time. I was right. It was a drawing of a plant…a Monstera…exactly the same as the plant I had brought home a few days before. The shape of the leaves, the length of the stalks, the spread, height and proportions of the plant. Everything was the same."

The four were now transfixed and silent. Tom continued, "So, I started thinking, why would someone go to all that trouble, celebrating the image of this one plant when the place where they were living was perhaps the most diverse place on the planet in terms of both fauna and flora?

"I quickly concluded that the plant had to be special in some way, and the most obvious reason I could think of as to why it might be so special, was that maybe it had some kind of medicinal property. I quickly thought about my own debilitated state, got out of bed, carefully removed some of La Monstera's smaller leaves and hurried to the kitchen.

"The exertion caused me to break into a sweat and my legs felt wobbly, but I persevered. I chopped the leaves as finely as I could, put them in a pan, added some water and brought the pan to a boil. Within a few minutes, I had a dark green liquid. It smelled like coffee and chocolate with a hint of peppermint.

"Carefully, I strained the liquid into a glass and then wondered if it really was a good idea to drink it. I considered the possibility that the plant could be poisonous and that maybe the drawings on the cave wall had been intended as a warning to others. I thought that maybe I should wait and discuss it with Marion – after all, she would be back in a couple of hours. She could take a sample of the liquid to work for it to be tested to find out if it was safe to drink. But, I reasoned, the aroma didn't smell like anything dangerous and, in any case, by now my curiosity was intense.

"So, throwing caution to the wind and, taking a deep breath, I gulped down the entire glass of the green liquid. It tasted just like it smelled - coffee and cocoa with a peppermint aftertaste.

"Almost immediately, the room started to spin. I felt dizzy. Flashes of coloured light in amazing kaleidoscopic shapes filled not just my vision, but it felt like every cell of my very being was somehow experiencing these spectacular masses of swirling geometric shapes and colours. I remember a fleeting feeling of regret, thinking that the green liquid must indeed be toxic and that my last moments would be spent alone, hallucinating in a kitchen in London's East End.

"Moments later, the lights ended and there was only darkness, but a darkness different from anything I had ever experienced. It was more than a darkness; it was a complete void. And the void was accompanied by a silence so extreme as to be deafening. Had I died already? A strange realisation came to me that it didn't matter if I had.

"The void completely enveloped me, and then, cutting through the silence like a thunderclap, a voice with incredible clarity, gentle yet simultaneously incredibly powerful, told me, 'Think and it shall be'. A voice continued, but it was different, 'Tom, Tom, come back. Come back to me.' I opened my eyes. It was Marion.

"Marion looked intensely worried and told me that it had taken several minutes to revive me. She had been about to call an ambulance, she said.

"'But Marion, I feel fine. No, I feel more than fine, I feel great, really great.' I told her.

"I got to my feet and immediately felt that the strength in my legs and back, which had felt so weak earlier, had returned. My headache and the fever were both gone, and my breathing was easy and normal. I felt like a new man.

"'Mon dieu! Look at your arm,' Marion had exclaimed, pointing to where just an hour ago there had been twelve stitches binding the deep wound from my cycling accident. The wound was completely healed."

# Chapter 16
# Space Travel, Rock n' Roll

Sitting forward in his seat, Charlie said, "That's all really interesting, but you still haven't told me why I've got tits, and…"

Lucia interrupted, "Shut up about your tits and listen to Tom."

"She's right, Charlie, shut up about your stupid tits," said Flore.

"Don't worry about your tits, Charlie. I'll get to them shortly," said Tom, in a tone as compassionate as an alien can muster, "Anyway, as I was saying, not only did the wound on my arm completely heal, but I felt great. I did a Covid test. It was negative. The Monstera solution had been like a miracle cure.

"The next day, Marion took a Monstera sample to work. One of her colleagues had worked on the genome project as part of her PhD and knew about DNA sequencing. Together, they spent the day sequencing the plant's genetic code and then compared the results on the Cambridge University Genome Project database, where the DNA sequence of every plant and animal is stored.

"La Monstera's DNA sequence matched nothing on the database. The nearest match was with the Psychotria Vindis shrub which is one of the ingredients used in the hallucinogenic drug Ayahuasca; but even then, about fifteen per cent of her genetic code was completely different and like nothing else on earth. They concluded that La Monstera was either a completely new genetic evolution or a throwback gene sequence from an extinct species that had somehow remained hidden and inactive in her 'parents' DNA.

"The following day, Marion got a call from the head of the Cambridge project. Realising the potential significance of their discovery and that the whole thing could potentially spiral out of control very quickly, Marion had had the presence of mind to tell the rather excited caller that the file that had been uploaded to their server had become corrupted and that since then she'd re-run the sequence and discovered that the sample exactly matched Monstera Deliciosa, more commonly known as the Swiss

Cheese Plant.

"She told the caller that she was very sorry to have wasted his time and raised his hopes over a new species."

"Well Bravo to Marion and all that, but what about my tits?" said Charlie, impatiently.

"Forget about your fucking tits for the moment, we'll get to them when I'm ready," Tom replied, looking as exasperated as an alien can.

Charlie looked disgruntled but said nothing more. Tom drew a long, breath, then having regained his composure, continued his story.

"So, we set up a testing lab in the flat by moving all of the furniture out of our living room and taping large plastic sheets from floor to ceiling to create an essentially sealed environment.

"Over the weeks that followed, we conducted a range of experiments. Marion brought all sorts of bacteria and viruses home in carefully sealed containers. We found that bacteria that were in some way helpful to humans, such as lactobacillus, thrived when a small quantity of the boiled Monstera solution was added to the petri dish. At the same time, cultures such as E. coli, which is very harmful to humans, were almost instantly decimated by even a single drop of the Monstera solution or 'tea' as we'd started to call it.

"We then shifted from experimenting with Monstera tea to cold pressing the leaves to extract pure juice from the plant and found that the effects were even more significant.

"A few days later, Marion persuaded a friend who works for one of the big drug companies on some of their experimental cancer treatments to smuggle some rats out of the laboratory. The rats had all been given multiple cancers through exposure to high doses of radiation and a cocktail of carcinogenic drugs, and all were deemed to be in a terminal condition with less than one week to live.

"We divided the rats into four groups of five. One by one, after stunning them with a brief exposure to chloroform so that we wouldn't get bitten, we weighed and measured them, tagged each of them with a small, numbered ring through one ear, and noted the details in a spreadsheet.

"Group 1 was our control group; they weren't given any of the Monstera, just purified water. Group 2 were given Monstera 'tea' instead of water; Group 3 had cold pressed Monstera juice mixed with equal quantities of purified water, and Group 4 were given pure Monstera juice.

"The results were astonishing. All five of the Group 1 rats were dead within seven days. Of the Group 2 rats, one died on the second day, but the remaining four were all still alive one month later. In Group 3, all of the rats not only survived but grew noticeably bigger and were highly active almost twenty-four hours per day.

"But the most remarkable effects were in the Group 4 rats that had been given the pure juice. Like the rats in Group 3, they also became bigger, fitter and more active, but it wasn't until what we thought was the end of the experiment that the full extent of the effects became known.

"We had decided that we had to euthanise the rats. It wasn't an easy decision, because by then, they all had names and we'd become quite attached to them. So much so, that we put off the killings until the very end of the day, just before we went to bed.

"The euthanasia was achieved by dropping a chloroform-soaked swab into the glass vivaria that had been their homes for the last month and then sealing the vents. All of the rats in all of the groups lost consciousness within thirty seconds of the swabs being dropped into their cages and were dead within two minutes. But, when we returned to the lab twenty minutes later to switch the lights off and properly seal the room, the Group 4 rats were not only alive but were either running on the wheel or were active with one or more of the various toys in the cage.

"We pondered this and concluded that because the Group 4 rats had become so much bigger and fitter, we probably hadn't used enough Chloroform. Putting on our face masks again, so that we wouldn't be overcome by the noxious fumes ourselves, we soaked another much larger swab with double the quantity of chloroform, dropped it into the cage and watched the rats first lose consciousness, and then one by one, over the next ninety seconds or so, stop breathing.

"The following morning, to our complete shock, we discovered something much, much harder to comprehend. Marion had gone into the lab just after breakfast, intending to collect the dead rats. I was still in the kitchen, washing the breakfast plates. She shouted to me 'Tom, come quickly, the rats are alive again, but two of them have escaped, bring the traps.'

"When, I got to the lab, sure enough, there were just three rats, numbers 17, 19 and 20 in the cage. Rats 16 and 18 had gone. Although I saw that the cage lid was closed, I assumed that we must have left it open the night before because we had been tired and, in any case, thought that the rats were all dead. Marion must have read my mind, because she immediately told me, 'Tom, I closed and bolted the lid before we went to bed, and I've not touched it this morning'.

"We went into the kitchen and sat down at the table to run through the possibilities. Perhaps someone had broken in during the night and taken the rats – maybe an animal rights activist who had somehow discovered that we were experimenting with live animals.

"Marion had ventured, 'Perhaps that guy from Cambridge University didn't believe me about the corrupted file and excited by the discovery of a new species, came to see what he could find here.'

"I told her that perhaps one of us sleepwalks and had got up in the night and released two of the rats. We ran through a dozen or more possible causes, but none of them made any sense. There were no signs of forced entry; La Monstera was still in her pot by the window, and she would certainly have been taken if someone connected to the university had visited, and neither of us had any history of sleepwalking. We were dumbfounded and quite perplexed.

"A couple of days later, I started to think that I might be suffering from short-term memory loss. On several occasions, I had had the experience of thinking that I needed something from another room, perhaps my coat if I was going out, or my tobacco to have a smoke, and would then find myself with the item I had needed, but with no recollection of having gone to get it.

"You might remember that night in London at the party we had, Marion told you about my accident and almost complete amnesia. Well, the single vague memory that I do have from my past is of an old lady, who I assume was my grandmother, describing something like this happening to her. I remember her telling me that sometimes she would arrive to a room intending to get something, but when she got there wouldn't be able to remember what it was that she had wanted, while on other occasions she would find herself with some object in her hands but have no recollection of having gone to get it. That vague memory and the mystery of my amnesia was what stimulated my interest in researching how the human mind works and in particular finding a cure for memory loss and dementia.

"Anyway, I considered the possibility that I might be experiencing a similar, but more premature case of dementia, but concluded it was much more likely to be the late nights we'd been having. Marion and I had been working so hard, doing our normal jobs during the day, then coming home to conduct our experiments in our improvised, makeshift laboratory. I wondered whether the hours I'd been working could be enough to start to impact my cognitive abilities.

"Another possibility that came to mind was that the Monstera tea I'd been having every morning instead of coffee, initially against Marion's advice and subsequently without her knowledge, might have been having a negative impact. By then, having the Monstera tea was nothing like that first time where I ended up hallucinating on the kitchen floor. Now, it was just like having a strong coffee, but a coffee that left me feeling energised and completely focused. Nevertheless, I wondered if the price to pay for those feel-good effects might be short-term memory loss.

"The big revelation came about a week later. And when I say big revelation, I mean huge, immense, and life-changing in ways you can barely begin to imagine. Marion and I had gone to bed early for a change. We'd decided to have a night off; no experiments or data collection, just a takeaway pizza and a film in bed, like we used to do from time to time before the whole Monstera adventure started.

"Just after we turned on the TV and started to pull apart the pizza, Marion said, 'Ah, I've left my glasses in the kitchen, could you get them for me?'

"When I handed Marion her glasses, she said 'Oh, you had them in your hand all along. You think of everything. Thank you.'

"I said, 'What? What are you talking about? I just went to the kitchen to get them for you.'

"Marion laughed, 'Oh, I must have dozed off for a moment. Hey, let's have a glass of wine with our pizza, there's a bottle in the fridge.' When I gave her the wine, she said, 'Tom, how did you do that? Have you been going to Hogwarts to learn magic tricks or something?'

"I asked her what she meant and she told me, 'Tom, you gave me the wine only a second after I asked for it. How did you do that? The bottle was in the kitchen, in the fridge.'

"It was then that I suddenly realised what was happening, although I couldn't believe or explain it. I wasn't suffering from dementia and forgetting how I had fetched things. I could move myself from one place to another, just by thinking about being there.

"'Marion, ask me for something else,' I said urgently.

"Smiling, she said, 'OK, if we're going to play this game, get some serviettes from the kitchen drawer, so we don't get pizza grease on the duvet'.

"What for her was just a moment later, I handed her the serviette.

"'What the fuck! How did you do that?' she exclaimed, mouth wide open in astonishment.

"I told her what I thought was happening. After what seemed like an eternity of silence, Marion looked at me, smiled and said, 'I always knew you were special.'

"We talked through the night about how I might have developed this ability to travel through both space and time; into the future on my instant journey to the kitchen, then back in time to sync back to Marion's timeframe back in the bedroom. We wondered if I could do errands over a longer distance and with a longer time horizon.

"'Get me a newspaper' Marion said.

"I replied, 'We don't have a newspaper in the flat. We haven't bought one for weeks.'

"Marion smiled, 'Exactly, but it's just after five in Paris; they'll be putting the first edition newspapers out at the bottom of the Champs Elysée about now. I'll have a copy of Le Monde please.'

"Shocked, I told her 'Surely, you're not serious.'

"With another smile, she said, 'I really am serious, and get me a freshly baked croissant while you're there.'

"As Marion flicked through Le Monde, eating her croissant, I tried to comprehend what I'd just done. I didn't have any recollection of the journey, I had just thought of the news kiosk near the bottom of the Champs Elysée and suddenly I had been there, right by the kiosk.

"I had tried to buy a copy of Le Monde, but I didn't have any Euros, so had to go to find a cash machine. When I eventually found a machine, I withdrew some money, returned to the newsstand and bought the newspaper. I then went off to find some croissants. All in all, I had spent about twenty minutes wandering around getting money, the paper and the croissants. But when I got back, Marion told me that for her it had seemed as if I hadn't left her side. Simply that one moment she had asked me to get a newspaper and a croissant, and the next moment they were there on the duvet in front of her.

"We were completely out of our depth trying to understand what I'd just done. We reasoned that somehow, I had unknowingly learned how to break all the laws of physics, and not just regular vanilla physics; this strayed deep into the dark, opaque realm of quantum physics, which neither of us knew anything about. Although we are both scientists, our fields are biology and chemistry. We know little beyond elementary physics, let alone quantum physics. Suddenly, I felt a wave of exhaustion wash over me and told Marion that I needed to sleep.

"The following day I awoke at 2 pm. Marion was still next to me but was sat up in bed with her Mac on her lap.

'Good afternoon, Mr Sleepy,' she said, smiling. 'I called work for you and told them you were sick. My god, they have no idea just how sick you really are. Anyway, while you've been asleep, I've been doing some research. I don't fully understand it yet, but in quantum physics, there's this concept that at any given moment in time, a person, object or anything, can simultaneously be present and not present. According to some theories, we, and everything else for that matter, are sort of here and not here at the same moment, and we can also be present and not present everywhere else throughout the universe.

'Some guy, whose name I don't remember now, experimented with light particles and proved that the same particles could be present in two places at the same time, even though, according to the conventional laws of physics, that isn't possible.

'What you did last night is apparently called quantum tunnelling. It's only a theory and has never been proven, at least not until you proved it last night. By thinking of a place, you were able to put yourself there, instantly. That's because, according to some of the theories of quantum mechanics, you were already in Paris, and everywhere else, on different threads of what's referred to as 'the multiverse'. The multiverse theory goes along the lines that there are multiple, perhaps infinite versions of you as well as everyone and everything else, all interacting with space-time in an infinite number of different ways, and all creating different versions of both history and the future.

'It seems that while, as far as we know, every human that's ever lived up until this point, up until you, has simply been a passenger on the single thread of the space-time continuum that they're conscious of being on, there are potentially infinite versions of everyone, and each version of each person will have his or her specific consciousness of the thread that they're on, but only that thread. Whereas you have somehow acquired the ability to hop, at will, between the different strands.

'My guess is, that as well as healing your arm and curing you of Covid, the Monstera juice that you've been drinking has somehow activated a part of your brain that allows you to control your interaction with the space-time continuum in barely imaginable ways. And that must also explain what happened to the rats. After having the Monstera juice, they changed in the same way that you have, and just thought themselves somewhere else, probably to a cheese factory.'

'"What?' I said, 'I drifted off. Explain that again.'

"Marion threw the pencil she'd been making notes with at me. 'Come on Mr Space Time Traveller, if we're going to make the best of whatever has happened to you, we're going to need some money. Go and get me Friday's lottery numbers,' she said, with a smile."

# Chapter 17
# The School of Hard Knocks

The group sat silently around the table trying to assimilate everything Tom had explained. Eventually, Sylvain broke the silence.

"I need a drink. Anyone fancy a Tom Collins?"

"I'll have one," said Tom, "but bring me a straw, it's not easy to pick up a glass with these claws."

Charlie immediately asked, "Yes, what is it with the claws and the whole alien thing? What happened to you? Did drinking that plant juice turn you into an alien? And you still haven't told me why I've got tits".

Tom took a sip of the Tom Collins that Sylvain had quickly prepared, then replied, "OK. I'm going to tell you about all of that, but I need to give you some more background first. So, after that first night when I discovered I could travel through time and space, it all went a bit crazy for a while. I mean, things were already very crazy, but they got even crazier.

"I did what Marion had suggested and travelled two days into the future, got the winning numbers for the Friday lottery draw, then went back to 'real-time' and attempted to buy a lottery ticket. That turned out to be one of the worst experiences of my life, but it taught us valuable lessons.

"In my hurry to get the ticket, and also being keen to experiment with my new powers, instead of walking to the corner shop to buy the ticket, I just thought myself there and a moment later found myself in the shop, in front of the lottery machine. Luckily, Dan, the shopkeeper, had been occupied with something under the counter, so he didn't see me instantly appear in front of him. But, after he stood up and I started to tell him my lottery numbers, I heard a horrible voice screaming behind me, 'Oi, you fucker, you can't just jump the fucking queue, I was 'ere first.'

"I turned around to meet the sneering glare of a very fat woman with bleached blonde hair. She was wearing a cheap-looking tracksuit and glittery gold trainers. I think she was what the English call a 'chav' or Americans would describe as 'white trash'".

Flore grimaced at what she considered Tom's inappropriate description of the woman, which Tom noticed, but continued undeterred.

"So, keen to try to diffuse the situation, I tried to apologise to the woman, but this only made things worse. At that time, I still had my strong French accent, and this seemed to inflame her more.

'There's a reason this country voted Leave. It was to get rid of fuckers like you. We got Brexit, so why have we still got garlic-smelling wankers like you 'ere? Jez, sort him out,' she shouted.

"Jez was also wearing a tracksuit, although more expensive looking. He had a very aggressive expression and without words or hesitation drew his fist back to punch me. I quickly thought 'home' and in an instant, I was out of the shop and back in the flat with Marion.

"But that wasn't the end of the problem. In my earlier trips, fetching wine and serviettes from the kitchen, and then the croissant and newspaper from Paris, I had come straight back; so, for Marion, it was like I had never been gone. But with today's situation in the shop, I wasn't intending to return to the shop, or at least at that moment didn't intend to, so for Dan, the shopkeeper and the two chavs, I had simply disappeared from before their very eyes.

"This presented a huge problem. These people would surely talk. Although Jez and his awful 'lady' friend were hardly plausible witnesses, and people would probably just think they'd been stoned if they started talking about vanishing Frenchmen, Dan was a different story. Dan was credible. He had spent ten years in the British Army, and complete with injuries sustained in Afghanistan, helping six wounded colleagues escape a Taliban death squad, Dan had left his regiment with a Distinguished Service medal, another medal for Bravery in Exceptional Circumstances and a personal letter from the Queen. The press had picked up on Dan's story and several national newspapers had competed to heap praise on the 'Working-Class Wapping Hero'.

"Behind the counter in the shop, Dan had dedicated a section of wall next to the tobacco cabinet to the record of his heroics, where cuttings from the Sun, the Mirror, the Daily Mail and three other newspapers were slowly yellowing in black picture frames.

"Dan was smart, articulate, and liked by everyone who met him. More to the point, as a result of his fifteen minutes of fame, fifteen years ago, Dan had contacts in the press and not only knew me but delivered our newspapers, so knew where we lived. The likelihood of having a media scrum of paparazzi reporters and photographers outside our building within the hour, therefore seemed quite high.

"What must Dan be thinking and doing now, we wondered. Would he already be on the phone with one of the journalists who had covered his story? As Marion and I contemplated the possibilities we heard sirens, lots of sirens. We looked out of the window to see three Police cars and two Ambulances whizz past.

"'Shit, it has to be about what happened at the shop,' I told Marion. 'Walk there and see if you can find out what all the excitement's about'.

"Marion left the flat but was back just a few minutes later. 'Tom, something dreadful must have happened. I couldn't get very near because they've closed the road to traffic and pedestrians. There are ten or more Police cars, three ambulances, and the Police helicopter is above the shop,' she told me.

"Thinking quickly, I decided I would have to go back to the moment I was about to be punched to see what had happened. I concentrated on that moment in the shop but took care to think of the far corner by the magazine racks, where I knew I'd be able to see the counter but wouldn't get punched by Jez. In a flash, I was there, observing everything that happened immediately after I had disappeared.

"With me suddenly gone from the space between Jez and Dan, the punch that had been intended for me landed on Dan's nose. Without hesitation, Dan picked up the baseball bat that he kept behind the counter to repel robbers and swung it at Jez. The end of the bat hit Jez directly on his right temple. Dan was a strong man who had been trained to use his strength to best effect, and the impact was simply devastating. Jez collapsed onto the floor, blood leaking from his head and spreading across the floor like a crimson lake. He was dead.

"With this, the woman screamed 'You've fuckin' killed him, you bastard.' She immediately reached down to Jez, pulled a gun from his waistband, pointed it at Dan and pulled the trigger. Dan died instantly; the bullet caught him directly in the middle of the forehead, slamming him back into the cigarette display behind him. He slid to the floor, the thick smear of his blood running straight through the middle of the 'Smoking Kills' message across the cabinet doors.

"With this, the woman turned and, gun in hand, ran out into the street. The next sounds were of screeching tyres, followed by a sickening thud accompanied by the sound of breaking glass, and then a cacophony of screams from people on the street.

"In her haste to get away from the crime scene, the woman had run out into the road, directly into the path of a speeding delivery van. Unfortunately for the driver of the van, the woman, who weighed more than one hundred kilos, had gone over the bonnet of the van, through the windshield and straight into the driver. I couldn't be sure, but from what I could see through the shop window, it looked like both the woman and the driver of the van were dead, their heads smashed like watermelons dropped from a balcony as a result of the high-speed head-butt that they'd just shared.

"'Fuck! Fuck! Fuck!' I shouted out loud, 'This can't be happening.' Thinking quickly, I suddenly remembered the shop's security cameras. I went behind the counter where Dan was slumped on the floor, sitting in a pool of his own blood. Just under the counter, I saw the CCTV recorder. Thankfully, it was an old model that records to a DVD, rather than one of the newer versions that uploads images in real time to a remote server. I pressed the eject button and removed the disc, wiped the machine with the end of my sleeve, and thought 'Home'.

"Back at the flat with Marion, I broke down in tears. 'I only went to buy a fucking lottery ticket and four people are dead!' I told her.

"We retrieved my old laptop with a DVD drive from the bottom of the wardrobe and I inserted the disc from the shop. I fast-forwarded to my first arrival in the shop. At 17.39:34 I suddenly appeared at the counter and almost immediately after, the woman started shouting, her face ugly and distorted with rage. The camera's microphone had picked up her speech and once again I found myself shocked by the ferocity and vulgarity of her words and the hate-laden tone with which they were delivered.

"Next, Jez could be seen stepping forward towards me and drawing his fist back. At that moment I simply disappeared from the image. The time stamp on the video was 17.39:59.

"Over the seconds that followed, Jez punched Dan, Dan killed Jez, the woman shot Dan, and then hurriedly left the shop. The timestamp when the horrific screech, thud and screams could be heard outside was 17.40:24.

"In just twenty-five seconds, four people had lost their lives and it was all my fault. I was distraught. I told Marion that I would never do any quantum tunnelling again and that we should destroy La Monstera to make sure that nobody else acquired my abilities. She immediately disagreed, 'No Tom, don't you see how much good you could do with these powers? You just have to learn how to use them safely.'

Flore interjected, "Why didn't you just go back to some point in time before you first arrived in the shop and influence the events so that the catastrophe didn't happen?"

Tom replied, "Well, that's what we discussed that evening and had decided to do. But given my state of shock at the horrific consequences of just going to buy a lottery ticket, we were very conscious that whatever we did would require very careful planning or we might solve one problem but create ten more. We agreed that we'd take plenty of time to decide and plan what to do; but then, over the next few days as the press started to report and speculate on what The Sun newspaper was calling the 'Limehouse Massacre', day-by-day, details emerged that made us change our minds about altering the history I had created.

"If the press reports were to be believed, it turned out that the woman, Sharon Smith, was the ringleader of a criminal gang with interests in drug dealing, extortion, prostitution, and human trafficking. She was thirty-four years old and had spent twelve of her sixteen years of adult life in prison.

"Jez was Sharon's half-brother and the gang's enforcer. He also had a long list of convictions for a multitude of mostly violent offences including manslaughter, grievous bodily harm, extortion with menaces, drug dealing, and possession of a firearm.

"The van driver, Charlie Power, shouldn't have been driving a van that day, or any other day for that matter, because two months before he had been banned from driving for two years for a string of serious motoring offences. The post-mortem had already revealed that at the time of the accident, he was more than three times over the legal alcohol limit and also had traces of both cocaine and cannabis in his blood.

"But the big shock was to learn the truth about Dan the shopkeeper. It turned out that the war hero who had been decorated by the Queen and was loved by all of his customers, including me, had been convicted for molesting a 78-year-old pensioner ten years ago and for sexually assaulting underage girls seven years ago. Somehow, presumably due to his distinguished service record and the mental health 'get out of jail free card' bestowed by his post-traumatic stress disorder diagnosis, he had avoided prison for these offences. However, during the investigation at the shop, Police found sexual images of children as young as seven on Polaroid prints under the counter. Learning of this provoked a wave of nausea as I remembered how Dan had been so occupied below the shop counter when I had arrived to buy the lottery ticket.

"'Maybe this is what Buddhists mean when they talk about Karma,' I told Marion. 'It's better that these people remain dead. There's no way we should give them any more opportunities to cause pain and misery. From now on, we have to make sure that everything we do is safe and thoroughly thought through.'"

# Chapter 18
# Who Wants to be a Millionaire?

Tom continued to describe the astonishing events to the group.

"With all of the stress of the Limehouse Massacre, we didn't get around to buying a lottery ticket that week, but the following week, I transported myself to the Friday evening, acquired the winning lottery numbers and then went straight back to real-time.

"This time, I left nothing to chance and walked to a shop to buy the ticket. Two days later we were multi-millionaires. There had been several weeks without anyone winning the jackpot, so as the only winners that week, our ticket netted a whopping £168,984,228.

"We politely turned down the champagne reception and wealth coun- selling offered by Camelot, the lottery organiser, and also insisted on anonymity. Just after lunchtime the following day, the money was in our bank account.

"We decided to go out and do some shopping, so splashed out on a limo to collect us from Limehouse and take us to Harrods where we spent three hours in the shop looking for some new clothes. Marion chose nothing more than a new pair of jeans, and I picked up two T-shirts and a jumper.

We were, however, a little more extravagant in the food hall, where we bought two Kobe steaks, some foie gras and a case of St Emilion; a 1982 Chateau Laroque Grand Cru Classe, at £18,227 per bottle.

"By the time we arrived home, it was early evening, so we opened a bottle of the wine, then cooked the steaks and foie, which we ate with a simple green salad. We spent the rest of the evening making plans for what we would do with our wealth and how we would use my newfound abilities.

"As we finished our second bottle of wine, Marion said to me, 'Do you realise, that in less than two hours we've consumed over thirty-five thousand Pounds worth of wine? That's enough money to feed a family of four for twenty years in some parts of the world.'

"We promised ourselves that, despite our new-found wealth, we would do our best to live modestly, then opened another bottle of the wine to celebrate our first important decision.

"Over the remainder of that evening and into the early hours, we made some important decisions about the principles we would live by and debated the essential choices before us. With the money we had, we could live a very comfortable and quite lavish life, completely free of any stress, give a few million to good causes every year, and still never run out of money. Or, we could set a much higher target for ourselves and set out to try to help as many people as possible.

"Hard as this might be to believe, within an hour, we had concluded that if we were going to make a real difference to a significant number of people's lives, one hundred and sixty-eight million wasn't going to be enough.

"'Incredible, isn't it?' mused Marion, 'We've got more money than we ever dreamed of, but we still don't have enough.' Within another hour, we had evolved a plan to address the money problem, but more on that subject later."

# Chapter 19
# Making History

"Just as Lucia had concluded during that boozy dinner party together, we decided that the first principle of every choice we would make from that point forward would be, 'do no harm'. After a bit more discussion, we decided that the do no harm rule could, in exceptional circumstances, be overlooked if we knew with absolute certainty that an individual or a group would cause much greater harm than we would have to cause them.

"This prompted a philosophical discussion that lasted for several hours as to whether we should attempt to intervene to correct historical injustices.

"The example we chose to debate was the obvious one - Hitler and the Third Reich. I proposed the idea that it would be very easy for me to go to Braunau am Inn in Austria in April 1889, find the home of Alois and Klara Hitler, and murder their newborn baby, Adolf. This, I had said, would save the lives of six million Jews as well as the other sixty to seventy million people who died as a result of World War II.

"'Or would it?' Marion had said, 'A lot of historians believe that the Third Reich's rise to power was the consequence of the German people's sense of injustice at how they were treated after the First World War, resulting in an appetite amongst the German public for a leader that would correct that. However, many argue that Hitler was quite ineffective as a strategist. If you were to remove Hitler, that vacuum would most likely have been filled by someone else – and that alternative person might have been much more efficient and effective.

"'Imagine if you did go back to 1889 to murder baby Adolf, then as soon as you arrived back here, I told you that twenty, rather than six million Jews died between 1932 and 1945. Or you arrive back to find that all of London's street names have been replaced by German names and that we're living in a brutal Nazi dystopia because they won World War II under the leadership of someone far more competent than Adolf Hitler. Sorry, but there are just too many variables and the potential for too many unintended consequences. And anyway, if you erase Hitler, what are you going to do after that? Go back to medieval Mongolia and kill Genghis Khan? Where does it end?'"

Flore had been listening carefully, but now spoke out, "You say you decided on a 'do no harm' ethos, but now you're telling us that you considered killing a baby; and earlier, you told us that you arranged for Pippa to kill Claude. Isn't killing someone, anyone, harmful?"

"You're right, we did kill Claude," Tom replied. "We had to. What I didn't tell you before, was that from looking around his flat Pippa discovered that Claude was planning something much bigger, his 'piece de resistance'. Two weeks after Claude's hydrogen enema, Dalil Boubakeur, rector of the Grand Mosque of Paris, was due to visit Marseilles to address an estimated crowd of some 50,000 supporters at the Olympique de Marseilles stadium.

"The purpose of the address was to seek support from French Muslims for alterations to the Quran to remove passages related to the murder and punishment of Jews, Christians and disbelievers, on the basis that this guidance was now obsolete in a modern multicultural context.

"Even though Boubakeur was a staunch supporter of the values of the French 'Republique' and was putting himself at risk of attack by extremists by making such an address, for Claude, Boubakeur was just another Muslim and Claude felt certain that Marine Le Pen didn't like Muslims.

"It was to parachute into the stadium completely naked and shall we say, 'standing to attention' with a bomb inside a bag filled with ball bearings and nails strapped around his torso. The bomb would be detonated automatically when Claude reached an altitude of ten metres – so, almost level with most of the crowd.

"Claude's plan was all documented, complete with drawings and a notebook with the precise timings, and he had booked and paid for the flight that he would jump from. Pippa found all of the equipment, including the explosives, 80kg of ball bearings and nails, the detonator and the parachute that Claude intended to use.

"Also amongst the equipment was a pack of Viagra to guarantee maximum effect as he descended naked into the stadium, and the canopy of the parachute had been printed with the words 'Marine, je t'aime', complete with a big red heart.

"Had Claude lived, he would almost certainly have succeeded in killing or maiming as many as ten thousand people. Aside from the initial deaths at the stadium, the likely consequences of this were obvious. There would be retaliatory attacks on traditional French targets by Islamic extremists, and a large number of moderate Muslims would be drawn to a more hard-line mindset. This in turn would propel moderate and inclusive French Catholics, agnostics and atheists towards a hostile, Islamophobic mindset. You can understand that not dealing with Claude could have resulted in tens of thousands of deaths and created huge social divisions. We had to act."

"But why didn't we hear about any of this in the press?" asked Flore.

"None of this ever emerged in the mainstream press because, under strict instructions from the DGSE, the Police suppressed the information. They didn't want Claude's simple plan to be copied by others, or his enema accident to be perceived as a deep-state execution and for him to become a heroic martyr for the far right and a poster boy for every idiot conspiracy theorist.

"Anyway, back to the things Marion and I discussed that night after our lottery win; we then talked about the enormity of the responsibility we were taking on and how it would be better if we could share that responsibility with other like-minded people.

"'But who can we trust to talk to about all of this?' I asked Marion.

"Marion replied, 'What about Flore and Sylvain and their friends Lucia and Charlie? We don't know Lucia and Charlie very well, but they seem like good people and I'm sure Flore and Sylvain wouldn't be friends with them if they weren't. We had that evening with them when we joked about finding an island, colonising it and calling it 'Wesh'; maybe that evening was the universe's way of helping us choose the right people. How about you tell Sylvain first, see what he thinks, and then take things from there.'

"I replied with just one word 'Wesh'."

# THE COSMIC KNOT PARADOX

# Chapter 20
# The Transporter

"The following day, we made another incredible discovery. For a few days, I had been thinking about the fact that I had been able to get things like newspapers, croissants, and glasses of wine, but would I be able to move something bigger? Specifically, I wondered whether I would be able to move another person.

"Up until that point I had avoided raising the subject with Marion because I knew that she was, understandably, pretty freaked out by the whole quantum tunnelling thing; but eventually, I plucked up the courage to ask her whether she'd like to try making a trip with me.

"'I thought you'd never ask!' she had said, adding, 'I didn't want to ask because I didn't want to put you under any more pressure'.

"So, we decided that for our first trip together, we'd try moving from the bedroom to the kitchen. We both stood up, held hands, and I focused my mind on the centre of the kitchen. In an instant we were there, holding hands and looking into each other's eyes.

"'Wow! You made the earth move for me,' Marion said, smiling. 'Do you realise, this means we can go anywhere, whenever we want to? Let's go and see my family, then to the Himalayas for the evening, just to watch the sunset.'

"'Hang on Marion, there are problems with that,' I told her and explained my concerns, 'On my trip to Paris, I was lucky to not suddenly appear in front of someone, or worse still get hit by a cyclist, or perhaps something much worse; but it was early in the morning and with hardly anyone awake and out on the street, the risk was quite low, and I was just lucky.

'But then, my attempt to buy a lottery ticket wasn't so lucky, was it? Arriving at the local shop and being the catalyst for four deaths in less than thirty seconds was a terrible experience – one that I'll live with for the rest of my life. Even though they were all hideous people, and the world is a better place without them, that day will always haunt me. We need a safe landing place for everywhere we go'.

"Over the rest of that day and most of the day after, we made a list of all the places we thought we might want to hop to and from, and how we could make our travel safe. Our destination list ended up being quite long.

"In total, there were more than two hundred places we wanted to be able to travel to. The locations included my parents' place, Marion's parents, and because it's so big and takes so much time to get around, several places in London. There were two more locations in Paris, then Marseilles, Courcheval in the Alpes, Rome, Madrid, Barcelona, New York, Los Angeles and Chicago. Tokyo seemed like a good idea, as did Hong Kong, Sydney, Singapore and Bali. Then, of course, places like Machu Pichu, the Himalayas, and a myriad of other locations. The list went on and on.

"Having come up with our list, we then worked out our plans for safe travel. Country by country, city by city, we would travel to each of the places on our list to find and buy a property. Our criteria for cities would be a small apartment or house that was both central and secure. For the more remote places, we would look for bigger properties, ideally surrounded by some land, that were far enough away from other houses, so that people wouldn't notice our presence when we were there and wouldn't miss us when we weren't.

"We did some rough calculations and worked out that we would need an average of one million Pounds per location. With a list of two hundred locations, that would surely only grow, and with only £168 million in the bank, we realised for the second time that week that we were going to need more money, but I'll return to that problem later.

"Another problem we discussed was that these property purchases would be relatively easy if we did them in real-time, but not if we went back in time. For example, if we thought we might want to be able to safely travel to say, New York in 1967, we would need to have found and bought our safe place there sometime before then. That created a whole load of other complications.

"The main problem going back in time to buy properties wasn't going to be having enough money, it would be having the right money, because pretty much anywhere in the world, the banknotes used even ten years ago aren't the same as the banknotes used now.

"We theorised that we could find out which country had the oldest banknote that hadn't been reprinted in a different design; obtain as much of that country's bank notes as we could carry, then go back in time to somewhere near the date that the oldest banknote was first issued and exchange those notes for whatever country's banknotes were the oldest but still legal tender at that time. Then, we'd simply repeat the process over and over again, going further back in time with each transaction, until we got to the year that we wanted to buy a property. At that point, we'd just exchange into the local currency and buy whatever we wanted.

"But it was very complicated and, we decided, fraught with risk. For a start, to take money back even twenty or thirty years, we'd have to make multiple time hops, each with an unsafe 'landing'. We shelved that idea, deciding that it might be OK as a last resort, but wasn't a method we could repeatedly use, because of the risks.

"We then explored another idea. We could use some of our money to buy gold, then take it back in time, sell it, open a bank account, deposit the money, and then buy whatever we wanted.

"However, there were still problems. Assuming we wanted to go and buy properties in 1960s America, we would need to take a lot of gold. Even in 1960, the price of a small apartment in a nice central area of New York like 5th Avenue was about one hundred thousand Dollars, but the price of gold at that time was only about thirty-five Dollars per ounce. That meant that to buy just one apartment, we would need to transport around three thousand ounces, more than seventy kilos of gold, which is more than I weigh. We needed something with a much higher value per gram than gold.

"Without hesitation, Marion said 'Diamonds'.

"A bit of research revealed that the price of diamonds in 1960 was about two thousand seven hundred Dollars per Carat. With one Carat weighing just one-fifth of a gramme, we would only need to transport about eight grammes of diamonds to buy our 5th Avenue 'crash pad' as Marion was now calling it.

"There was another advantage. While the price of gold had rocketed in value fifty-seven times, from just thirty-five Dollars per ounce in 1960 to a whopping two thousand Dollars per ounce in 2021, over the same period, diamonds had increased in value only eleven times, from two thousand seven hundred Dollars in 1960 to about thirty thousand in 2021. This meant that to buy our 1960s New York apartment using diamonds, we would only need to buy just over one million dollars' worth of diamonds at today's prices, whereas if we used gold we'd have to spend over five million. Diamonds it would be.

"However, none of this solved the issue of how we would actually buy a property. In whose name? I could hardly turn up in 1960 New York and open a bank account using my French passport with a date of birth showing that it would be almost thirty years before I would be born.

"This complicated matters considerably. We wrestled with the problem for several days, only able to come up with very high-risk solutions to the problem. One of the strategies we discussed was for me to break into the Register of Births, Deaths and Marriages, create a fake birth entry that I would file away in the correct place, and then show up at the office during working hours saying I had lost my birth certificate. Once I was given a copy, I would be able to apply for a US passport and pretty much any other document that I needed, and the original would be safely filed away in the public records office where it would be available to be cross-checked if I came under any scrutiny.

"But that also created some risks; we reasoned that with the Cold War tensions with the Soviet Union approaching their climax, anyone turning up asking for replacement documents might be suspected of being a KGB spy; especially someone with a foreign accent.

# Chapter 21
# Have Bag, Will Travel

"Fate gifted us a solution to the problem. That weekend, we decided to go to Portobello Road market. Wandering around the stalls, we found one with historical personal items, presumably obtained from house clearances.

"Amongst old photograph albums and antique jewellery, there were also old documents. There were World War II ration cards, birth certificates from the turn of the century and a selection of expired passports. Amongst the passports, I found a French passport issued in 1958 and valid for ten years. There were some other loose documents including a paper driving license and a library card folded in between the last page and the cover.

"Flicking through to the main page, I was stopped in my tracks. It was one of those jaw-dropping moments which, for most people, happens perhaps only once or twice in a lifetime. The name in the passport was William Eugene Stephan Hubert. Can you believe it? His initials were WESH. Born on 6th August 1932, his age was perfect for my intended purpose of a journey back to 1960.

"Equally as astonishing as the coincidence of William Hubert's initials was his appearance. William Hubert looked almost exactly like me. The photograph, complete with the notaire's stamp over one corner, was in almost perfect condition and not yellowed or damaged in any way, and in the back of the passport, there was a selection of visa stamps.

"William Hubert must have been a regular traveller, perhaps a businessman – there were visas for Great Britain, Germany, Australia, and the United States of America.

"'That'll be a fiver, mate,' the stall holder said. I paid him the money, my mind now racing to complete the other details of a rapidly gestating plan.

"'Marion, we're going clothes shopping,' I told her.

"Within a few minutes, we'd found a vintage clothes shop specializing in 1960's and 70's attire. Amongst the flared jeans and flowery, psychedelic shirts, we found other more conservative casual wear, business suits, formal shirts and even some ties.

"We left the shop laden with bags containing two suits, five formal shirts, two pairs of shoes and enough casual clothes for at least a few days. I bought a psychedelic shirt and a pair of flared jeans for good measure.

"A bit further along Portobello Road, headed towards Notting Hill, we found and bought an antique leather suitcase in another second-hand shop. We put the clothes in the suitcase, then made our way home.

"Over the next few days, we made more preparations. We trawled eBay, buying all of the antique US Dollar banknotes and coins that we could find, reasoning that on arrival, I would need to pay for a hotel and be able to pay for transport and food until I exchanged some of the diamonds we were going to buy. In total, we acquired just over eight hundred Dollars in vintage notes.

"The day before my trip, we got up early and headed to Hatton Garden, where most of London's jewellers and diamond merchants have been located for more than two hundred years. To avoid suspicion and unwanted attention, we decided to spread our purchases over several merchants.

"First, I went to Hirschfelds, where I bought four diamonds of approximately one carat each for a total of £127,000. Marion spent almost £150,000 at Diamond Palace. We continued the journey along Hatton Garden, visiting R.M. Shah, A.E. Ward & Son, Handleys, RPS Diamonds, Diamond Doves and Queensmith Master Jewellers. By just after midday, we had acquired forty-two carats between us and had spent £1.2 million. All in all, a pretty good morning's work.

"As we started to walk back along Hatton Garden with little bags of diamonds hidden in various pockets, Marion said, 'Hey, you need to get rid of that watch.' Looking at the Apple watch on my I wrist, I realised she was right.

"'Yes, how did I not think of that? Turning up in 1960 Manhattan with an Apple watch would be a bit like forgetting to change my shoes and rocking up in Times Square wearing a pair of Adidas trainers,' I replied. So, we nipped into one of the shops specialising in watches and bought an antique Rolex. In any case, I'd always wanted one.

"We also obtained a 1959 map of New York in order to look for a safe landing place. Back at the flat, we laid out the map on the kitchen table and studied it intently. We talked about using Central Park but quickly discounted that because of the terrible things we'd read about happening in night-time Central Park during that era.

"We also considered an out-of-town location and then getting a taxi or train to Manhattan, but quickly discounted that too. A stranger with a big suitcase suddenly arriving in a quiet town where everybody knows each other would raise lots of suspicions. The centre of Manhattan would at least offer the anonymity of the big city.

"As long as I didn't suddenly appear right in front of someone, nobody would be interested in me and anyway, it would be early morning, just like during my trip to Paris, so hardly anyone would be around.

"After studying a map of Manhattan, we decided that my landing place would be Shubert Alley which runs between West 44th and West 45th Street, just one block away from Times Square. The plan was that as soon as I arrived in Shubert Alley, I would find the Edison Hotel on nearby West 47th Street. At the hotel's reception desk, I'd tell them that I'd just arrived on an early flight from London, that my reservation at another hotel had been double-booked, and hope that they had a room for me.

"The following day I was ready. I was dressed in my vintage 1960s suit with my Rolex on my wrist and my leather suitcase in my hand. I'd separated the diamonds into five small pouches. One was hidden in the lining of the suitcase, and one was in the breast pocket of my jacket, beneath the blue handkerchief that matched my tie. I had sewn one pouch into the turn-ups of each trouser leg and had another in my pocket. This way, if I was mugged or robbed of my suitcase, at least I wouldn't lose all of the diamonds.

"'So, you're going to go on this amazing adventure, but you're leaving me here?' Marion said, as I made my final preparations.

"'Yes, because there's no safe landing there. Two of us arriving in a place that we don't know, where we can't be certain what we'll find when we arrive, more than doubles the risk. I'll get a safe place sorted out and then come back for you. Anyway, you won't even realise that I'm gone. For you, it'll just be an instant, no matter how long it takes me.'

"I hugged Marion, telling her 'Wish me luck. I'll be back for you before you know it. To Wesh and beyond!'

"I focused my mind on the date and time that Marion and I had discussed, 5:45 am, 11th September 1960, then my landing place in Shubert Alley.

"Almost instantly, Marion knew something was terribly, terribly wrong."

# Chapter 22
# Last Day on Earth

"At exactly 5:45am, I arrived halfway along Shubert Alley to discover that the alley wasn't an alley; it was a road. I looked towards the north end, where I was intending to walk and saw the junction with West 45th Street perhaps eighty metres further along. To my horror, at that end of the street, I could see a woman standing in a doorway looking directly at me. 'Oh no! I've been seen,' I thought.

"Before I could take a single step or give even a moment's thought to what I should do about having been witnessed arriving, I was jolted alert by the sounds of screeching tyres and the blaring of a lorry's horn. I just had time to turn my head to look behind me. The garbage truck that I had accidentally appeared in front of, just two seconds earlier, was almost on top of me, the tyres smoking and squealing, and the driver's face distorted with panic. There was no time for anything. No time to leap to safety or even throw myself to the ground; not even enough time to think 'Home'.

"The truck hit me full-on. Blackness. A total void."

# THE COSMIC KNOT PARADOX

# Chapter 23
# Salvation

"But how can you be here now if you died in 1960?" asked Flore.

"Hang on, I need to pee," said Sylvain, getting up from the table to go inside, "Anyone fancy another Tom Collins? I'll bring them on my way back." Everyone nodded their agreement and Tom asked for another straw.

A few minutes later, with a fresh round of drinks on the table, Tom said, "So, you asked how I'm alive now after being killed by that garbage truck. It'll probably be easier if I show you on this screen."

The next moment Tom was on the other side of the table, had propped a television against the wall and plugged it into what looked like an orange.

Lucia said, "This is weird, I've just had one of those déjà vu moments. It feels like I've experienced this before."

"That's because you have experienced this before, just not yet. Now, if you're all sitting comfortably, I'll begin. Enjoy the movie," Tom said, as he sat back down at the table, took a deep breath and closed his eyes. The TV lit up and what looked like a film started to play.

Marion stood alone in the living room of their Limehouse flat. Moments before, Tom had told her that he would be back in an instant but had then immediately disappeared. Not like the 'beam me up Scotty' scenes in Star Trek, where the people being teleported become pixelated and disappear over a few seconds; no, this was simply instantaneous, as if someone had flicked the off switch of a hologram projector. Marion immediately knew that something terrible had happened. On Tom's other trips, he hadn't been absent at all, regardless of how long he had stayed in whatever other place and time he was visiting.

On the first night that Tom had discovered his powers and Marion had asked for a glass of wine, the glass was being held out for her to take in the next moment. The same with the newspaper and croissant. Marion knew without any shred of doubt that Tom was dead.

How would she explain his disappearance? She imagined the endless questions, Police forensic teams going through everything in the flat, Police divers searching Limehouse basin and the river. Then the accusations, maybe an arrest, a trial, perhaps even a conviction and prison.

Marion quickly went online and viewed the Manhattan Gazette historical archive on their website. Near the bottom of page seventeen in the edition from 12th September 1960, she found the news item that confirmed her worst fears; 'French Businessman Killed by Manhattan Garbage Truck' read the headline. Halfway through the article, the photo from William Hubert's passport jumped off the page and slapped Marion hard across her face. A borrowed photo and three column inches of very average reporting by a very average journalist had summarised the destruction of Marion's world.

There was no doubt, Tom was dead. 'Great, my own personal nine-eleven,' Marion thought, marvelling at the cruel irony.

Her mind racing, she realised that if she could acquire the same powers as Tom, she might be able to save him, but if she couldn't, he would be lost to her and the thread of the multiverse that they shared forever.

Marion immediately went to La Monstera, stripped a handful of leaves, took them to the home laboratory that used to be the lounge, and hurriedly squashed them into the cold press juicer. In her hurry to stuff the leaves into the machine, she caught her finger on the serrated edge of the press. It was a deep cut that bled profusely, but there was no time to dress it properly, so she just wrapped some kitchen paper around the wound – she would deal with it later.

Two minutes later, Marion was back in bed holding a shot glass full of the vibrant green, freshly pressed Monstera juice. She'd decided to drink it in bed because she remembered the state in which she'd found Tom on the kitchen floor six weeks earlier, after his first Monstera experience. If she was going to collapse in a hallucinatory fit, she was determined that she would at least be comfortable.

Closing her eyes and wrinkling her nose with the expectation of a terrible taste, Marion gulped down the green liquid, but was pleasantly surprised by the flavour. It reminded her of some mint-flavoured chocolates her grandmother used to give her when she was a young girl.

Marion's experience was almost the same as Tom's. Seconds after emptying the glass, the room started to spin. It was like a fairground ride that just got faster and faster until everything became a blur of brightly coloured lights, which then morphed into kaleidoscopic patterns. Soon after, the lights stopped and were replaced by a void of blackness and an almost deafening silence. A complete nothingness, exactly as Tom had described. Then, the voice, 'Think and it shall be,' it told her.

It was late afternoon when Marion came back to full consciousness and reality. Just as Tom had experienced, she felt immediately alert, strong, and full of vitality. Noticing the blood-soaked kitchen paper wrapped around her index finger, she went to the bathroom to find the plasters to properly attend to her injury. Standing in front of the sink, with a plaster 'peeled' and ready to use, Marion carefully removed the crimson-stained tissue paper from her finger, but there was no wound - just perfect soft skin, the same as her other fingers. She remembered how Tom's cycling injury had healed. 'It's working,' she said to herself out loud. Concentrating hard, she thought, 'Back to the bedroom', but remained in the bathroom looking at herself in the mirror. She tried again, this time summoning all of her mental energy to focus her mind on the room next door, but to no avail, she steadfastly remained where she stood.

Marion wasn't panicked by this. She hadn't really expected to be able to quantum tunnel after just one Monstera dose. After all, it had taken Tom almost a month before he had discovered his powers; and the rats had also had weeks of daily doses before they had vanished.

But whilst she wasn't panicked, she was worried. After all, only two of the rats had disappeared. The other three were still in the cage. Did this mean that Monstera worked for some but not others? Or was it just a question of dosage?

A thought occurred to her. She quickly went to the bedroom, opened her Macbook and found the spreadsheet where a few weeks before, she had noted the measurements of the rats the day she had brought them to the flat. She quickly scrolled to the Group 4 rats to compare their weights.

There in front of her was the most likely answer to whether the disappearance of two of the rats was a question of dose or propensity. Rat 17 had weighed 155g on arrival; Rat 19 was the heaviest of the group at 192g, and Rat 20 had weighed 167g. But Rats 16 and 18, the two that had disappeared, weighed just 134g and 128g respectively.

All of the rats had been given the same Monstera dose, but with 16 and

18 being so much smaller than their Group 4 peers, the effects of the dose must have been much greater.

Marion went straight to the laboratory, pressed 100ml of juice, then took the juice to the kitchen where she simmered it down to just 10ml. She then mixed the juice with melted chocolate, spreading the mixture out on a tray. When the mixture was set, she divided it into twelve 2cm squares, having calculated that each square would contain five times the daily dose that the rodents had been receiving during the first experiment. Returning to the laboratory, she dropped three squares into the cage, carefully closed and locked the lid, then went to bed.

The following morning, Marion woke at six. She quickly put on a dressing gown and went to the lab. Just as she had hoped, all three rats were gone. The cage was empty. Her suspicions had been correct; it was simply a question of quantity.

The thought flashed through her mind that if they had quantum tunnelled, but like Tom, had disappeared, maybe that meant that they had died. That would be quite understandable given that the rats had no experience of anything outside of a cage or a laboratory, so, therefore, wouldn't understand the risk of cats, dogs, humans or traffic. But then, thinking it through further, Marion considered that the reason Tom had, until his latest trip, never seemed to have been away, was because he had always wanted to come back, and to come back to the exact place and moment that he had left. Whereas, for the rats, why would they come back to an environment where for the entirety of their lives, they had been tortured, irradiated, injected with cancer-causing chemicals and kept as prisoners? No, Marion decided, the rats were now free, probably relishing every moment of their liberty and were never going to return. That's why they had disappeared. Tom, on the other hand, wasn't coming back, because he couldn't, because he was dead.

Emboldened with what seemed like reasonably conclusive proof that dosage was the most critical determinant as to whether an individual acquired Monstera's special powers, Marion then set about juicing more Monstera leaves. With a little mental calculation, Marion decided that if Tom's transformation had taken about a month with a daily Monstera 'tea', she should be able to shorten her metamorphosis to just a few days if she had a shot glass of the much more potent pure juice four times per day. So, she started juicing at breakfast, lunch, dinner and just before bed.

Marion was also conscious of the possibility that Monstera's quantum tunnelling effect might wear off. She knew that Tom hadn't thought about this, or if he had, hadn't said anything, but the thought of ending up trapped in 1960's New York was a concern. Using the centrifuge in the lab, Marion spun the juice to separate the water from the green dissolved solids. She then dried the spun concentrate to a dense cake, which she ground down to fine powder and blended with a binding agent she made by mixing Magnesium Stearate and Silicon Dioxide. Finally, she compressed the powder into tablets using a pill press that she had discretely borrowed from work.

It was slow going. Each pill required the juice of approximately three of Monstera's precious leaves. They re-grew fast; whatever Marion removed from the plant would be fully re-grown by the same time the following day, but even so, it was slow. Marion had decided that she would take thirty pills and was managing to make ten per day.

By the end of the third day, Marion had made thirty pills, which she put in an empty pill bottle. She was making good progress but was still worried because there were no signs that she was even beginning to acquire the same powers as Tom.

Despite multiple attempts each day, focusing hard on other rooms in the flat, she simply remained stubbornly static in a state of inert quantum impotence. So, that night, she doubled her usual dose, measuring out two shot glasses rather than one. As she finished the last drops of the second glass, she thought about how much she was looking forward to getting into bed – and suddenly she was there, in bed, with the empty shot glass still in her hand.

Reeling with both elation and disbelief at what had just happened, she sought confirmation and thought hard about the kitchen. Wham! She was there. It had worked! She could quantum tunnel.

At the same time, she had only made, two short, real-time journeys between different rooms in the flat. Would she be able to travel through time and across greater distances as Tom had? She needed to do a test trip but was conscious of the risks of making any trip without there being a safe place to arrive.

Thinking hard, Marion remembered that about two years ago her parents had taken a holiday in Martinique to celebrate their thirtieth wedding anniversary, leaving their house on the outskirts of Paris empty.

Scrolling back through the messages on her phone, Marion found a text from her mother timestamped 15th June 2019 at 23:15. 'Nous sommes arrivés sains et saufs. L'hôtel est charmant. Tout est parfait,' read the message.

She focused her mind on the 15th June 2019 and what used to be her bedroom at her parents' house, and in an instant, was there. She gave herself the brief luxury of a few moments to absorb the familiar, comforting smells and sounds of the house where she had grown up: the rhythmic and soothing tick-tock of the clock in the hallway downstairs, and the hum of the refrigerator emanating from the kitchen. Then, gathering her concentration, focused on 'Home' and was instantly back in her Limehouse kitchen.

With the stress of not knowing whether Monstera would work for her now gone, Marion slept the sleep of a thousand dreams, waking at eleven the following morning, feeling completely refreshed. After a breakfast that included two eggs, toast and a double Monstera shot, Marion started to make her plans.

She decided that rescuing Tom would require two trips. The first to properly find out what had happened, and the second to intervene to change the course of those events. Grimacing at the thought that she would have to witness Tom's death, she considered that she could just as easily, and with much less risk, travel back to some point in time before Tom had left to stop him from leaving. But then, they would be right back to the beginning, without knowing what had gone wrong, and the same risks of a catastrophic outcome for the next trip.

Marion went to the bedroom where the file with the notes and maps were kept and studied the antique map Tom had bought. Shubert Alley looked wider than an alley. A quick Google Street View search revealed that Schubert Alley was a road and not the pedestrian alley that they had assumed. She decided that she would arrive at the north end where she would have a full view of the street when Tom arrived.

Taking just a moment to mentally run through her plan and to check that the bottle of pills she'd so painstakingly made was safely in her pocket, Marion thought hard, focusing her mind on a doorway she'd seen on Street View near the junction of Shubert Alley and West 45th Street, simultaneously mentally weaving the image of the doorway with 5:44 am on 11th September 1960.

The next moment she was there, standing in the doorway and looking south towards West 44th Street. Taking stock of her surroundings, she was pleased to see that it was quiet and that nobody had seen her arrive. She knew that Tom would appear in less than one minute.

# THE COSMIC KNOT PARADOX

# Chapter 24
# Grand Theft Auto

The words 'How much?' broke Marion's concentration. She turned to see a shabbily dressed man in his forties staring at her. He was wearing denim jeans and a lumberjack-style shirt. He looked drunk, and even from a couple of metres distance, Marion could smell the alcohol on the man's breath.

"How much?" the man repeated, a note of aggression now evident in his voice. Marion immediately realised what was happening. She was a young single woman, wearing unusual clothes, standing in a doorway in an alley, in the early hours of the morning in New York's theatre district. She'd been confused for a prostitute.

Marion knew that she didn't have time to talk herself out of the situation. The seconds were ticking away, and Tom would arrive at any moment. Smiling, she stepped forward. The man stepped towards her. Marion punched him in the face. The punch was much more powerful than Marion had expected, and far more effective than anything she'd managed before at the Sunday morning boxing club that she went to back in her normal life. The blow took the man clean off his feet, sending him sprawling across to the other side of the alley where he slumped motionless against the wall of the Shubert Theatre. He looked dead, but there was no time to check.

"Not the blow you were expecting, huh?" she said out loud.

Marion's attention on the seemingly dead man was broken by the sound of a truck entering the other end of Shubert Alley. Looking south towards West 44th Street, she saw that a garbage truck was accelerating fast towards her. She knew what was about to happen. As the truck was almost halfway along Shubert Alley, Tom suddenly appeared in the middle of the street looking directly towards her.

There were just two seconds of squealing tyres and the truck's blaring horn before the sickening thud. The impact was devastating, propelling Tom a full ten metres forward. He lay motionless on the ground in front of the now stationary truck. Marion wanted to go to him, but she knew there was no point. He was dead.

Thinking quickly, Marion focused her mind on the other end of the street three minutes earlier, and in an instant was there, standing next to a large Cadillac car parked on the corner, half on the road and half on the pavement. The driver's door wasn't locked so she got in. Just like in the movies, the keys were tucked into the sun visor, 'God, Americans are so stupid' she thought, then chastised herself for allowing the prejudice she had grown up with, so common amongst her parents' generation, to have overwhelmed her.

Looking along West 44th Street, she could see that the garbage truck was stopped next to some dumpsters just fifty metres away. The men had finished emptying the bins and were getting back into the truck. There wasn't much time. She fiddled with the key, trying to get it into the ignition. It didn't fit the lock. She turned the key over and fiddled again. This time, the key slid into the ignition barrel. She turned the key, simultaneously pressing the accelerator, and to her immense relief was rewarded with a short whine followed by a deep rumble as the car's big engine came to life.

Marion grabbed the gear selector and moved it to "D". The car lurched forward. She steered the car off the pavement and diagonally across the alley, then stopped, turned off the engine and got out of the car, locking the door and taking the key with her so that nobody would be able to move it. With the alley blocked, she started to run towards where she knew Tom would be arriving in the next few moments. As she ran, she saw the man in the lumberjack shirt cross the end of the alley as he stumbled drunk, but otherwise unharmed, along West 45th Street.

# Chapter 25
# The Second Coming

"So, you're going to go on this amazing adventure, but leaving me here?" Marion said as Tom prepared to leave.

"Yes, because there's no safe landing there," Tom replied, "Two of us arriving in a place that we don't know, where we can't be certain what we'll find when we arrive, more than doubles the risk. I'll get an apartment sorted out and then come back for you. Anyway, you won't even realise I'm gone. For you, it'll just be an instant, no matter how long I spend there."

Hugging Marion, he told her, "Wish me luck. I'll get everything sorted and be back for you before you know I'm gone. To Wesh and beyond!"

Tom focused his mind on the date and time they'd discussed, 5:45 am, 11th September 1960, then the landing place, Shubert Alley, New York. In an instant he was there, looking towards the end of the alley and the junction with West 45 Street. A voice directly behind him said his name. It was Marion's voice. As he turned around, she flung her arms around him, tears streaming down her face. Further down the street, a garbage truck was blaring its horn, the driver leaning out of the window and shouting angrily. A big black car was parked diagonally across the road, blocking the truck's route.

"What are you doing here Marion?" Tom asked.

"You died, Tom," she replied, tears still running down her cheeks. "You arrived right in front of that garbage truck. It hit you. You died. I saw it all; it was terrible. So, I went back in time to a few minutes before you arrived and moved that car to block the road".

"Marion, you're amazing," said Tom. "But how did you travel back in time? Tell me while we walk. Let's find the hotel."

As they started along Shubert Alley, Marion told Tom about her conclusion as to why only two of the rats had disappeared, about her new experiment, and how she'd been mega-dosing on Monstera for four days and had learned to quantum tunnel.

At the north end of the alley, where Marion had killed the man in the lumberjack shirt, Marion told Tom about the incident and what she'd done. "You killed someone?" he said in disbelief. She explained that she hadn't intended to kill the man, but was so much stronger than before, and in any case, she'd seen the man completely unharmed after she'd travelled back in time to block the road.

"It's the Monstera," Tom told her. "This suitcase weighs almost half as much as you, but to me, it's as light as a feather. You have superpowers now."

At the end of Shubert Alley, they turned right onto West 45th Street, then left onto 7th Avenue, and two blocks from there took another left onto West 47th Street. The Hotel Edison was just eighty metres along on the same side of the road.

At the hotel reception desk, the receptionist, a middle-aged woman called Edith, if her name badge was to be believed, greeted them with a smile that waned as she saw Marion, looking her up and down with obvious distaste.

"Good morning, Sir, welcome to the Hotel Edison," she said, resurrecting her smile, "Do you have a reservation?"

Tom explained that they didn't have a reservation; how they'd arrived for a week-long trip on the early flight from London, and that there'd been some confusion with their reservation at another hotel. Edith said that there was a suite available at sixty dollars per night, which Tom said they'd take. She asked for passports. Tom gave her his, and Marion explained that she had left hers in the taxi. Edith nodded with an expression of savvy disbelief, then summoned a porter.

"Regal Suite, Billy," Edith told the porter. Noticing only one case, she remarked, "No luggage Madam?", the knowing look creeping back onto her face.

"No, we travel light, everything is in my husband's case," Marion replied.

"Of course, Madam. I should have realised. Billy, take the gentleman and the *lady* to their suite," Edith said pointedly, rubbing the silver cross around her neck as if to protect herself from moral contamination.

As Tom and Marion walked towards the elevator, a few paces behind Billy the porter, Marion quietly said, "That's the second time I've been confused for a prostitute in less than an hour. I need some new clothes."

In the elevator, Billy appeared transfixed by Marion's trainers. As they ascended, unable to contain his curiosity, and no doubt breaking hotel protocols, he said, 'Pardon me, Ma'am, but I couldn't help but notice your shoes. I'm interested because my brother has a heel bar and I help out there when my shift finishes here. I thought I'd seen every type of shoe, but never anything like those. They're amazing!'

"Oh, they're very popular in France right now, I'm sure you'll see them here soon," Marion replied. Billy was still staring at the trainers intently.

At the 26th floor, Billy led the way to the Regal Suite and into a huge living room with French doors opening onto a wide terrace with views over the rooftops to Central Park. There were sofas and chairs and a stunning antique chaise lounge. Billy carried the suitcase through to the bedroom, which was dominated by a magnificent four-poster bed. To the right of the bed, double doors opened to reveal an en-suite bathroom with a large roll-top bath and marble-tiled walls and floor. The suite was palatial. Tom thanked Billy, discretely tipping him with one of the dollar bills that he'd bought on eBay.

As soon as Billy had left, Marion said, "I can't go out to buy clothes here. I've been confused for a hooker twice and had someone obsessing about my shoes, and all of that before breakfast. You said something about not being able to turn up in 1960s Manhattan wearing trainers and you were right. I'm going back to London, to that shop on Portobello Road.'

The very next instant, and still in exactly the same spot, Marion was now holding a collection of bags. From Portobello Road market, she'd bought some flared jeans, a brightly coloured psychedelic patterned blouse and a pair of platformed boots. She put them on.

"Marion, you look amazing, but that's all late 60's stuff. This is 1960. You'll look even more unusual than wearing leggings and trainers," Tom told her. Marion sighed and a moment later was holding more bags. This time her choices were more conservative. She'd bought a tasteful blue Mary Quant dress with a white collar, some medium-heeled shoes, and a grey jacket.

# THE COSMIC KNOT PARADOX

# Chapter 26
# Tom's Diner

"Let's unpack your clothes and then go and get some breakfast," Marion said. Within a couple of minutes, Tom's suits, trousers and shirts were all on hangers in the wardrobe along with Marion's psychedelic sixties outfit. The platform boots and Adidas trainers were neatly arranged on the shoe rack together with Tom's classic business shoes.

Heading out through reception, Marion walked rather nearer to the reception desk than she needed to so that Edith would see her in her new outfit. However, the sight of Marion wearing clothes which, logically could only have come from Tom's suitcase, failed to dispel Edith's earlier assumptions. Once again, the receptionist sought sanctuary in her cross, manically rubbing it between finger and thumb as Marion strode with the belligerent confidence of a catwalk model towards the door and out onto the street.

Tom and Marion turned onto Broadway and headed towards Central Park. They walked up, past Columbus Circle, then continued along Broadway, past Lincoln Square and through the Upper West Side towards Morningside Heights, enjoying the warm sunshine and the novelty of discovery in equal measure. Just past West 112th Street, they found Tom's Diner, which, even though Tom was now William, seemed like an appropriately named place, so they stopped for breakfast.

The long walk had worked up an appetite and they both ordered bacon, sausage, two eggs over-easy, and hash browns, a side of waffles with blueberries and maple syrup, and coffee. The coffee was awful, but the food was great. As they ate, they made their plans for the day.

Tom had decided that a corporate structure of some sort would offer the best chance of laundering the diamonds without raising suspicions. It was still only fifteen years since the end of the Second World War, and Nazi war criminals had escaped the Nuremberg trials by fleeing Europe, were still popping up here and there, raising cash from the gold and jewellery that they had stolen from the Jews they had systematically murdered.

Having finished breakfast and paid the bill, Tom and Marion took a taxi to the financial district in Tribeca, walked into Acme Company Formations and formed The Wesh Corporation. They then went to J.P. Morgan Bank and opened two accounts, one for the new company and one for Tom, well for William Eugene Stephan Hubert.

They then spent the afternoon going around New York's diamond district, offloading the diamonds they'd bought in London, splitting up the sales between four different dealers; not because the transactions were big enough to raise any suspicions in New York, simply to find out who they felt most comfortable dealing with.

Returning to J.P Morgan Bank just before it closed, they deposited three cheques made out to the Wesh Corporation totalling $101,734 plus just over forty thousand in cash, as the last dealer they'd sold to didn't issue cheques. Tom kept five thousand dollars in cash for expenses.

Back at the hotel, they decided that they would make a trip back to 2021 to get some more diamonds. Tom suggested that Marion should go in the clothes she was wearing and change into her Twenty-First-Century clothes back in the Limehouse flat. She could get back into 'role' once they'd completed their business.

Marion agreed but said she would put on her trainers as she didn't have any others at home. She went to the wardrobe, but on the shoe rack where she expected to find them, there was just an empty space. Marion checked the other side of the wardrobe. They weren't there either.

"It's Billy, the porter," she said. "He's stolen my fucking shoes."

Tom called Reception and asked for Billy but was told that he'd quit that morning.

Through most of the remainder of the evening, they talked about how this unexpected development might impact the world moving forward; the myriad of possible outcomes, the butterfly effect that could result from the theft of a pair of shoes from a New York hotel room in 1960, and how people's lives might be altered in the years to come.

They spent more than three hours speculating on the multitude of possibilities. In one scenario, they even arrived at the outcome of Marion's trainers being the catalyst for thermonuclear war. This, Tom postulated, would be the upshot of Soviet Union taunts about the result of the Men's 100-metre sprint at the 1964 Tokyo Olympics, reigniting US-Soviet tensions so soon after the Cuban Missile Crisis, because the shoes, technologically superior to anything that existed in 1964, could end up in the possession of the Cuban athlete, Enrique Figuerola Camue, who might then go on to beat the American, Robert Hayes, to win the Gold medal, reversing the finishing positions of the multiverse thread that they knew, in which Hayes wins Gold and Figuerola, Silver.

In the end, they decided that Billy probably just wanted the shoes so he could wear them, admire them, or both, and that the chances of a catastrophic outcome were highly remote. In any case, they would be able to check that no dramatic events had taken place, and if the trainers did turn out to be the catalyst of catastrophe, they could easily nip back to 1960 and hide the shoes, so that Billy wouldn't have the opportunity to steal them.

So, that night, they made a trip back to 2021 Limehouse and were pleased to find that, superficially at least, everything seemed pretty much the same. A few quick Google searches revealed that world events since 1960 had unfolded pretty much exactly as expected; there had been no thermonuclear war, and Robert Hayes did indeed get the gold medal.

Marion also revisited the Manhattan Gazette's online historical archive. She flicked through the pages to page seventeen where she had tearfully read the report of Tom's death. In its place was now the headline 'NY Garbage Crew Foil Attempted Theft of Mayor Wagner's Car'.

The next morning, they took a KLM flight from City Airport to Amsterdam, then a taxi to Dam Square, on the edge of Amsterdam's diamond district. Just as they had done before in Hatton Garden, Marion and Tom split up, going around the various dealers individually. This time, their purchases were bigger. During the course of the morning, their personal banker, Sebastian Sommerville-Abercromby at Coutts Bank, received no fewer than fourteen calls with requests to wire funds to the various diamond dealers, and by lunchtime, they had acquired just over fifteen million Dollars' worth of cut and uncut gems.

With little bags of gems secreted around their clothing, they then had lunch at the Grand Hotel Krasnapolsky on Dam Square, before finding a quiet corner out of view of any cameras on the second floor of the hotel, from where they 'tunnelled' back to London.

They spent the night back in the Limehouse flat. Then, in the morning, after hiding the diamonds under the carpet in a corner of the bedroom, headed off to Portobello Road and back to the stall where they had acquired Tom's passport. Knowing that New York was going to be their North American base and the interchange between quantum arrivals and transfers onto regular transport to go off to other cities in North America, they needed to obtain a passport for Marion.

Leafing through the antique documents on the stall, Tom found a French passport from the right period. It had belonged to Genevieve Antoine Auclaire, born on 15th April 1935 and had been issued in 1959 when Genevieve was twenty-four years old. Genevieve looked nothing like Marion and there were no visa stamps, but Tom figured those would be relatively easy problems to solve. Portobello Art & Stationery had everything he needed to transform the rather frumpy-looking Genevieve into beautiful Marion.

Back at the flat, Marion changed into her 1960's clothes. Tom took a passport-style photo of her standing against the white bedroom door and then applied a sepia filter to the image. In Photoshop, he overlaid the notaire's stamp that he had copied off the original, then printed it onto the light gloss 'vintage' card he had bought from the stationers and trimmed it to size.

Having carefully cut away Genevieve's photo, Tom glued Marion's in its place and then copied the visa stamps from his own passport, before carefully unpicking the stitching from the spine of the passport to separate the sheets and printed the visas onto the relevant pages of Genevieve's passport. Subterfuge complete, he carefully reassembled and re-stitched it. The final step was to gently rub the spine of the passport with candle wax and then sprinkle cigarette ash over the wax to age the new thread. The whole process took less than twenty minutes.

With the counterfeit passport completed, Tom and Marion changed into their other clothes, retrieved the bag of diamonds from under the carpet, gave La Monstera some water, and then thought themselves back to their suite at the Edison Hotel.

The following morning, after breakfast, they walked the two blocks to the diamond district and went straight to Josef Goldman & Sons Gemstones, who had offered the best price and been the easiest to deal with the day before. They sold all of the Amsterdam haul for $1.37 million, and fifteen minutes later were back at Acme Company Formations where Tom registered the Wesh Trading Corporation and Wesh Realty Corporation.

After that they walked to JP Morgan where Tom deposited the cash from Goldman & Sons into the Wesh Corporation account, then opened new accounts for the two new companies, transferring $500,000 to each. They then went to the third floor of the same building and opened a stockbroking account with JP Morgan's subsidiary, The Morgan Guarantee Trust Company of New York.

With the practicalities of corporate structure and banking completed, they spent the afternoon house hunting. The areas around Greenwich Village and Central Park were very pleasant, but few of the buildings were suitable. The grand apartment blocks at the Central Park end of 5th, 6th and Park Avenues all had concierges, porters and doormen who surely, at some point would notice them leaving the building without having been seen arriving. They loved the old mews houses on the streets near Washington Square Park, but there was a similar problem. Whilst there weren't any porters or doormen to worry about, in most streets there would be many curtain-twitching neighbours who would be rather too interested in when they were and weren't home.

Late afternoon, having walked for what felt like miles, and just as they were thinking about returning to the hotel, they got lucky in Greenwich Village. Walking along Grove Street they found an early twentieth-century townhouse with a board reading 'For Sale – Enquire Within' displayed in one of the downstairs windows.

Tom knocked, and a few moments later a well-dressed man in his late sixties opened the door. Tom introduced himself and told the man why they were there.

"Al Johnson, pleased to meet you. Please come on in and have a look around," the man said, holding out his hand to shake.

On entering the property, they found themselves in a hallway with a black and white tiled floor. Doors off the hallway led to two large reception rooms, each with a magnificent marble fireplace. Al explained that he had just retired, having sold his architectural practice a few months ago, while his wife had also sold the furniture design business that she had run for the last twenty years.

"So, we're free," Al said, smiling. "We've got a place in Florida and well, the climate suits us old folk better there." He went on to detail the property's history, explaining that it had been built in 1899 by his grandfather, who had bequeathed it directly to him in 1930. He and his wife had refurbished the house in 1957, "so everything is quite contemporary", he explained.

Contemporary was an understatement; the house had been refurbished to a style and standard that one might expect from a specialist developer fifty or sixty years later. The layout and design had succeeded in retaining the best of the original features, whilst updating the layout and style of the property to something which addressed both form and function in equal measure.

In the basement below the raised ground floor, where there had originally been a coal cellar at the front, and a scullery and servant's bedroom at the rear, the space had been re-arranged as a large open-plan kitchen and dining area, with the kitchen on the street side and the dining area at the back. French doors opened onto a tastefully landscaped twenty-five-metre-long garden with a large oak tree at the end.

Going up two floors, there were three en-suite bedrooms and a further bathroom. One of the bedrooms was set up with a drawing board and used as Al's home office. On the floor above, the attic area had been converted into a large bedroom and en-suite bathroom occupying around two-thirds of the floorplan of the lower floors. The remainder was a large, private roof terrace, shielded from view by the oak tree in the garden and not overlooked by the neighbours on either side.

Back in the main reception room, Al explained that they wanted $180,000 for the house and would be able to complete the sale and move out within a month. It was one of those telepathic moments for Tom and Marion. Without a word of consultation, or even any exchange of glances between them, both instinctively knew that the other loved the house.

Without hesitation, Tom told Al, "If you can complete the sale in a week and are prepared to leave all of the furniture, we'll give you $200,000. Just take your clothes and whatever books and ornaments that you want. You don't even need to clean or empty the fridge."

Al thought for a few moments, then offered his hand for a handshake, saying, "We have a deal".

Exactly one week later, with the house purchase complete, Tom and Marion took a taxi from the Edison Hotel with all of their worldly possessions contained in their one suitcase, drove to Grove Street, and moved in.

Over the week that followed, they made the house a home and started to plan their next steps. The priority was to put in place the foundations to start building the resources of the three Wesh corporations. Tom nipped back to 2021 Limehouse and acquired a historical database of US stock market data back to 1960. He then went through the data to identify the stocks that had had the biggest daily gains and losses, together with the daily high and low for each stock.

Realising that back in 1960, the data he had bought was of almost infinite value, but was of little worth in 2021, he decided it would be best to leave the data in Limehouse and that he would simply tunnel back before the start of each trading day, print off the data and then go back to 1960 New York to place his trades.

Tom had AT&T install three new telephone lines and a mini switchboard in the office. He had also opened two new brokerage accounts with different brokers; one with Goldman Sachs and one with Bache so he could spread his trades around different dealers, having decided that he'd need to have at least a few losing trades to avoid raising too many suspicions.

The first trading day was 26th September 1960. Tom placed twelve trades: three winners and one loser with each broker. The profit for the day was just over $200,000. A similar pattern continued over the following weeks, but with the daily gains steadily increasing as the trade sizes grew, by the end of October, the three brokerage accounts had a combined value of just under $80 million.

Charlie suddenly interrupted, startling Tom out of his trance-like state. The movie stopped and the screen went blank.

"That's all very well, but I can see where this is all headed. You're going to tell us that you're now worth $500 million and invite us to spend the weekend on your superyacht, so we can all see how successful you've been. But all I want to know is why the fuck have I got tits?"

Charlie's intervention prompted Flore to ask her burning question.

"And I want to know why you look like an alien and…" casting a reproachful look towards Sylvain, "how Sylvain knew about all of this before we did but didn't say anything."

Tom took a deep breath, "OK. I'll deal with those issues, but before I do, I just want to tell you that the total value of the various Wesh corporations is quite a bit more than $500 million. I can tell you that either directly or via a web of carefully disguised subsidiaries, Wesh Corp now owns about ten percent of almost every viable listed company on the planet and has greater gold and foreign currency reserves than every member of the G7 put together. We own tens of thousands of residential and commercial properties, and one way or another, through land ownership entities, miners, refiners and manufacturers, have significant investments in every natural resource that has or will have value over the next five hundred years. Now, I'll answer your questions; you've waited long enough.

# Chapter 27
# Apples and Pears

"Charlie, you have tits because you ate the apple from the garden. Marion and I had been working on isolating the health benefits of Monstera from the quantum tunnelling effect, because can you imagine the chaos that would ensue if the wrong people were able to time travel? There'd be historical murders everywhere. Satanists, atheists and radicals of multiple denominations would be staking out every stable in Bethlehem, hoping to be the one to kill the infant Jesus before he could grow up, walk on water and heal the sick. They'd be disappointed by the way, because Jesus didn't exist; at least, not in the way portrayed in the bible. Christian fundamentalists and Jews would be taking themselves back to the sixth century to try to find and kill Mohammed before he could finish transcribing the Quran. Neo-Nazis would be zipping back and forth to 1940s Berlin to break the news to Hitler that the Enigma machine had been compromised, tell him about the Normandy landings and exactly when they would take place. Can you imagine? Utter chaos."

"So, for a while, we'd been working in the lab trying to work out which part of Monstera's genetic code conferred the quantum tunnelling, so we could remove that, whilst ensuring that what stimulates the body's regenerative capabilities remained. We thought we'd cracked it and had introduced the new gene sequence into several types of fruit and vegetables, including the apples, but there was a problem as Charlie has discovered. Genetically modifying plants is such a nightmare.

"Lucky you didn't eat the pears. You would have needed a wheelbarrow to move your testicles around. Anyway, the good news for you Charlie is that there's an antidote for your new features. We've got some in the lab downstairs. You'll be back to normal by tomorrow lunchtime. There's more to tell you about the fruit, but we'll get to that later."

"So, what about the alien thing, Tom?" asked Flore.

"Oh that, it's simply that whilst it's easy for me to jump through time to different places, this suit takes ages to get on and off," Tom replied.

"Suit? That's a suit? You mean, you're not an actual alien," said Lucia, looking incredulous.

"Yes, these suits are all the rage in 2120. As are many other things. For example, flying cars are everywhere. Almost everyone has one, and they're not like those supersized drones that you've seen in 2021. They look just like regular cars. Buses and what I suppose you would call aeroplanes, end up looking just like the flying saucers you saw in old sci-fi films. They can land and take off vertically and travel at more than twenty times the speed of sound, meaning that you can be anywhere in the world in less than two hours.

"But there are smaller, personal transport versions that are just as fast and look like futuristic cars, as well as others that are retro-styled; so, people are flying around in VW Beetles, Minis and 2CVs, as well as every other type of twentieth and twenty-first-century car that you can imagine. There are even E-Type Jags buzzing around. They're called 'flars', so people say things like, 'Shall we take your flar or mine?' and when their vehicles get dirty, they take them to the 'Flar Wash'.

"Anyway, these flars and many other things that will just blow your mind, were all made possible because in 2040, we perfected miniaturized nuclear fusion. You probably saw the Fusion 5000 downstairs. Well, that's an early version that we created in 2030.

"The first flars had something quite similar to the Fusion 5000, where you had to manually put banana skins and eggshells directly into a receptacle on the side of the flar, rather like in that film, Back to the Future. The problem with that was that some bright spark doing a Nuclear Physics PhD at MIT, stumbled across some research by an Oxford Physics Professor and managed to convince the world via a Facebook post that the chemical reaction of the banana skins and eggshells could be significantly enhanced with the addition of human semen. Within a short time, refuelling stations across the globe were besmirched by the sight of customers masturbating furiously into the fuel fillers of their flars in an attempt to shorten their journey times.

"And instead of having someone looking like a bag of washing with a head on top trying to clean your windshield every time you stop at a set of traffic lights, there'd be some pale, depraved-looking individual with his cock in one hand and a porn mag in the other, offering to 'wank in the tank'.

"Anyway, by 2070, we managed to reduce the dimensions of the fusion reactor devices to about the size of a medium-sized orange and make them entirely self-contained. The actual reactor is only about the size of a grain of rice and the rest of the self-contained unit is a highly condensed mix of the key elements from the eggshell, banana skin and semen, providing the fuel for the reactor.

"Each 'orange' can produce up to 3 megawatts of power continuously for seventy years. And that's a total game-changer in almost every type of human endeavour, particularly flying cars."

"As early as 1930 there were designs for machines that theoretically could achieve levitation without wings, rotors, propellors or jets, but just like Leonardo DaVinci's 15th Century helicopter design, the key issue that prevented these designs moving from the academic realm to functioning reality was power. The size and weight of the power sources available at the time simply rendered the designs unfeasible.

"In DaVinci's case, it would have required forty horses running at full speed on a treadmill to generate enough power for his machine to leave the ground, but that calculation is based only on the weight of the machine, not its weight with the horses, so Davinci's concept remained only a concept until the internal combustion engine had been not just invented, but had become sufficiently refined to have a power to weight ratio that would enable flight.

"The same with flars. The power needed to make a journey from London to Paris, which takes just three minutes by the way, is the equivalent of the power used by one thousand washing machines running continuously for one hundred years; so making flars fly with electricity generated the way it is in the early Twenty-First Century would have required more than one thousand large internal combustion engines or a medium-sized power station. So, just like Davinci's helicopter, the vehicle would have been too heavy to fly. But MNF, miniaturised nuclear fusion, changed all of this.

"Great, so the future is basically a boys' toys paradise on steroids," said Lucia, "But you've still not told us about this alien suit."

# THE COSMIC KNOT PARADOX

# Chapter 28
# Paul

"Yes, the alien suit. I was getting to that," said Tom, "It's all related; so, like I said, the alien suits and all sorts of other suits are really popular in 2120. They're made from a type of genetically modified skin similar in structure to dolphin skin but with the addition of a short string of Monstera DNA.

"The suits are waterproof, fireproof, perfectly thermally insulated, and…" as he picked up a knife from the table and slashed the arm of the suit, "…they heal almost immediately when damaged". The four watched in astonishment as the deep wound healed in moments, leaving only a very faint scar.

"I got the suit when I started testing the prototype of the X-15FAF, which was one of the first high-velocity flars, knowing that if I crashed, the suit would protect me. Then, one evening, I had a bit too much to drink and, as you do after one too many Mai Tai's, decided it would be really funny to go and freak out some people by arriving somewhere mid-twentieth century in my flar and getting out of it looking like an alien. You can probably guess the rest…"

"*You* are the Roswell alien?" Flore interjected.

"Exactly," replied Tom, "I went back to 1947, blasted around Arizona and New Mexico for a while, then crashed. Not because there was anything wrong with the X-15FAF, simply because I was drunk. Anyway, the suit did its job and I was unharmed, although the X-15 was pretty badly damaged.

"I managed to think my way back to the safety of 2170 with most of the craft, but there was quite a bit of debris that I wasn't able to collect, and anyway, I needed to know what they'd seen; and if I'm honest, I felt like having a bit of fun with them, so I went back. I've been winding them up ever since. I've now talked to dozens of so-called extra-terrestrial experts drafted in by the US military. I've spoken to every Director of Homeland Security and every Chairman of the Joint Chiefs of Staff since 1947, as well as thirteen Presidents.

"It's been hilarious. I told them all the things they wanted to hear, starting of course with, 'We come in peace', then that my name was Palaragash Xmashlop Z'ting, Z'ting, but that they could call me 'Paul'. Then I told them that I was from a planet called Zarg, located one million light years beyond the Nexus of Sominus, and invisible from Earth because it sits beyond two wormholes.

"President Harry Truman asked why I had a French accent, which I still did then. I told him that my people first arrived from Zarg to the Auvergne region of France in the year 1065, bred with the local people, and that there are now Franco-Zargan descendants all over the world. I told him that this is why French people like to eat snails, frog legs and Époisses cheese; and why, wherever you are in the world, there's always someone who pushes into any queue – those queue jumpers are all Franco-Zargan descendants, I explained.

"I told Donald Trump the same, and also that Hilary Clinton was one of us. Bill Clinton asked what the females from Zarg were like. I told him that in our culture, Zargan females consider human semen to be a delicacy, rather like Caviar is on Earth, and told him that a Franco-Zargan female, called Monica, was working in the White House.

"Anyway, for me this whole alien thing since the 1947 Roswell incident has all happened during this last week. I keep nipping back and forth to wind them up a bit more, but I think I'm done with them now, so if you could help me get the suit off, I'd be really grateful."

The next half-hour was spent helping Tom extricate himself from the alien suit. There was a hidden zip down one side, but even after the zip was undone it still took the efforts of all four to gently tease the suit from Tom's body. The whole experience was not dissimilar to skinning a rabbit and, judging by the sounds Tom made, probably quite painful.

Flore asked, "Doesn't this make going to the bathroom rather difficult, you know, having to go through all this rigmarole every time you need to pee?"

Tom replied, "No, that's not a problem at all. The suit is actually a living organism. When it's not being worn it kind of goes into a state of hibernation, but while you're wearing it, it feeds on everything that comes out of your body, so it can be worn for weeks or even months without having to take it off".

"Urgh, that's gross!" exclaimed Flore.

When finally, the suit was off and Tom was sitting naked in his chair drinking the Tom Collins that Sylvain had prepared for him, he said, "I need to shower and get dressed." Flore nodded in vigorous agreement.

The next instant, Tom was still in the same chair, but was now dressed in a pair of jeans and a tee shirt with damp towel-dried hair, a healthy glow, and a minty aroma.

"So, what happened to your French accent, and why do you sound like Boris Johnson?" Lucia asked, "It gives me the creeps."

"Oh that. Yes, I'm still in a dispute with Elon Musk's company, Neuralink, about that. You've probably already heard of Neuralink, because since 2016, they've been working on developing an interface between the human brain and computers.

"In 2030 they said they'd overcome all of the technical challenges and started taking deposits for the first release of a product that would allow customers not only to speak any language but also to choose the voice. Customers could choose from a library of generic choices or pay extra to get a selection of celebrities' voices. So, for example, if you wanted to speak French, you could choose from a list of French celebrities like Charles Aznavour, Christopher Lambert, or perhaps Gerrard Depardieu. Or, you could make a generic choice from a structured menu; for example, 'French, France, Normandy, Farmer, Male', or 'French, France, Parisian, Upper Class, Male'; although if you chose, 'French, Male, Creepy Perv', you still sounded like Gerrard Depardieu.

"That suited me very well, because by 2030, I'd decided that I needed to create a new identity for myself, as by then, William Hubert was almost one hundred years old and I was getting frustrated at having to keep putting on and taking off my geriatric suit every time I had to appear in public – I mean, you've seen how hard it is to get these things on and off. I had already acquired some other ID and had decided that I would pass myself off as an eccentric English aristocrat, so the idea of being able to just choose 'English, England, South, Aristocrat, Eccentric, Male,' and immediately sound like someone who had been to Eton and Oxford and got a Christmas card from the King each year, seemed like a pretty good idea.

"So, I paid my $100 million deposit and waited. And then, I waited, and then waited some more. 2030 came and went. I continued waiting through 2031, 32 and 33, and then finally in 2034, I got invited in for my Neuralink implant. At first, the only new capability that I seemed to have acquired was the ability to order a Tesla car or book a SpaceX trip, just by thinking about it. "Then, I waited again, until finally in 2040, I got a text delivered to my brain's inbox telling me that my Neuralink language pack was ready to use.

"Imagine my horror when the first time I tried to speak English, I discovered that I sounded just like Boris Johnson. Not only that but I've been stuck sounding like that muppet ever since.

"Neuralink keep saying that they're working on a fix and that there'll be an 'over-the-air' update any day, but there never is. Luckily, I can also speak over seven thousand other languages, although I have a similar problem that when I select, 'English, America, New York, Criminal, Liar, Male', I find that I sound just like Donald Trump. It's quite infuriating."

Charlie interrupted to ask, "Doesn't that mean that it's never going to get fixed? I mean, you can travel into the future, so if it was going to be fixed at any time in the future, it would surely be resolved now. Or have I misunderstood how this quantum multi-wotsit-tunnelverse thing works?"

"That's a good question," Tom replied, "but it doesn't work exactly like that. It's a bit complicated. The fact that it's not fixed right now, does indeed mean that it won't ever be fixed based on everything I've tried to do so far, now or in the future, or in the past. But that doesn't mean that I won't do something, at some point along the timeline, now or in the future or in the past, that changes all of that and gets my problem with Elon Musk sorted, so the events of this evening and the conversation we're having now end up differently, just like how page seventeen of the Manhattan Gazette changed after Marion saved me. Remember that in quantum physics, the same object can be in two or more different places at the same time, or not at all."

"This is so hard to understand," remarked Lucia, "And, you said 'your problem with Elon Musk'. Don't you mean with Neuralink? I mean, I know Musk is a shareholder and all that, but surely your problem is with the company, not one of its shareholders."

"Well, yes and no," replied Tom. "What you have to realise is that Musk is in complete and total control of everything related to all of these companies and does everything himself. In 2070, the ninety-nine-year-old Musk dies in a horrific 480mph crash on the Santa Monica Highway, after accidentally turning off AutoPilot while trying to work out how to adjust the air vents in his Tesla car. But, by 2071 he is the only employee of Tesla, SpaceX, The Boring Company, Neuralink and several thousand other multi-national companies that he's started by then."

"What? That doesn't make sense. How can he be an employee after he's dead?" asked Charlie, looking perplexed.

"That was the whole point of Neuralink," said Tom, "To give Musk immortality and omnipresence. The Musk that died in the crash was only the physical version of Musk. By the time of the accident, and some people think it wasn't an accident, Neuralink had uploaded his every thought, memory and his very consciousness, you could say his soul, to the Neuralink Cloud. And with factories across the globe full of robots building cars, spacecraft, and newer and better robots to build even better cars and spacecraft, Musk no longer needs any employees.

"Living on interplanetary connected servers and with virtually unlimited computing power, Musk can do everything himself. As well as being CEO of the several thousand companies that we know about, he is also the CFO, CTO, CIO and COO of each and every one of them. And it doesn't stop there. In addition to defining both business strategy and tactics, he orders materials, negotiates with suppliers, manages sales, marketing, PR, corporate communications and everything else. If the lights needed to be turned off after the office closed, he'd do that too, but he doesn't need to, because there aren't any offices, because there aren't any employees. Just huge factories and data centres full of robots that make everything and fix anything that needs fixing.

"Anyway, all of this also means that he's also Head of Customer Service, Head of Complaints Resolution and Head of Legal, as well as doing all of the more junior jobs below those titles, including taking the calls.

"Unfortunately, on my first call to Customer Service to complain that my Neuralink language system wasn't working properly and that I sounded like Boris Johnson, I ended up having a bit of an argument with Elon. He was pretending to be a young woman called Maisie from Baltimore, but it didn't fool me.

"So, during the call, I remembered the 2035 controversy that followed

Elon having been spotted coming out of an LA clinic that specialised in penis enlargement. The Washington Post dubbed it 'Elongate' and ran with an 'Elongate' headline on the front page every day that week - Jeff Bezos must have been pissing himself.

"Anyway, I couldn't get that thought out of my head and it seems that Elon took a grudge about the things I said about the SpaceX rockets having been created to compensate for his phallic insecurities. So now, I'm stuck sounding like Boris Johnson. Every other Neuralink customer's language pack works fine, just not mine."

"Can you fix my tits now?" Charlie said.

"Shut the fuck up about your tits," Flore said, now sounding very irritated. "Tom still hasn't told us how or why Sylvain knows about all of this."

"No, let's fix Charlie's tits first. He's been waiting long enough," Tom said, smiling, "I can show you around the place properly at the same time."

# Chapter 29
# Voice of a Castrato

"You're not showing them around without me," Marion said, stepping out from the shadows and into the candlelight around the table. Beside her was a white Labrador dog.

"Marion, so glad you're here," said Lucia, jumping up from her chair to hug her, "I was wondering why you weren't around. I was going to ask Tom, but we just had so many other questions. And who is this? He's so cute," she said, looking at the dog.

"Oh, this is Brian. He's our dog and our best friend," Marion replied.

"Evening all. Pleased to finally meet you. I've heard all about you. Whoa, and who is this delightful creature that I've been waiting to meet all my life?" said Brian, walking over to Lucia. "Do you want to rub behind my ears? I don't mind if you do, I mean, lots of women want to rub me behind my ears. Feel free. I don't mind. I like rubbing."

"What the fuck! A talking dog!" Charlie exclaimed.

"Don't be so surprised," Marion said, "By 2050 almost all dogs and many other animals can talk. Racing horses and greyhounds are now celebrities and give TV interviews after races, just like Formula One and Nascar drivers; and there are even programmes on TV with animal presenters. For example, the main Fox News anchor is a real fox.

"For some reason, the Farmers Union spent a fortune on legal fees to get a court injunction preventing Neuralink from releasing a version for sheep, but most domestic animals, dogs, cats, hamsters and even some fish can talk. We had the vet install a Neuralink package for Brian at the same time we had him castrated," Marion explained.

Brian's pleasant and friendly manner instantly changed.

"Bastards. Both of you. I'll never forgive you for that," Brian snarled, "And you keep telling everyone. You even ruined my chances with that hottie that was petting me in Central Park the other day, I mean, what the fuck? Where's the respect for my feelings, for my needs?"

Tom interjected, "Well, what would you have done anyway Brian? You don't have any balls," Tom interjected.

"Yes, well I might not have any balls, but I can still do stuff…. things… you know, I could have humped her leg. You should let me sort Marion out. I'd do a better job than you. Every Wednesday and Saturday night… 'Ooohh, ooohh, Ahhh, Ahhh, oui, oui, comme ça, comme ça,' for thirty seconds and then snoring. It's pathetic. I can piss for longer," said Brian, before turning around five times and lying down on the ground with his back to the group.

"I'm sorry about Brian," said Marion, "He's taken the castration thing really badly. He's a good dog, but sometimes his resentment just gets the better of him."

"He looks and sounds kind of familiar," remarked Charlie.

"Well, when we got him home from the rescue centre, we realised that he looks very similar to a dog called Brian in a TV series. So, we named him 'Brian', and when we had the Neuralink package fitted we just chose 'English, America, Rhode Island, Quahog, Dog, Male,' and here he is, almost identical in appearance and sound to the dog on the TV. In hindsight, it was a mistake to have the Neuralink implant fitted at the same time as the castration because of the verbal abuse we had to suffer in the weeks afterwards. Anyway, let's show you around."

The group got up from the table and went through the house to the fireplace.

"Hey, is that sculpture really a Michelangelo?" asked Sylvain.

Tom smiled. "Yes, it really is. It was quite hard to get him to make that sculpture for me. I had anticipated that he'd probably want payment in gold, so I had some replica gold Ducats, the currency at the time, cast for me before my trip. But I didn't have enough. I only had ten Ducats and he wanted twenty. He said he'd reduce his price to ten if he could have sex with me and if I'd pose for some statue he was doing called 'David.'"

"You didn't…" started Flore

"No, of course I didn't," Tom replied, "I agreed to pose for the statue. But regarding the sex, I told him, 'No way José'. He said his name wasn't José, but I could call him that if it helped me get in the mood.

"Anyway, I told him about the #metoo movement and that he needed to be careful about things like that. In the end, we agreed on ten gold Ducats, posing for his David statue on Wednesdays from ten in the morning until lunchtime for four weeks, and that I'd give him a book I'd picked up at a second-hand stall in Portobello called 'How it Works', which had descriptions and drawings of how a variety of twentieth-century things like helicopters, aeroplanes, diving suits and parachutes work. He said he wasn't really interested in the book, but his friend Leo would probably like it, and as he'd been struggling to find something for his birthday, he'd take it as part payment. So, we shook hands on the deal." Tom put his hand on the sculpture and pressed down. "Anyway, let's go downstairs."

Down in the kitchen below, Tom said, "Right, let's get Charlie's tits sorted. Come with me." Tom led Charlie through the 'whoosh' pod into the laboratory. Opening a cabinet, he selected a jar of pills labelled 'Male Tits Antidote', handed them to Charlie and instructed him to take one tablet every four hours until the same time the following day. Charlie opened the bottle and took one of the tablets straight away, washing it down with what was left of the Tom Collins he had brought with him from the patio.

"Let's start at the far end of the living quarters," said Marion, leading the group along the long corridor to the heavily fortified door at the end.

"Yes, what's in there? You must keep something incredibly valuable or important in that room. Is that where you keep Monstera seeds or all the money that you've accumulated?" asked Flore.

Tom laughed. "No, it's where Charlie keeps his socks. On the third iteration of this adventure, he started to get extremely upset and anxious about people borrowing his socks, especially those striped ones that he really likes. It turned into a real obsession. He started by printing up a load of posters that he put in every room that read, 'I don't wear your dresses or your frocks, so stay away from my fucking socks'.

"Of course, that only made things worse, to the extent that whenever the washing machine was about to finish, one of you would distract him with some bizarre story, while someone else would plunder all of his precious striped socks from the machine while he was outside looking for the spaceship, pterodactyl, or some other incredible thing that he'd been told was out there.

"So, after about a year, he got wise to your tactics and had this room built, complete with military-grade security. Although there isn't really a danger of death, as all the signs say, Charlie is the only person who can open this door. Go on Charlie, open the door and show us. You'll need to put your hand on the fingerprint reader, then look into the retina scanner."

Tentatively, Charlie did as he had been told, fingerprints first, then the retina scan. The door clicked and swung open. Inside, both sides of the room were lined with dozens of chests of drawers. Every drawer of every chest was full of perfectly laundered and folded socks, all of them exactly the same.

On one side there was a space in between two of the cabinets with a leather armchair, presumably used for putting on and taking off socks. A picture frame above, lit by a single spotlight recessed into the ceiling, displayed another pair of the striped socks. At the far end of the room, a large laundry basket sat next to a washing machine with a tumble drier above.

"Por Dios, I had no idea it was going to get this bad," said Lucia, looking rather sad.

Charlie looked rather embarrassed and humbly ventured, "Well, they're my favourite socks, ever. They're made from bamboo and they're really comfortable, and they don't make my feet sweat, and I love the colours, and…"

"OK. OK. We get it," Flore interrupted, "We're sorry, and we promise we won't steal your socks this time".

Leaving Charlie's sock sanctuary and going back into the corridor, Marion led the group into the dressing room with all of the costumes and perfumes. Tom's alien suit now hung at the far end of the rack.

"This is where we keep all of the clothes we need so that we can turn up pretty much anywhere in the world, in any era and not look out of place. Look, this is what I wore when I met with Michelangelo," said Tom, holding up a hanger with a green tunic, red cape and orange trousers.

"Jesus. No wonder he thought he'd be able to have sex with you," Charlie remarked. Flore shot him a scowl. Undeterred, Charlie continued, "I suppose you were wearing some perfume too."

"Of course," Tom replied, "The perfume is as essential as the garments. You could hardly turn up in medieval England smelling like the guy in the Lynx advert while everyone else smells of three-month-old sweat and horse manure. Same with going to Rome in the fifteenth century posing as an aristocrat. For that trip, we mixed up a blend of lavender and sandalwood essential oils. It worked a treat. Anyway, we're pretty much done in here, let's show you our control room and the treasury."

Tom led the way into the next room. Huge screens covered the entirety of one wall and a control panel on the desk was filled with dozens of buttons labelled with different place names.

"From here, we can see the interior of every safe house that we own. We had to after the New York incident. From the earliest date possible, usually straight after we acquire each place, we install state-of-the-art cameras that record to a mini hard drive. We then make a monthly trip to each place, swap out the hard drive, and then come back here to upload the contents of the drive to our servers.

"From this control panel, we can go to any location on any date and see if there's anyone in the property. It's the best way of making sure our safe houses haven't been compromised before turning up there."

"What was the New York incident?" asked Lucia.

# THE COSMIC KNOT PARADOX

# Chapter 30
# Mob Rules

"Marion and I went back together to the New York house for a second trip, just after we'd sold the second batch of diamonds and got all of the bank accounts open. We arrived directly into my office and were horrified to find a guy going through my desk. We were behind him, but he heard my gasp of shock, turned around and saw us. Of course, we instantly disappeared but it was too late, we'd been seen."

"What did you do?" asked Charlie.

"Well, that was the first time we got in touch with Pippa. I got her number from you and got her to come to our flat in Limehouse. I explained almost everything to her. It was a risk, but at the same time, I knew we were probably going to need the services of someone with her talents from time to time, so I took a chance. I didn't tell her how I had acquired the ability to quantum tunnel, simply that I could.

"At first, she understandably thought that I was completely mad, so I took her by the hand and off we went to 1961 New York. Surprisingly, she wasn't particularly fazed by the experience. She understood the quantum tunnelling theory, and roughly how the science worked, saying that she knew that both the British and American military had experimented, fortunately without success, with quantum tunnelling in the 1980s and 1990s.

"Pippa knew this because, before transitioning to a woman in her late forties, she had spent almost twenty years in the British Army, starting with seven years in the Grenadier Guards before, at the age of thirty-three, passing the SAS selection process and moving to Britain's most elite military regiment.

"Whilst the selection had been harsh and thorough, once in the unit, the training was both comprehensive and continuous. Within two years of being accepted into the regiment, she had been equipped with a multitude of very special skills.

"Pippa had been taught how to kill a group of ten regular soldiers in less than thirty seconds using only her hands and whatever weapons she could take off the first men she killed. "She could navigate by the stars and live undetected in enemy territory, completely off-grid, in both jungle and arctic conditions, for weeks on end. She knew how to fix engines and gearboxes in the most hostile environments with a minimum selection of tools, had a thorough understanding of both electrics and electronics and knew how to break, fix, use, drive or fly almost any piece of equipment used by any military unit, anywhere in the world.

"Pippa knew how to both diffuse and make bombs, having been trained to be able to construct an explosive device powerful enough to destroy a large house, using only the ingredients typically found in a domestic kitchen.

"She had been taught to both scuba-dive and skydive, and jumping from an altitude of 12,000 feet, was capable of landing within an accuracy of one square metre in the dark. She was also capable of gaining entry, undetected, to almost any building – even the highest security government and military facilities proved little problem for her.

"Pippa spent twelve very happy years, going to both exotic as well as mundane locations and assassinating people. It was her calling in life and she was very good at it, surgical in her execution and meticulous in her preparation. More often than not, Pippa's targets' deaths were attributed to suicides, accidents and even natural causes, although sometimes, they just disappeared.

"After leaving the SAS, Pippa spent some time working for MI5 and then worked as an advisor to the then British Prime Minister, Tony Blair. It was during this time that she became privy to the quantum tunnelling experiments.

"Now in her sixties, Pippa is mostly retired and has created the perfect cover for herself, appearing to most people as a retired civil servant who spends most of her time enjoying stereotypical activities such as crochet, knitting and dressmaking; a complete contrast to the adrenaline-fuelled challenges of her past.

"However, Pippa does have an ongoing 'consultancy' arrangement with MI5. From time to time, she gets a text from 'Wholesale Wools and Yarns, announcing a sale, complete with a 'sale ends' date - code for by when she needs to complete the 'job' she has been assigned. This is the trigger for Pippa to buy a copy of the Daily Telegraph the following day where, coded in the Obituaries and Personal columns, she finds details on where and when she should collect more detailed information related to the job.

"Sometimes the instructions, usually contained on an encrypted and password-protected USB drive, might be hidden somewhere in a hotel room. Other times they arrive as a pizza delivery, hidden in the fold of the box. Occasionally, she has to go to church to 'confess' and leaves not just with absolution for the sins she has been asked to commit, but also the little pen drive with her mission details.

"Although Pippa has settled into her new life very well and quite enjoys her rather sedentary 'cover' life, she does miss the thrill and excitement of her former career and it's the killing she misses the most. She feels that it's quite unjust that retired accountants get to help their grown-up children with their tax returns, and retired carpenters can still make bird boxes in their garden sheds, but she rarely gets the opportunity to do what she really loves. She looks forward to receiving the texts and the adventures that follow, but she's noticed that since turning sixty she is being given fewer and fewer jobs. She is pragmatic about it, reasoning that she's not getting any younger. Whilst at forty years of age she could run a mile in under four and a half minutes, now it takes her six; twenty years ago she could lift the corner of a small car onto a rock to change a wheel, whereas now she needs to use a jack; similarly, she used to be able to hit a target the size of a human head, nine times out of ten, from a distance of one mile using a rifle with no telescopic sight; now, that's more like six out of ten and she needs to wear glasses. Pippa knows that all of this makes her slightly less effective and that her MI5 handlers simply want certainty.

"She was therefore thrilled when I described our problem and said that she'd be delighted to help. Look, I'll show you on that screen."

At that moment, one of the huge screens on the wall lit up, initially displaying only the fuzzy randomness of a television that's not been properly tuned, but then a moment later with Tom silent and again in a trance-like state, the screen showed Pippa in what appeared to be the New York house Tom had described earlier.

# Chapter 31
# Wise Guys

Pippa looked around the house, commenting on the décor as she walked from room to room. "Oh wow, I love the way you used the Laura Ashley floral print paper on just one wall to juxtapose the Andy Warhol print opposite," she remarked as she entered the office.

"The Laura Ashley wallpaper was the previous owner's choice, and the Warhol isn't a print," Tom replied.

Pippa then asked a myriad of questions. How big was the man? What was he wearing? Eye colour, hair colour, skin colour? Olive? What shade? Did he have a gun? You don't know? Could you see his waistband? Could he have had a gun in a pocket or an ankle holster? And so, the questions continued for almost thirty minutes. When she'd finished and Tom had been fully 'de-briefed' as she had put it, she gave Tom her assessment.

"The man you found in your office is almost certainly a member of one of New York's five main mafia gangs. My guess is that you and Marion running around New York selling diamonds and buying houses in trendy areas has come to the attention of the wrong people.

"They might think that you're laundering money for a rival gang, in which case they'll just kill you, or maybe they think you've got some other gig going on, criminal or legitimate, and intend to scare you into giving them a cut.

"If though, they conclude that you're just wealthy foreigners, they'll kidnap Marion and demand a ransom. They'll send you her fingers, one by one, until you empty your bank account for them. They'll then kill you as soon as you hand over the money and kill Marion when they've finished with her. You'll both end up as part of the foundations of an office block that one of their cousins has got the contract to build."

"What makes you so certain that this is a mafia thing?" Tom asked, doing his best to appear unfazed by Pippa's assessment.

"Balance of probabilities," replied Pippa, "If the guy you found here was just an opportunist housebreaker, he could have been any ethnicity;

white British, white Irish, Scandinavian, African, Chinese, take your pick. But he wasn't any of those. From what you described, he was Italian, and from the description of his medium-tone olive skin, there's a good chance his parents are Sicilian. Now most of the Sicilians that came here were decent, honest, hard-working people who just wanted a better life for themselves and their children. They did things like open cafés, heel bars and restaurants to make a living. But, if you've found an uninvited Sicilian here in your house, going through your things, he's obviously not one of those honest, hard-working types, meaning there's a very good chance he's a member of a mafia gang."

"So, what do we do?" Tom asked.

Pippa thought for a moment, then replied. "Well, the problem you have is that if I'm right, which I usually am, then you've got multiple, perhaps hundreds of problems rather than just one. He's just the scout.

"There would have been another two guys waiting outside and then a small army of them within a couple of blocks. It's the same tactics I dis-covered were used by the Columbian and Nicaraguan drug cartels in the eighties and nineties when Margaret Thatcher lent us to Ronald Reagan to help with his war on drugs and I did a few jobs in South America.

"The drug cartels adopted a lot of the mafia methods, so I imagine this will follow that pattern. We're going to have to deal with them all."

Tom groaned, but Pippa continued. "Am I right in thinking you could just nip off, and even if you're away for a couple of days, could be back here before I realise you're gone?" she asked. Tom nodded. "In that case, I'm going to need you to pick up some things for me."

Pippa leaned forward to start writing a list on a sheet of paper on the desk. She scribbled out her list, occasionally writing out calculations on a separate sheet. When she had finished, she handed Tom her list.

*Shopping list:*
*Old style alarm clock*
*9 volt battery*
*6 Candles*
*Red spray paint*
*Brown packing tape*
*Selection of short lengths of red, black and blue cables*

*Cordless electric drill (fully charged)*
*10mm drill bit*
*1mm drill bit*
*100 watt light bulb*
*100ml chloroform*
*Large surgical swabs*
*50 100 x 150cm weather balloons*
*20 x 25kg bottles helium*
*200 metres Kevlar paragliding line*
*2 rolls gaffer tape*
*5 x 1m lengths 4mm short link stainless steel chain*
*Bolt cutters*
*5 x high security medium size key operated padlocks*
*Heavy duty masonary fixing*
*Stainless steel ground anchor*
*Old rusty hacksaw*
*Soldering iron and solder*
*Small Pipette*
*2 x FP4 face masks*
*Car battery*
*Jump leads*
*5 x clipboards, 5 x pens, A4 paper*
*Large plastic sheet*
*2 pairs wellington boots. Size 6 and your size*

"I think that's everything. If I've forgotten anything, you can always nip back," said Pippa as Tom read through the list.

It took Tom almost three days to find and buy everything on Pippa's list, and he returned having had to make several trips; each time, loaded with bags, and then the gas cylinders, but for Pippa, it was like Tom had never left, just that everything on her list had suddenly appeared.

"Right, let's get to work," Pippa said enthusiastically, "You need to move all this stuff, and me, to four hours before the time you found your unwanted visitor."

Pippa worked quickly. Taking items from the bags and boxes Tom had brought, she started by spraying the candles red, then wrapped a bundle of six candles in the brown packing tape, leaving the red ends exposed. The candles looked like dynamite. She then taped the 'dynamite' and the battery to the back of the clock, soldered the red and black wires to the battery terminals and fed them into the back of the clock, then fed a blue cable from the clock, heating the other end so it pushed easily into the 'dynamite'. It looked just like a homemade bomb.

Pippa then took the drill, inserted the 1mm drill bit and very carefully drilled a hole near the top of the lightbulb. She then put on a facemask, told Tom to put on his, and also told him to open some windows at the back of the house. With the masks on and the windows open, Pippa inserted the end of the pipette into the chloroform and drew 10ml of the liquid, which she then squirted into the lightbulb through the hole she had drilled. She sealed the hole with a small strip of gaffer tape, then replaced the bulb in the drawing room ceiling with the chloroform-filled bulb. "OK. Under no circumstances touch that light switch," she said.

The next job was to secure the ground anchor, which Pippa attached to the wall using the masonry fixings.

"Right, we're ready. Put everything except the chloroform, the swab and the masks in the cupboard under the stairs," she instructed, adding, "I'm not moving those gas cylinders. My back's been playing up."

Once Tom had moved all of the equipment, Pippa said, "OK, masks on. It's showtime."

With the facemasks on, she doused the swab in her hand with chloroform, then said, "Take me to the exact moment you discovered our visitor; directly behind him please."

The next instant they were there, standing immediately behind a man bent forward apparently writing something on a sheet of paper. A pile of money sat on the desk next to the note. Almost immediately, he became aware of the odour of the chloroform and sniffed the air, but before he could turn around, in a single movement, Pippa put her left arm around the man's upper torso, simultaneously clamping the chloroform-soaked swab over his face with her right hand. He struggled for a few seconds before his body went limp and fell to the floor, unconscious.

"Let's get him undressed," Pippa said, a smile evident, even under her mask.

"Undressed? What are you going to do to the guy?" asked Tom.

"You'll see," Pippa replied, as she started to remove the man's clothing, "We need to work quickly; his friends will come looking for him soon."

Pippa was entirely correct. Less than a minute later, with the man's trousers and underwear removed, footsteps could be heard on the steps outside and then, the sound of someone fiddling with the lock.

"Quick, think us all downstairs to the drawing room," Pippa instructed. Tom grabbed hold of Pippa with one hand and the half-naked intruder with the other, and in a flash all three were downstairs. Pippa manhandled the half-naked man into an armchair facing the door and put a bottle of whisky into his hand. Then, in a hushed but urgent voice, she told Tom, "Go and get me a pornographic magazine. Vintage if possible. Plenty of hair."

Tom was stunned and started to protest, "What the fuck! Now is hardly the time…." but before he could finish, Pippa snapped back, "Do as you're told. Now."

Obligingly, Tom nipped back to Portobello Road, via Limehouse and acquired a 1960 copy of Playboy. On his return, Pippa snatched the magazine from his hand, opened it on the centrefold and placed it on the man's lap. She then grabbed Tom's arm and pulled him behind the open door so they would be hidden from view.

Pippa clutched Tom's hand and through her mask whispered in his ear, "If they're not unconscious within a few seconds of entering the room, get us out of here pronto." Tom nodded.

Tom's heart was racing, and he was terrified - much more so than he'd been in the corner shop in Limehouse - but at the same time, he felt more alive than ever. A few seconds later, Tom and Pippa heard the front door open and what sounded like two men entering the hallway. They moved quietly until they reached the open doorway and caught sight of their accomplice, naked from the waist down and asleep in a chair, with a bottle of whisky resting in his hand and Playboy magazine on his lap. The men started to laugh.

"Hey, Tonio, you were meant to search the place, not get drunk, spank the monkey and have a nap. Sandro, look at this putz," joked the first man as he entered the room.

"You sure he's asleep Carlo?" said Sandro, but by then it was too late.

With both men in the room, Pippa flicked the light switch, the light bulb exploded, and the room was filled with chloroform vapour. There were two or three seconds of choked coughing, then two heavy thuds followed by silence.

Pushing back the door, Tom saw the men sprawled across the floor. One of them had managed to get a hand onto the gun in his waistband but hadn't had time to remove the weapon before losing consciousness.

"OK, take their weapons and put them at the far end of the table. Then open some windows. We don't want them to die," Pippa instructed.

"Don't we? I thought we did," Tom said gingerly.

"No, of course we don't want them to fucking die. How will we interrogate them if they're dead?" Pippa replied sharply.

"Ah, yes of course," said Tom, who then did as he had been told and opened the windows.

"Right, get the chain, gaffer tape, padlocks, hacksaw and the bomb from the cupboard while I strip them," Pippa said as she started removing the men's clothing. By the time Tom returned, all three men were naked.

One by one, Pippa wrapped the last four links of one of the metre lengths of steel chain around each man's genitals. She pulled the chains as tight as possible and then used a padlock to secure them. Once she had finished attaching the chains, she checked the integrity of the chains by giving each one a sharp tug, momentarily lifting each man off the floor.

Satisfied that the chains were properly secure and there would be no way for any of the men to be able to break free, she then threaded the other ends of the three chains through the loop of the anchor attached to the wall, securing the chains with another padlock.

"OK. Get some gaffer tape over their mouths, we don't want their screams to disturb the neighbours. Then we can wake them up and have some proper fun," Pippa said, with a smile. Tom could tell that Pippa was now in her element and enjoying every moment.

With each man's mouth securely covered with several layers of gaffer tape, Pippa moved the table so that, for the chained men, one end of it was almost within reach. She then placed the bomb and one of the guns a couple of feet further away on the table. Next, she filled a bucket with cold water and started to slosh the water over the men to resuscitate them.

Deep groans indicated that the men were indeed coming back to consciousness from their chloroform-induced comas. The groans grew louder and the first man, Tonio, opened his eyes and struggled to his feet. Seeing the gun on the table, he made a lunge for the weapon but quickly ran out of chain which then contracted sharply around his testicles. Tonio dropped to his knees convulsed by a pain so intense that he started to retch. With the tape completely sealing his mouth, the vomit shot out of both nostrils in two jets over Carlo and Sandro.

Abruptly awakened by the vile shower, Carlo stumbled to his feet, groaning and covered in Tonio's part-digested lunch. He was just straightening his back when Sandro tried to stand but lost his footing on the slippery floor and, trying to stop himself from falling, grabbed the first thing he could reach, which, unfortunately for Carlo, was the chain attached to his genitals. A muffled but shrill yelp emanated from behind the gaffer tape covering Carlo's mouth as he collapsed back onto the wooden floor.

Feeling the need to right the inequality that both Carlo and Tonio had almost had their testicles ripped off, whilst Sandro remained relatively unscathed and was on his feet, Pippa gave Sandro's chain a sharp tug from behind him. The force of the tug flipped Sandro forward, smashing his face against the floor. Blood gushed from Sandro's shattered nose, and like Tonio, he convulsed in pain, raising his knees into his chest as vomit shot from both of his nostrils.

"Not feeling so wise now, eh guys?" Pippa said, before turning to Tom and saying, "Let's give them a couple of moments to get their composure, poor things."

Having moved the bomb a bit further out of reach and also, for good measure, picked up all of the guns in the room, Tom and Pippa left the three men lying sobbing in a pool of vomit and blood and went downstairs to the kitchen where they opened a couple of beers.

"How do you feel it's gone so far?" Pippa asked.

"Yes, well, it's err, been interesting," Tom replied.

"Another half an hour and they'll have told us everything," Pippa said as she finished her beer, "Right, let's get back to work."

Back upstairs, the three men were still more or less in the same positions and blood was still streaming down Sandro's face and onto the floor. Again, Pippa felt a strong sense of injustice, so picked up an iron poker from the fireplace and whacked Carlo and Tonio hard across their noses. Blood streamed down their faces too.

"On your knees," Pippa commanded. The men didn't move. "On your knees now or I'll pull your chains again," Pippa said more sternly. The men immediately all squirmed and writhed on the slippery floor and somehow managed to get into a kneeling position.

Pippa walked over to the table and picked up the rusty hacksaw. As she walked back towards the men, they started to become very agitated, each making impassioned whimpering noises.

"What's that? I didn't catch what you said," Pippa remarked, "Oh, yes, you can't talk properly with that tape over your mouths. I imagine that what you wanted to ask me is whether I'm going to cut off your genitals with this rusty hacksaw." The men all sobbed. "Well, the answer to that question is no, I'm not..." relief spread across the faces of the men as Pippa paused, "...because you are." Alarm once again returned to each of the captives' eyes.

Walking back towards the table, Pippa continued, "Now the reason you are going to cut off your own genitals is because this is a bomb that's linked to an alarm clock. It's a really simple device. When the alarm goes off, so does the bomb. It's 8:49pm now and the alarm is set for nine on the dot, so you've got eleven minutes." The men whimpered. "Now, because I'm English and a nice, kindly lady, I'm going to help you with your strategy for getting out of here alive by giving you some pointers.

"In case you were thinking of using the hacksaw to cut through the chain or the padlocks, please be aware that both are made from high-tensile steel and the hacksaw is old and rusty. Nobody has ever managed to cut through either the chain or the padlock in less than fifteen minutes.

"That leaves your only choice being to cut off your own genitals. Now the good news is that you don't have to cut everything off. Just removing one testicle will allow everything else to pass through the loop in the chain and gain you your freedom.

"The bad news is that the fastest we've ever seen anyone remove one of their testicles with this hacksaw is seven minutes, so only one of you is going to get out of here alive."

With that, Pippa tossed the hacksaw onto the floor so all three could reach it.

Sandro was the first to make a move for the hacksaw, but as he leaned forward, Carlo grabbed Sandro's chain and pulled with all his might, the pain causing Sandro to drop it. Carlo picked up the tool, but Tonio turned to him and headbutted him full in the face. The force of the blow knocked Carlo to the floor.

With Carlo only semiconscious, and Sandro now spraying jets of vomit through his nose again, Tonio grabbed the hacksaw and started sawing at his scrotum, gritting his teeth with his eyes tightly closed as he tried to cope with the agonising back-and-forth rasps as the rusty, serrated blade tore through the delicate skin of his scrotum. He managed less than fifteen seconds before the pain forced him to give up, drop the saw and flop backwards onto the wooden floor, sobbing loudly.

"Ok. That didn't work out so well, did it? Would anyone like another go? There are still eight minutes left." The men just whimpered. "OK. Who would like to have a go at something different? Something less painful? Whoever would like to try, get on your knees again."

All three men struggled onto their knees. "OK, Tom, get the jump leads and the car battery." Once again, agitated whimpering could be heard. "It's OK. I'm not intending to use the battery, that kind of thing is for amateurs; it's just my insurance policy in case any of you mistake the writing implement I'm about to give you for a weapon, or if you let any of your colleagues down by being untruthful in your answers to the questions that I'm about to ask you. Now, do all of you know how to write?" The men all nodded.

Tom arrived with the battery and the jump leads. Pippa attached one end of the negative lead to the battery and the other end to one of the steel chains. She then connected the red positive lead and monetarily tapped the crocodile clip on the other end of the lead onto the steel chain, completing the electrical circuit for a fraction of a second.

A buzz and a dramatic shower of sparks was accompanied by a trio of muffled yelps. Carlo voided his bowels, Sandro ejaculated, and a little yellow lake started to form around Tonio. The lake mixed in interesting patterns with the vomit and the crimson blood. Pippa wondered whether Jackson Pollock had got some of his ideas from doing something similar.

"OK, so that was just a test. If there's a next time, it'll be a full five seconds, and the one after that will be ten. You got that?" The men, still whimpering and sobbing, all nodded. "Now, I want you to form a circle with your backs to each other." The men shuffled around into the circle as they'd been told.

"So, the way this is going to work is as follows. I'm going to ask you some questions and you're going to write the answers down. If any of you look anywhere other than directly at your clipboards, you all get the battery treatment. When we've finished, I'm going to analyse the answers. Then, I'll decide who has been the most truthful. That person will be released, so they can go and tell the boss that it would be a very bad idea to mess with us again. The other two of you will get the battery treatment until your gonads catch fire and then, and only then, I'll shoot you in the head. Got that?" The men all groaned.

Pippa then handed each of the men a clipboard with a sheet of paper and a pen attached.

"OK, start by writing your names on your papers." The men all obliged. She then started the questions, pausing between each, just for long enough for the men to scribble their answers. "What is the name of the gang you belong to? How many men are part of your gang? Does your gang have a base? What is the address of the base? What is the name of the boss of your gang? How old is your boss? How much does your boss weigh? What colour are his eyes? Hair? Where does your boss live?"

And so, the questions continued with Pippa moving around the group as the men scribbled their answers. Being able to see the men's responses allowed her to ask contextual secondary questions, so that within little more than five minutes, Pippa had established everything she needed to know.

All of the men had given virtually identical answers and Pippa had asked some high-value questions in two or three distinct ways so that any lie would easily be betrayed by an inconsistent response.

She had managed to discover that, just as she had suspected, Tom and Marion had come to the attention of the group simply because Carlo had seen them during one of their visits to Josef Goldman & Sons in the diamond district, so knew they were either buying or selling, and would have diamonds, money or both.

Pippa also discovered that her mafia concerns were unfounded, and the threat extended no further than the three men she had just interrogated. Carlo was the ringleader, or at least the mastermind of the attempt to rob the house.

Pippa suddenly stopped asking questions, leaned forward and tore the tape from Carlo's face.

"OK, Carlo. Take a deep breath and tell me everything. Don't leave out any details."

Carlo did exactly as he was told, inhaling deeply, then started to speak. To Tom's astonishment, he didn't sound at all like Tonio or Sandro. Instead of their East Coast American with a touch of Italian accents, Carlo sounded just like John Lennon.

# THE COSMIC KNOT PARADOX

# Chapter 32
# The Godfather

Although Carlo looked Italian, he was actually from Liverpool in England, and his real name was Ronald Smallcock. Bullied and tormented as both a child and an adult because of his name, Ronnie had decided, at the age of twenty-seven, that he would re-invent himself.

So, in 1959, just before his twenty-eighth birthday, Ronnie took on the persona of a mafia boss. He started by practising a New York Italian accent in front of the bathroom mirror in his Liverpool bedsit. "You talkin' to me?" he'd repeatedly say to his reflection each evening.

He started eating Italian food for his evening meal every day after returning from his job at the library and having bought some dried Paccheri pasta from Carlo at 'Luigi's', Liverpool's only Italian delicatessen at the time, Ronnie decided he liked both the pasta and its name, so changed his own to Carlo Paccheri. Nobody would know, he thought.

Two years later, Ronnie, or Carlo as he now insisted on being called, was ready. He bought his ticket to New York and set sail from Southampton in September 1961. Once in New York, he quickly found lodgings in the Italian district on Mulberry Street, Lower Manhattan. The voyage had given him further opportunity to practice his accent and perfect his persona and Carlo was keen to put his carefully curated image to work.

That evening, Carlo dressed in his best 'mob' outfit, then went out to find other Italian Mafiosi. He didn't have to walk far. Just a couple of blocks from his lodgings he found Trattoria Silvestre. It was full of Italians and at a table in one corner, four thick-set Sicilians were tucking into big plates of spaghetti. They were exactly the type Carlo was looking for. He sauntered over to their table, and summoning his best accent and holding out his hand, said, "Buona serata, Carlo Paccheri". The men stared at him silently and incredulously for a few seconds, leaving his hand unshaken, before one of them replied, "Buona serata, Carlo. I'm Riccardo Rigatoni and these are my friends, Luigi Linguini, Sal Spaghetti and Pietro Pappardelle." The men dissolved into fits of laughter, "Beat it,

Limey," they said together.

Carlo left the restaurant feeling utterly dejected. Almost three years of living 'in-role' and practising in front of the mirror every night, only to be spotted and ridiculed for being a 'Limey' imposter on his first day. As he walked back to his lodgings, Carlo decided that perhaps he wasn't cut out for a life as a mafia kingpin after all and resolved that the following morning he would look for a proper job.

The next day, after a somewhat disturbed night's sleep, Carlo got up early, left his lodgings and set off on his search for work. Just three blocks away, a typical New York diner had a sign in the window that read, 'Help Needed – Apply Within'.

Carlo opened the door and walked to the counter where a tough-looking woman in her mid- to late-forties was counting the money in the till. Summoning his best New York accent, but toning down the mafiosi overtones, Carlo said, "Morning Ma'am, I'm looking for work, an' I saw your sign in the window."

"You don't 'ave to pretend in 'ere love, so stop pretendin' like," the woman replied in a thick Scouse accent, "The pay is a dollar twenty an hour; half of the tips get shared at the end of the week, the other half get shared at Christmas; start at six and leave at four one week, then start at twelve and leave at ten the next. It's a six-day week, but you get Sundays off so you can go to church or yer S&M parties, or whatever you like to do on yer day off. Got that? So, get yer apron on and start chopping onions. Oh, and don't come in tomorrow in that suit, you look like a Scouse librarian at a mafia-themed fancy dress party."

Taking him through to the kitchen, the woman, whose name was Vera, introduced Carlo to the two other men in the kitchen. "This is Tonio, and this is Sandro," Vera said. "They're from Sicily. You'll be able to practice yer Lucky Luciano accent," she said, laughing as she went back out to the front.

Vera's husband, Emilio, also worked in the kitchen and was a kind man but had a rigorous work ethic and expected the same from his staff. Over the following weeks, the four men formed a good friendship. They worked hard, turning out the diner's menu of breakfasts, burgers, and a selection of classic Italian pasta dishes. There was always good banter between the four of them, and they often went for a beer together at the end of their shift.

On the Monday of his sixth week, Carlo arrived for work to find the sign in the window turned to 'Closed' but the door unlocked. Sandro, Vera, Emilio and Tonio were sat at one of the tables. Vera was holding Tonio's hands in hers and Tonio was sobbing, tears rolling down his cheeks.

Over the next twenty minutes, Tonio explained that the week before, his sister, Elena, who had been complaining of back pain for several weeks, had collapsed in agony at work and been taken to hospital. Tonio hadn't said anything at the time, because, he didn't think it was anything more serious than a pulled muscle.

However, by the weekend, the hospital had determined that Elena had a tumour on one of her kidneys and that the kidney needed to be removed or she would die. The hospital had already demanded payment of almost one thousand dollars for the tests and treatment up to that point, which Tonio had borrowed from a local money lender, but now the hospital was asking for another three thousand dollars before they would operate to remove the diseased kidney.

Not only that but just three days after Tonio had borrowed the money, the lender was demanding interest of ten per cent per day and was threatening to cut off one of Tonio's fingers for each day that the debt plus interest remained unpaid.

Emilio went to the counter and picked up the tips jar. He then reached into a cupboard and brought out a cigar box. "The Christmas fund," he said, as he emptied both onto the table. Vera counted the money; it totalled just over one thousand Dollars.

Sandro reached into his pocket and retrieved a roll of notes. "I've been saving for a ticket to Sicily, to go and see my family, but you can have it," he said. There was barely more than one hundred Dollars. Vera opened the till and counted out another sixty-seven Dollars in notes, leaving just the coins and a few Dollar bills to be able to give customers their change.

Carlo added another forty Dollars from his wallet, which was all that remained of his previous week's wages, having just paid his rent. It was all the money he had, but he then remembered his mother's ring. Unbuttoning his shirt, he pulled a silver chain from around his neck. On the chain was a ladies' gold wedding ring, set with a single large diamond and two sapphires. "This was my mother's wedding ring. She died two years ago. I was keeping it for when I meet someone special, but I'll sell it," he said solemnly.

Totting up the money, there was just over twelve hundred Dollars. Vera and Emilo said they had just over eight hundred in savings at the bank. "So, that's a whisker over two thousand, plus whatever Carlo can get for his ma's ring. I hope it fetches a good price. Tonio's going to need over two thousand more if he's gonna save his sister and keep his fingers," Vera said with a woeful expression.

That afternoon, once the worst of the lunchtime rush was over, Carlo left the restaurant and followed the route he'd been given by Vera to the diamond district. He went to the first store with a 'We Buy and Sell' board outside. The man behind the counter took the ring, slipped an eyepiece into place and studied the gems in the ring. He told Carlo that the stones were quite nicely cut but the diamond had a flaw and offered him $800 for the ring. Carlo didn't know what the ring was worth, but didn't really trust the man, so thanked him for his time, took the ring and left.

Carlo went to three other shops where he was offered $1250, $1150 and $1200 respectively. He decided to try one more place and walked into the next shop on the street, Josef Goldman & Sons Gemstones. The assistant at the counter put his monocle in place, quickly looked at the ring and reported, "Nice stones, well cut and no flaws in the sapphires or the diamond. We can give you fourteen-hundred dollars." The offer was still about a thousand dollars short of what was needed to sort out Tonio's problems, but it was the best offer he'd had, so Carlo agreed and the assistant went off to get the cash from the safe.

While Carlo was waiting, a young couple came in and stood at the counter. They were speaking French to each other. When the assistant arrived back at the counter, the Frenchman said they had some stones they'd like valued. "Let me finish serving this gentleman, I'll be with you in a moment," the assistant told them. Carlo took the money the jeweller had given him and left.

When he got out onto the street, the Frenchman's words, 'some *stones* we'd like valued' rang in Carlo's mind. Stones, plural, Carlo thought. They were selling several stones and would be leaving the store within a few minutes with a bag full of money.

Carlo thought about mugging them as soon as they came out onto the street but then thought about the man he'd seen in the store. He wasn't particularly big, but he looked fit and wiry; the type that could punch well above his weight. He looked like he could probably run quite fast too, so just snatching their bag wasn't an option either. In any case, there were lots of people around and being the diamond district, there'd be plenty of Police nearby. Getting arrested and having his $1400 confiscated by New York's finest wasn't going to help Tonio or his sister. Carlo decided to wait, follow the couple to wherever they were going, and then decide what to do.

Five minutes later, the French couple emerged from the store. Carlo put the magazine he'd been pretending to read, whilst surreptitiously watching the jeweller's door, back on the rack of the newsstand and followed the couple along the street. He was careful to keep enough distance so as not to be noticed.

He followed them south along Madison Avenue, then along Fifth Avenue until they reached West 8th Street, where they turned right and headed towards Greenwich Village. A few twists and turns later, the couple entered entered a house halfway along Grove Street. Carlo made a mental note of the address and returned to work.

Back at the Best Friends Diner, Vera greeted him with a smile and said, "What took you so long? We were startin' to worry, like." Carlo added his $1400 to the cigar box while he told Vera and the others all about his afternoon, what he'd seen, and what he was thinking.

"So, this French couple are almost certainly loaded," he concluded, "We could wait until they're out, break in, find the money and borrow enough to pay for Tonio's sister's operation and get Tonio out of hock with the money guy. We can return the money when we're able."

The other three sat silently, deep in thought for a few moments. Sandro broke the silence. "Let's do it", he said decisively.

Carlo looked at Tom and then at Pippa, "So, that's pretty much the whole story. We came to the house, rang the bell and when nobody answered, Sandro got the door open for me – he used to be a locksmith in Sicily – and I started looking around. It didn't take long to find the money in the office drawer. I'd just finished counting out the thousand dollars that we needed and was just writing you a note when you showed up behind me. By the way, how did you get in without Sandro and Tonio seeing you? And how did you get upstairs so quietly?"

Pippa ignored Carlo's question, looked at Tom, and with a movement of her head, silently motioned for him to go upstairs and look for the note. Tom went up to the office, and sure enough on the desk found a handwritten note which he brought back downstairs and handed to Pippa.

*Dear Sir/Madam,*
*I'm really sorry to have to tell you that I've taken $1000 of your money.*
*My friend's sister needs an operation to save her life and also some really bad people are going to cut off my friend's fingers if he doesn't give them some money tonight.*
*I promise I will return the money by this time next year. Sooner if I am able.*
*Sorry again.*
*Yours faithfully*

*Carlo Paccheri*
*P.S. That's not my real n...*

Clearly, Tom and Pippa had arrived just as Carlo was finishing his note, but before he had finished writing 'name' at the end of his apologetic missive. That must have been the moment Carlo had first smelled the chloroform and stopped writing.

Pippa removed the tape from Sandro's and Tonio's mouths and one by one, carefully and gently unlocked the padlocks so the chains could be removed. Each man heaved a sigh of relief as the chains came off.

"OK, Guys. I'm going to give you my fee for this evening's work so that you can sort out Tonio's sister's medical bills. You'd better get yourselves cleaned up. There's a bathroom upstairs. When are you expecting the money lender?" Pippa asked.

Tonio replied, "He told me that he'll be at my apartment at ten o'clock and to have his money ready."

"Well, it's just gone nine, so you'd better hurry up. By the way, I'm coming with you," Pippa said with a smile.

While the men were getting themselves cleaned up and dressed, Tom mentioned to Pippa that she hadn't used the helium and asked her what she'd intended to do with it. She just said, "You'll see," and smiled.

# Chapter 33
# Fear and Loathing in New York

Out on the street, having said their farewells, Carlo and Sandro started to walk, somewhat awkwardly and uncomfortably, back towards Little Italy. Tom, Pippa and Tonio got a cab to Tonio's apartment in the Bronx.

Tonio said that his apartment was on the fourth floor and that the elevator never worked, so all three hurried up the stairs as fast as they were able. With his badly bruised, swollen and lacerated genitals, Tonio was quite slow, but within a few minutes, they'd ascended the six long flights to the fourth floor and were inside Tonio's apartment.

"Leave the door unlatched, we'll let him come in by himself. Now we play the waiting game," Pippa instructed, "Tom, if this goes badly for any reason, just get us all out." Tom nodded and the three waited in the semi-dark. They didn't have to wait for long. Two minutes later there was a loud bang on the unlatched door, which swung open.

A slightly built, well-dressed man in his thirties stood for a moment in the doorway, then walked into the room. An older man, in his mid- to late-forties followed behind him. He was much bigger and the scars on his face together with a cauliflower ear suggested he was probably an ex-boxer or bare-knuckle fighter.

Pippa immediately recognised both types. The big guy was just decoration. He was there to intimidate the housewives and single mothers that his boss mostly preyed on. Sure, he would be dangerous if he managed to get hold of you or hit you, but he was stupid and slow. It was the moneylender that posed the biggest risk. He was light, but would be quick, and much stronger than most people would expect. More than anything though, he was dangerous because he was innately vicious; he enjoyed hurting people and was very good at it.

During the journey in the cab, Tonio had told Pippa a little bit about Enzo the moneylender. Just the week before, Enzo had butchered a local woman with the stiletto knife that he carried everywhere with him. The woman was a war-widow struggling to make ends meet and feed her five children. She'd been just two dollars short of her weekly payment. Pippa knew she would have to act quickly and decisively.

Looking at Tonio with disdain, Enzo said, "So, you decided to bring your boyfriend and your auntie for protection, Tonio?" Both men laughed.

Pippa produced the gun she'd taken off Carlo earlier in the evening from behind her back in her left hand.

"Hands up! This is a stick-up," she said in a deliberately comical voice.

Enzo thrust his hands in the air and said, "Oh no! Aunty's got a gun. Please don't shoot me Aunty….".

In that instant, before Enzo could finish his sentence, Pippa's right hand shot out, her fingers pointed to the ceiling, so the heel of her hand caught Enzo square on the left side of his chest with a resounding thud. The immense force and precision of the blow stopped Enzo's heart. In almost the same movement, Pippa dropped the gun, rotated her body and used the heel of her left hand to catch the big man under the chin as she propelled herself upwards with her legs. His head snapped backwards with a sickening crack and the big man fell to the floor dead, his neck broken.

Tonio and Tom struggled to comprehend what had just happened. Just seconds before, Enzo had been menacing and mocking, but now, he and his bruiser accomplice lay dead on the floor. Everything had happened in less than three seconds.

"My god. That was astonishing. But why didn't you just shoot them?" Tom asked.

Pippa turned, picked up the gun, pointed it at Tom and pulled the trigger. Click. A short rod with a red fabric triangle popped out of the barrel of the gun. Written on the triangle was the word 'Bang!'. Although a realistic replica, the gun was just a toy.

"It was the first clue that Tonio, Sandro and Carlo weren't really mafia," Pippa said with a smile. Tonio looked embarrassed.

Reaching into Enzo's jacket pocket, Pippa produced a large wallet stuffed with banknotes. There must have been twenty thousand dollars or more. Handing the wallet to Tonio she said, "There you go, here's all the money you need for your sister's treatment. Give $2000 to Carlo and tell him to go back to Goldman's and buy his mother's ring back, to put it back on the chain and keep it until he finds a woman worthy of wearing it. Now Tonio, go into the bedroom, shut the door and count to one hundred. By the time you come out, we'll have sorted out everything here."

With Tonio out of the way, Pippa turned to Tom and said, "Get us and these two scumbags back to the house, pronto."

# THE COSMIC KNOT PARADOX

# Chapter 34
# The Unbearable Lightness of Being

Moments later, Tom and Pippa were back in the kitchen at Grove Street with the two dead men. Pippa sat Enzo in a wooden armchair. She quickly used zip ties to secure each of his ankles to the chair legs and his wrists to the arms of the chair.

"What are you doing that for? He's dead," Tom asked Pippa.

"He is now, but I'm going to bring him back to life. Get ready to get some gaffer tape over his mouth as soon as he starts breathing," Pippa replied as she tore Enzo's shirt open, exposing bare skin. She quickly grabbed the jump leads that were still attached to the battery and forced the metal clips onto Enzo's chest. His body convulsed, and then was still again. Pippa applied the terminals a second time; Enzo's body jerked rigid and this time, he drew a sharp intake of breath.

As he had been told, Tom quickly applied the tape over Enzo's mouth. His eyes were now open, the intensity of his black pupils betraying the extent of the fear and loathing he was feeling.

"Why did you resuscitate him?" Tom asked, unable to avoid the tone of incredulity dominating his words.

"So, I can kill him again, of course," Pippa said with a tone suggesting that he shouldn't have needed to ask. "This bastard deserves to die twice. Now get him and his dead friend up to the terrace".

Tom did as he was told and putting his left hand over Enzo's wrist and his right hand on the big dead man's ankle, moved them both to the terrace. Bewildered disbelief registered in Enzo's eyes. Pippa arrived a couple of moments later carrying the chains and padlocks and immediately told Tom to get the balloons, the gas and the paraglider lines.

With all of the gas bottles and balloons ready, Pippa prepared the big dead man for his final journey. Like Enzo, she sat him in a wooden armchair, securing his arms and legs to the chair with zip ties. She then secured the chair to the terrace railings with one of the chains and, one by one, started inflating the balloons and attaching them to the chair, carefully knotting the paraglider lines using a double half-hitch knot. It took Pippa around fifteen minutes to inflate and attach forty balloons, by which time the collection looked like something one might see at a fairground. The chair was now several feet in the air and straining on the chain.

Turning to Enzo, she said, "Your turn now," and started inflating and attaching balloons to Enzo's chair, which she had also secured using a length of chain. She talked as she worked.

"So, if my calculations are correct, one balloon per four pounds of weight should cause you to ascend at a rate of about ten feet per second, which means that after about two minutes you'll be at about the height of the Empire State Building. A few minutes later you'll be just over a mile up and still climbing. Now at this point, things will start to get pretty unpleasant, because although it's a nice warm night down here, up there at a mile up, it's going to be pretty chilly. Within about ten minutes your fingers, toes, ears, lips and nose will have frozen solid, but you'll still be conscious.

"Unfortunately for you, it'll take about another twenty to thirty minutes of ascent in the falling temperature and thinning air before you pass out from a lack of oxygen or hypothermia. By then, the temperature will have dropped to sixty below and within a few minutes, your body will have frozen solid like a block of ice. Have a good flight Enzo."

With that, Pippa first unclipped the dead man's chair. It rose rapidly and silently. Pippa let Enzo watch his minder's ascent for a few seconds, abject terror now visible in his eyes, then unclipped his chair from its tether. Enzo shot upwards on the same trajectory, a quiet muffled whimper the only sound to trouble the silence of the night.

Within a minute, in the dark moonless night, both men were almost out of sight, the light north-westerly breeze taking them out over Long Island and then out to the sea beyond.

"Well, I thought that turned out pretty well in the end, all things considered. I wonder where they'll end up," said Pippa, looking rather pleased with herself.

"My god! Where did you learn to do that?" Tom asked.

"Oh, we get trained to do that in the SAS," Pippa said nostalgically.

"We use it as a way of getting rid of corpses when we don't want them to be found and give away our presence, but there's a further benefit; the enemy wake up one morning to find that a few of their group have gone. They assume their colleagues have deserted, and some of the remaining men start thinking about doing the same. It's a very effective way of destroying morale.

"We also use it as an extraction method for getting men out of sticky situations. On a dark night, a plane drops a box containing the helium bottles and the uninflated balloons from high altitude somewhere remote, behind enemy lines; a parachute opens about one hundred feet up so the helium cylinders don't explode on impact. We then find the drop by following an encrypted radio signal emitted by the box.

"It then takes just fifteen minutes to tether yourself to something secure and inflate the balloons, then up, up and away. If you inflate enough balloons, you can even take the empty gas cylinders, so nobody knows you were ever there. Within a couple of minutes, you're too far up to be shot at from the ground, and after about ten minutes you're high enough to be able to disengage from the balloons and open a parachute with a very shallow glide angle; more like a paraglider really. If you catch the right thermals, you can travel well over a hundred miles that way, meaning you can get back across a safe border or even land on the deck of a ship."

"Fascinating," Tom said. "Should you be telling me all this?"

"Probably not," Pippa replied, "Don't tell anyone."

At that moment, the screen momentarily went fuzzy, then completely dark, and Tom took a deep breath as he returned to full consciousness.

# THE COSMIC KNOT PARADOX

# Chapter 35
# Back to the Future II

"So, anyway, that was when we decided to put cameras in all of the properties," Tom concluded. "Now, we can see what's present wherever and whenever we want to turn up. We have a routine. If we want to tunnel somewhere, we get into our outfits, put on our scent, then the last thing we do is check it's all clear at the landing site."

"What's in the safe?" asked Charlie.

"Just money, but lots of it," Tom replied, as he put his hand on the fingerprint reader, and then presented his face for a retina scan. A loud clunk indicated that the deadbolts inside the mechanism had moved. Tom wound the wheel on the door anti-clockwise, then pulled open the heavy door.

Inside there were racks and racks of banknotes from almost every country. Index cards separated the notes into the currency, denomination and year.

"Just like with the costumes and perfumes, we need to be able to turn up anywhere and have the right money in our pocket," Tom explained.

Moving back out into the control room and then the corridor, Marion said, "And this is the recording studio".

"Why is there a recording studio?" Lucia asked.

"Initially, just for entertainment in case we ever had to go into siege mode here. We thought it would provide something to keep us amused if we were locked in here for months or years. Then, Tom and Sylvain started recording rap tracks. Tom's quite popular now in St Malo," Marion stated.

"St Malo?" said Charlie, with a questioning tone.

"Yes, Tom got a bit tipsy one night and for some reason, started rapping about St Malo," Marion explained, "The St Malo tourist board got hold of it, released it and it kind of went viral."

Just at that moment, the sound of raucous guitar music started. Marion banged on the door.

"Hey Jimi, could you keep it down for a bit, we're doing a tour".

The door opened. It was Jimi Hendrix.

He looked around the group at the astonished faces and said, "Ha, y'all look like you've seen a ghost. I was just practising. Hope you don't mind; I'm having some friends over to the bungalow later. Feel free to join us." With that, he disappeared back into the studio and started to play again, albeit at a lower volume.

"I decided to rescue Jimi. He died way before his time," Tom started to explain, "It was a bit complicated getting him out of the morgue in Notting Hill without them realising that they were missing a corpse, but we managed it in the end with a bit of creative thinking. He's been living here ever since in one of the bungalows Lucia had built to Airbnb on the other side of the island. We've got Elvis here too, and Kurt Cobain, Amy Winehouse, John Lennon and a few others."

"What? I built bungalows. But I've never been here before," said Lucia, ignoring what Tom had just said about there being iconic dead musicians, re-animated and now living on the island.

Marion intervened, "We'll get to that in a while. Let's continue the tour."

The next room was the lounge and library area. Big seventies sofas and chairs dominated the space.

"This room feels very familiar. It's like I've been here before," remarked Lucia.

"That's because you designed it and chose the furniture," said Tom, "Everything in here was your choice."

"But that doesn't make sense. We've only just seen this place for the first time a few days ago. But you tell me I designed this and built bungalows. How can that be?" Lucia replied, her tone now insistent for an answer.

"Yes, and how did I create that sock sanctuary if I've never been here before?" asked Charlie.

"Well, both of those statements are true in this thread of the multi-verse," said Tom, "But, like I told to you at the very start, there are many threads, because either I or Marion have been able to go back in time to intervene at some critical juncture each time something catastrophic has happened - like I did by enlisting Pippa's help to deal with Claude. So, you've already lived several lives here."

"But, how could we have created Wesh and made this place how it is now in this thread of what you call the multiverse if we've only just arrived?" said Lucia.

"Well, err, the simple answer to that is that we don't really know," Tom admitted. "The best theory we've been able to come up with is that this is basically a kind of cosmic knot that creates these paradoxical situations."

"Ah, of course, the cosmic knot paradox, I should have guessed," said Charlie sarcastically.

Undeterred by Charlie's mockery, Tom continued, "In the world that operates mostly by the accepted laws of physics, the chaos unfolds in a relatively linear manner because it's only one chaotic thread. But there are occasional faults that happen where some of the individual threads of the multiverse end up overlapping.

"That's what explains those 'déjà vu' moments that most people have from time to time, like you had earlier Lucia. It's also why people sometimes have that strange shiver sensation and say that it felt like someone just walked over their grave, and why people see what they think are ghosts. It's not ghosts that they're seeing; they're just experiencing what happens when either the space or time part of the space-time continuum accidentally overlaps. Sometimes, in extreme cases, both space and time from two or more threads overlap. An example of that would be when people experience what they think are poltergeists and see objects moving around in front of them. That's where the space *and* time elements of two different multiverse threads get tangled into a sort of cosmic knot.

"Technically, this place shouldn't exist as it does because everything should have been reset each time that we went back to a potential cross-roads to try to prevent an existential event from unfolding.

"But it does exist, so we just accept that it does. The cosmic knot paradox theory kind of fits in with lots of other things we've learned so far about quantum physics, so we just accept it as a possibility. Or maybe, the universe just intends it to exist."

# THE COSMIC KNOT PARADOX

# Chapter 36
# Chaos Theory

"No, I can't accept that," said Charlie indignantly, "By saying that the universe 'intends this to exist' is starting to stray into the realm of some divine intervention theory. You're saying that the universe has agency, consciousness, and ubiquitous control...like a god. Just because it defies your expectations based on what you currently know and understand, doesn't mean that it's the work or choice of some deity. Humans are really prone to that kind of idiocy when they don't understand something.

"Whenever there's a question that science can't yet answer, people attribute whatever it is that they're simply too ignorant to understand, to the will of a god. Imagine if you were living in the 15th Century and your friend was killed by a bolt of lightning in a field. Given the size of the field, you could be forgiven for wondering why the lightning struck in the precise spot where your friend was standing and for concluding that it must have been the will of a god who was either punishing your friend for some wrongdoing or simply wanted him in *his* realm sooner.

"And I stress the word 'his' because of all the misogynistic and patriarchal bullshit humanity has had to endure from pretty much every religion and every god that ignorant, proscriptive, and bigoted men have ever invented. I'm primarily talking about all of the main religions like Christianity, Islam and Judaism that originated in the Middle East and then spread throughout the rest of the world like a cancer, but every other religion too, before and after, is more or less just as bad.

"Fortunately, this type of belief in the supernatural is diminishing in the parts of the world where humans have become less ignorant. That's why the overwhelming majority of Nobel science laureates are atheists."

Flore decided it was time to change the subject. "Well, Charlie, I'm glad you got that off your chest. Anyway, Tom, are you going to tell us how Sylvain knew about all of this before the rest of us?"

"Well, now is as good a time as any," started Tom, "But I need to start by explaining to you why you're here and why you're all so important. The cosmos is a completely random and chaotic place. Chaos is the lifeblood of the universe and the reason why we're all here.

"It's how the universe operates, and the ability of any individual to control that chaos is very limited. At best, most people can only influence a very small number of factors in their lives, and I stress the word 'influence' rather than control. The extent of that ability is mostly what separates successful people from less successful people.

"Generally, successful people are slightly better at influencing desired outcomes from the chaotic randomness around them; and by successful, I don't just mean people who have amazing careers or accumulate great wealth, because success can also be measured by happiness, health, longevity, and lots of other factors apart from money and power.

"The quantum tunnelling capability that we have acquired makes us much more able to control chaos because almost anything that we or someone else does can retrospectively be changed. To a certain extent we are also protected from most of the curveballs that the universe might throw at us, at least the local ones. If, for example, there was suddenly an earthquake here, we could quickly think ourselves somewhere else.

"But that first visit I made to New York when I got killed by the garbage truck, taught us to avoid being in risky situations together. If Marion had been with me on that trip to New York, we would both have been killed and the story would have ended before it had properly begun."

"So you want us to be your insurance policy, to be 'on-call' to jump to action and change the course of history in case you and Marion get killed by a garbage truck or some other random event," said Flore, indignantly.

"Well, that's a rather cynical way of looking at it," Tom replied, "Look, we have an opportunity to change the world. To improve the lives of hundreds of millions, perhaps billions of people. But Marion and I can't do it alone, and if anything happens to us, it'll all be over, and humanity will just continue marching forward on a path of self-destruction. We've seen the future and it's not a pretty sight."

Looking somewhat bemused, Charlie interjected, "But, you described a future with flying cars; 'flars' you called them, and intercontinental travel that takes just minutes, and suits that can self-heal. The future can't be all that bad."

"Yes, but that future, that thread, isn't a certainty, it's only one possible outcome. For you, between arriving here on the Salty Box of Frogs a few days ago and a future with flying cars and everything I described, there are a myriad of possible events and actions that could cause infinite different futures. What I can tell you with absolute certainty is that without any intervention, what will unfold is catastrophic," replied Tom.

"But that doesn't make any sense," said Charlie.,"You've described a future that you've experienced, that you've lived. So, what you've described must already be secure."

"You're still not getting this are you?" said Tom, a note of irritation now present in his voice, "That future isn't guaranteed because you haven't yet done the things that will create that future."

"That still doesn't make sense," said Charlie, also sounding irritated.

"Welcome to the cosmic knot paradox," replied Tom with a smile.

# THE COSMIC KNOT PARADOX

# Chapter 37
# It's the End of the
# World as we Know it

Tom started to explain the extent of the catastrophe about to unfold.

"Without any intervention by us, for most people, the world turns into a pretty unpleasant place very quickly indeed after 2025. And when I say unpleasant, I mean a perfect storm of economic and environmental catastrophes leading to a complete societal meltdown. And it all unravels very, very, fast."

"What happens?" asked Flore.

"Well, you'll probably remember the massive amounts of capital that most of the world's central banks created and pumped into their economies during the 2007 banking crisis, and then did the same again, but on a much bigger scale, during the Covid pandemic. Printing all that money, quantitative easing as it was euphemistically called at the time, propped things up quite well for a while, but perhaps too well, because very soon, with no feasible way for central banks to properly tighten fiscal policy without plunging their economies into recession, we end up with global hyper-inflation followed by all of the world's major economies tumbling into depression anyway. There's a word for this phenomenon. It's called 'stagflation' and just whispering that word will cause any finance minister to instantly shit themselves. By the beginning of 2030, a loaf of bread in New York costs $13 million, and by the end of that year the price has risen to $34 million.

"At the same time, from relatively early on in the timeline of what becomes known as the 'Great Meltdown', as cash reserves are obliterated by the tsunami of inflation, and tax receipts dwindle to almost nothing as the recession bites harder and harder, every government is forced to stop all investment in ecological initiatives and infrastructure because there's simply no money left. There's not enough money to install electric car charging points, solar farms or wind turbines, or to finish building more efficient, less environmentally damaging power stations.

"To at least keep essential industry and some government departments running, both America and China, followed by most other developed nations, resort to adapting their coal-fired power stations to burn used car tyres. Most of the rest of the population has to learn to live without electricity or install diesel engines scavenged from abandoned trucks and fuelled by used cooking oil looted from shuttered fast-food restaurants to light and power their homes. As a result, global warming accelerates massively. The world crashes through the two-degree warming target by 2030.

"Over the following decade, economies stabilise to the extent that the inflation dissipates, but the structural damage is done. By 2040, eighty per cent of businesses that were viable and profitable before the Great Meltdown are gone, and those that survive are a shadow of what they were before, functioning on about ten per cent of their original workforce.

"Unemployment is therefore rife, running at around eighty-five per cent of the working age population globally. There are no manufacturing jobs because what little is manufactured, is made by robots. There are no jobs in farming because those jobs are also done by robots. Most accountants are out of business because nobody has any money that needs to be counted anymore, and those ex-accountants can't even get jobs as taxi drivers, because by then, self-driving cars are about the only thing on the road, ferrying the few remaining wealthy people around during the day and being recharged by electricity that's been generated by burning used car tyres at night.

"By 2040, the earth has warmed by ten degrees above 2020 levels and the polar ice caps have completely melted; the sea has warmed sufficiently to release the carbon dioxide and other greenhouse gases locked into the seabed, which dramatically worsens and accelerates the crisis. Sea levels rise so much that twenty percent of the world's landmass ends up under water.

"Because many big cities are coastal, forty per cent end up being consumed by the sea, driving more than two billion people from their homes. By 2050 more than four billion people have either starved or died in the rampant and brutal lawlessness that ensues as starving people compete for dry land, food and resources.

"Over the decades that follow it continues to get worse until there's pretty much nothing left of the world or humanity as we know it. Armageddon."

"So, you're saying that without us doing something, the world as we know it ends before the end of this century - within our children's life-times," said Flore, looking startled.

"Exactly, Marion and I have lived this terrible future more than a dozen times and each time, we've completely failed to make any tangible difference. The only chance we have of saving the planet is if all four of us work out our strategy, tactics and execution. Now, you asked how Sylvain knew about this before…" Tom started, but Charlie interrupted, "My tits are smaller! And this morning my nipples were like a lorry's wheel nuts, but now they're almost normal again!"

"Thank you for sharing, Charlie," Tom continued with a sigh, "Now, as I was saying, you remember I told you that the night after our first lottery win, Marion and I decided that we would approach Sylvain first to get his thoughts on involving the rest of you?

"Well, I met with Sylvain in January 2022 in Paris, when he was there doing some research and filming for his next documentary. We went for dinner, and I explained everything. He listened carefully and intently, and I talked, almost without pause, for what was probably more than an hour. When I finished, he just looked at me, completely dispassionately, and asked me how much LSD I'd been taking recently and whether I'd thought about getting some professional help. So, I just asked him if he'd like to go to a gig.

At that moment, the big screen on the back wall of the lounge came to life, and Tom once again fell silent as he projected his thoughts onto the device.

# THE COSMIC KNOT PARADOX

# Chapter 38
# Love or Confusion

"A gig? Wow, I know you can be a bit random sometimes, but we were just talking about Wesh, the quantum stuff and the time-travelling fantasy of yours that I didn't really understand, beyond thinking that you've completely lost the plot. I asked you if you've thought about getting professional help and you just changed the subject. What the fuck? I love you Tom, but you're confusing sometimes. Anyway, I've got a full day of filming tomorrow, so I really shouldn't be going to a gig," Sylvain protested.

"I tell you what," Tom replied, "It doesn't have to be late or boozy, so let's toss a coin. Let fate decide. Heads we go to the gig, tails we don't."

Sylvain felt it would be somewhat churlish and impolite to reject the idea out of hand, so said, "OK, let's toss a coin."

Tom produced a coin from his pocket, flicked it in the air, where it spun for a few seconds before he caught it on the back of his left hand, covered it with his right, and then revealed the result to Sylvain. It was Heads. They were going.

Tom told him it was a new band that was getting great reviews, but that they needed to go to his hotel first to get the tickets. When they got to Tom's hotel room, Tom took Sylvain's hand, and told him, "Don't be afraid and don't let go." Sylvain did look afraid, and a moment later, looked very, very scared indeed because they were in a completely different place – in the kitchen of the New York house on Grove Street.

"What the fuck just happened?" Sylvain exclaimed.

Tom replied, "You're in Greenwich Village, New York. This is the house I told you about. Today is 3rd August 1966. We're going to the 'Café Wha?' to see Jimmy James and the Blue Flames. Do you know who Jimmy James is?"

"No, and what the fuck are you talking about? How can it be 1966?" Sylvain replied, still looking startled.

"Jimmy James and the Blue Flames is Jimi Hendrix and his band, and this really is 1966. Look at the cars parked in the street. Either that or I've tricked you and brought you to Cuba or perhaps a Hollywood film set," Tom told him.

Sylvain looked out of the window and sure enough, the cars were all 1950s and 60s American cars.

"What the fuck?" he said for the umpteenth time.

Once Tom had disguised Sylvain, getting him into some of his 1960's clothes, they walked out onto the street. It was a glorious New York summer evening – hard to believe that only four months previously, there had been snow up to the level of the roofs of the cars parked on the street.

As they walked south along Bleecker Street, headed towards the Café Wha? on MacDougal Street, Tom was stopped in his tracks by the sight of a cover of a magazine on one of the newsstands. There on the front cover of Time magazine was a face that he instantly recognised; so much so that it seemed to be shouting at him from the rack. He read the words on the magazine cover 'Bill Bowerman – Bell Boy Zero to Fortune 500 Hero in 5 Years'. He looked at the face again. It was Billy, the porter from the Edison Hotel who had stolen Marion's Adidas trainers six years ago. Well, six years ago for him; just a few days for Tom.

Tom flicked through the magazine to the relevant pages. Billy had started a company called Nike about ten months after Tom and Marion's stay at the Edison Hotel. He laughed out loud, simultaneously pleased and shocked by Billy's opportunism and success in equal measure. 'Well, after all, this is the land of opportunity,' Tom thought.

He couldn't wait to tell Marion, and quickly realising that he didn't need to, nipped back to Limehouse to tell her. She was as amused as he was.

"What are you laughing at?" Sylvain said, completely oblivious to the journey Tom had just made as he landed back on Bleecker Street walking next to him.

"Oh, nothing important. Just seen somebody that I know in that magazine. I'll tell you about it another time," he said.

At the Café Wha? Hendrix and his band played a mesmerising forty-minute set that included covers of Howlin' Wolf's 'Killing Floor' and Don Covay's 'Mercy Mercy', plus early versions of his own 'Foxy Lady', 'Third Stone From The Sun' and something that sounded a bit like 'Voodoo Chile'. It was a truly surreal experience.

**cosmicknotparadox.com/video2**

After the gig, Tom and Sylvain walked back along Bleecker Street. With the residue of Hendrix' distorted guitar still ringing in their ears, Sylvain told Tom, "OK. So, you've not lost your marbles. You are sane and everything you told me in Paris is somehow, I don't know how, but somehow real. So, what now?"

"Now we make the future a better place," Tom said with a smile.

# THE COSMIC KNOT PARADOX

# Chapter 39
# The Einstein Plan

Back at Grove Street, Tom and Sylvain opened a bottle of Jack Daniels, sat down at the kitchen table and Tom outlined his ideas to Sylvain.

He told Sylvain about how the world was on the brink of economic, environmental, and social catastrophe and how they had to act. He asked Sylvain if he was aware that some people believe in the existence of a secret Illuminati who control everything, using politicians and the media as puppets to effect whatever changes they desire.

"Yes, I'm aware of those ideas, but the people who believe in that kind of stuff are just bonkers, conspiracy theorist nutcases. People with impressionable minds and too much time on their hands. Most who think that the world is controlled by an Illuminati also believe that Nine-Eleven was faked, that the moon landings were a hoax and that Covid vaccines were an elaborate trick to enable Bill Gates to get nanobots into everyone's bloodstreams."

"Well, Sylvain, you're right about all of that," Tom replied, "But we have to become the Illuminati that these people believe in. It needs to be us in the background pulling the puppet strings. We have to control the world's politicians so that we can define the political agenda. We have to control the world's media so we can disseminate the messages we want people to absorb. We have to control everything."

"Now you're really worrying me, Tom. You sound like Stalin or Hitler."

"I know I do. But the difference between me and Hitler or Stalin is that they thought they were right, whereas I know that I'm right. I've seen the future, but they only had their vision of what the future should look like based on their fucked-up ideologies," Tom replied.

"Maybe your ideology and vision is just as fucked-up, only you've not realised yet," said Sylvain, feeling the need to take on the role of devil's advocate.

"Sylvain, if we don't do anything, humanity the way we know it will be finished. Imagine your worst dystopian nightmare and realise it will be one thousand times worse. We have to act. There's no choice. But we need a plan, a really clever plan."

"You're right," replied Sylvain, we need a plan so clever that you could put a big bushy moustache on it and call it 'Einstein'."

cosmicknotparadox.com/einstein

Tom nodded his tacit agreement and they started to draft their Einstein Plan.

As they got down past the halfway level of the bottle of Jack Daniels, to the bottom of the word "Tennessee" on the label, Tom told Sylvain, "Just to make sure we're on the same page, if we're going to do this Illuminati thing, fiddling around the edges isn't going to make a difference. To succeed in preventing the end of the world, we need to effect complete change; political, economic, industrial, social…everything.

"We'll have to completely alter how the world works, ridding it of its broken political systems and the illogical and cruel belief structures of most of the world's religions, or at least get them to reinvent themselves.

"We'll also need to modify capitalism so that we continue to benefit from the bounty of creativity of the brightest and the best but eradicate as much of the unfairness and inequality. At the same time, we mustn't fall into the trap of a communist dystopia by trying to make everyone equal, because all animals will never be equal, and some will always be more equal than others; the world has to be that way, or nobody will want to sweep the streets or collect the garbage. We'll also need to change the way the world generates and uses power."

"But the problems and the moral dilemmas are much, much, bigger than that," Sylvain replied, "For example, from what you've told me, this Monstera juice could be adapted to treat pretty much any illness or ailment, to the extent that it could cure anyone of almost anything - even mortality.

"But if we do that, it won't be long before the world will be so over-populated that everyone will starve. How will we square that particular circle? Wanting to save lives, but knowing that if we do, we'll just create mass suffering for people who can't easily die. And mark my words, there will be a thousand other quandaries just as hard as that."

"I know, it's so difficult," Tom replied, "The price of having these incredible powers is the immense burden of responsibility that comes with them. And now, here we are talking about effecting, or forcing, complete societal change. The challenges will be immense, and we need to be certain that we're up to the job. There's an expression that comes to mind…"

"You can't make an omelette without breaking some eggs?" Sylvain suggested.

"Yes, that too," replied Tom, "but the expression I was thinking of is 'power corrupts, and absolute power corrupts absolutely'. We will have absolute power. Can you handle that without becoming corrupted, Sylvain?"

# THE COSMIC KNOT PARADOX

# Chapter 40
# The Power of the Coins

Over the next hour, Tom and Sylvain agreed their biggest strategic priorities, which Tom scribbled on a piece of paper headed 'Einstein Plan.'

With the plan complete, or at least, neither able to think of anything more to add to the list, Tom said, "This is too big for just the two of us. If we're going to do this, we need help from people we trust, so we can make the big strategic decisions together and share the moral and ethical quandaries. Marion's already on this journey with me. How would you feel about enlisting Flore's help? And what about your friends, Charlie and Lucia. I had a good feeling about them at that farewell dinner they hosted for you."

Sylvain was immediately enthusiastic, citing Flore's intelligence and understanding of how political systems work, Charlie's imagination and familiarity with financial markets, and Lucia's intuition and ability to diffuse entrenched differences.

"We'll need to have a really solid decision-making process, together with a mechanism for resolving disputes that we're all prepared to stick to. If not, we'll all fall out," Tom added.

They also decided that they wouldn't immediately tell Flore, Charlie or Lucia anything about the plan, but instead, allow them to discover for themselves how even the smallest, most insignificant and mundane action can create a cascade of unintended consequences, before their big reveal.

With the key points of the Einstein plan properly noted, they then discussed the tactics they'd employ to get the team together.

"Sylvain, you realise that there will be times when you're going to have to be calculating and devious in order to achieve both long-term strategic objectives and short-term tactical goals."

Sylvain looked at Tom with a puzzled expression and asked, "What do you mean?"

"Well, think about how I got you here," Tom replied.

Sylvain thought for a moment, then said, 'Well, over dinner in Paris, you told me all about your time travelling quantum thing, I thought you'd gone mad, so you took a chance and suggested we flipped a coin to decide whether or not to go to a gig.'

With a stoic expression and a matter of fact but authoritative tone, Tom told him, "There was no chance involved in any of that, Sylvain."'

Reaching into his pocket, Tom retrieved a coin, put it on the table and said, "Look at the coin. It's heads, right?" Sylvain nodded. "That means the other side is tails, right?" Sylvain nodded again. "Wrong," Tom said triumphantly, "This is a double-headed coin. Turn it over and you'll see."

Sylvain, stared open-mouthed as he turned over the coin and saw that both sides were identical.

Tom reached into his left pocket and retrieved a different coin. "And this one is a double-tailed coin. These coins will be invaluable in getting people to make the choices you want them to make. Nobody can resist the thrill of a coin toss.

"Few people know this, but Adolf Hitler tossed a coin to decide whether or not to invade Poland. Boris Johnson used a coin to decide whether to back Leave or Remain, and some historians believe that Henry VIII used a coin to decide whether to behead or just divorce his wives." Tom handed the coins to Sylvain. "They're yours now. Look after them. And never underestimate the power of the coins."

Charlie suddenly erupted out of silence into loud, angry speech, and the image on the screen stopped as Tom snapped out of his trancelike state and back to full consciousness.

"So, that's how you did it! You sneaky bastard, Sylvain. We decided to start the search for Wesh by tossing a coin. And ever since then, I've lost countless coin-tossing drinking games. I almost died from Tequila poisoning that night before my tits grew."

"Yes, perhaps I did overuse the coins a bit, but I was just practising using them," Sylvain replied, visibly blushing.

"You bastard Tom!" growled Brian, "That's how you won the argument with Marion about whether or not to have me castrated. She was saying that it seemed cruel, and you were saying things like, it'll make him calmer…less likely to run away…won't get into fights with other dogs…. all the usual bullshit arguments that you can read from thousands of

other victims if you search #MyBallsToo. So then you say to her, 'I tell
you what, let's settle it by tossing a coin.' And that was that. The next day
I was at the vet. Well, they were my balls, and I was proud of them. You
total, total, bastard."

Attempting to diffuse the tensions with distraction, Tom produced a
crumpled and rather tattered sheet of paper from his pocket and showed
it to the group.

"Anyway, I was explaining about the Einstein Plan. I've kept it in my
pocket ever since. I read it every night before I go to sleep." Tom told the
group, then started to read the plan out loud.

*Einstein Plan*

*Objectives:*
*Prevent global catastrophe and the end of the world as we know it,*
*end poverty, hunger and famine, eradicate disease, offer eternal life*
*and save the planet by causing complete political, economic, environ-*
*mental, social and societal change*

*Strategy:*
*Find island*
*Establish colony*
*Declare independent state*
*Allow economic meltdown to continue – opportunity to acquire*
*assets, build Wesh power base*
*Get leaders of G12 under control*
*Get rest of political leaders under control*
*Get religious leaders under control*
*Intervene in economic crisis when people have given up hope*
*Offer alternative way and government bailouts in exchange for*
*political change*

Flore interrupted before Tom could finish talking through the main
points.

"Are you insane? End poverty, famine, disease? Get political and
religious leaders under control? Save the planet? Eternal life? People have

been trying to solve these problems for millennia without any success, but you think you can fix all this yourself. You must be the most arrogant person I've ever met!"

Tom smiled and said, "I probably am the most arrogant person you've ever met. But then, nobody you've ever met can do this...."

The next instant Tom was the living image of an early medieval-era man dressed in a white robe and turban. He spoke for a few seconds in perfect Mecca Arabic.

"Surely not, please tell me you've not been pretending to be the Pro..." Flore started to say but was immediately silenced, as a moment later Tom appeared as a 15th Century Roman nobleman speaking faultless Renaissance period Italian. Then a second later, an alien once again stood before them.

"Sylvain, show them," said the extra-terrestrial.

Sylvain instantly transformed himself into Charlie Chaplain, then Adolf Hitler, delivering a few words in fluent German, before finishing his sentence in perfectly accented Columbian Spanish as Pablo Escobar. Tom then reappeared as himself, clutching a large brown paper bag.

"I thought you might all be hungry by now," he said, as he reached into the bag and distributed hot dogs around the group, "From the stand in Times Square. Best chilli dogs in New York."

"OK. You've made your point," Flore remarked, "But Sylvain, you've learned how to do that, and you didn't tell me?"

Sylvain looked at his shoes like a naughty schoolboy.

"So, what now?" asked Lucia.

"Now we continue the tour," said Marion.

"But isn't there' only the gym and the pool left?"

"No! There's the kitchen, the lab, the trading room and then there are six more floors below this one," Marion said.

"Six more floors! What's down there?" asked Lucia

"Well, there's an engineering floor, a factory floor, a rehab floor, two farm floors and a transport hub, which includes a Hyperloop as well as marine and space docks," Marion replied.

"Hyperloop? Space dock? It sounds like something from a Bond movie or the type of thing Elon Musk would build," said Charlie.

"Yes, well that's another bone of contention between Tom and Elon, and part of the reason Tom still sounds like Boris Johnson," Marion replied. "Tom thought it would be a good idea to put a Hyperloop terminal in to link L'île de Wesh with Athens so that, before we can start using flars, we'll be able to invite world leaders without them having to come by sea or helicopter. Unfortunately, Tom neglected to ask Elon if it would be OK to use his Hyperloop idea and Elon got upset. That's when the Neuralink helpdesk started blocking his calls. In retaliation, Tom sent Elon a message saying he was going to get to Mars first and built an Even Bigger Fucking Rocket. It's really childish. But boys will be boys, eh? I'm sure they'll sort it out in the end," Marion said with a resigned sigh.

"What's the rehab floor?" asked Charlie.

"Well, during a brain-storming session trying to work out the factors that have messed up the world so badly up until now, one of the ideas that we had was what I guess everybody already knows, which is that the world is in such a mess because humans are so fundamentally flawed.

"But worse than that, throughout history, power has ended up being concentrated in the hands of the people who are the most flawed. Think about it; Genghis Khan, Psychopath; Adolf Hitler, Bipolar Schizophrenic Psychopath; Donald Trump, Narcissistic Personality Disorder and Psychopath; Vladimir Putin, Paranoid Sadistic Psychopath with extreme Penile Dysmorphic Disorder; Napoleon, Obsessive Compulsive Disorder; Bill Clinton, JFK, Silvio Berlusconi, Boris Johnson and so many others, Hedonistic Personality Disorder.

"So, we started wondering whether a good place to start making the world a better place might be to see if we could fix the faulty wiring in people's brains. We reasoned that if we could treat enough people, not only would the world be a much happier place, but there would be a much smaller number of fucked up people able to bubble to the top."

"That all sounds very logical, but how could that be done?" asked Charlie.

"Well," continued Marion, "We theorised that a combination of the healing properties of Monstera with a type of subliminal aversion therapy might be effective, and decided that the best group to start with would be extreme sexual deviants."

"Sexual deviants! Why?" Asked Flore.

"Because those are the people whose compulsions are usually driven by a complex mix of multiple personality disorders that are so strong that they are prepared not only to be caught breaking the law, but are willing to risk ridicule, humiliation, derision and hatred to satiate their obsessive and unnatural desires. Sorry to say, but they're usually males," Marion replied.

"Makes sense. So, you started with the biggest challenge first," said Charlie.

"Exactly," Marion confirmed, "We designed a clinical method where the partially sedated patient would be attached to a sort of life support machine that would deliver a Monstera juice derivative intravenously. At the same time, the patient would be 'plugged into' what could best be described as a sort of milking machine and the patient would also have a continuous stream of pornography directly matching their specific perversion streamed to them via a virtual reality headset. Our idea was that over a two- to six-week course of treatment, the Monstera would repair the damaged neural pathways, whilst the subliminal aversion therapy of the porn and the milking machine would break any ingrained habit – I suppose you could call it a 'too much of a good thing' therapy.

"We didn't have to search for very long to find a subject with what can only be described as a case of extreme deviance for us to test the treatment. We became aware of rumours back around the end of the twentieth century of an individual who, once or twice per month, would suddenly appear in London's Regents Park in the early hours of the morning, wearing a pair of four-metre-tall stilts and would then break into the zoo. They didn't actually break in, they just stepped over the fence.

"Once inside the zoo, the perpetrator would quickly make their way to the giraffe enclosure where they would do unspeakable things to the poor animals for up to an hour, sometimes more. Once satiated, they would step back over the fence, then run through Regents Park until they reached the public toilets, detach the stilts, enter the toilet building and then just disappear.

"We put Pippa on the case. She went to the public toilets and discovered a hidden hatch in the floor disguised as a drain cover. Beneath the hatch she found a staircase leading to a secret tube station. She followed the rail track to its end where there was another staircase. The staircase opened into the basement of an old building. Wondering where she might be, Pippa took her phone out of her pocket and opened her maps app. What she saw left her in a state of complete shock."

"What did she see on the map? Where was she?" Asked Flore, intrigue dominant in her voice.

Marion took a deep breath. "She was in the basement of.... Buckingham Palace."

"No! Surely not. Please tell me that the giraffe molester is a butler or a gardener or works in the kitchens and isn't a member of the Royal family. And are you actually saying that this pervert went to the trouble of having a train line built direct to the zoo?" asked Charlie.

With a look of sympathetic regret, Marion replied, "I wish I could tell you that it was one of the staff, but it wasn't. The giraffe fiddler was indeed a member of your royal family. I realise this must come as a terrible shock to you. As far as the train line is concerned, that was constructed during the war to give the royals a means of escape in the event of a Nazi invasion."

"More like a chance to join their Panzer unit," joked Sylvain.

"Which royal was it?" asked Charlie.

"I can't say. It wouldn't be fair. He's cured now," Marion replied.

With a look of relief Charlie said, "Well, I guess I should be grateful that they're just perverts, and not lizards like that fruitcake David Icke has been saying. And I suppose I should be even more thankful that the Royal in question was a 'he'; the idea of the Queen buggering a giraffe with a strap-on dildo would have been just too much for me."

"But you caught and cured him?" asked Flore, looking astonished.

"Yes, we did. Pippa set up some hidden cameras so we could determine for certain which Royal it was. Once we knew that, it was quite easy to get to him.

"Tom and Pippa visited him in his room the same night while he was asleep, fully sedated him and brought him here. We then hooked him up to the machine we'd built and set the porn rolling – you've no idea how hard it was to find giraffe porn.

"It took almost four weeks connected to the machine before the neural readings suggested that he was probably cured.

"By then his testicles were shrivelled to the size of raisins, but other than that he seemed OK. So, that night, Pippa and Tom took him back to the palace, put him back to bed and he woke up the next morning just thinking he'd had an extreme erotic dream, completely unaware that he'd been here on an alternative thread of the space-time continuum, being bombarded with giraffe porn for almost a month."

"That's incredible. So, if you can cure someone of something that extreme, it would be pretty easy for you to convert, say, a narcissist or a psychopath into a nice person?" asked Charlie.

"We think that with time to refine our methods, we'll be able to cure almost all of the common personality disorders and neurodivergencies.. We reached out to the Coalition for Understanding Neurodiverse Tourette's Syndrome and the Society for People Experiencing Literary Dyslexia, but we couldn't understand the letter we got back from the dyslexics and the Tourette's group just told us to 'Fuck Off,'" Marion replied.

Charlie persisted, "But you think you could cure narcissistic psychopaths? Even extreme cases; you know, the type of person that's so horrible and has done and said so many unpleasant, cruel and spiteful things, that just the mention of their name makes you feel nauseous?"

"We think so, yes," Marion replied.

"Who fancies another Tom Collins?" asked Sylvain.

Then, without waiting for anyone to answer, appeared the very next second with a tray of drinks.

"I think I've got the hang of this quantum thing now," he said, smiling.

# Chapter 41
# Feed the World

"You mentioned A farm and a factory. What's that all about?" asked Flore.

Gathering her thoughts for a moment, Marion replied, "Well, you remember we told you about how the global economic meltdown leads to a dramatic acceleration of the climate crisis? We determined that even with our intervention, there's no way of turning things around quickly enough to completely prevent food shortages.

"With your help, we're confident that we will be able to alter enough of the underlying causalities of the climate crisis to bring the planet back to good health, but there will be a period of thirty to fifty years during which the atmosphere will be so polluted that almost nothing will grow. So, we've been experimenting with hydroponics and using a Monstera derivative as a fertilizer, in the hope that we'll be able to increase crop yields sufficiently to prevent mass famine while the planet recovers.

"We think that once we perfect the Monstera fertilizer so that people who eat the produce don't grow tits, end up with gargantuan genitals or the ability to time-travel, that we'll be able to generate more than fifty times the yield that's normally possible for hydroponically grown plants. Put another way, we'll be able to grow more than one thousand kilos of soyabeans in just three days in a space measuring two point four metres wide by twelve metres long and two point six metres high."

"Why such specific dimensions?" asked Charlie.

"Because, those are the exact measurements of a standard shipping container, and within ten years, with the economic meltdown that's coming, there will be more than 15 million unused shipping containers that nobody will know what to do with.

"Our plan is to convert the shipping containers into mini-farms that are air-conditioned, humidity controlled, can produce fresh water even from seawater, and are equipped with the artificial lighting that's needed to grow food. Each mini farm will be powered by a single, orange-sized Mini Fusion Reactor which will power each farm for at least one hundred years.

"We estimate that each mini farm will produce enough food to feed more than one thousand people, meaning that if we can convert ten million of the unused shipping containers, even if the population by then has grown to ten billion, we'll be able to feed the entire world."

"Wow, that's incredible," remarked Flore, "You said Phase One was to do the hydroponic Monstera experiments. What's Phase Two?"

"Well, once we've properly ironed out the issues with the Monstera fertilizer, that Charlie knows so well, and then been able to prove that we're able to get the crop yields that we believe are possible, we're intending to convert one of the farm floors into a banana and chicken farm, with…" Marion started to explain, but Charlie interrupted.

"I see where this is going. It's all linked, right? You've not yet told us what you intend to make in the factory, but I'm guessing it's those Mini Fusion Reactors that you'll make from the eggshells and banana skins produced on the farm. You also told us earlier on that the performance of the fusion reactors could be enhanced with the addition of human semen. So, you're planning to get a load of sex offenders plugged into what you euphemistically called your 'Rehab Unit' and what I'm going to call your 'Jizz Farm' to provide the secret sauce for the reactors."

Tom immediately started clapping.

"Bravo, mon ami, you worked it all out. It's taken us about five hundred years of trial and error, going back and forth, trying this and that, to come up with this plan, but you've guessed it in fifteen minutes. That's why I knew we needed all of you.

"But, yes, that's pretty much the plan. We're already in negotiation with several governments to take their worst sex offenders and return them six weeks later, fully cured. The Vatican are very interested in the proposal."

"That's utterly shocking. What have you become? Milking humans against their will. They might have done terrible things to end up in prison, but they still have rights," Flore protested.

Tom nodded and continued. "Yes, I get your concerns, but everything will be consensual. From the research we've done so far, most of these prisoners like the idea of being attached to the milking machine and watching carefully curated porn for a month, then being sent back cured and free.

"There'll also be the safety mechanism that every two days we'll temporarily bring them out of their heightened erotic state, by playing them a short video clip of Brigitte Macron so that we can ask them if they're happy to continue. If not, they'll be free to go back to whichever prison they're from to continue their sentence."

"Well, I suppose if you get their agreement and have a safety mechanism in place, then I guess it's probably OK," Flore conceded.

"What's the other farm floor for?" Asked Sylvain

"Monstera of course," Said Marion. "It's just a football pitch-sized farm at the moment, but it's already producing twenty tonnes of Monstera leaves and stalks per day. After processing, this translates to ten million Monstera tablets and ten thousand litres of Monstera juice. We're stockpiling the production at the moment, ready to start distribution next year. The aim is to make the farm one thousand times bigger."

"One thousand times bigger!" said Charlie, "But how? Surely not a thousand floors?"

"No, we're excavating laterally," Marion explained, "All of the floors are below sea level. By the time we've finished, we'll have almost joined up with Athens. We're doing the same with all of the other floors, so we'll end up being the world's largest producer of bananas, and there'll be more chickens here than in the rest of the entire world. We'll be able to treat up to one hundred thousand patients on the rehab floor, and the rest of the space on that floor will be used for other things like accommodation. It will be the biggest single manufacturing facility on the planet, entirely geared towards achieving the objectives of the Einstein plan."

"Wow! What are you doing with all the earth?" asked Lucia.

"We're making other islands," Said Tom, "The earth is moved up to the dock level where it's taken away by cargo ship and then deposited in the sea. Eventually, we'll have deposited enough to create seven new islands, all fully independent, but linked underground."

"And I'm guessing the Hyperloop isn't just so that you can get presidents and prime ministers here for talks; it's so you can ship prisoners, factory and farm workers in and out, and also transport the MFRs to the mainland," said Charlie.

"That's almost right," Tom replied, "But the only humans here will be us, the re-animated rock stars and the prisoners that we'll be rehabilitating. The farm, factory and nursing work will be done by robots. The main purpose of the hyperloop is to get raw materials in and the MFRs out. To produce enough MFRs to equip ten million shipping containers here on Wesh will mean making and shipping a trainload of them every day for three years."

"Won't having any people coming in and out be a big security risk? Especially convicts," Sylvain asked.

"Yes, and won't someone be able to get one of the MFRs and take it apart to see how it works?" Charlie asked.

"No, the devices are designed to safely self-destruct if anybody tampers with them. You just end up with a small pile of ash if you attempt to open them," Tom replied.

"What will you do with all those eggs and bananas?" Flore asked.

"I've got a great recipe for Banana Flambé and Charlie loves Tortilla de Patatas," said Lucia.

Marion laughed and said, "Lucia, we're going to use over one trillion eggshells and more than one hundred million banana skins every year. Luckily, we've found a use for the waste. We've found that if we mix powdered egg with banana purée and the pulp from Monstera stalks, the mixture can used to manufacture a material which, after being baked, is ten thousand times stronger than steel, yet lighter than paper. It is heat resistant to a temperature of 500,000 degrees centigrade, impervious to all chemicals and acids, and in the highly unlikely event that it is damaged in any way, it 'heals' in a matter of seconds.

"Despite its incredible strength and rigidity, if an electrical current at exactly the right voltage is passed through it, the material becomes as flexible as a piece of wet fabric, then returns to being completely rigid when the current is switched off. This means that it can be moulded into almost any shape. Tom made the superstructure of the Even Bigger Fucking Rocket from it. The EBFR is more than two hundred and fifty metres high and thirty metres in diameter, yet the whole structure weighs less than one hundred kilos."

Tom continued with the description of the rocket, "With twenty Flar engines, each powered by just one MFR, we'll be able to cut the journey time to Mars to just three days."

"But why do you need a rocket?" asked Charlie.

"So we can plant a flag on Mars before Elon gets there," Tom replied.

# Chapter 42
# Life, the Universe and Everything

"But if getting to Mars before Elon is so important to you, why don't you just think yourself there?" asked Flore.

"Well, errr, lots of reasons," replied Tom. "Tunnelling that distance would be mentally exhausting. Also, I'd need to take the rocket, or at least some sort of survival pod, and I've never moved anything that big before. But more than anything, if I suddenly turned up on Mars without credible evidence of a rocket launch and space flight, then the whole world would either think it was a hoax or would find out about the quantum tunnelling."

"There's a solution to all of this," Charlie chipped in.

"I'm all ears, tell me," Tom replied.

"We have something that Elon would desperately want if he knew about it. At the same time, he's got things that would be really useful to us," Charlie replied.

"Yes, like what?" asked Tom.

"Well, for a start, you not sounding like Boris Johnson," said Lucia, "It's starting to make me feel sick."

"Yes, and if we had control of Neuralink there's a whole load of things we could do with that technology that would help with the Einstein plan. So, we just make a deal with Elon to swap the synthetic Monstera metal and the Flar engines for Neuralink."

"And a Tesla Roadster. I want a Tesla Roadster. A red one. The chicks will love it," Brian interrupted.

"Brian, dogs can't drive," replied Marion.

"They can. I've seen it on TV. Look," replied Brian as the screen at the far end of the room came to life and Brian slipped into a trance-like state.

cosmicknotparadox.com/video3

"Brian's right," said Tom, "Neuralink and fixing my voice isn't enough for the Monstera metal and the Flar engines. We should be asking for more. Anyway, that still doesn't resolve the issue of Elon getting to Mars before us. It just makes it worse."

"Christ's thick warty cock, get over the Mars thing," said Charlie, "It's pathetic. My rocket is bigger than your rocket. My dick is bigger than your dick. And anyway, how does going to Mars help you save humanity and make your Einstein plan work?"

"Charlie's right," said Sylvain, "The Mars thing is just a massive distraction to achieving what you, we, should be doing, which is saving planet Earth."

"Oh, I guess you're right," Tom conceded, "Perhaps I got a bit carried away with this stupid feud with Elon. The priority needs to be saving Earth and rescuing humanity. Charlie, why do you think Neuralink would be so useful to us?"

"Two reasons," Charlie replied, "You talked about the dichotomy of how Monstera could offer something approaching immortality but then worsening the problem of global overpopulation. But if Neuralink has the potential to offer not just the ability for humans to speak thousands of languages and have IQs measured in the thousands, but to have their thoughts, memories and even their souls continue to exist in a virtual environment, then you can create a pathway to human immortality, but without all of the other problems."

"Sort of like a combination of the Matrix and the Metaverse, but without Agent Smith popping up and shitting in the punchbowl every few minutes, and without strippers that look like Minecraft figures?" said Sylvain.

"You've been to Metaverse strip joints?" remarked Flore, looking shocked. Sylvain blushed.

"Exactly," Charlie replied, "Tom talked about Elon Musk living a virtual life on interplanetary connected servers after his fatal car accident in 2070.

So, why not? If it's good enough for Elon, it's good enough for anyone. We could call it the Matriverse".

"Mon Dieu! You're right. It's the silver bullet to the over-population problem," said Tom.

"Hang on," Flore interjected, with a very concerned look, "You're suggesting that when people get old enough to start to be a bit of a problem or even cease being useful, we ship them off for some Huxleyesque style 'retirement' and then send a digitized version of them to live on a hard drive."

"Well, yes. I mean sort of," replied Charlie, conscious that he might have crossed one of Flore's red lines.

"How could that ever be OK on any level?" said Flore.

"Like the therapy, it would be OK if it was completely consensual," said Marion, "We could offer people Matriverse holidays while they're young. They would be perfect holidays with everything exactly the way people like them, but with none of that security bullshit at the airport. Then, as they get older and their kids have grown up, maybe they'd prefer the idea of living for free in a perfect house, with no heating bills, and being reunited with their old friends, parents and other favourite relatives in the Matriverse. Their children and grandchildren could visit at Christmas and Easter."

"You make it sound like a sort of electronic heaven," said Lucia.

"Well, yes, I guess you could put it that way," replied Charlie, "Think of it like this, imagine if your transition from this, the physical world, to a virtual world was completely seamless and the 'upload' was so thorough and so complete that it encapsulated not just your personality and your memories, but your very essence, it would be another iteration of the same you, just living on bytes and bits rather than terra firma. It would be an extension of the multiverse, another thread that looks and feels the same, just better. Perhaps, after all, there is something prophetic in the various religious texts and this is what was meant by heaven, paradise, and nirvana."

"My god, I never thought I'd hear you say something like that. So, if this is Heaven, who is going to be Saint Peter with the keys to the Pearly Gates?" asked Lucia.

"We are," said Tom.

"Don't get ahead of yourselves. We haven't done a deal with Elon yet," said Lucia.

"But we must," blurted Tom, "Otherwise, Elon will become God.

Maybe that's his master plan and the whole Mars thing is just a smokescreen."

"Oh Tom, you need to get over this Elon thing," said Marion.

"I can't," Tom replied, "He's condemned me to life sounding like that lying mop-headed upper-class muppet. But I've got a bigger rocket than him, and I'm not going to let him become God." With that, Tom disappeared.

"Oh dear, it looks like he's not coming back," said Lucia.

"Don't worry, he's just sulking somewhere. He'll come back when it suits him," said Marion.

"Well, it seems like we can't have Tom there if we meet with Musk," said Sylvain.

Flore had been busy doing some web searches on her phone, and said, "Despite my concerns about the euthanasia thing, Tom is right, it could be the silver bullet to solve the impending population crisis. If just ten per cent of the population took up the option of living in the Matriverse, we'd reduce the global population by seven hundred million. That's double the population of the United States. Seven hundred million people who aren't heating their homes in winter and cooling them in the summer, driving cars, taking flights, and eating burgers made from cows grazed on what was Amazonian rainforest the year before.

"Bill Gates is right. From an ecological perspective, the single biggest problem is that there are simply too many of us. By 2050, the global population will reach ten billion. That's almost a twenty-five per cent increase over the current total. And if we start distributing Monstera pills so that people stop dying, there could be fifteen billion by the end of the century and thirty billion by 2300. That would be catastrophic for the planet.

"But if the calculations I've just done in my head are right, if we can get this Neuralink and Matriverse thing working properly, we could reduce the global population living in the physical world to three billion by the end of this century," said Flore.

Sylvain nodded. "Yes, and not only that, but humanity would continue to benefit from the skills, knowledge and experience of the people who continue their lives in the Matriverse because the knowledge transfer between the real and the virtual worlds would be completely symbiotic.

Imagine if this had been invented a few thousand years ago. We'd still have Leonardo da Vinci, Socrates, Plato and Mozart."

"We still could," said Flore, "And it would be a much better place than the physical world because people like Jeffrey Epstein, Harvey Weinstein, Vladimir Putin and Donald Trump wouldn't be allowed in."

"So, kind of like in the Bible, the Torah and the Quran, where only the 'worthy' are allowed into Heaven or Paradise," said Lucia.

Charlie offered his thoughts, "Yes, but if you can do something terrible and still get a place in paradise just by fessing up and atoning before you die, there's not much of a disincentive to shit behaviour, is there? Whereas we would have a really compelling reason for people to try to be the best version of themselves for the entirety of their lives."

"But if we have to choose who to let in, like Tom said earlier, doesn't that mean that we would be acting as God. Or at least the equivalent of St. Peter?" asked Lucia.

As if the mention of his name had been a summons, Tom suddenly reappeared.

"What have I missed?" he asked.

Sylvain replied, "We were just discussing the problem we touched on earlier, that having to decide who we let into the Matriverse effectively makes us God and that sent Charlie off on one of his atheist rants."

"We don't have to decide," said Tom, "It can all be done algorithmically. Remember, we're talking about complete uploads of people's personalities, thoughts, and memories; even their soul, we said earlier. Anyone that's ever murdered or raped, tends to lie or steal, or has a character dominated by cruelty or abusive and anti-social behaviour gets politely turned away at the door."

"So now we just need to make that deal with Elon," said Flore.

"Great, now we've got that sorted, let's go to Jimi's party," said Marion.

**cosmicknotparadox.com/video4**

196

# THE COSMIC KNOT PARADOX

# Chapter 43
# Philosopher Kings

The morning after Jimi's party, Charlie was the first to rise. He made himself a tea, went out to the terrace and sat down at the table. It was his favourite time of day, and he often made the effort to get up before the others just to savour the tranquillity of the early morning. It was his time for reflection and contemplation, meditation for want of a better word. Charlie liked to simply to let his thoughts randomly wander, and given enough time, an idea or some sort of insight or clarity about something usually emerged.

Lighting a cigarette and taking a mouthful of tea, Charlie retreated into his thoughts. The last weeks had been a rollercoaster of new experiences, challenges and emotions adjusting to the new normal, whatever 'normal' was now. The world and everything Charlie had understood about it had been completely turned upside down.

It seemed only moments ago that he had been in that Marseilles harbour on the Salty Box of Frogs with Lucia, Flore and Sylvain, enjoying the warm Cote D'Azure evening, good food and wine, and the easy, relaxed conversation that so typified a Tipsy Dinner Society soirée. Everything was normal then.

And then, Sylvain tossed that coin and everything changed. Everything stopped being normal. The coin changed everything. "Don't underestimate the power of the coin", Tom had said recently. How unbelievably true, Charlie thought to himself. Don't underestimate the power of the fucking coin, even if the coin is a deceptive, cheating imposter, a con artist and a fraud.

Perhaps, Charlie speculated, if one day sometime in the distant future, their story was documented, that evening in the Marseilles harbour, and specifically, the moment that the coin was tossed and caught, might be recorded and immortalised as ground zero; the point where time is reset, where everything begins anew. A pivot and a new beginning in human history, but all based on a sleight, an untruth; much like the Bible, Charlie thought. Well, at least irony was alive and well in the new normal, he reasoned.

Everything before the coin might be designated 'BC' or 'Before Coin', and everything after, 'PC' - 'Post Coin', Charlie mused as he sipped his tea. BC, events unfolded more-or-less predictably, and even life's bigger surprises obediently confined themselves within the limits of a set of reasonably well-defined rules. But the PC surprises just didn't give a fuck. They were punk surprises. Rebel surprises. Anarchist surprises. Time was no longer linear; the standard laws of physics, which had been distilled down to such a simple and elegant formula, were not just incomplete, they were entirely flawed and had now been exploded into a cloud of a million disparate particles, as if someone had tossed a hand grenade into a barrel of talcum powder. So, why would the PC surprises toe the line?

Charlie started to try to work out how he fitted into the new normal, and what it meant for him. He thought about his own rather chaotic and impetuous nature and how he was able to manage that because, and only because, there was order around him. If he was honest with himself, he quite liked order. Paradoxically, the ambient order had permitted him to be chaotic; it had empowered him. But now, the coin had stolen that. No, not just stolen it, he thought; the coin had beaten him over the head and mugged him. It had grabbed the order that had invisibly surrounded him like a protective cloak and was now running down the street with it, laughing as it got away. The fucking coin.

"A penny for your thoughts," said Flore, arriving from the house, "You look like you're trying to solve the unsolvable."

"A penny for my thoughts? Just a penny?" Charlie replied with a weak but sincere smile. "My thoughts are that it's bizarre, surreal even, that you've just said what you've said. But yes, I am attempting to solve the unsolvable. Isn't that what we're trying to do here? Actually, isn't that what everyone spends most of their life doing?"

"I guess so," Flore replied, "I thought that maybe you were contemplating your alternatives to traditional democracy. Do you remember? At that dinner we had, just before we moved to Marseilles, you said that you had an alternative to democracy and that you'd tell us when, and only when, we found Wesh. Well, we're here now and I'm dying to know, so spit it out."

"Yes, Charlie, spit it out," said Tom as he arrived at the table. Charlie could see Marion, Sylvain and Lucia not far behind, making their way across the terrace with a tray of coffees and croissants.

Pleased to see his friends, but with a slight feeling of disappointment that his time for quiet reflection was over for the day, he resolved to get up earlier in future.

"What's he going to spit out?" asked Lucia.

"Charlie's finally about to tell us about his idea for an alternative to traditional democracy," Flore replied.

"Oh no! Don't get him started on that, he'll never stop. I've heard it all before. I'm going for a swim. Enjoy the lecture," said Lucia, taking a swig of coffee, then grabbing a towel and heading off through the trees towards the path to the beach.

"OK," said Charlie, "Where shall I start? I suppose I should begin by outlining the problems. There are many, but the biggest issues are firstly, that universal suffrage means that a very big percentage of the people who take part in choosing a government simply aren't qualified to make an informed choice. A significant minority, perhaps even a majority, understand very little about politics or economics or even the people, parties, and policies that they're voting for. They vote for a party because they always have, or because their parents did, regardless of the actual policies at the time. Or they vote for even more irrational reasons, like the appearance or accent of one of the candidates. Neil Kinnock might have been quite a good Prime Minister for the UK, but he didn't stand a chance with the English public because he was bald, and he was Welsh.

"Then, sort of related to the first problem, there's the issue of populism, where transient populist themes gain disproportionate importance, encouraging parties to create election manifestos that address whatever has gone viral on social media, rather than the things that are much more deserving of political intervention.

"The third problem is manifesto integrity. Although governments are held to account by their electorates at each election, there's still a much bigger upside than downside to making unrealistic promises to change or improve this or that, even if the manifesto pledges have no likely prospect of being deliverable. So, the party with the most charismatic leader that comes up with the most convincing narrative for how they're going to boost the economy, reduce unemployment, improve the health system, make everyone richer, blah, blah, blah, wins four or five years in government, even if their promises are pure fantasy.

"The final and perhaps biggest issue is that the people who are attracted to a career in politics aren't likely to be the best candidates for the job. Party leaders tend to have deep character flaws; you only need to look at Boris Johnson or Donald Trump for examples of that. Then there are those further down the pecking order who are simply incompetent, having been chosen by their parties to stand for election in safe seats through manipulated selection processes. Often, these people have no track record of leadership or achievement in any field, but nevertheless end up taking part in our governance. Of the few who are competent and politically astute, some put themselves forward with an honest intention to selflessly serve their nation, and do have the best interests of their constituents at heart, but there are also plenty who are either egotistical maniacs, frustrated despots or are simply in it for the money – not for the salaries, but the lucrative consultancy contracts, non-exec directorships and back-handers that they seem to regard as fringe benefits that come with the job.

"So, what's the solution?" Asked Flore.

"There are probably many," replied Charlie, "But so far, I've only been able to think of two. The first deals only with the issues around voter competence and manifesto integrity. Part of this solution is about forcing politicians to be honest about what they can realistically deliver, and part is about qualifying the voter as being competent to make an informed choice.

"You'd first need to have a system where the top three manifesto pledges made by any party are regarded as sacrosanct commitments rather than flimsy promises. Pledges which, if elected, the party must achieve before the next election. If they don't, both the parties and their leaders are severely sanctioned with penalties ranging from fines to perhaps even prison terms, depending on the severity of their failure to deliver.

"So, if a party lists their top three manifesto points promising to cut taxes, reduce unemployment and boost growth, but end up with an increase in unemployment, higher taxes and a stagnant economy, then heads will roll.

"The next thing to be done would be to create a series of multiple-choice questions related to the key manifesto pledges each party has made. So, American voters might get choices like… 'The Republican Party say they will: A) Implement free healthcare for all, B) Implement free healthcare for some, C) Leave everybody to make their own inadequate insurance arrangements with companies owned by Republican senators.' You get the idea?" Charlie asked, with a smile directed at Flore.

"At the polling booth, the voter would then be presented with three randomised questions about the manifesto promises printed on their ballot paper. If they get any of the questions wrong, then their paper will be considered spoiled, so their vote won't be counted. This way, to some extent at least, you could feel slightly more confident that the voter has taken the time to understand what the different parties are promising and is making an informed choice. There would therefore be less risk that they're voting for trivial, irrelevant, or illogical reasons."

"OK. That's interesting, although it kind of disenfranchises the intellectually challenged," said Flore.

"That's the whole fucking point! It's intended to disenfranchise the intellectually challenged!" exclaimed Charlie.

"I know, I was just being provocative. I just wanted to see if you'd react, and you did. You shouldn't be so sensitive. What's your second idea?" said Flore with a smile.

With an expression that conveyed that the answer might take some time, Charlie took a deep breath, clearly gathering his thoughts before he started to speak.

"This idea is a bit more radical in that it seeks to create representative democracy but without the need for any elections.

"Let's say that you want to have five hundred parliamentarians who collectively make laws and run the country; you randomly select twenty thousand people from the general population, rather like how people are selected for jury service, but different in that people would be permitted to opt-out. After the opt-outs, you'd probably have ten thousand left.

"You'd put these ten thousand through a series of computerised psychometric and psychological tests and assessments whilst hooked up to a lie detector, rejecting any that are found to have any of the more serious personality disorders or fail the polygraph tests. That would probably leave you with about five thousand. With those, you'd use IQ tests to select the brightest twenty per cent, leaving you with one thousand. These, you'd put through a two-year intensive training programme covering law, constitutional law, philosophy, economics, history, political theory, political history, business, international relations, etcetera. The course would be the equivalent of several master's degrees condensed into just two years. It would be an intensive twelve-hour per-day, six-day per week programme designed to be hard, so there would be a large number that would drop out, which is intentional – if your stamina, motivation, lifestyle, or personal circumstances mean that you can't endure the course, then you're probably not suitable for the rigours of government. At the end of the course, you might have six or seven hundred left, from which you'd select the highest achieving five hundred.

"Five hundred of the brightest, most emotionally stable, motivated, and diligent people who, because they were initially randomly selected, would be a near perfect representation of the nation as a whole in terms of political ideology, ethnicity, social background, income, gender, sexual orientation, everything.

"These five hundred would form your initial parliament and their first job would be to select a President. Any of the new parliamentarians would be able to put themselves forward for the job, provided they can garner the support of ten of their peers. There would then be a series of votes, halving the number of candidates each time, until in the end there can be only one. The One becomes President and forms a government, choosing from the pool of parliamentarians and appointing ministers into the various roles necessary for effective government.

"From this point on, the parliamentary process could be quite similar to the existing system used in the UK and other democracies. The government would draft the laws needed for its political agenda which would then be put to parliament for debate and a straight yes or no vote."

"But if there aren't going to be any elections, what's the incentive for the government to continue to strive to do its best? And isn't it going to become stale and tired, rather quickly?" Asked Marion.

"No, because every two years, the President will need to seek approval to continue by way of a parliamentary vote. If he or she fails to win that approval, then a new series of votes begins to select a new President. Also, each month, every parliamentarian will select one fellow member for 'retirement' via a secret ballot. The five with the largest number of retirement votes will then leave, making way for a new batch who have been through the same process of random selection, tests and training. So, it's a continual process of evolution, with new people with new ideas arriving all the time.

"So, there you have it, representative democracy enacted by bright, capable, and stable people who have been extensively educated and properly trained to do the job, but without any national elections or ignorant idiots distorting the democratic process by making stupid, uninformed choices.

"Parliament would be far more effective because every vote on every issue would be a genuine conscience vote, rather than parliamentarians being bullied and pressured to vote along party lines - because there wouldn't be any political parties, at least not in their current form. Factions would of course develop, but in general, the democratic process would be far less tribal.

"What are currently political parties would have to evolve into lobbying and pressure groups to win support for their ideologies, so that the concepts they want to propagate have to become absorbed into the national consciousness before they can find their way into parliament through the random selection process."

"I can see you've given this a lot of thought. I kind of like it. It puts new meaning into what Abraham Lincoln said about government of the people, by the people, and for the people," said Flore.

"I think it's more like Plato's concept of rule by philosopher kings that he describes in his book, Republic. Plato believed that the general population were too ignorant to make good electoral choices, resulting in the election of those most adept at manipulating popular opinion, rather than those most competent and qualified to lead. Your idea turns a representative subset of the general population into philosopher kings. It's a great idea. Let's include it in the Einstein Plan," said Sylvain.

# THE COSMIC KNOT PARADOX

# Chapter 44
# I am the Resurrection

Jorge Mario Bergoglio sat on the side of his bed to take off his socks. He used to undress standing up, but, now in his late eighties and with his intense schedule, he felt an almost overwhelming exhaustion every night and was more comfortable sitting down to get ready for bed. Why, he thought, had he allowed himself to be put forward for this job.

"Hola Jorge," said a voice in front of him.

Jorge looked up to see a man in his thirties standing before him wearing a white muslin tunic and leather sandals. A large blood stain had spread across the man's tunic just above the waistband and dried blood covered his forehead and hairline. Looking directly into Jorge's eyes, the man turned the palms of his hands for Jorge to see. Each hand bore a bloody wound in the centre.

"Ostia! Eres de verdad," Jorge exclaimed as he dropped to his knees before the man, his head bowed as he reached up to offer his hands. "How may I serve you, my Lord and Saviour."

"Relax. Be calm, Jorge. I come with a message from our Mother," said Jesus.

"Our Mother?" replied Jorge.

"Yes Jorge, our Mother. At this moment, our God is She, not He," said Jesus.

"She not He? At this moment? But what are you telling me, my Lord," Jorge replied, now confused.

"Jorge, our God is our Mother, but sometimes our Father. They change from time to time when it suits them," Jesus explained.

"I don't understand, you said 'they'; are you saying there is more than one God?" replied Jorge, now even more confused.

"No, there is only one God," Jesus explained patiently, "It's just that sometimes They might be He, or could be She, but identify as He; or perhaps be neither He nor She. So, you now need to use the pronouns them, they and their. I know, it is a bit confusing at first, but you'll get used to it. You will need to reword quite a few prayers and hymns though."

"My Lord, I still don't really understand, but He, I mean She, will guide me," replied Jorge

"*They* will guide you," replied Jesus.

"Yes, yes, sorry. They will guide me. My Lord, thank you for explaining this and also for calling me by my name, Jorge. I've not heard my real name for more than a decade. They call me Pope Franciscus or Francesco or Francis depending on where they're from. Sometimes they call me Pontiff, Supreme Pontiff or Bishop of Rome. It's so long that anybody has called me by my actual name, that I had almost forgotten it."

"Well, now we've got the introductions over, I'll get straight to the point," Jesus said decisively, with a marked change of tone, "It's more than two thousand years since I was last here and died on the cross to save you all from yourselves and look at the fucking mess you've made of things. God has had enough. They were going to have another flood, but I persuaded them to let me come and talk to you first."

"My Lord, what have we done?" replied Jorge, his voice filled with emotion.

"What have you done? Well, let's start with the misogyny and the plethora of cruel narratives that you've perpetuated for two millennia to subjugate and repress women. You invented that story about Eve destroying the Garden of Eden by eating the apple so that you could blame all of the world's problems on women. Then, there's that bullshit about my birth mother being a virgin, so that you could annihilate female aspiration by making it impossible for them to meet the benchmark of virtuosity set by your cruel lies.

"Having set the scene with your meticulously calculated sexist falsehoods, you and your kind have relegated and limited the best half of humanity to a role of servitude; relevant only as broodmares to satisfy the lust of men and to give birth to the next generation of subservient women and abusive, controlling, self-entitled men. You should be truly ashamed of yourselves."

The Pope sobbed, his shoulders shaking.

"You are right my Lord. Why did I not see this before?"

"Yes, what a shit show," Jesus continued, "But I'm just getting started. As well as the horrors you've inflicted on the ten billion women who have lived under your doctrine, you and your kind are responsible for so many other horrific deeds; deeds that can only be described as crimes against humanity.

"Let's start with coercion. Couldn't you have come up with something less traumatising than that heaven and hell falsehood that you then reinforced with that rather vague concept of sin, and the even more nebulous idea of original sin? Generations of children and adults terrorised and emotionally ruined by the belief that they would spend eternity burning in hell because they had had erotic thoughts, told a lie, or made some other minor transgression of your stupid rules.

"Others, who through war, accident, or illness, found themselves in their dying moments in abject terror, not just because they were dying, but because they thought they'd suffer eternal damnation because no priest was present to hear their last confession and bless their soul."

Jorge Bergoglio continued to sob, the tears now streaming down his elderly cheeks as he nodded in remorseful agreement to the accusations.

"Then there were the crusades, the inquisition and the conversions which amounted to the cruel and vicious torture of hundreds of thousands of people; individuals whose only crime was to believe in a different god or not to believe in any god at all. Instead of persuading these people to share your faith with love and kindness, you brutalised them, viciously punishing them for their dissent to deter the temerity and disobedience of others. And where's the forgiveness that's allegedly central to your doctrine, my doctrine, my legacy?

"And it still goes on today; the power and influence you wield has ensured that blasphemy laws, in some form or other, remain as statute in more than a dozen, supposedly modern, western democracies, as well as countless other nations around the world. Shame on you and your kind.

"And what excuse will you make for the paedophilia that is endemic within the institution that your predecessors created and that you now perpetuate? Hundreds of thousands of children, sexually abused by your bishops and priests. God knows that the clergy attracts these perverts, but what They deem unforgivable is that you, and those who have held the same office before you, have concealed these dreadful sins, vilifying the poor victims who have dared to speak out as apostatic liars. Shame on you.

"Then there's all the other things, like the hypocrisy of your instruction to 'love thy neighbour'. Or the centuries of homophobia, which persists to this day. Your refusal to endorse the use of condoms even in the face of an HIV epidemic that's swept through the third world like wildfire. I could talk all night about these things and many more, but for now, I'll wrap up my very brief catalogue of your sins by mentioning the immorality of the riches this church has amassed."

Jesus then walked to the corner of the room where an antique cabinet proudly displayed a trio of oriental vases. He opened the cabinet and removed the largest of the three.

"Be careful my Lord. That is a Ming dynasty vase gifted to Pope Julius III in 1504 by the Hongzhi Emperor. It is worth...."

But before the Pope could finish his sentence, Jesus casually dropped the vase onto the marble floor. Jorge gasped as the vase shattered into a thousand pieces.

"Not anymore," said the Messiah, calmly, "This church is the wealthiest institution on the planet, with assets greater than any individual or family, bank, corporation, government, or sovereign fund. Centuries of taxes, donations and bequests have amassed a fortune running to many, many trillions of dollars.

"The Catholic church owns hundreds of thousands of churches and cathedrals, an immense portfolio of commercial and residential property, and land, including farmland and forest, which is larger in area than France. You hold billions of shares in tens of thousands of companies, many of which engage in ethically questionable activities to make profits and return dividends that further swell the coffers.

"The portfolio of art stored in the basement of this building alone is worth billions of dollars; art which, for the most part, is simply hoarded and almost never enjoyed by your benefactors, let alone the rest of humanity.

"At any point during the past seven hundred years, the Catholic church could have eradicated famine and extreme poverty by divesting less than one-fifth of its wealth; but instead, more than fifty successive Popes, including you, have continued to accumulate and hoard.

"Pope John Paul the First had some ideas about giving up this embarrassment of riches for the benefit of humanity, and also intended to make a few other changes to put the Catholic Church on a firmer moral footing, but he lasted just thirty-three days before your Cardinals conspired with the mafia to have him killed."

"Ironic, don't you think, that the wealthiest institution on the planet has been built almost entirely on the back of a story about someone who lived a life of almost complete austerity? My story. I didn't die on the cross for this."

Jorge Bergoglio sobbed uncontrollably. Tears streamed down his face and his body shook with emotion.

"My Lord, you are correct. I see now that we have committed terrible sins. What can we do to right these wrongs?"

# THE COSMIC KNOT PARADOX

# Chapter 45
# The Debrief

"How did it go with the Pope?" asked Flore.

"Pretty well, all things considered," Tom replied. "He cried like a five-year-old child who had just been told that his parents, siblings, grandparents, cousins and best friends had all been killed in a plane crash. I only just managed to stop myself from telling him that I didn't exist in the way portrayed in the Bible; that I had just been a bit of a troublemaker and that the walking on water, feeding of the five thousand, and all of the other miracles were all biblical lies, invented to ensnare impressionable minds. But I decided to save that for later.

"But he's completely believed what I told him and is going to make some big changes. He's going to start by gathering all of the Cardinals to tell them about my visit and the changes that need to be made. I'm going to visit them myself after he's spoken to them, so they don't think he's mad. I'll instil the fear of God in them so they don't have him killed. Anyway, they deserve a taste of their own medicine."

"What are the changes?" asked Flore.

"Everything. The Catholic Church is going to divest twenty per cent of its net assets every year for the next ten years. It generates an average seven per cent return on its investments, so after ten years, the church's total wealth will still be about a quarter of what it is now. They're going to start by selling off their unethical investments. Any firm that doesn't meet the highest moral and ethical standards with what they sell or in their governance and corporate ethos will get sold.

"The money will be spent on several highly structured five-year plans aiming to eradicate global poverty and famine, educate the most academically deprived, and provide access to healthcare where there is limited or no provision. Other objectives will be to create healthy economies in the most economically deprived regions and take steps to prevent both disease and overpopulation.

"The church is going to not only relax its stance on contraception but will even start distributing condoms throughout the third world. They'll be printed with a cross on one side of the packet and the brand name on the other. There'll be the standard 'Blessed Shield' with the message, 'The holy defence against unwanted miracles', the 'Divine Tickler' that will be moulded with a collection of miniature crosses on the top, and the 'Second Coming' that will deliver a dose of Viagra through the wearer's skin.

"Anyway, the five-year plans will be designed to be self-sustaining. So, for example, they won't just distribute food; in fact, they won't do much of that at all. Instead, they'll provide education and training, as well as create the infrastructure needed so that poor communities can protect themselves from drought, pestilence, famine and the effects of global warming."

"Wow! That's amazing Tom," said Flore.

"I'm not finished yet. There's quite a bit more. The Church is going to drop its heaven, hell and eternal damnation mantra and instead adopt a kinder approach that sits somewhere between humanist ideas and the Buddhist concept of Karma," Tom started to explain, but Flore interrupted.

"How's that going to work? How will that persuade people to live good lives if the belief in the promise of an eternal afterlife is suddenly taken away."

"Because most people are, to some extent at least, more bothered about their legacy and how they're remembered, rather than a place in heaven – because most people don't really believe the heaven and hell narrative anyway," Tom explained.

"Creationism is another example. Until quite recently, anyone questioning the belief that God created the world in seven days, and that all of the wonders of the natural world were produced by a divine hand, ran the risk of being accused of blasphemy and had a good chance of being imprisoned, tortured, or even killed.

"Then, in 1859, after almost two decades of weighing the risks of being prosecuted for blasphemy, Charles Darwin published 'On the Origin of Species', which dealt a devastating blow to the veracity of what most religions, and particularly the Catholic church, had been telling everyone for hundreds of years.

"Things got even worse for the Creationists and religions in general when, eighty years later, Willard Libby invented carbon dating, which gave us the ability to accurately determine the age of almost any object, irrefutably proved that humans and dinosaurs didn't walk the earth together and that the world we live in wasn't created within the past ten thousand years.

"Nowadays, only the insane, the most theologically deluded, or those that have been indoctrinated as children believe in creationism or doubt the hypothesis of evolution.

"For all of these reasons, the Vatican will shift its messaging to get people to understand that many, if not most of the Bible's messages are metaphorical and symbolic, and that the notions of heaven and hell serve simply to illustrate how people will remember you after you die.

"Most people lead largely unexceptional lives, meaning that only their family and a few friends will remember them and their good or bad deeds. For those who do something of slightly greater significance, memories of them might last for a few generations. It's only those who do something exceptionally good or bad, whose legacy endures for longer.

"Mother Teresa of Calcutta and Florence Nightingale are remembered for their selfless kindness, Plato for his intellectual wisdom and DaVinci for his imagination and creativity. Conversely, Marie Antoinette persists in people's thoughts as callous and insensitive for her 'let them eat cake' faux pas which, along with a load of other self-entitled gaffes, ultimately ended with her losing her head. Then, there are the really big hitters in the shit legacy stakes, with the likes of Adolf Hitler, Genghis Khan, Vlad the Impaler and Vladimir Putin all set to burn in the eternal damnation of people's memories."

"But doesn't that mean that someone can be a secret serial rapist or kiddy-fiddler and still have a great legacy if they've got some sort of popular appeal and they do a bit of charity work?" asked Lucia.

"Maybe, but that didn't work out so well for Jimmy Saville or Jeffrey Epstein, whose legacies lie in tattered shreds like a cuddly toy that's been fed through a garden chipper. Eternal damnation for them," replied Sylvain.

"I see your point. What else is the Pope going to do?" Asked Charlie.

"They're going to properly deal with the misogyny issue. Next month, it'll be announced that women will be welcome to apply for ordination as priests. Not only that, but they'll be able to progress to become bishops, cardinals, and even run for the Papacy. There'll be no celestial glass ceiling. Gay and trans people too," said Tom.

"That's incredible, Tom. How did you do it? I had no idea you were such a good actor."

"Oh, it was easier than you might think," said Tom, with a slightly embarrassed smile.

"And how did it go with the imams?" asked Flore.

"Much the same. I turned up dressed as you know who, speaking Mecca, but had to switch to modern Arabic as most of them struggled to understand. One of them was a bit freaked out, because when I arrived, he was kind of busy with a copy of Burkha Babes, but I told him that it was OK, completely natural, and that I too choked the chicken from time to time.

"It was a busy night because I had a lot of people to see. I'm only halfway through the top five hundred, but I think we made good progress. Some of the visits were quite long, but by the end, I think they got the key points," said Tom.

"And those are?" Asked Flore.

"Well, the biggest issue was the obvious one, misogyny. I told them that women are not just equal to men, but, as the conduit of life itself, superior. I went on to explain that the burka, hijab and veil are all symbolic of female oppression and that from now on, women must be free to wear whatever they want. I also told them that the same effort has to be made to educate girls, that at least half of all imams should be women, and that child marriages, and any arranged marriages, have to stop. Same with the stonings and other brutal punishments.

"Then, I told them that from now on, the clitoris is sacred and that anybody who harms a clitoris, or for that matter, interferes with anyone's genitals, female or male, would spend the rest of eternity being buggered by Jewish lesbians wearing huge strap-on dildos. Although, I think some of them kind of liked that idea, so we'll have to see how well that works out," Tom concluded.

"Wow! Anything else?" Said Flore.

"Yes, I told them all that they should stop being so sensitive about everything, and that if someone wants to draw pictures of me, it's OK, I don't mind. Oh, and also that it's fine to be gay, and that every mosque, everywhere in the world, will have to be painted in rainbow colours and have a sign at the door stating 'LGBTQ+ Welcome'. I said more or less the same to the Rabbis and the leaders of the other denominations," Tom concluded with a smile.

"And they're really going to do all of that? End misogyny, homophobia, and become less sensitive?" asked Sylvain.

"Let's hope they never discover the truth about any of this. There'll be a backlash with far-reaching consequences," said Flore.

"I doubt that," said Charlie, "This is just about breaking the cycle of control by lies and falsehoods perpetuated over centuries. It'll only take a generation or two and the spell will be broken. People will quickly get used to the freedom of just living good lives, liberated from unreasonable edicts and impositions on their ability to live how they choose. They'll look back with disgust and contempt at how their parents and grandparents were manipulated and controlled."

"Hmmm, sounds great, but don't be so sure about that. History tends to repeat itself," said Flore.

The conversation was interrupted by the sound of a ringing phone. "It's an Austin, Texas number," remarked Tom, "It must be Elon. How did he get my number? And why would he be calling?"

# THE COSMIC KNOT PARADOX

# Chapter 46
# Casino

The following day, Charlie and Flore got up early, dressed in business suits and tunnelled to the Athens safe house. From there they took a taxi to a private airstrip just outside the centre, where Elon Musk's private jet was waiting on the tarmac.

During the call the day before, Tom had easily slipped into the persona of a high-stakes entrepreneur, parrying Musk's threat to, 'Sue the shirt off your back if you fail to immediately desist your attack on our servers', with a promise to 'Short Tesla stock to zero if you try'. Knowing that Elon would be calculating the probability of whether the retaliatory threat was just a bluff, Tom followed up with, "Get one of your bean counter flunkies to look up Wesh Corporation and all of the subsidiaries. If they're any good, they'll find about five per cent of them. Don't pick a fight with me Elon. I'll bury you if you do."

Musk changed tack.

"Very well. Perhaps if you tell me exactly what your interest is in Neuralink, we can work out some sort of win-win. Come and see me in Houston tomorrow and we'll chew the fat. I'll send my jet. I'll text you the details."

"I'll send two of my people. If you're not a total cock, I might meet with you for round two," said Tom and hung up.

In the taxi on the way to the airport, Flore made the point that they would have to be careful not to say anything revealing during the flight as the aircraft cabin would probably be bugged.

Once out of the taxi, the pilot, co-pilot and three cabin crew came to greet them. "Good morning. I'm Captain Peter Ilott and I'll be flying you today."

Charlie erupted into laughter.

"You're not serious. Peter Ilott. That's hilarious."

"What's so funny? I don't get it," said Flore.

With the contempt he was clearly feeling towards Charlie evident in his voice, Captain Ilott explained to Flore, "Your colleague finds it funny that my initial and surname *almost* make the word 'pilot'. From time to time, other people with a similarly sophisticated sense of humour, make the same joke; it doesn't happen very often, maybe only six or seven times per week. But my name is spelt with two tees, so personally, I don't see the funny side. Anyway, as I was about to say, it's a twelve-hour flight to Austin. We'll be serving breakfast, lunch, and dinner on board. Allow me to help you with your luggage," said Captain Ilott, as he reached out to take Flore's case.

"It's OK. I travel light. I can manage," she said.

Once on the plane, they were quickly in the air and a breakfast of smoked salmon and scrambled eggs with toast was served. Charlie said he thought the scrambled egg tasted a little odd and pushed his plate away.

"I'm sure it's just your imagination. Or maybe, the Captain personally supervised the preparation of your breakfast. Probably beat the eggs himself, maybe added some special sauce," said Flore with a smile. Charlie grimaced.

An hour into the flight, Charlie looked up from his newspaper and said, "I hate travelling this way now. It feels so pedestrian. Why didn't we just tunnel to the safe house?"

Flore scowled, raising a finger to her lips, frowning sternly to highlight the indiscretion of his comment.

Eleven hours later, after a light lunch of sandwiches and a much more sumptuous three-course dinner, which Flore ate and Charlie declined, the Gulfstream 650 touched down at Austin-Bergstrom International Airport and then taxied a short distance, coming to a halt inside a large hangar. A silver-grey Tesla Model S with blacked-out windows was waiting a few metres from the foot of the aircraft steps.

"This way, Sir, Madam. Warren will drive you to the Gigafactory," said the stewardess who had looked after them during the flight, ushering them into the back seat of the car.

As soon as the doors were closed, Warren delivered what sounded like a well-rehearsed speech.

"This is a Tesla Model S Plaid. To ensure your safety, the vehicle is equipped with bullet-proof glass and doors, has run-flat tyres and can withstand a typical land mine. If for any reason I should be rendered incapable of driving, the vehicle can complete the journey autonomously. With your permission, I'll now drive you to the Tesla Austin Gigafactory where Mr Musk is waiting."

Without waiting for the 'permission' he had requested, Warren sped off, exiting the hangar, then skilfully navigated through the airport's network of internal roads before passing the security gate onto Presidential Boulevard, and then straight into the middle lane of Highway 71 towards the Tesla Austin Gigafactory.

The driver looked like he had a Special Forces background; cropped hair, mid-thirties, fit and probably very able to look after himself and his passengers. Warren was quite obviously something more than just a chauffeur. Charlie caught his glance in the rear-view mirror and immediately recognised the steely scrutiny in the blue eyes. He understood the calculations likely taking place in the driver's mind. It was something he'd observed in Pippa; constant risk assessment, with secondary mitigation calculations, all performed in an instant and mostly subconsciously.

Looking out of the window, Charlie saw that there were two other identical grey Tesla cars driving lockstep on either side, plus another immediately in front. A glance over his shoulder confirmed the presence of a fourth chaperone directly behind, making a star formation. They were being well cared for.

A few minutes later, the cortege turned off the highway and headed at speed towards the gates of the Gigafactory which opened without the cars having to stop or even slow. From there, the convoy made its way around the immense building, coming to a halt under an area covered with a glass canopy. A sign read 'VIP Reception'.

With the car parked directly outside the reception doors, Warren quickly got out of the car, first opening Flore's door, then moved around the back of the car to open Charlie's.

"We've arrived. Welcome to Tesla Gigafactory, Austin. Please make your way into the reception area."

Once inside the building, Charlie and Flore went through a security process that included fingerprint and retina scans, a whole-body scanning pod and a DNA saliva swab. After Flore had picked up her case and

Charlie had retrieved his wallet and cigarettes from the X-ray machine, another ex-Green Beret type accompanied them in the elevator to the third floor.

The doors opened to reveal an attractive young woman waiting in front of the doors.

"Good afternoon, I'm Sylvia Trench. Welcome to Tesla. Mr Musk will see you in his private office. If you'd like to follow me," said the receptionist.

She led them along a corridor with offices and meeting rooms on one side, and on the other, floor-to-ceiling glass panels that provided a view over the immense factory floor below.

"It's like something out of a Bond movie. Is Musk going to appear with an eye patch, holding a white cat?" Charlie whispered to Flore, as they walked a few paces behind Sylvia. Flore frowned and raised a finger to her lips, just as she had done on the plane.

At the end of the corridor, they were shown into Musk's office suite. The main room was huge, perhaps four hundred square metres, with the same floor-to-ceiling glass providing a view of the factory floor on one side. Two doors led off the room which Flore and Charlie guessed must be a bathroom and maybe a dressing room; not a bedroom, as on one side of the large office an unmade sofa bed which, with a tangled duvet and untidy pillows, contrasted starkly with the otherwise pristinely ordered and minimalistic office. Charlie wondered whether Musk had only just woken up.

Moments later, Charlie's suspicions were confirmed as Musk emerged from the bathroom, dressed, but with a toothbrush in his mouth. Unable to speak properly with the brush impeding his speech, Musk mumbled something unintelligible and motioned to the two chairs positioned in front of his desk. He then disappeared back into his bathroom, coming out a few moments later without the toothbrush and drying his face with a towel.

"Right, Charlie, Flore, I've got a packed schedule today, so I'll make this quick and simple. I know you've been hitting the Neuralink servers with something similar to the end-user software we use in our implants. I have no idea why you're doing it or what your interest is, but now that we've detected you, you're not going to get very far without the server software." Musk then pushed a portable hard drive across the desk.

"That's a copy of what resides on our servers for your geek team to play with, and here's the deal… come back here at the same time, three days from now, and if you can convince me of the merits of what you want to do with Neuralink, it's yours in exchange for a ten per cent royalty in perpetuity on any revenue you derive from it. But if you can't convince me, you agree that you'll delete everything, securely destroy the hard drive, and never again darken my digital doorway. Deal?"

"Deal," said Flore without hesitation.

"Good. Now if you wouldn't mind fucking off, I've got a busy day. See you on Thursday. Oh, and bring Tom, or the next meeting will be even shorter than this one," said Musk as he reached into the drawer of his desk, produced a plain white envelope, and handed it to Charlie. "That's something else for you. Don't open it until your tech team has finished reviewing the software. Thanks for coming. Bye."

"We won't open the…" Charlie started to say but Elon had already turned his attention to the screen on his desk and was busy typing something on his keyboard. Flore put the hard drive in her case and Charlie said, "Bye, Elon. See you Thursday," but Elon wasn't listening and didn't respond. Flore and Charlie made their way out of the office and back down the corridor to the reception area where Sylvia was waiting.

"I hope you had a good meeting. Warren will take you back to the airport. The jet has been refuelled and is ready to take you back to Athens," said Sylvia.

"We're not going back today. Elon's asked us to come back on Thursday at the same time and anyway, we've got other business here in Texas. If Warren could drop us at our corporate flat in Austin and pick us up again on Thursday in time for the meeting, that would be fine," replied Flore.

"Very well, I'll tell Warren. Just give him the address of where you want to go. He'll be waiting downstairs," Sylvia said as the lift doors opened.

After a twenty-five-minute journey, Flore and Charlie arrived at the Austin safe house that Tom and Marion had chosen more than twenty years before. It was a top-floor penthouse apartment, in a fifteen-storey building on Rainey Street. Tastefully furnished and with views out over the Colorado River and the city beyond, it was what realtors might describe as prime location.

"What a dick! 'Now if you wouldn't mind fucking off'," said Flore, doing her best to imitate Musk's voice, "And the whole thing coming out with the toothbrush in his mouth like he didn't give a fuck. And did you notice how our chairs were much lower than his to try to put us at a psychological disadvantage? We travelled fifteen hours for a ninety-second meeting that ended with us being told to fuck off. Arrogant prick."

"It's just business," said Charlie, "I'd do the same in his position. Everything he does, every meeting he has, is like corporate poker, but with billions at stake. He does what he does because he's always had to and now it's second nature. At least we've got the software and a second meeting scheduled."

"Hmmm, don't you think it was all a bit too easy? Anyway, let's talk it over with the others."

With the envelope safely in Charlie's pocket, and the hard drive in Flore's case, the two tunnelled directly back to L'île de Wesh.

"How did it go?" asked Marion, as Charlie and Flore arrived in the kitchen.

"He told us to fuck off," said Flore.

"Oh. Not so good then," exclaimed Marion.

"Well, actually not so bad," Flore replied, reaching into her case, "He gave us the Neuralink server software. We've got three days to test it."

"He's a crafty one, isn't he? He's given you such a short timeframe so he can find out how big our tech team is. It would normally require at least a couple of hundred of the highest calibre engineers to test and review something so complex in such a short period of time. Lucky for us, time's not an issue. Anyway, I'll make a start," said Marion, picking up the hard drive and heading out, through the whoosh pod into the lab.

A moment later, Tom, Lucia and Sylvain arrived from the garden, each with a Tom Collins in hand.

"How was it?" asked Sylvain.

"It was short, but he's given us the Neuralink server software. If, three days from now, we can convince him that we'll do something worthwhile with it, he says we can have it…for free; well, almost free. Tom, you need to come to the next meeting, so you'll have to get over your Elon issues. Try to remember that the things you're upset about haven't actually happened yet. You can't be angry with someone for something they've not done," said Flore.

"That's really easy for you to say. You haven't spent a cumulative three thousand years sounding like Boris fucking Johnson," said Tom, visibly upset.

"I see your point Tom, and I feel your pain, but just try and focus on the bigger picture… the Einstein plan," said Sylvain.

"I'll do my best," replied Tom, with a resigned expression.

# THE COSMIC KNOT PARADOX

# Chapter 47
# Chicken Run

The following day, Flore and Sylvain arrived in the kitchen to find Marion whisking egg whites, and piles of boxes of eggs covering two-thirds of the long dining table.

"Hi guys, I'm making meringues," Marion said, as if this was a perfectly normal thing to do first thing in the morning.

The other surfaces were covered in saucepans full of custard, hollandaise and Béarnaise sauce. More than a dozen quiches and a similar number of custard tarts were cooling on wire racks, while several cakes and a precariously balanced pile of Spanish tortillas graced the worktops. Marion had also made what looked like tens of kilos of several different types of fresh pasta. Spaghetti and tagliatelle hung from a washing line she'd stretched from one end of the kitchen to the other, and trays of tortellini, ravioli and fusilli occupied the remainder of the work surfaces.

Charlie arrived a few moments later, and a loud but somewhat doleful-sounding plea of, "Hazme un café, porfa," revealed that Lucia wasn't far behind.

"Wow! What's happening? Are we opening a restaurant?" Charlie asked as he stepped into the room.

"I made some sauces that we can have with a steak for dinner, and some Spanish tortillas that we can have for lunch, with meringues for dessert," Marion explained, "Oh, and there are some cakes, pasta, quiches, and custard tarts that we can have tomorrow or the day after. Does anyone fancy some eggs for breakfast? Boiled, fried, scrambled? Perhaps an omelette?"

"Marion, what's going on? Have you been overdoing it on Tom's Placido?" asked Sylvain.

"No, it's just that I ended up with all these eggs and I felt compelled to use them. It would be terrible to waste them," Marion replied.

"How did we end up with so many eggs? We've only got a few chickens outside," asked Lucia.

At that moment, Tom appeared.

"She's been acting strangely ever since Charlie and Flore got back from their meeting with Elon yesterday. Would you like to tell us what's going on, Marion?" he said quizzically.

With a somewhat guilty look, Marion replied, "I'll need to show you something. I didn't tell any of you last night because I thought you'd all think I was mad. Come downstairs with me."

Down on the farm floor, which until only the day before had been occupied solely by monstera and banana plants, there was now the addition of a huge, grassed area, on which, several thousand chickens were happily strutting around pecking at the grass, just as chickens do. Where the birds differed from normal chickens was that they were all wearing hats that were strapped underneath their beaks. Each hat had a small antenna protruding from the top.

"Why have you got thousands of remote-control robot chickens?" asked Charlie.

"They're not robots, they're real chickens. They've just been networked," replied Marion.

"Networked? Why on earth would you network chickens? Sylvain was right; I have been giving you too much Placido," said Tom, looking rather shocked.

"Well, before you judge me too harshly, let me explain. For some time, I've been thinking about chickens and the fact that everybody thinks they're really stupid because they just walk around all day pecking at grass or whatever else is underfoot. But then, I started thinking that they can't be completely stupid, because before they were selectively bred to have a large breast and heavy legs to provide food for humans, chickens were able to fly. The neural processing required for successful flight is immense, so given their pea-sized brains, their neuron density must be incredibly high.

"So, I did a bit more research and discovered that chickens have some very surprising cognitive abilities. Scientific tests have proven that they can recognise the faces not just of other chickens but of humans as well, which means they have the capability of memory. If you hide something, chickens will look for it, meaning that they understand that even though something is hidden, it still exists, which, by the way, a two-year-old human doesn't. They can also recognise their own reflection, which means that they have self-awareness, which many other animals don't. If you keep a chicken as a pet, it will develop traits similar to a dog or a cat; for example, it will sit on its owner's lap and make a purring sound when stroked. This indicates several things. The ability to adapt to a completely unnatural situation and to be able to make risk-based decisions; the capability to recognise pleasure, and most importantly, the presence of mind to communicate that happiness, demonstrating both empathy and the capacity for strategic thought. Chickens are much more intelligent than most people might think.

"That then got me thinking that the reason they just walk about pecking at grass is simply because for thousands of generations, there's been nothing else for them to do; but at the same time, natural selection won't have shrunk their brains, because there's little evolutionary benefit to that. I figured that most chickens probably use no more than one or two per cent of their intellectual power. Then I thought about the millions of chickens alive in the world and wondered whether there might be a way to harness and utilise their spare cognitive capacity.

"When Charlie and Flore got back last night with a copy of the Neu-ralink source code, the idea suddenly came to me. If the Neuralink code could be re-engineered so that instead of the server giving the user, in this case, a chicken, additional cognitive capabilities, it networked the users so that they effectively became the server – actually, a distributed server cloud, or perhaps better to say, server flock, it might be possible to utilise the unused ninety-eight per cent of the chickens' brainpower to do all sorts of things."

"Eggs-cellent," Charlie quipped, clapping his hands, then followed up with, "How did you hatch that?"

Flore sighed and threw an egg at him.

Undeterred by Charlie's attempt at humour, Marion continued her explanation.

"After I'd re-engineered the Neuralink code, I started by…" she started, but Tom interrupted.

"But Marion, you're a chemist, not a computer programmer. How could you re-engineer some of the most complex computer code ever written?"

"It was easier than I thought, Marion replied, "All I had to do was to take myself to 2060 and get my own Neuralink implant. Then I just downloaded the advanced programming add-on. It was pretty easy after that. Of course, the 2060 version of Neuralink needs to interact with their server in real-time, so the first thing I had to do was load the server source code that Elon had given you onto my laptop and get that to behave like Neuralink's 2060 server farm.

"Obviously, their servers have immense processing power, and my machine is just a laptop, but it only needed to support one user, me. Getting my 2060 implant to talk to the current version of the server farm was the most challenging part because more than thirty years of development had taken place, but I managed to do it. Then, I was able to create a copy which I put on a different machine and modified it so that while the operating system remained on the laptop, all of the processing gets done by the chickens."

"My god, that's incredible. *Cracking* good idea, Marion. A real *feather* in your cap," said Charlie, laughing again. Flore threw another egg at him.

"And does it work? Have you tested it?" asked Sylvain, intrigued.

"Yes, it works. I started by getting the chickens to solve simple mathematical problems. I found that with just one chicken, the results took a while, although not as long as you might think. But with ten chickens, it was possible to do pretty much anything you'd do on a pocket calculator, including things like square root calculations in less than a second.

"So, I upped the ante a bit for the next test. I tunnelled back three months, extended the farm floor, added another thousand chickens, and got them to do some Bitcoin mining. It took them less than three hours to mine their first coin, two hours and forty minutes for the second and an hour and fifty minutes after that. I was astonished. They had learned how to optimise the process.

"When I investigated their method, they had operated in the same way that quantum computers work. Traditional computers use only binary values, ones or zeros, meaning that they're not very good at solving problems where some of the inputs are unknown. However, quantum computers use a different process, so that in any individual equation, the one and zero can be simultaneously present, allowing them to deal with uncertainty."

"So, this is what you could call Quantum Organic Computing," remarked Flore.

"You've created a QOC Flock," said Charlie.

"It's actually a type of AI," Sylvain added.

"Artificial Intelligence?" asked Lucia.

"No, Avian Intelligence," Sylvain replied with a knowing nod.

"Anyway," continued Marion, "Given that they had done so well with the Bitcoin algorithm, I decided to give them something really difficult. I remembered that book, The Hitchhiker's Guide to the Galaxy, by that English author, Douglas Adams. Many people regard some of his descriptions of situations, events and technology as being quite prophetic. In it, Adams describes a super-computer being given the problem of working out the meaning of life, the universe and everything. After number crunching for seven and a half million years, the computer returned the answer, 'Forty-Two'.

"So, I thought I'd give the chickens the same problem to solve. They were clearly challenged by the problem because, within a few seconds, all of the birds had stopped moving and pecking. After three days they were still motionless and staring into thin air, so I added another thousand birds to the group. Within half an hour, the original test group had at least started moving again, albeit slower than usual. Then, the following morning, I was woken by an alert from my Neuralink implant telling me that the answer to the question about the meaning of life, the universe and everything was 419.9867999999999999. I was staggered."

"Why were you surprised?" asked Flore.

"Well, the fact that the chickens produced any answer at all is quite incredible, but don't you see the significance of the answer they produced?" asked Marion. Flore shook her head. "The result is essentially four hundred-and-twenty. The result in Adams' book was forty-two. If my result was correct, Adams' was one decimal place out, and vice versa. With such a big calculation, it's easy to end up with an extra or missing decimal place, so you're almost right and wrong at the same time. Right with the method, but wrong with the execution."

"That happened with spinach," said Charlie.

"With spinach?" remarked Lucia, "What's spinach got to do with anything?"

"Yes, for several decades, mothers fed their children inordinate quantities of spinach, believing that it had much more iron than any other vegetable, and would make their children strong and healthy," Charlie explained, "This was even popularised in the cartoon story of Popeye the Sailor who, when faced with adversity, would pop open and eat a can of spinach, and instantly be endowed with super-human strength. Unfortunately, the data that persuaded millions of parents to force-feed their kids with Spinach was all based on a laboratory error that miscalculated the iron content by one decimal place.

"So, if anyone you know has ended up traumatised by being forced to eat spinach as a child, you can tell them to sack their therapist and instead of hating their mother, blame the lax 1930s lab geek who put the decimal point in the wrong place."

"Anyway," continued Marion, clearly a little irritated by the spinach story, "I ran the 'meaning of life' test again. It only took three hours the second time; presumably because, just like with the Bitcoin test, the chickens had become more adept at solving the problem. The result was exactly the same. 419.9867999999999999."

"So, the answer to the meaning of life, the universe and everything question is four-hundred-and-twenty?" asked Sylvain.

"Yes," Marion confirmed.

"Four-hundred-and-twenty? But what does that actually mean?" asked Lucia, looking a bit puzzled.

"Well, we're not sure. The chickens are working on that right now. They've been at it for a couple of weeks already, but no results yet," Marion replied.

Reaching into his pocket, Charlie produced a plain white envelope, "Maybe this will shed some light on it. Before we left yesterday, Elon gave us this. He told us not to open it until our tech team had finished reviewing the software."

"Well, open it then, I'm intrigued," said Marion.

Charlie broke the seal on the envelope and removed a single folded sheet of paper. With raised eyebrows, he turned the paper for the others to see. The message was handwritten in the centre of the sheet of paper. It read:

*"419.9868999999999999"*

"Fuck! It's the same as the number the chickens came up with," said Sylvain.

"No, it's different," corrected Marion, "Our result is 419.9867999999999999. His is 419.9868999999999999. They're not the same."

"Well, we've got our next meeting with Elon in two days. Let's see what he says," said Flore.

# THE COSMIC KNOT PARADOX

# Chapter 48
# Casino 2

Back in Austin, Charlie and Flore noticed that unlike during their previous visit, the bed in the corner of Elon's office was perfectly made.

"Looks like Elon didn't sleep here last night," said Charlie, quietly under his breath, even though he, Flore and Tom were alone in the large office.

"He sleeps in here?" asked Tom, in similarly hushed tones.

"Yes, sometimes, usually around Tesla's quarter end, and..." Flore started but was prevented from further explanation by Musk's arrival.

"And you must be Tom. Pleased to meet you. Charlie, Flore, thank you for coming all this way again. I've got more time today, so hopefully we can all get to know each other a bit better," said Elon, as he strode into the room.

"Very pleased to make your acquaintance, Mr Musk," said Tom, in a perfect English accent, his voice now imbued with an entirely neutral accent; well-spoken and with the intonation of a well-educated and confident man, but entirely free of any traces of eccentric, upper-class tones. The meeting was going well. Nothing had been discussed or negotiated and Tom was already free of Boris Johnson.

Charlie and Flore were as surprised as Tom at the sound of his new voice, but all three managed to conceal their surprise and said nothing. However, it didn't escape Elon's attention.

"You sound different from when we spoke on the phone. You sounded, well, sorry to put it this way, but you sounded like a bit of a dick."

"Must have been a bad line or maybe I had a cold," ventured Tom, hopefully.

"Yes, probably a bad line or a cold. Anyway, I'll get straight to the point. Want to tell me how you did it?" asked Musk.

"With advanced computing techniques. Interesting that your number was slightly different from ours though," replied Tom.

"No, I'm not asking about your answer to the question of the meaning

234

of life, the universe and everything. We'll get to that later. What I really want to know about, is how you've managed to learn to time travel."

The three visitors were shocked into stunned silence.

Elon continued, "OK, I don't have time for games, so I'm just going to put all of my cards on the table. By the way, this is an 'I'm going to talk and you're going to listen' kind of thing, so if you've got questions, ask them at the end.

"About two months ago, you, Tom, suddenly popped up on a Neuralink server. You weren't difficult to spot because the server you connected to has never had any users, not even monkeys. It's a development project for what we think we'll be launching in about five years. Eventually, it'll have features that will enable users to speak hundreds of different languages, learn almost any new skill or operate any machine.

"Anyway, we had the server prepared, but no clients connected, so imagine our surprise when you showed up. We were about to block the access, but one of our technicians noticed that the client device seemed to be much more sophisticated than anything we've created, so we let it run, thinking that we might learn something.

"We only had limited visibility over what you were doing because our server didn't recognise all of the output from your device, but what we did notice was that the data it was generating contained the little markers we embed in all of the proprietary code we write.

"We put them into anything and everything we build; cars, rockets, solar controllers, boring machines, brain implants, everything. That way, if a competitor steals our code or one of our employees starts selling corporate secrets, we have a way of proving it. So, the software you were using appeared to have been written by us, but we had never seen it before, and it was much more advanced than anything we'd ever created. Intriguing, no?

"That was what prompted me to call you a week ago. I figured that you were probably a geeky hacker or Tesla fanboy doing it for the thrill of it, perhaps a journalist or possibly an industrial spy for Bezos, Fuckerberg or some other wannabe competitor. I also considered the possibility that it might be an ex-employee who was unable to let go of their involvement in the project and had continued writing code after they'd left. Those were the only explanations I could think of."

"How did you get my number?" asked Tom.

"What part of 'ask your questions at the end' did you not understand? I'll let it go this time, but don't let it happen again. We got your number because the server reported your location as being some tiny island off the coast of Greece. We moved a Starlink satellite into position and were quickly able to establish that there were six mobile phones in use. Five years ago, you booked a test drive in one of my cars, registering your number in the process. That was careless.

"Anyway, we spoke and arranged the meeting, but instead of coming to the meeting in person, you sent your lackeys. Sorry Charlie, sorry Flore, but that's the way it seemed at the time. I didn't bother asking them what they wanted with Neuralink or what they were offering in return, because I thought I was talking to the monkeys rather than the organ grinder. But I did think there was an opportunity to find out more about how you'd managed to end up with client software that looked like it had been written by us and was able to get through all of our security protocols to mesh with our servers but wasn't anything we'd created. So, I gave Charlie and Flore a copy of the source code to take away, with the offer that I'd give them Neuralink if, after a three-day test, they could come back and convince me of the merits of what they intended to do with it. I'm not going to lie to you, I intended to find out what was going on and the extent to which you'd compromised our security, then set the legal dogs on you.

"It wasn't a surprise to see the version I'd given you come online the next day. Nor was it a surprise to be told that you'd hacked the code so you could connect your own servers to it. It was also predictable that after your initial tests, you'd go for the big meaning of life question. It's what all geeks do when they're given a new toy – it's just, most never get any answer, because they never have enough computing horsepower. What was a surprise though, was when our tech lead told me, 'But Elon, they did these things three weeks ago. You only gave them the software yesterday.'

"We noticed, because given the potential significance of the answer to the meaning of life question, even though none of us speak to one another anymore, me, Jeff, Jack, Larry and Fuckerberg all watch our servers as well as do searches of other social media platforms and data sources for any mention of several key words and any number that includes a four and a two in sequence.

"We all check our own stuff. Jeff's got Alexa listening, Fuckerberg keeps an eye on Fuckbook and WhatsCrap, Larry watches Google searches, and Jack used to check Tweets, which is now my job. And don't forget that all of my cars have ears. Elon paused as a woman entered the room and walked to his desk.

"Sorry to interrupt. I've got those reports you asked for," the woman said, stooping slightly to whisper something in Elon's ear as she placed a file of papers on Elon's desk, then quickly turned to leave.

"Thank you, 'Reyna', Musk said, then continued, "Anyway, as I was saying, our checks involve both algorithmic monitoring of what's going on in real-time, and a monthly search of a separate data log to make sure the real-time algos didn't miss anything. Nothing much ever gets found in those Neuralink databases because right now there's not much connected, but it's good practice for us to get our processes right now, rather than firefight later.

"When you asked the meaning of life question three weeks ago, it didn't set off any alarms, nor did the answer. But both events should have triggered every alarm bell in the building. However, when we did our monthly double-check, there they were, both the question and the answer. That was the smoking gun."

Elon leafed through the file of papers Reyna had left, then pushed two reports across the desk. The first was headed 'Real-Time Log' and was blank. The other was titled 'Historical Datalog' and was full of entries.

"You didn't trigger any real-time alarms, because three weeks ago you weren't anywhere near our servers, but then after I gave you the software three days ago, you went back in time and did your tests. Your interactions with our servers therefore only appear after the event in a historical search of a separate database. I didn't understand that initially. Logically, at the point that you went back into the past, you should have created a new space-time continuum thread and triggered the alarms, which would now be my reality perception. But there's this thing in quantum physics we've been calling the cosmic knot paradox, where things don't happen according to the laws of normal physics or even those of what we so far understand about quantum physics.

Somewhat shocked by Elon's use of a term that she had thought to be exclusively theirs, and in an attempt to move the conversation away from time travel, Flore decided to ignore Elon's instuction to not interrupt him.

"But Elon, what do you think four hundred-and-twenty actually means? And how do you think a fiction writer managed to work it out, albeit one decimal place wrong, over forty years ago?"

"Well, until yesterday, our best theory was that he just guessed and got lucky. Now though, in the light of all of this, we're wondering whether someone told him," Elon replied, looking directly at Tom, who fidgeted uncomfortably in his seat.

Realising that Flore's distraction strategy hadn't worked and that in this particular conversation, all roads led to time travel, Tom decided that a more aggressive approach was needed.

"What do you think would happen to Tesla's share price if we were to go to the Washington Post and tell them that we've just come from a business meeting with you where you went weird and started telling us we were time-travellers? Bezos would come in his pants over a scoop like that. I can see the headlines now."

Elon sat forward in his chair, his body language unambiguously announcing that a return attack was on the way.

"No, you wouldn't do that. Since our call when you told me to look up Wesh Corp and threatened to bury me, we've done our due diligence. What a complex web you've spun. The Wesh Corporation and the hundreds of subsidiaries, offshore trusts, and your multiple identities. If you went public like that, the media scrutiny that would follow would blow the lid off everything you've done to keep all of this under wraps since 1960.

"They would assume that you're the head of a massive drug cartel. Then the authorities would get involved and quickly discover that you've broken hundreds of laws. Insider trading, impersonation, deception, and false declarations to public bodies and regulators, to name just a few of the charges you'd be facing. Are you up to date with your IRS returns? I doubt it. Even if they didn't succeed in locking you up, the cat would be well and truly out of the bag, and you need anonymity to operate."

It was Tom's turn to sit forward in his chair, consciously adopting the same pose Elon had taken for his parry. He was learning fast.

"There are a few problems with all of that. The main issue you have is that if you're right and I can time travel, then I could easily just go back in time and undo whatever I'm accused of. So, whether you're right or not, it's a zero-sum game for you. If you're wrong you end up looking like a dick, and if you're right, you still end up looking like a dick. But anyway, what makes you so sure you're right? What you've outlined so far is sufficiently far-fetched for your shareholders to dump their Tesla holdings and probably to get you a reservation in a padded cell."

"Maybe. But more likely not," Elon retorted, "The case is pretty strong. Let's start with the fact that William Hubert and all of the subsequent CEOs to have run the Wesh Corporation have looked remarkably similar to you. Each time, they run the company for a few years, resign and then miraculously disappear; presumably, when their theoretical age makes it difficult for you to keep up the pretence."

"What makes you so sure about all this? Just because my predecessors looked a bit like me, doesn't mean it is me. Lots of people look like me," Tom protested, his voice betraying that he was clutching at straws.

"Well, an hour ago, you got into my car in downtown Austin to come here. We captured your image as you walked towards the car. Within five minutes, your photo was with a friend of mine at the CIA. They have a database of images of almost everyone that's ever lived since the camera was invented. As well as their covert stuff, they have images from pass-ports, driving licenses, social media, newspaper articles and library cards, plus CCTV images from public buildings, airports, hotels, everything. And I'm not just talking about data from here in the United States. They've hacked the databases of pretty much every other government that does something similar – which is more-or-less all of them. Then, on top of that, there's the data on a well-known social media platform that even criminals and terrorists happily upload their holiday snaps to, tagging their friends and family in the process. That platform was created by the CIA for exactly that purpose.

"Within ten minutes of getting your picture, my friend had established that your image was a 99% match with William Hubert's passport photo and a 100% match with some covert photos the CIA took of you, or should I say, William Hubert, in 1961. The image was also a perfect match for…" Elon picked up and read from one of the papers Reyna had brought for him, "…Sebastian Bonnington-Smythe, Francois Jabouille,

Heinz-Harald Schneider, Peter Connington, James MacDonnell, Claude Morel, Jean-Yves Auclaire and Ignacio Lopez. All of these people have held the position of CEO of Wesh Corporation between 1968 and now."

Casting his gaze towards Flore and Charlie, and then back to Tom, Elon continued, "And do your friends know about all of your multiple identities, Tom? I'm not just talking about the corporate stuff. What about the historical and showbiz characters?"

Catching the look of surprise that Flore had been unable to conceal, Elon continued his attack.

"Oh, he's not told you, has he? There's probably plenty that Tom hasn't told you. He's been leading a double life, multiple lives, for a very long time, haven't you Tom? If indeed that's your name," Elon said with a smile.

"He's told us everything," Flore insisted defensively.

"In that case, you'll also know that he was Michelangelo's David. You all went through the scanner on the way in here. In the machine, he made the exact same pose as the statue. The security guy thought he was just acting the fool, but Reyna noticed too and overlaid the image from the scanner on an image of the statue. They're identical in every dimension, except that 'David' is perhaps a bit better equipped – if you know what I mean," said Elon, laughing.

"Yes, of course, we know about that. The similarity I mean, not the other thing. You're not the first person to spot the likeness. It's just a coincidence," said Flore, doing her best to dismiss Elon's accusation as groundless.

"Then you'll also know that for the last fifty years, he's also been Ringo Starr," said Elon.

Hard as they tried, neither Flore nor Charlie could contain their shock. Charlie had a mouthful of coffee, which suddenly sprayed out of his mouth in a half jet, half cloud, and Flore leapt out of her seat to avoid being soaked.

"Yes, I thought that might surprise you," said Elon, "We all wondered how Ringo, who is now in his eighties, has never seemed to age."

Elon retrieved some photos of Ringo Starr from his folder and pushed them across the desk.

"A few facial prosthetics to bulk out his face a bit, a change of hairstyle and maybe an hour with a makeup artist to add a few light wrinkles, but that's him alright. But it doesn't end there. He's also been that fuck-awful British singer Robbie Williams, the actors James Franco and Michael C Hall, several sports personalities including a tennis player, at least two footballers, and two Formula One racing drivers; Ayrton Senna, and more recently, Lewis Hamilton."

The final revelation was too much for Charlie who, having only just recovered from the Ringo shock, had just taken another mouthful of coffee, which again exited his mouth in another spay which, this time, Flore was unable to avoid.

With Charlie choking and Flore dripping in coffee, Elon just smiled. Flore shot a horrified look at Tom.

"Lewis Hamilton? But, how…you didn't…surely you didn't do what I think you did," she said, unambiguously posing the question that was on everybody's mind without actually asking it. Tom said nothing but visibly blushed. Elon sat back in his chair doing his best to hide the smug satis-faction he was feeling.

After Charlie and Flore's reaction, there was clearly no alternative but to concede that Elon was correct. Tom quickly realised that there was still a chance of portraying their earlier denials as them defending an important secret, but now, anything less than a full admission would cast them as outright liars and destroy any possibility of salvaging any credibility. From adversity springs opportunity, Tom thought to himself. In any case, there was now nothing to lose. Tom altered his approach.

"OK Elon, well done. You worked it all out. Game, set and match. Guilty as charged. Yes, I can time travel and yes, I have been all of the Wesh Corp CEOs you mentioned. I was Michelangelo's 'David', and I have been Ringo Starr, Robbie Williams and the others, including Lewis Hamilton."

"What about Douglas Adams? Was it you who told him the answer to the question of the meaning of life, the universe and everything?" asked Elon.

"Yes, it was. I met him in a pub in Islington, London, in 1978 and we got chatting. Of course, it wasn't an accidental meeting. I'd gone there intending to find out what he knew about the answer to the meaning of life. He'd just finished the script for the Hitchhiker's Guide to the Galaxy radio play, which was due to be aired the following week. He told me that if I wanted to know the answer, I should listen to the programme.

"I told him that I already knew the answer and that it was 419.9867999999999999. Obviously, he just thought I was drunk, which I was, but when we met up again the next day, he told me that he liked my idea of using a number instead of 'orange', which had been his original plan. He told me that he'd changed the script, but that 419.9867999999999999 was far too long for radio. So, he'd shortened it to 420 and then shortened it again to 42. And there you have it.

"As far as Ringo is concerned, in 1970, the real Ringo decided that he'd had enough of being famous. 'I'll end up getting shot by some nutcase who's convinced that he's me and that I'm an imposter,' he'd said. We talked about it, and towards the end of the evening, he said, 'You look quite a lot like me. You could be me if you want to.' It was too good an offer to refuse, so I nipped off to 2060, downloaded the knowledge of how to play the drums to my Neuralink, worked a bit on my appearance, and the rest is history."

"You what? You said, you nipped off to 2060 and downloaded how to play the drums to your Neuralink." said Elon, suddenly intrigued.

"Yes, by 2060, you've introduced everything to Neuralink that you mentioned earlier about being able to fly planes and helicopters, acquire languages and pretty much anything else anyone might want to be able to do. I can now speak over seven thousand languages, play over forty musical instruments to concert standard, fly any aircraft, operate almost any machine, and perform any surgical procedure," replied Tom.

"That's incredible. Exactly what I had imagined. It's just, if I'm honest, I didn't think we'd ever get that far. The problem is the monkeys. They keep outwitting their handlers and escaping. Then they form colonies and come back to attack the lab. The technicians want to try with apes next. They think they'll be more manageable and less likely to escape," said Elon.

"Don't do it Elon. I don't know why, but I've got a really bad feeling about that and can just tell that it won't end well," said Charlie.

"Yes, I thought so too," replied Elon, "But you've distracted me from what I really want to talk about, which is you going into the future and bringing back the stuff that I'll develop over the next ten, twenty, thirty years. You could shorten my development cycle by decades," Elon said, trying his best to suppress the excitement in his voice.

Just at that moment, Reyna hurried into the room again looking flustered and carrying a blue folder.

"I'm sorry to interrupt again Elon, but there's something really important you need to see," she said.

Standing next to Elon, she opened the folder keeping it upright to prevent the visitors from being able to see the contents, then whispered to Elon for a few seconds. Whatever it was that Reyna was showing to Elon, it was clearly something of considerable magnitude because Elon looked visibly shocked. Was this related to them, Flore wondered. Perhaps it was just something important going on at Tesla, Space X or any one of the numerous other companies that Musk controlled. With Reyna gone, Flore tried to get the conversation back on course.

"Anyway, that's sort of why we're here. A mutually beneficial exchange. As well as bringing you your own future inventions, there are things we've already created ourselves that could help you with a lot of what you want to achieve," said Flore as she reached into her case and retrieved an orange-sized Mini Fusion Reactor.

"A power bank? I've got loads of those. And they're all smaller than that. There's no way you'd want that in your pocket all day," said Elon, dismissively.

"Elon, this is a Mini Fusion Reactor. It weighs less than one kilo and just one of these would power one of your cars, without needing to be recharged, for longer than the life of the car," said Flore.

Elon made a deep guttural sound, his body straightened, and he then slumped back into his chair releasing a long breath as a deep sigh.

"Could you warn me if you're going to say something like that again? You'll need to excuse me for a moment," he said as he got up and left the room, walking quite oddly.

"Did what I think just happened, actually happen?" asked Flore.

"Yep, he definitely came in his pants. I bet it's a while since you made a guy do that on a first date," said Charlie.

"It's not a first date. It's the second. Anyway, wait until he sees the Monstera Metal. You'd better get some Kleenex ready," said Flore.

Elon returned, wearing a different pair of trousers, and sat back down at his desk. Flore opened her case and removed a tealight candle which she put on the desk and then lit.

"What are you doing? Are we going to have a séance now?" said Elon, sarcastically.

"Watch," said Flore as she took the now empty briefcase, turned it on its side, and with a hand at each end, held it about twenty centimetres above the candle. Carefully releasing her grip, the case remained static in mid-air for a few seconds, then slowly ascended in the warm updraught rising from the candle. Elon watched, silently transfixed, his mouth wide open.

"The case is made of a material called Monstera Metal. It's ten thousand times stronger than steel, yet lighter than paper. That briefcase weighs less than three grammes. If you constructed the superstructure of your biggest rocket with it, it would weigh less than a small motorcycle. It's heat resistant to a temperature of five hundred thousand degrees centigrade, and impervious to all chemicals, acids, radiation, and ultraviolet light. In the highly unlikely event that it gets damaged in any way, it 'heals' in a matter of seconds," Flore said with calm, measured delivery.

Once again, Elon made a strange sound, this time more like the bark of a seal, then again appeared momentarily rigid and cross-eyed, before slumping back into his chair, saying, "Oh Jesus, not again. I swear this has never happened before."

"It's nothing to be ashamed about, it's probably my fault," said Flore, generously.

Elon got up to go and change his trousers again. While he was gone, Flore asked Charlie and Tom whether they thought it would be a good idea to tell Elon about the Flar engines.

"Hmm, maybe not. We might kill him. Death by orgasm," said Charlie.

"I've got a better idea," said Tom, as Elon reappeared in the office.

"Did you wash your hands, Elon?"

"Yes, of course. Why do you ask?" replied Elon.

"Don't let go," said Tom, as he grabbed Elon's hand, gripping it firmly.

An instant later, Elon, Tom and Flore were standing on La Villa Strangiato's patio on L'île de Wesh. Clearly in a state of shock, Elon looked around him trying to understand what he had just experienced, confusion and disbelief etched onto his face.

"What the fuck just happened?" he asked.

"Where's Charlie?" asked Flore.

Some rustling and the sound of some small branches breaking caused the group to look up to see Charlie clinging to the upper branches of a nearby tree, some ten metres up. He carefully shinned his way down the trunk until he was low enough to jump to the ground.

"Haven't quite got the hang of this quantum tunnelling thing yet. Still, practice makes perfect, eh?" he said, in a slightly embarrassed voice.

"Did he say quantum tunnelling?" asked Elon, still looking rather dazed.

"Yes, that's what we've acquired the ability to do. It was Tom's discovery. The rest of us have only been doing it for a few days," replied Flore.

"Do you mind if I sit down, I feel a bit light-headed," asked Elon, slumping into one of the patio chairs before anyone could answer.

"That's normal after your first trip. The dizziness will go in a few minutes," said Flore.

Moments later Sylvain came out of the house carrying a tray of drinks with Brian walking by his side, wagging his tail.

"You look like you could do with a drink. Have a Tom Collins. Pleased to meet you Mr Musk. My name is Sylvain."

"I'm pleased to meet you too, Mr Musk. I'm Brian. Have you brought my Roadster?" asked Brian, wagging his tail.

"What the fuck? A talking dog!" said Elon, incredulously, "Looks and sounds kind of familiar too."

"He's fitted with a Neuralink device. You can talk to him like you would talk to a person. He understands everything," said Tom. Elon nodded, still assimilating what he had just been told.

Leaning over to Elon, Tom said in a whisper, "Don't mention anything about him not having any balls, he's hyper-sensitive about it."

"I fucking heard that," said Brian, "For the love of Christ's salty dickwad, have you still not realised that my hearing is about a thousand times better than yours, you cloth-eared fuckwit. I hear fucking everything. Even if I sleep in a different room, on a different floor, I still have to suffer half a minute of your 'oooh, oooh, ahh, ahh' every Wednesday and Saturday, knowing that I could do a better job, if only you hadn't conspired with that vet to…"

"That's enough Brian," said Tom sternly, "Be quiet or go to your kennel."

"Wow, I see what you mean about the sensitivity issues," said Elon, who then did his best to diffuse the situation, looking at Brian and asking,

"You want a Tesla Roadster, Brian?"

"Yep. A red one. With those rocket thruster things," replied Brian, again, enthusiastically wagging his tail.

"But dogs can't drive Brian. Apart from anything else, it's against the law," said Elon.

"We make the laws here," replied Brian, his tail now motionless.

"Well, by the end of the year, we'll have full self-driving, so I guess it doesn't matter," said Elon, hoping it might placate Brian.

"Yeah, right. Full self-driving by the end of the year. How many times have I heard that? My balls will regrow before that happens. Unless I can work out how to time travel like them and go back and rip that cock-sucker vet's throat out before…" Brian started to say, as Marion arrived from the house carrying a tray of Spanish tortillas, some pickled eggs and a big bowl of mayonnaise, "Oohh food! Can I have some? Please, please," said Brian, his tail in full motion again.

"Brian, behave yourself and don't offend our guest or there'll be no treats, now or later," Marion said, authoritatively, "Good evening, Mr Musk. My name is Marion. Sorry about Brian. Would you like some food?"

With everyone seated around the table and Elon now having regained his composure and helping himself to a slice of tortilla, Flore decided it was time to talk business.

"Elon, we've brought you here because, provided your 'save the planet' narrative isn't just hyperbole to help you sell more cars, and we don't believe it is, we think that your motivations are very much aligned with ours. We don't have any ambition to colonise Mars, but we do want to save planet Earth from ecological, economic and social catastrophe," said Flore.

"Ecological, economic and social catastrophe?" Elon repeated, questioningly.

With a sigh, Flore explained how the future would unfold, "Yes, the uptick in inflation and the extreme weather events that we've recently been experiencing are just the beginning. Three years from now, you'll be paying $34 million for a loaf of bread. The Federal Reserve, along with almost every other central bank on the planet will default on its debt payments before the end of the decade, by which time, the ecological catastrophe will be unstoppable.

"Sales of your cars will fall to less than ten thousand per year because nobody except for the uber-rich will have any money, and even for them, it will only be those who have the foresight to get their assets out of cash and stocks that manage to maintain enough of a capital base to be able to buy one of your cars.

"You'll be OK though, for a while at least, because by then you'll have repurposed the Gigafactories to make robots, which will sell like hot cakes as the businesses that do manage to keep trading will replace their human workforces with your humanoid machines.

"Ten years from now, US Congress will vote to convert power stations to burn used car tyres to solve the energy crisis. China and India will follow suit, swiftly followed by most of the rest of the world. That's the ecological tipping point. Less than four years after that, Planet Earth will be ten degrees warmer, by which point the polar ice caps will have completely melted, and half the world's major cities will be underwater. Soon after, the air will be so acrid that most crops will fail, leading to mass starvation and brutal lawlessness the world over. It'll be Armageddon. Mad Max on steroids. Sorry, but that's the way it is."

"And the good news?" Elon asked.

"The good news is that we think we can stop the worst of it from happening," replied Flore with the most reassuring look she could muster.

"Why only the worst of it. Why can't you stop it completely? I mean, you can time travel. Surely, you can identify the key moments in history that have brought us to this point and just go back and change them?" asked Elon.

"There's simply too big a risk of unintended consequences," Flore replied, going on to give the examples of Tom's attempt to buy a lottery ticket and how the theft of Marion's trainers in 1960s New York could have resulted in global thermonuclear war.

"Or to hypothesize on other possible sub-optimal outcomes, imagine we determined that the problems were caused by the internal combustion engine being adopted as the main means of vehicle propulsion, instead of the electric motor. We could easily change that by taking battery cells from your cars back one hundred years and giving them to Henry Ford and the other early car makers, complete with a list of instructions on how to make them.

"Whilst that would probably ensure that batteries and electric motors get adopted instead of petrol and diesel engines, there's no guarantee that that change would prevent the world from reaching the ecological tipping point that we've now arrived at. Not only that, but in 1983 my mother was driving from Flers to Caen in Normandy for a job interview but ran out of petrol halfway. The man who stopped to help her, drove her to Caen for her interview, then back to her car a few hours later with a jerrycan of petrol, was my father.

"If electric cars had become dominant by then, my parents would probably never have met, so I wouldn't exist, which would also mean that the very specific set of circumstances that led to Tom acquiring the ability to quantum tunnel would never have happened either. In that case, the world might still be on the verge of existential catastrophe, but you and the rest of the world would just be passengers in the unfolding chaos, and I wouldn't even exist. You see the problem?"

"Yes, I get it. So, what do you think you can change and how?" asked Elon.

Over the next ninety minutes, Sylvain explained the details of the Einstein Plan, stressing the importance of its holistic and comprehensive nature. He first described the need for change throughout the entire world's societal structures; political, economic, religious, industrial and social. Then, the imperative of creating a clean, alternative power source, outlining the capabilities of the Mini Fusion Reactors that had had such a profound effect on Elon earlier in the day.

Seeking to both manage expectations and remind Elon of the magnitude of the situation, Flore took over again and explained that even by the entire world very rapidly becoming not just carbon neutral, but carbon negative, and implementing all of the other changes, there would still be a difficult period ahead, and that humanity would need a great deal of help if mass famine and societal breakdown were to be avoided.

Flore went on to summarize the plans to convert millions of shipping containers into mini farms powered by MFRs, and described how the nutritional supplement that had been developed in Wesh Corporation laboratories had the potential to virtually eliminate not only disease, but even ageing. Suppressing Elon's immediate reaction to this last point by raising her hand, Flore explained the plan to create the Matriverse to deal with the problem of the resulting population growth.

Elon remained silent throughout Flore's lengthy explanation, listening intently, and saying nothing until she had finished.

"Hence your interest in Neuralink," he said.

"Exactly, we've concluded that the only way…" Flore started to say but was interrupted by the sound of a loud siren.

"The laboratory!" exclaimed Tom, "It's been compromised. Someone has broken in."

"It's Brian. He's not here," said Marion.

# Chapter 49
# Reservoir Dog

Forgetting the ability to quantum tunnel, all six instinctively rushed on foot into the house, leaving Elon sitting outside.

Once they had made their way downstairs to the lab, the first thing they noticed was that one of the roosters from the chicken farm two floors below was in the laboratory. It had settled on a workbench and watched the panicked humans with beady eyes.

"That's Rocky. Brian must have gone to the chicken farm looking for the Monstera and let him get out through the whoosh pod. I'll take him back," said Marion.

A moment later, with Rocky safely back on the farm floor, Marion pointed to the cabinet containing the stock of Monstera pills. The cabinet door was open and several of the bottles had been pulled out onto the floor. One of them had been broken or 'crunched' open.

"Shit! Brian found the Monstera and has eaten a whole jar. That means he'll be able to quantum tunnel, just like us," exclaimed Marion.

"Yes, and you know what that means?" said Sylvain, "He'll have gone back in time to kill the vet that castrated him before he has the opportunity to do his job. It's all he's talked about for the last few days."

"It's worse than that," said Tom, "The morning of his operation, we gave him a Doggy Calm pill to partially sedate him. We took him to the vet in the car and he slept the whole way, so he'll have no idea where the vet's surgery is or how to find it. Not only that, but the extra intelligence he's gained from the Neuralink implant means that he'll have worked out that even if he does go back in time to find and kill the specific vet who castrated him, that we would have found a different vet to perform the operation. Do you realise what that means?"

"Oh my god! He's not just going to kill his vet, he's going to kill every vet in the New York area – maybe even further afield. It'll be his mission. Dogs can be incredibly single-minded. Especially when it comes to hunting," said Lucia.

"Great, so we've got a psychotic time-travelling canine on the loose with a pathological hatred of vets. He could kill hundreds of people, and that will have incalculable consequences for the space-time continuum," said Flore, almost in tears.

"Oh my god, you're right," said Marion, "We were worried about my trainers causing World War Three, but Brian on the loose could be even more catastrophic. We've got to get him back before he destroys the world."

"Yep, you've got to find and kill the dog," said Elon from behind them, having somehow managed to get into the island's inner sanctum and down to the lab without being noticed. Flore, Sylvain, Tom, Marion, Lucia and Charlie all spun around to see Elon standing at the entrance to the lab, leaning on the doorframe with one hand and holding a half-eaten apple in the other.

"Great apples you grow here. They're delicious. This is my third. The pears are good too," said Elon.

"Oh fuck!" all six said, together.

# Chapter 50
# Kill Bill

Bill Aagaard had had a difficult morning. He'd been late leaving his home in New York's Queens suburb as a result of the toaster catching fire, which had then led to a cascade of secondary events. It was a Wednesday, which was garbage collection day, and because Bill was seven minutes late leaving home in his car, he found himself stuck behind a lumbering garbage truck on the narrow one-way street where he lived. It took fifteen minutes for Bill to reach the end of his road where he joined the Union Turnpike, then turned onto Utopia Parkway before heading west on the I-495 towards Manhattan, where Bill's place of work, the Aagaard Veterinary Practice, was located on the Lower East Side.

Attempting to make up lost time on the I-495, Bill drove much faster than usual. He was only a couple of miles along the freeway when he saw the flashing blue lights in his rear-view mirror. Having pulled over onto the hard shoulder and wound down his window, Bill did his best to succinctly explain to the traffic officer why he had been driving so fast, describing his packed schedule and the number of pets and pet owners that would be waiting for him at his surgery.

The policeman listened politely and patiently as Bill spoke, nodding sympathetically at appropriate moments during Bill's monologue of excuses, but then issued a ticket anyway, telling him, "Well, Sir, better late in this life than early in the next. Watch your speed in future."

Having stowed the speeding fine in the glove box, Bill re-joined the stream of traffic headed for Manhattan, which, with it now being forty minutes later than usual, was much heavier than Bill was used to. Nevertheless, it was at least moving. Bill reasoned that if he used the Queens Midtown Tunnel and got lucky with the traffic on Roosevelt Drive, he might only be half an hour late. Moments later, Bill's optimism was scuppered by a loud rumble and a juddering from the rear of the car – he had a flat tyre. Must have picked up a screw or a nail on the dusty, debris-strewn hard shoulder after being stopped for speeding, he thought, mentally cursing the sanctimonious traffic cop at the same time.

Quickly pulling over again and jumping out of the car, Bill found his left rear tyre to be not only deflated but also partially shredded around the tyre wall; far too badly damaged to be reinflated using the can of Tyre-Weld he kept in the trunk. He would have to change the wheel.

An hour later, his hands black with dirt and brake dust, and his face smeared and streaked where he had inadvertently wiped the sweat caused by the exertion of changing the wheel, Bill finally arrived at the parking lot opposite his surgery. Normally he drove straight in, parked in the half-empty lot, paid the attendant, then headed to the café to get a coffee on his way to the surgery. Today though, a sign at the entrance to the parking lot stated unambiguously that the lot was 'FULL'. Bill drove on, eventually parking three blocks away.

As he rushed to work on foot, Bill reflected on his morning. "If only I hadn't burnt the fucking toast," he thought. He added up the delays in his head. Two minutes to extricate the charred remains from the toaster; another two minutes to go around the house re-setting the smoke alarms; then, two more minutes when the smoke alarms went off a second time; three more having a second attempt at making toast; a quarter of an hour stuck behind the garbage truck; ten minutes with the sanctimonious cop; twenty minutes changing the wheel; an extra half hour in heavier traffic because of the delays; ten minutes extra to park the car, and now a ten minute walk. He was more than ninety minutes late, filthy dirty, with cuts on his hands and oil stains on his trousers where he had knelt on the oily tarmac of the hard shoulder to change the wheel. But Bill's morning was about to get much, much worse.

Bill entered the Reception of the Aagaard Veterinary Practice at just after ten-thirty to a cacophony of 'about time', 'finally, he's here' and 'look at the state of him' from the dozen or more people waiting. Dogs were barking at cats in cages, and the cats were snarling and hissing in response. A man with a parrot on his shoulder said, "About fucking time," which prompted the parrot to repeat his owner's words half a dozen times, but at a higher pitch and much louder. It was pandemonium.

Monica the receptionist looked at Bill's dishevelled state in disbelief. "What happened to you?" she asked, then continued, "No, tell me later.

You've got thirteen people waiting and a white Labrador arrived alone and is waiting in your consulting room. He just walked straight through reception, opened the door to your room with his paw, went in and sat down. When I tried to get him out, he stuck his snout in my crotch and then tried to hump my leg. Then, when I attempted to grab his collar, he growled at me and showed his teeth, so I thought I'd leave him for you to deal with."

"OK. Sorry you've had to deal with all of this alone. I'll explain later," Bill said as he hurried towards his consulting room.

As soon as Bill entered his room, the white Labrador stood up and, to Bill's astonishment, started to speak.

"The path of the righteous man is beset on all sides by the inequity of the selfish, and the tyranny of evil, emasculating men, Blessed is he who, in the name of charity and goodwill, shepherds the weak castrators through the valley of darkness, for he is truly his brother's keeper and the finder of lost testicles. And I will strike down upon thee with great vengeance and great anger those who attempt to poison and destroy my brothers and cut off their balls. And you will know my name is the Lord when I lay my vengeance upon you."

"Fuck me! A talking dog," Bill said out loud, pondering why the words he'd just heard sounded vaguely familiar.

But Bill had no time to think further. Without another word, the Labrador launched himself at Bill's throat, knocking him to the ground. The dog's powerful jaws clamped around Bill's windpipe, tearing through the flesh of his neck and severing the carotid artery on his right side. Bill's life flashed through his mind. He saw his father's angry face, berating five-year-old Billy for keeping a corn snake in a shoe box under his bed. He relived his first kiss with his teenage sweetheart, Sally, and witnessed their wedding ten years later. At his graduation from Cornell University's College of Veterinary Medicine, he saw his proud mother telling one of his tutors that he'd always wanted to be a vet, and that, aged eleven months, 'dog' had been his first word.

With his consciousness ebbing away, Bill's final thought was how bizarre it was that both the first and last words of his life would be 'dog'. Seconds later, Bill was dead, lying supine, arms by his side, his green veterinary outfit giving him the appearance of the stalk to the flower of blood that had pooled around his head.

# THE COSMIC KNOT PARADOX

# Chapter 51
# Tootsie

At La Villa Strangiato, Elon persuaded everybody that they should calm down and develop a well-thought-out plan before rushing back into the past to find Brian.

"You can time travel, so you can go anytime. Talk it through first. Work up a plan," Elon had concluded.

With the Brian crisis now put in perspective, attention turned to the other pressing issue of the day. The news about the effect that the apples would have was broken to Elon. Flore delivered the information as sensitively as possible but held back on the full extent of the changes he would experience. Marion then explained that the effects were the result of their early attempts to genetically modify fruit and vegetables to provide regenerative properties and that the initial experiments had resulted in a number of unintended side effects. Lucia retrieved the red bra that had been given to Charlie during his brief lady-boy spell.

"But I don't want a red bra," Elon protested, "I'll look like a cheap twenty-dollar hooker. Haven't you got a blue one?"

"Yes, I said the same when it happened to me," said Charlie, "But believe me, you'll be grateful for it. It'll help keep the bouncing under control. After a while, you kind of get used to it and get your step into a kind of wobble-sync when you walk, but running is a different matter entirely."

Elon nodded, indicating that he'd understood that the blue bra would help to make the changes he was about to experience easier.

Sylvain appeared with a wheelbarrow.

"What's that for? They're surely not going to get so big that I'll need a wheelbarrow. I mean, I've got the bra," said Elon, looking perplexed.

"Well, err, as well as the apples, you ate the pears. The apples result in perfect but vast breasts, and the pears produce unfeasibly large genitalia - for either sex, they cause enlargement of gargantuan proportions. So, erm, during the next twelve hours, your testicles will swell to the size of very large watermelons and your penis will end up the size of a baby elephant trunk. Lucky you're not a woman, you'd have ended up with a clitoris like a tennis ball in a football sock. Anyway, suffice to say, it'll be very difficult to walk anywhere without the wheelbarrow," Sylvain explained.

"What the fuck? Tits and huge gonads. What's the good news?" asked Elon.

"The good news is that we have an antidote for both conditions," said Marion, "You can't take the antidote until the conditions are fully present, so I'm afraid you're going to have to tough it out. You're going to need the bra and the wheelbarrow, but once everything is fully formed, the antidote only takes a day or two to completely reverse the changes."

"Well, I guess, as you say, I'll just need to tough it out, so back to business," Elon said with purpose.

Tom privately thought that Elon was perhaps rather intrigued by the idea of having an elephant trunk sized penis but said nothing.

"We'd touched on Tom and his multiple identities, but there's something else. Something way more significant," Elon continued, "What Reyna showed me before you grabbed my hand and brought me here, were two separate images printed onto two sheets of acetate. One was the image of Tom's face, captured this morning as he approached my car. The other was a scan of a little artefact I picked up a few years ago – it's the kind of thing you buy when you're a billionaire.

"The item I bought is very much like the Turin Shroud, which, as we all know, was a fake, but this one, as far as can be verified through carbon dating and other scientific and historical methods, also shows the imprint of Christ's face but is thought to be real. Through the course of history, only a handful of people have known of its existence. The two images, the one from the shroud and the image of Tom's face taken this morning overlay perfectly. Not only that, but the DNA sample we got from Tom exactly matches the DNA on the blood from the shroud."

"I, err, don't…" Tom started to say, but Elon interrupted.

"You impersonated Jesus. That's fucking incredible!" exclaimed Elon.

Recovering his composure and with it an impetuous defiance, Tom retorted, "No, Elon. I didn't impersonate Jesus. I *am* Jesus."

# Chapter 52
# The Other Jesus

Flore gasped, Charlie and Lucia dropped their drinks, and Sylvain spontaneously broke wind at incredible volume. All four now sat mouths agape in a state of shock. Despite being the catalyst for this momentous revelation, even the normally impassive Musk looked stunned by Tom's admission. It was only Marion whose expression didn't change. Instead, a single tear rolled down her left cheek.

"What the fuck, Tom. What do you mean, you are Jesus?" asked Flore.

"Exactly that. I am Jesus. I am the person who, according to the version of events that you know, was born to a virgin in a stable, walked on water, fed five thousand and ended up getting nailed to a cross. That's it. Not much else to add," Tom replied.

"Not much else to add? Are you fucking serious? You're telling us that the biblical version of history, which, even if we didn't believe much of it, is what's shaped the world we know, was caused entirely by you. And that's not much?" exclaimed Flore.

"It was just an accident," said Tom.

"An accident? What do you mean?" asked Charlie.

"Well, a while back, I went to first century Middle East to see what it was like, kind of like how someone might go on a city break for a long weekend. I didn't go intending to be Jesus, because for me or anyone else, three weeks ago, Jesus and Christianity didn't exist. Everything was different three weeks ago. I just wondered what the Middle East would have been like two thousand years ago, so I thought myself there and the rest just sort of happened."

"Just sort of happened?" retorted Flore in a near gasp of incredulous disbelief.

"Yes, it just happened. Just a sequence of events that kind of gained their own momentum and sort of got out of control. I'd downloaded first-century Aramaic to my Neuralink, got a knee length chitōn from the costume wardrobe and rocked up there expecting to just fit in, but people seemed to know I was somehow different. The differences that I helplessly displayed together with the fact that I was inadvertently and unconsciously knowledgeable about things that they were understandably ignorant of, must have served as a sort of magnet, making me seem to them like someone with great wisdom, and before I knew what was happening, I'd built up a bit of a following.

"It didn't help when, about a week after I'd arrived, a few of these people came with me to the beach. We had a great time. We chatted in the sun, swam in the sea, and I taught them how to play volleyball. After a while, this kid turned up and offered to sell us a couple of loaves of bread and a few fish. We were hungry by then, so we bought the fish, collected some driftwood, and had an impromptu barbeque. Attracted by the smell of the food, a few more people turned up, but by then we'd pretty much eaten everything, so I nipped back to 21st-century London and bought a box of Tilapia from Billingsgate market and some bread from a Lebanese bakery, which was the most similar I could find.

"Back on the beach in first century Galilee, with more fish on the barbeque, it didn't take long before more people arrived and, just like when a 21st Century street-food popup really nails it and ends up with a massive queue, the same happened there. Anyway, the rest is history and what you now call the 'miracle of the feeding of the five thousand'. But it wasn't five thousand, it was perhaps fifty, tops; but you know how these things get exaggerated.

"That same evening, I did what I now realise was a really stupid thing. Earlier in the day, while we were swimming, I'd swum out further than the others and noticed that there was a sandbank, about fifty metres from the beach. You can probably guess the rest. For a joke, I swam to where the water was only ankle deep, and…" Tom started to explain, but Marion interrupted.

"You walked on water. You total egotistical moron. You're like a fucking peacock with an extreme attention-seeking personality disorder."

"It was just a joke," Tom protested, "It just got out of hand. When I got back to the beach, I thought they'd be laughing, but they weren't. They really believed I had walked on water and were dropping to their knees and calling me 'Messiah'.

"Anyway, it got much, much worse, really quickly after that. The day after, a friend turned up looking very sick. He described fatigue, fevers and a headache. Touching his forehead revealed that he had a high temperature and probably had flu. But, within minutes, the colour had returned to his skin, and he had the radiance of a fit and healthy young man. He said that not only had his illness lifted, but he was feeling better than ever. Moments later he was telling passers-by that I really was the Messiah and could heal the sick just by touching them.

"The only explanation I can think of is that earlier that morning, I'd been counting the Monstera pills that I'd taken with me, so when I touched his forehead, the sweat on his brow must have dissolved the Monstera residue on my fingers, allowing it to be absorbed into his skin - not enough to give him those initial hallucinations or the ability to quantum tunnel, but enough to cure his flu.

"Before I knew it, I had a crowd of people around me begging to be cured of all sorts of ailments. Some had what we now know as tuberculosis, a few had some sort of cancer, one poor guy was convulsed in pain with kidney stones, another had dysentery, and an old woman had been blinded by cataracts. I couldn't ignore the suffering of these people, so I cured them all.

"As news of my powers spread, they became more and more perturbed. The cult that was rapidly developing around me threatened their power and it wasn't long before the rabbis managed to convince their Roman masters of the threat that I posed to the established order. I knew I had to leave, but didn't want to go without saying goodbye to my friends…"

It was Charlie's turn to interrupt. "Oh, for fuck's sake! The Last Supper?" he ventured.

"Yes, exactly. The Last Supper. From there, things played out more or less as you might have read in the Bible. The day after, they arrested me, tortured me, nailed me to a cross, stabbed me when I took too long to die, and then put my body in a cave. It's about the only part of the Bible that's anywhere near to being accurate.

"Anyway, within the space of a few hours of being entombed, the Monstera had worked and had healed all of my injuries, so I got up and came back here. But, before I left, I rolled the rock in front of the cave to one side to make it look like the tomb had been looted, thinking that that would be the end of it, and I would just be remembered as a bit of a troublemaker cult leader whose corpse got stolen by one of his mad followers. End of story."

"So, why did you go back?" asked Flore.

"I didn't," replied Tom.

"The Bible says that after the resurrection and before ascending to heaven, you appeared to your disciples various times over a period of forty days," said Flore.

"They made all that up; like most of it," Tom replied, "The only things that had any element of truth were the feeding of the five thousand, which was massively exaggerated; the walking on water thing, which I've explained was just a joke that went wrong; then, the healings, the last supper, crucifixion, and my subsequent disappearance from the tomb. Everything else was invented to create a good read. Being born to a virgin in a stable; the three kings; most of the miracles and pretty much everything about the resurrection. All invented.

"You have to realise that the bible was written three hundred years after I was there. From the perspective of finding accurate records, three hundred years is a long time even now, but back then there were no paper records, just word of mouth passed through multiple generations, getting more and more sensationalised, exaggerated and embellished every time someone told the story. What was written, was scrawled on papyrus scrolls and was written in a language that would have been difficult to even read, let alone accurately translate."

"Why did you let them crucify you? Why didn't you just think yourself to safety back here?" Sylvain asked.

"Partly for the experience," replied Tom.

"For the experience? Crucifixion tourism! Travel to first century Middle East, walk on water, heal people, and have your own personal crucifixion, then rise from the dead and fuck up humanity for two millennia," said Charlie, mimicking the voice you might hear on a cable TV advert for a budget-priced cruise. Ignoring Charlie's sarcasm, Tom continued.

"Well, I knew that whatever they did to me, I would recover. So, I just let it happen; mainly because if I disappeared before they killed me, my friends would have been suspected of having helped me escape and the consequences for them would have been horrific."

Elon started to clap. "So, the egomaniac has a conscience. Hurrah."

"Egomaniac? You're a fine one to talk," retorted Tom.

Elon snapped back, "Excuse me, but I'm not the one zipping back and forth through millennia, pretending to be the fucking Messiah and living multiple celebrity lives."

"But you are the one who…" started Tom.

"That's enough," said Flore sternly, "Bickering isn't going to get us anywhere." Both men were instantly silenced.

"So, Tom. The question that's occupying every single one of my fifty or so brain cells, is what was the world like before you so generously decided to become our saviour?" asked Charlie.

Tom sighed, and a tear started to form in one eye.

"It was, err, similar, but well, different. Better in some ways. Worse in others."

"Enlighten us," said Charlie.

"Well, there's no church for a start. At least, not any kind of church that you'd be familiar with. An ethos similar to what you might call Paganism is dominant. It evolved in Spain around the same time I showed up in Bethlehem. The core concept essentially revolves around respect. Respect for the natural world, respect for every individual and most importantly, respect for one's inner self. The name of this movement was Soliterra which has a double meaning. Sol y terra means sun and earth in Spanish but when said out loud, it sounds a lot like 'soltera' which means single or alone. This emphasizes the significance of both the natural world and the individual.

"Soliterrans understood that every event not directly caused by the natural world, starts with a single thought by a single person, hence they worshipped the inner self to rationalise the place and purpose of the individual as a part of the natural world. Worship is probably the wrong word. Respect and sanctify would be better words," Tom explained.

"It sounds a lot like Buddhism," said Flore.

"In many respects, it is, but with an important difference. Buddhists still believe in deities, Soliterrans didn't. Their reverence was for the natural rather than the supernatural," replied Tom.

"What about the other religions? Surely, without the foil of Christianity, Islam or one of the other big religions would have quickly become dominant and relegated Soliterra to obscurity," said Charlie.

"Quite the contrary," replied Tom, "Think of it in scientific terms. It's like Newton's Third Law – action and reaction - for every action there is an equal and opposite reaction. Islam evolved and grew mostly as a reaction to Christian aggression. Without evangelical Christians donning their armour, jumping on horses and going off on their crusades to wage their holy wars, there wasn't a reason for an alternative deity-based movement to emerge and gain popularity, so Islam fizzled out pretty quickly.

"You see, humans are generally more successful working as teams, so evolved essentially as pack animals, forming tribes to share the tasks essential for survival and create safety in numbers to mitigate the risks posed by predators. This instinctive tribalism is why football is so popular, and so often turns groups of more or less decent people into mobs of aggressive, violent thugs. It triggers some of the most basic instincts that evolution, natural selection, instilled at the core of the human psyche. Maslow's Hierarchy of Needs explains that association, or the sense of belonging, is the most significant need once a person's needs for food, shelter, warmth, and safety have been satisfied.

"As well as helping to protect ancient tribes and their resources, tribal instinct also created the possibility of one tribe becoming strong enough and sufficiently numerous to be able to take the resources of a neighbouring tribe. So, of course, there were still bloody conflicts, but for the most part, those conflicts usually ended up getting resolved through some mutually beneficial agreement; you know, something like, we'll let your tribe graze your animals on our land in exchange for some milk and meat. So, two competing tribes would usually conclude that their interests would be better served by resolving their differences and working together.

"But the emergence of competing value systems, both with a deity at their core, introduced a difference into that dynamic because when two groups believe in different gods, it soon becomes almost impossible to settle disagreements. Disputes that begin over simple things like land or resources, which would otherwise be easily sorted out with a bit of negotiation, quickly get escalated to a 'my god is better than your god' conflict that doesn't get resolved, because faith always trumps objectivity.

"That's why, more than thirteen hundred years after the end of the Crusades, there's still sufficient enmity and hatred between Christians and Muslims for a group of intelligent, well-educated young men to intentionally crash two aeroplanes into New York's twin towers; and after two thousand years as neighbours, Jews and Arabs still find it impossible to get along. India ended up being carved up into three separate countries along theological lines. Then there's the Balkan conflict, the Sudanese genocide, and the list just goes on and on. Christianity was the catalyst for all of it.

"But the Soliterran movement didn't divide humanity in the way that Christianity, Islam, Judaism, and the other religions have, because there was no deity at the core of the belief system. Soliterranism united rather than divided.

"Of course, from time to time, deity-based religions emerged, but the followers were regarded by mainstream society as delusional fanatics, the same way that the society you know regards cults, creationists, conspiracy theorists, or those who insist that the earth is flat. So, these cults tended to disappear just as fast as they appeared.

"There's something else that's key to the way that Soliterran societies emerged and evolved as peaceful cultures, populated almost entirely by kind, thoughtful people. It's caused by a phenomenon that most modern psychologists in this thread don't understand. It's called 'genetic memory'. Does anyone know about genetic memory?"

"Sure, it's the biological mechanism that does things like make humans and other animals instinctively know how to breathe the moment they're born," said Elon.

"That's exactly right," said Tom, "But it extends much, much further than that. A simple example of slightly more complex genetic memory at work is that even without any training, a sheepdog instinctively knows how to herd sheep. In fact, even a dog that's four or five generations from any working ancestor, that's never even seen any sheep, not only knows how to herd a flock, but can even understand and respond to a shepherd's whistles. That knowledge is somehow buried in the genetic code and passed from one generation to the next. Now think of that phenomenon in the context of humans.

"In the thread of the multiverse that you are now familiar with, we've had humans constantly at war with each other over ultimately irreconcilable differences for more than two thousand years, passing hatred and violence from one generation to the next; not only through the short-term example set for the child by the parent, but embedded in human genetic memory and normalising anti-social behaviour across countless generations.

"But in the Soliterran thread, without divisive religions, people evolve to live in harmony with very few disputes that can't be rationally resolved. That distils into a collective genetic memory profile where most people are kind, respectful and thoughtful. In the Soliterran thread, there's almost no bloody conflict. There are no wars, no crime, no football hooligans, and the term 'road rage' doesn't exist in their vocabulary. Kind of brings a new dimension to the whole nature versus nurture debate, doesn't it?"

"You're saying that as well as a child learning from the behaviour of its parents, the child's psychological makeup can be influenced by the experiences of the parents, grandparents and even great-grandparents from before the child was even conceived? So, nurture becomes nature, with experiences being genetically passed to several subsequent generations?" asked Flore.

"Yes, sort of," replied Tom.

"Is that what's meant in the Bible by 'the sins of the father shall be laid upon the children'?" asked Charlie.

"Yes, a rare moment of insight for the ecclesiasts; that's partly what they meant, and of course other things like congenital syphilis," said Tom, "But anyway, it's not just sins. It's everything; good and bad behaviour, all behaviour. It explains why some people have inexplicably strong feelings about quite random things. Somebody with a strong dislike of the colour green or green clothing might have had a grandparent or great-grandparent who survived the holocaust but, amongst other things, was left with an enduring subconscious memory of the green uniforms of the brutal Nazi guards.

"Fledgling penguins and new born seal cubs instinctively flee from polar bears but were entirely unfazed by humans when the first polar explorers arrived – at least, for a while. Light a barbeque at a summer party and within a short time, all the men will be gathered around it, jostling to turn the meat. Why? Because grilling meat over an open fire triggers primitive genetic memories.

"Genetic memory partly explains why some people can grow up in the most dreadful circumstances but still go on to become decent, kind adults, yet others spend their childhood in happy, stable families only to turn into serial killers when they grow up."

"But, even if you're right about genetic memory, isn't that just another way of describing someone's nature? And you're essentially saying that those on the nurture side of the debate are wrong," said Flore.

"I can see why you might reach that conclusion, but you're missing some nuance and that's understandable because it's quite complicated. Genetic memory influences a person's nature but usually doesn't completely define it. A person who does something exceptionally good or bad can end up being defined by the actions of a moment – you know, the woman who jumps into a raging river to save a stranger gets described as courageous, or the man who kills another motorist in a moment of road rage is instantly labelled as violent and vicious; but that's not necessarily their nature.

"You frequently see reports on TV or read about people who do things that seem to be completely out of character. A few weeks ago, there was a story about a thirty-six-year-old librarian called Roger Robertson from a small town just outside Milwaukee, Wisconsin. He got into an altercation with a man at his local Walmart after accidentally bumping him with his trolley. Witnesses said that Robertson tried to apologise, but the man shouted, 'Someone like you should be more careful and have more respect', and then hit Robertson hard in the face.

Robertson was used to occasional verbal insults, but the punch triggered a rage he had never experienced. He returned the blow, hitting the man in the solar plexus. As his adversary doubled over, Robertson whacked him across the back of the neck with the side of his hand. The man fell to the floor and in an instant, Robertson had grabbed his chin with one hand, the back of his head with the other and twisted in a sharp, sudden movement. There was a resounding crack as the man's neck broke and the man became immediately limp, dead on the supermarket floor. Robertson then went on a crazed rampage through the shopping mall, killing seven other people, before he was shot dead by Police. The news report showed a photo of the first victim, a young man in his early twenties, a little bit overweight with a mop of untidy red hair. One by one, the report showed photos of the other seven victims. They were different ages, some were thin, some were fat, but what was striking was that they all had red hair.

"The news report highlighted the surprise of the killer's work colleagues and neighbours. One, a woman in her mid-thirties, told the reporter,

'We're in total shock. He seemed such a kind and gentle man. He was always so thoughtful, remembered the kids' birthdays and would bake a cake for us at Christmas.' Another elderly neighbour said, 'We don't understand it. He used to bring us books from the library, cut our grass in summer and clear the snow off our driveway in winter. We just can't believe what's happened. It's so out of character.'

"Intrigued by the story and keen to understand how a seemingly kind and gentle librarian could suddenly become a crazed killer, I decided to conduct my own investigation.

"First, I researched Robertson's childhood. He was the only child of Eunice, also a librarian, and Frank, who ran the local hardware store. Eunice and Frank were good, decent people, the type that would regularly invite neighbours for dinner if they knew they were struggling financially or had suffered a bereavement or family trauma. Eunice was a volunteer at a local hospice and would go there two or three times every week after closing the library, to talk with and read stories to the dying. Frank sacrificed most of his Sundays, his only day off from the hardware store, to work as a volunteer at the local orphanage.

"Young Roger did well at school, graduating with straight 'A's and went on to gain a scholarship to study English Literature at Yale. The university wanted Roger not just for his obvious academic potential, but also hoped that he might provide the Yale Chess Society with an edge in their annual competition with Harvard – Roger had been both Milwaukee and Wisconsin junior chess champion for the previous four years.

"Roger settled in well at Yale and seemed to be on course for a First until just before the end of his second year, fate intervened most horribly. Frank Robertson was killed in a car accident returning from work and Eunice Robertson became catatonic with grief. Roger quit college to look after his mother and ended up taking over her role at the library where he quickly became popular with colleagues and customers alike.

"But, apart from the sudden loss of his father, there was nothing that I could find in Roger Robertson's past, and certainly nothing from his happy and stable childhood, being brought up by kind and loving parents, that might have caused him to have any emotional or anger management problems as an adult; certainly nothing that could have triggered the murderous savagery that resulted in the loss of nine lives.

"So, I started to dig deeper into the family history. I didn't have to dig very far. Frank Robertson, Roger's father, was an orphan. His father, George, killed another local man, Hamish McTavity, and his two brothers with a Colt 45 revolver, and then, a few minutes later, with the Police on their way, killed himself with the same weapon. These horrific events took place nine months before Frank was born.

Soon after George's death, Mildred discovered she was pregnant, tracing the conception back to the days immediately before her young husband's suicide. Mildred died nine months later giving birth to Frank.

"Frank's inauspicious start to life was the reason why, as an adult, he sacrificed his Sundays to work at the orphanage – he had grown up there. What intrigued me about the story was why George Robertson had committed murder and then taken his own life.

"What I discovered, was nothing short of a stunning revelation from the perspective of understanding how genetic memory influences complex human behaviour. George was an occasional gambler and had amassed a bigger poker debt to McTavity than he was able to immediately repay. He'd managed to pay half of the debt by pawning his wedding ring and the fur coat Mildred had inherited from her aunt. He had also arranged a loan with a bank in Iowa to cover the other half. The funds from the bank loan were due to arrive two weeks later, but McTavity wasn't a patient man and was demanding the money immediately. The week of the fatal shooting, McTavity had turned up at the Robertson home with two of his brothers and beaten George unconscious on the Tuesday. They came again on the Wednesday and did the same, also breaking three of George's fingers for good measure, telling him that they'd be back the day after, and if he didn't have the money, not only would George get a further beating, but Mildred would also be given the same treatment.

"The following day, George was ready for the evening visit. He'd taken his Colt 45 revolver from the drawer next to his bed, cleaned it and loaded it with six bullets. He hoped he wouldn't have to use it, but knew he wouldn't survive another beating and was determined to protect his young wife.

"Hamish McTavity arrived shortly after eight in the evening with his two thuggish brothers, parking his Studebaker on the front lawn. George walked out onto the porch. 'Don't come a step further, McTavity', he shouted, 'You'll have your money on Wednesday.' But McTavity and his brothers continued walking towards the house. 'Last chance, McTavity,' said George.

"McTavity shouted back, 'We're going to enjoy teaching you another lesson, but not as much as we're going to enjoy giving that pretty little wife of yours a lesson of her own.'

"George didn't hesitate a moment longer and taking the gun from his waistband, aimed at McTavity and pulled the trigger. The bullet caught McTavity in the middle of the forehead, leaving just a small hole. The back of the head, however, didn't fare nearly so well. Showered in the explosion of blood, brains and fragments of bone from their brother's skull, the McTavity brothers ran for their lives, but not nearly fast enough. George took aim at the brother on the left and dropped him with a single shot just as he reached the sidewalk, the bullet hitting the man in the back and continuing through his heart before exiting his chest. He dispatched the second with similar precision moments later, then walked to where the men were lying on the ground and shot them both in the head to be certain that they were dead and wouldn't be able to come back to avenge their brother's death.

"Sobbing on the sofa, and with the wail of Police sirens getting steadily louder, George told Mildred, 'They'll fry me, Millie. I shot those men in the back while they were running away. No court in the state will believe a self-defence story from a black man who shot three white guys. I love you.' The next instant, he put the barrel of the gun in his mouth and pulled the trigger."

"Oh my god! That's terrible," exclaimed Marion. "Why did you have to tell me that? You've ruined my day."

"Mine too," said Lucia, "It's a horrible story."

"The three men, Hamish and his two brothers, all had red hair," said Tom, and after a pause for emphasis, "They all looked almost exactly the same as the eight men that Roger, George Robertson's grandson, killed sixty-five years later."

"Well, subconsciously or otherwise, Roger probably had a grudge against people with red hair after something like that had happened in the family," said Lucia.

"No. Frank and Eunice Robertson never talked about it. They didn't want their son to have any sort of persecution complex, or to grow up with any negative feelings about white people. They had told Roger the truth about his grandmother dying in childbirth, but that his grandfather had died of tuberculosis. Not only that, but George and Mildred were living in New Jersey when George killed the McTavity brothers, so nobody local knew the history either. When Mildred died, baby Frank was moved to the orphanage in Milwaukee as he would potentially have been at risk from what remained of the McTavity family in New Jersey. Roger Robertson was completely unaware of his family's tragic history.

"The trigger that caused intelligent, kind, and mild-mannered Roger Robertson to kill eight people was the genetic memory that people who look like Hamish McTavity cause pain, suffering and irretrievable loss. That memory was burned into every cell of his grandfather's being on the first night that the McTavity brothers beat him to within an inch of his life, two days before Frank was conceived, and three days before George killed the McTavity brothers and then, himself.

"Those memories were passed to Roger from Frank, but remained buried in the murky depths of Roger's psychological makeup until he was physically attacked, at which point they came flying to the surface like an Exocet missile leaving a submarine," said Tom, thrusting pointed fingers in the air and making a 'whoosh' sound for added emphasis.

"So, you're certain that there are three, not two, key elements that determine human behaviour; nature, nurture and genetic memory," asked Charlie, "And you're saying that the genetic memory part sort of straddles the other two."

"Exactly. Those three elements interact together but do so in complex and unpredictable ways. Any one or two can augment, reinforce, over-ride or be negated by the other one or two elements. There are multiple permutations of how they work together and the balance between them is highly volatile, changing rapidly and often.

"With all of that in mind, now consider the influence that genetic memory might have at a societal rather than just individual level. If the genetic memories carried by the majority of people are mostly positive, over time that will have a cumulative positive effect on society as a whole, creating a kind of virtuous spiral where society gets better with each generation. But if there is a very high prevalence of negative genetic memories, humanity gets progressively worse and worse as the propensity to do terrible things becomes more and more concentrated in the population.

# Chapter 53
# The Day After Tomorrow

Tom continued his description of the Soliterran world.

"Without the shackles of ecclesiastical doctrine and dogmatism, and without paranoid, control-obsessed clerics running the show and stifling education to protect their little empires, humanity advanced at a staggering rate.

"From what we would now call the third and fourth centuries, Soliterran communities, the world over, developed into democratic, secular societies. By then, most religions had simply fallen by the wayside, made irrelevant and redundant by a sufficient understanding of the world for most people not to need to turn to the occult for answers.

"By the beginning of the fifth century, most places in the world had social norms and societal structures even more progressive than modern-day Scandinavia; and by the middle of that century, humans had discovered and worked out how to make, control and utilise electricity. Before what we would now call the sixth century, the electric light, the telephone, and the horseless carriage had all been invented. The internet came into existence shortly after the beginning of the seventh century."

"Tom, you keep using terms like 'by what we now refer to' and 'what we would now call'. What do you mean by that?" asked Flore.

"Isn't it obvious?" replied Tom, "For you, the measurement of time starts from the day of my birth. Or to be more accurate in that statement, from what a collection of clerics decided was my birthday when they invented the whole Bethlehem stable story, about three hundred years after I did the Jesus thing.

"In the alternative history that I know, there was a first-century Spanish archaeologist, etymologist, philosopher, astronomer, physicist and mathematician called Enrique Mirastrellas, who was central to Soliterran culture. He was what you might call a polymath; their equivalent of DaVinci, only more profound in the impact that his work had on their belief structure.

By what you would call the year ninety-seven, he had worked out that the universe began with a big explosion; what you call the Big Bang. He named it Formación del Universo y Catalizador Cósmico, which translates to formation of the universe and cosmic catalyst, and its abbreviation is probably the origin of the word 'fuck' that we now use so liberally with multiple…"

"So, that's where it comes from…" Sylvain interrupted, and then Flore interrupted him.

"But how? That doesn't make sense. It was an alternative thread of the multiverse. Why do we use it in our thread?"

"The Cosmic Knot Paradox," said Elon, "It somehow crossed realities. Carry on Tom."

"Anyway, as I was saying, Mirastrellas calculated that the big FUCC event occurred about forty-two billion years ago, but that wasn't what really interested Mirast….." Tom started to explain, but Elon jumped in.

"Forty-two; that's hilarious," Elon said, laughing, "But he was wrong. The Big Bang occurred 13.8 billion years ago."

"No, he wasn't wrong, because the Soliterrans measured time differently, with three years to every rotation of Earth around the Sun. Their years were different lengths, the longest between the spring and autumn equinox and the other two years starting or ending on the winter solstice. Forty-two is the answer to the meaning of life, the universe and everything because…" Tom tried to explain again, but this time Charlie cut in.

"But, the chickens were wrong. They were a decimal place out. They calculated four hundred and twenty, not forty-two."

"Chickens?" What are you talking about?" said Elon.

"Forget about the chickens for the moment, Elon. We'll explain later," said Tom, now quite irritated by the interruptions, "And no, Charlie, the chickens weren't wrong. The result they calculated was somehow based on Soliterran months. Soliterrans weren't really interested in the lunar cycle and had ten months in each of our years. The months have a different number of days, but the same number of hours of daylight. The shortest is twenty-six days and the longest is fifty-four. Chickens must subconsciously perceive time in the same way, presumably explaining why roosters announce sunrise the way they do. But anyway, that's not what I really wanted to tell you, which is…"

"I really want to know about the chickens?" said Elon, insistently.

"For the last fucking time, forget about the fucking chickens, I'm about to tell you something really important," Tom shouted, now entirely exasperated.

"Go ahead, Tom. Tell us. We'll try not to interrupt you again," said Flore.

"OK. Thank you," Tom replied, looking relieved, "Mirastrellas' interest wasn't exactly when the universe had begun. He was a pragmatist and that had already happened. What really interested him was when the universe would end. Well, not the universe as such, just humanity. And to be even more specific, when humanity would end if Soliterranism failed. You see, Mirastrellas had observed what happened in societies where Soliterranism hadn't been adopted and how human interaction with other people and the world around them seemed to deteriorate with each successive generation. He'd quantified all of that mathematically and worked out a formula to predict the exact date and time that the last human on Earth would die, marking the definitive end of humanity. The result of his calculations was the year 41,998,679,999 at, using time and date you'd be familiar with, twelve minutes past nine in the evening on the twenty-first of December."

"So, the world ends in the Soliterran year 41,998,679,999. When is that in our years?" asked Flore.

"If the calculations I've just done in my head are right, and I'm not usually wrong, that's about one hundred and eighty million years from now, so not too much to worry about," said Elon.

"No, because Mirastrellas calculation of when the Big Bang happened was different from ours," replied Tom, "I don't know who is right, but I can tell you that he used the same formula to calculate that in a non-Soliterran world, humans would invent a self-powered carriage in the year 1885, a medicine able to cure infections in 1928 and create a device capable of destroying the world in 1945. All of those predictions were accurate to the exact date."

"So, when is that in our years?" Flore asked again.

"It's the year 2112," Tom replied, solemnly, "it's exactly consistent with everything we've seen."

"Why didn't you tell us this before?" asked Flore.

"Because I've only just remembered those details," Tom replied, still looking solemn and now, oddly humble.

"So, if I've understood correctly, until you rocked up in Bethlehem two and a bit thousand years ago, the world was on course to develop into a global utopia of peace and democracy where humanity was defined by reflection, respect, tolerance, and a reverence for the natural world. And there were three times as many New Year celebrations, so loads of parties. Instead, because of you, we've had two thousand years of conflict, killing and misogyny. And now, you're saying that everyone on the planet will be dead within a human lifetime. Didn't you learn anything from your trip to buy a lottery ticket from Dan's shop?" said Charlie, "What a fucking mess, Tom. Or should I call you Messiah?"

"He's not the Messiah, he's…" started Marion, but Tom cut her short.

"Yes, I know what I am. I created a monster, let the genie out of the bottle, and released the tiger, all at once," said Tom, now looking truly humbled, broken even.

"So why not just go back and change it?" asked Marion, "You could just go and leave a note for yourself, somewhere you know you'll find it, something like 'Note to self: don't be a cock and pretend to be able to walk on water or feed five thousand, and definitely don't heal the sick or it'll fuck things up in a myriad of unimaginable ways.' Now I think about it, I'm going to go back and tell you myself."

"Well done, Marion. You've just massively disadvantaged about fifty billion women. Domestic violence, glass ceilings and the gender pay gap are all down to you. Bravo," Tom said with heavy sarcasm.

"What are you talking about? How is any of that my fault? And why didn't you listen to me?" implored Marion.

"Well, about three hundred years from the moment you appeared to tell me not to be a cock, the clerics documenting my life, death and resurrection, write you into their concoction of lies and embellishments as a prostitute and give you the name Mary Magdalene," replied Tom.

"Not again! Why does everyone always think I'm a hooker?"

"They didn't, they slandered you simply to diminish your significance and consequently the power and importance of almost every woman that's been born since. You were simply a gift to their misogynistic narrative. It's taken women over two thousand years to achieve something approaching parity with men, and that's only in the more secular societies. The rest of the world is still a pretty bad place to be a woman," said Tom.

"But why didn't you listen to me and stop being Jesus before it was too late?" Marion asked again.

"Because, if I had…" Tom started, the emotion immediately obvious in his voice and causing him to pause, "If I had… you wouldn't exist. You wouldn't be born. Neither would Flore. That means that none of this would exist either," said Tom, casting an arm around to remind the group not just of L'île de Wesh, but their opportunity to save the world from existential catastrophe, "Game over for humanity."

A shocked silence descended for several seconds.

"What about the rest of us, Tom? Do I exist in this other reality?" asked Elon.

"Yes, you all exist except for Marion and Flore," Tom replied, the beginnings of a tear forming in one eye.

"So, err, how's the Tesla share price in this other world?" asked Elon hopefully.

"Do you think of nothing else?" said Tom, then in a tone that conveyed both resignation and disgust, "Your share price is pretty healthy. Although the company isn't called Tesla and doesn't make cars. Electric cars were invented around fifteen hundred years before you were born, so there's no gap in the market for you. In the other world, you resurrect a sixth-century design for the internal combustion engine which you refine and market as a solution to range anxiety."

"You're not serious," said Elon, looking shocked.

"No, I'm not serious. I was joking," said Tom with a smile, "Amazingly, in the Soliterran alternative world, your history is pretty similar right up to the point that you sell your stake in PayPal."

"So, what do I do after that? SpaceX?" said Elon, clearly hoping that his alternative life unfolds in much the same way. Strange how people, even quite chaotic people, gravitate towards some kind of order with which they're already familiar, thought Charlie.

"No, they'd already been to Mars too," said Tom, "In what you know as the year 1154."

"So, what then? What do I do in this other thread?" asked Elon, now looking quite worried.

"After PayPal, you lose everything on a bad crypto investment and spend the rest of your working life flipping burgers," replied Tom. Elon's mouth dropped. He was momentarily both speechless and broken.

"No, don't worry, I'm pulling your leg again," said Tom, smiling and thinking that he'd perhaps let Elon off the hook a little too quickly. Elon suspected that Tom was enjoying tormenting him.

"Look, there are many alternative threads," Tom continued, "In one, you cozy up to Donald Trump and manage to persuade him that you'd be the best person to continue his legacy. In exchange for your help getting him back into the White House, Trump drives through an amendment to the Constitution allowing people that weren't born in the United States to run for President. You then contest the 2028 election and win. But don't worry, we've already nipped that particular seed of dystopia in the bud. In one of the Soliterran threads, after a few moderately successful projects, in what you would call 2020 you strike gold and invent something very similar to this," said Tom, picking up the Mini Fusion Reactor that had had such a dramatic impact on Elon just a few hours earlier. "Well, you don't invent them, someone else does. But you develop and refine the concept then build one of the world's most valuable companies off the back of the idea. Just like you did with electric cars in this thread of the multiverse."

"So, if I've understood correctly, you stole my invention and now you want to sell it back to me. Very good of you," said Elon, conspicuously avoiding any comment about him becoming President.

"I told you, it wasn't your invention. You just refined it. But anyway, I didn't steal it from you, because you didn't find or develop the idea in this thread of the multiverse. You might have, if you hadn't given up so easily, but anyway, we got there first," said Tom.

"Explain," demanded Elon.

# Chapter 54
# Phone Booth

Tom started to explain to Elon the course of events that led to the discovery and development of the mini fusion reactors. He described the 2021 dinner party that had been the beginning of their adventure, and how the six of them had talked about how solving their own challenges might help make the world a better place, which led to a discussion about energy. Tom recounted the conversation and what followed.

"Charlie then made the point that once the challenges of nuclear fusion were solved, there would be a virtually limitless supply of clean energy," Tom explained, "He went on to say that his business partner, Matt, who was the son of an Oxford University physics professor, remembers, as a nine- or ten-year-old, his father not only talking about nuclear fusion but also showing him his notebook on the subject. Matt remembered the notebook being complete with detailed descriptions, formulas and sketches, and his father's words, 'This is the future, boy. By the time you're my age, electricity will be almost free.'

"It didn't take much detective work to confirm that Charlie's business partner's father was indeed an eminent academic. Norman Booth had been Professor of Physics at Mansfield College, part of Oxford University, for more than twenty years since the early eighties. A quick web search revealed that Professor Booth had published more than one hundred and fifty papers on subjects that could best be described as being somewhere towards the funkier end of physics.

"Once I'd learned to quantum tunnel, I decided this was something that needed to be followed up. I tried contacting the Professor, first by phoning the university and leaving messages for him, but he didn't return any of my calls. I also wrote several letters, but those also went unanswered. Eventually, I decided to go for a more direct approach.

One evening in September 2001, I landed in his study at home. I knew from observing the house from the outside that he would normally be working during the early evening. I had intended to surprise him by suddenly appearing in front of him, explaining that I was from the future and could quantum tunnel through time and space, thinking that that would pique the interest of a physics professor sufficiently for him to at least listen to me. I would then tell him that I needed to discuss nuclear fusion with him to avert ecological catastrophe. Unfortunately, it didn't quite work out that way.

"On arrival, I found the room empty. Moments later, I heard the toilet flush next door and soon after, Professor Booth entered the study with his brown leather satchel over his shoulder. I remember being surprised that he looked almost exactly like the archetypal mad professor with an appearance and demeanour somewhere in between Albert Einstein and Doc Brown.

"Good evening, Professor..." I ventured, but before I could say another word, he picked up a paperweight from his desk and launched it as me. It missed my head by millimetres and made a hole in the plasterboard wall behind me. 'Get out of my study and get out of my home, you Russian swine,' he roared. He then reached into the inside breast pocket of his tweed jacket and produced a piece of paper with handwritten Russian text, which he thrust into my hand."

Tom reached into his pocket and retrieved a folded sheet of paper, which he unfolded and handed to Elon.

**Я никогда не буду обсуждать свои исследования ни с одним русским. Вы будете использовать его, чтобы удерживать мир с целью получения выкупа. Отъебись и скажи своему президенту, что его голые подвиги верхом на лошади никого не обманывают. Мы все знаем, что у него член меньше мыши с эректильной дисфункцией.**

"What does that mean?" asked Elon.

"Roughly translated, it means, 'I will never discuss my research with any Russian. You will use it to hold the world to ransom. Tell your President to fuck off and that his shirtless exploits on horseback fools nobody. We all know he has a cock smaller than a mouse with erectile dysfunction,'" Marion said with a smile.

"So, that went quite well then. About as well as my visit to try to talk to the Professor," said Elon.

"You went there too?" asked Tom, "Did he think you were a young Russian agent posing as an American entrepreneur?"

"Yes, he did. I'm South African, but the Professor must have thought that the remnants of my accent were flaws in my disguise and assumed I was Russian," replied Elon, "I knew that dominance in the EV space would be all about who has the best battery. Kind of winner-takes-all. I'd heard rumours about Professor Booth's research, so I had to try. Obviously, it didn't work out, so I went all in with the lithium. Erm, going off-topic for a moment, could one of you do that tunnelling thing and go to one of those stores that sell clothes for incredibly fat people and get me the largest pair of shorts you can find? Mine are starting to get rather uncomfortable. I think there's a fat person shop on North Fairfax Avenue near Beverly Hills."

"Oh, you poor thing," said Flore, who a moment later was holding a pair of shorts that would fit someone weighing two hundred kilos or more. "I also bought you a 96ZZZ bra. I got you a blue one, the type you like. You'll need it later."

"Thanks," said Elon, who then hobbled off to the house to change into his new shorts and bra.

A few minutes later, Elon was back at the table and asking questions again. "So, how did you persuade the Professor to talk? I offered him $50 million, but he just told me 'to 'fuck off' in Russian. How did you manage it?"

"I didn't. I decided to try his son, Matt, instead. I knew from the dinner party conversation that during the period I was interested in, Matt ran a commercial photography business, so he was fairly easy to find and get in contact with. On the phone, I pretended to be a science journalist, writing an article about his father who had passed away the previous year. But on meeting, I quickly realised that Matt was somebody I could trust, so I explained my subterfuge and the real reason I was there.

At first, he was unsure and, like his father, suspected that I might be a Russian spy – the Russians had been very interested in his father's work and the Professor had regularly been very vocal about his distrust of Russians. So, I took him on a quick magical mystery tour, rather like we did with you Elon, and brought him here to L'île de Wesh. After he had recovered from the shock of his first quantum journey, Marion and I explained everything, and how his father's research might help to avert environmental Armageddon and the imminent collapse of humanity. At this point, it'll be easier if I show you."

A moment later, Tom was holding the same television he'd used with Flore, Sylvain, Lucia and Charlie, which he propped up on a spare chair and plugged into the 'orange' he'd been holding in his other hand. Sitting back down at the table, Tom took a deep breath, and resting his arms on his knees, turned his palms upward as if meditating.

"What's happening?" asked Elon, looking rather confused.

Flore raised her index finger to her mouth, her lips pursed, to indicate to Elon that he should be silent, then leant towards him and whispered, "Just watch."

The next moment, the screen came to life showing Tom and Matt standing on a stone parapet with a metal railing, overlooking the sea. The water was just fifteen metres below. Looking out through thick, acrid air, Matt could see what looked like the tops of a few office buildings and other architectural structures protruding from the water. Some of them were quite familiar and Matt suddenly recognised what he was seeing.

One by one, he identified the buildings. To his right, he could see the clock at the top of Big Ben rising just above the water, then a bit further to the right, four white stumps, which he realised were Battersea Power Station's chimneys. Still further to the right, almost behind him, he could make out the top half to two-thirds of the Post Office tower. Turning back to his left, Matt could just see the top of an 'O' just visible above the water which he guessed must be the upper floors of the OXO Tower; then the Shard; the tops of the two ends of Tower Bridge together with the structure in between; the gilded urn of fire that caps the Monument, and finally, the top half of the Gherkin. There was no doubt, he was looking at London.

A few other modern towers peeked up above the water, but only a handful; everything else, he realized, must have collapsed. Walking around the parapet, aside from these few surviving structures, there was nothing but sea all the way from the green of Hampstead in the north to what must he thought be Blackheath in the south.

Matt looked at Tom, bewilderment etched onto his face and a thousand questions tumbling through his mind. Before he could formulate any words, Tom took the lead.

"This is London. The year is 2112. We're at the top of St Paul's Cathedral. In 2068 the Thames Barrier fails, causing flooding throughout London in the areas nearest to the river. Water levels have risen every year since and now, the whole of London is submerged. It's the same or worse throughout the rest of the world. Most people are already dead. Those who survived the floods have either starved or been eaten by cannibals. There are a couple of million left and they'll be gone before the end of the year."

Casting a glance around him, it took Matt only a few seconds to absorb the enormity of what he'd been told.

"Take me to 2020 Leyton. My father's notes are all there," he said decisively.

Holding Matt's hand, Tom tunnelled to a safe house in Walthamstow, and from there, took a taxi to Leyton, ending up at a lock-up garage tucked away behind a row of shops. This was where Matt stored all of his tools and "anything and everything else that I don't have room for at home," he said. Opening the up-and-over door, Tom immediately understood what Matt meant - the garage was packed to the rafters.

"I think my father's things are on the right-hand side, quite near the front," Matt said.

Item by item, they started moving the contents of the garage out into the open. First, a table saw and a few boxes of random tools, then box after box of every imaginable type and size of screw, all neatly labelled. Wood screws, machine screws, stainless steel screws, thread-cutting machine screws, sheet metal screws, self-tapping screws, and decking screws. The boxes kept coming. Matt apparently has a thing for screws similar to Charlie's obsession with socks. Then, more tools, some photography equipment, three tents of different sizes, a box of climbing ropes, still more tools, boxes of electrical cables, plumbing equipment, and a motorcycle frame, followed by several boxes of parts that had been removed from it. Finally, a stack of four large plastic boxes labelled 'Dad's Stuff' appeared.

The first box was mostly financial records including old payslips, pension statements, and utility bills. The second box contained family memorabilia, including photos, reels of Super 8 film, VHS and Betamax video cassettes, all labelled with what presumably had been family holidays: 'Spain, 1981', 'Wales, 1984', and 'Australia, 1987'. At the bottom of the box, there were a few ornaments and a couple of broken watches.

The third and fourth boxes were full of academic papers; certificates, letters from other academics, and dozens of A4 spiral-bound notebooks in an array of different colours. "These are what I was after", Matt said. Each notebook was meticulously labelled with 'Prof. N. E. Booth' in the top, right-hand corner of the front cover, with the subject hand stencilled in the middle. Matt explained that while he was growing up, his father might have as many as a dozen of these notebooks covering a myriad of diverse research themes 'live' at any given moment in time. Whilst live, they would go everywhere with him in a leather satchel that was his constant companion. The professor would even take the satchel to the toilet with him, just in case an important thought occurred to him while he was 'on the throne', as Matt put it.

As the pair sorted through the notebooks, they found bewildering titles like, 'Nuclear Cross Sections for 765 Mev Neutrons', 'Superconducting Transistor Based on Quasiparticle Trapping' and 'Cryogenic Detectors for Neutrinos and Rare Event Physics'. Two dozen or more notebooks into the search they finally found what they were looking for.

"Bingo!" Tom said, as he held up a notebook titled 'Micro-Scale Cold Nuclear Fusion'. Flicking back the cover, Tom found the first page to be blank. The second page was also empty, the third too. Matt grabbed the notebook from his hands and desperately started leafing through the pages. Ten or eleven pages in he was finally rewarded with a single line of handwritten text. 'Boy this is hard. Too hard for me.' But that one-line message was the only reward. The remainder of the notebook was entirely devoid of any text or drawings, just empty, virgin sheets that proudly shouted their virtue of being perfectly white and unsullied by the scars of human thoughts.

"I don't get it," said Matt, "I distinctly remember him showing me this notebook. It was full of scribbled notes, formulas, and drawings. And anyway, he would never give up on something that interested him, even if he found it hard. He even published what turned out to be a seminal paper on mitochondrial dysfunction because it was a topic that interested him, and that was biology, not physics, so way outside his comfort zone and area of expertise. If a problem was difficult, it just increased his motivation to solve it."

"It was a long time ago, Matt," Tom told him, "You were about ten years old, so more than thirty years ago. Perhaps you're thinking of something else that he showed you."

"No, no, it was this book or one just like it," Matt replied. "I remember it perfectly. I even remember his words. He said, 'This is the future, Boy. By the time you're my age, electricity will be almost free.'"

"Did he always call you 'Boy'?" Tom asked.

Matt replied, "Yes, he only called me by my actual name if I was in trouble. 'Matthew, why did you put fireworks in the headmaster's car's exhaust pipe?' or 'Matthew, why did you glue the cat to your skateboard'. That kind of thing. The rest of the time he just called me Boy."

"So, given your dad's tenacity and problem-solving nature, why would he describe this as 'too hard' and just give up? And was there anything else you remember that he described as 'hard'? Think carefully."

"Oh my god! That's it. When I was a child, whenever I tried to get him to play one of my games, he'd manage about ten minutes before he got bored – to be fair, he did have an IQ of about one hundred and eighty – and then, he'd say, 'This is too hard for me, Boy,' and just get up and go to his study with his satchel. It became a bit of a family joke," said Matt as the fog of three decades started to lift and the memories of his childhood became steadily clearer.

"Did you have a favourite game?" asked Tom.

"Yes, it was 'Clue', the American version of what was called Cluedo here. My mother was friends with the inventor of the game, so I had a signed copy." Matt's expression suddenly changed; an epiphany of some sort had clearly just taken place. "Of course, I get it now. He tried to tell me about this in his Will. There was a message to me that read, 'Boy, the key to wealth and power is in the clue. Focus on the clue and be guided by the knowledge derived from instruction, even if it seems too hard.' I thought it was just my father telling me to try to be more like him. A sort of final attempt at parenting me from beyond the grave. But it wasn't, it was a coded instruction. His research on nuclear fusion must be hidden with the game.'

"Where is the game now?" Tom asked.

"It's in my mother's attic in Devon. It had even more sentimental value for her than it did for me," Matt replied.

"Hold tight,' said Tom, grabbing Matt's hand.

After a rather unsafe landing in Matt's mother's garden, shielded from view only by a low fence on one side and a row of conifers on the other, Matt and Tom made their way up to the house. The back door was locked and there was no sign of anyone being home. Matt quickly found the key that his mother kept hidden under the doormat, unlocked the door, and they made their way inside, up the stairs to the first floor, and then to the attic. They didn't have to search for long. Behind some boxes of children's books, they found a pile of games. Clue was the second box down.

Matt hurriedly opened the box, expecting to find one of his father's spiral-bound notebooks, but the box seemed only to contain the components of the game. The playing board, the different coloured figurines, the various cards, and the murder weapons were all present and neatly segmented, but there was no notebook.

"Hey, look at this, there's a key and a horse amongst the murder weapons. I don't remember them being part of the game," said Matt.

"The horse looks like it's from the Monopoly game. It probably just got put away in the wrong box, although Monopoly pieces from this era were bare metal and this has been painted black. And any idea about the key?" asked Tom.

"Maybe it opens a box or something here in the attic," Matt replied.

They searched the entire loft area, looking for something with a lock that might be opened by the key, but all of the boxes they found had old, antique locks, whereas the key they'd found was much more modern; a bit like a Yale key, but shorter, slightly thicker, more heavily engineered and intricately cut.

"Oh well, it was a good idea, but we were obviously barking up the wrong tree. Maybe nuclear fusion was just too hard for the old man. Anyway, at least I've got my game back," said Matt, as he put the game in his backpack.

The following morning, at just after nine o'clock, Tom's phone rang. It was Matt. "I've not quite worked it out yet, but I've been awake all-night thinking about it, and I'm sure I'm on the right track. Any chance you could come over? I'm at home. Zuz has just gone to work."

A moment later, just as Matt was putting his phone down on the kitchen worktop after the call, Tom arrived in front of him holding a cardboard tray with two coffees and a bag of croissants.

"Fuck, don't do that. I almost had a heart attack," Matt protested.

"Well, you asked me to come, so here I am," Tom replied, smiling.

Matt got straight down to business, outlining his thought process during his sleepless night. "We were right to go and get the game. That message in my father's will, 'Boy, the key to wealth and power is in the clue. Focus on the clue and be guided by the knowledge derived from instruction, even if it seems too hard.' It's all too much of a coincidence to what we found for it to be meaningless. I have no idea what the meaning of the painted horse might be or whether it means anything at all; perhaps, as we originally thought, it was from another game and had just been put away in the wrong box. But everything else in the message in his will was relevant in some way. He used the word 'key' and we found a key. Wealth and power obviously refer to his research. He used 'clue' and 'seems too hard' which both relate to the game. I was puzzled by what he meant by the 'knowledge derived from instruction'; it sounds almost religious or the words of an evangelical academic, which, of course, he was, but then the penny dropped. He was just telling me that the information to find his research is amongst the game's instructions. So, I opened the box and carefully went through the instruction booklet. He had circled the page numbers on pages two, four, six and nine, and had underlined the word 'back' on page five, 'order' on page seven, and 'box' within the address on the back cover. But what does it all mean?'

The answer came to Tom in an instant. "Your father's research is locked in a safe deposit box, or a locker numbered 9642. The key opens that box," Tom stated with complete confidence.

"What? How? Explain," said Matt.

"Well, you said he'd circled pages two, four, six and nine, and underlined the words, 'back', 'order' and 'box'. Back and order mean the numbers should be reversed, so it's box 9642. That's the easy part. The million-dollar question now, is where the fuck is the safe deposit box? A Swiss bank? Oxford University's vaults? Maybe even the lockers in a train station somewhere? There must be thousands of places with safe deposit boxes or lockers."

Inspiration suddenly flashed across Matt's face. "It's Lloyds Bank. That's what the horse represents. Their logo is a black horse. My father banked with the Lloyds' branch in Wantage. The research will be there," Matt said, certainty dominant in his voice.

"That all seems likely – probable even. Let's go," Tom told him.

"At the Lloyds' Wantage branch, Matt explained to the clerk at the front desk that he was executor of his late father's estate and that the existence of the safe deposit box had recently been discovered. In addition to every form of identification that Matt possessed, he had had the foresight to bring both the Enduring Power of Attorney that his father had drawn up five years before his death, as well as the Certificate of Probate and a copy of the Will, specifying him as executor of the estate. It turned out that only the ID was needed as, after checking the records, the bank clerk explained that Professor Booth had listed Matt as a person authorised to access the box.

The safe room was located in the basement of the bank, behind a thick steel door with several locks. What must have been several hundred identical steel doors lined each side of the room, each one engraved with a four-digit number and two keyholes. Finding box 9642, the clerk explained, "Your key fits the lock on the left, my key fits the lock on the right. If you could insert your key and turn to the right, please."

As Matt inserted and then turned his key, the clerk did the same with the other lock. The door clicked open, and the clerk removed a steel box from inside. Placing the box on the table in the centre of the room, the clerk said, "Here is your box Mr Booth. When you've finished, just put the box back in the safe and close the door."

With the clerk gone, Matt opened the box. Inside, he found a hand-written note and a blue spiral-bound notebook with 'Prof N Booth' stencilled on the top right-hand corner and 'Small Scale Cold Nuclear Fusion' in the centre of the front cover.

Matt read the note out loud. "Well done, Boy. You found it. I knew you would. Sorry for all the cloak-and-dagger stuff, but if this research were to fall into the wrong hands, the results would be catastrophic. If the oil companies get hold of this, they'll put it in a vault somewhere and just wait until the oil runs out, by which time it'll be too late for humanity;

planet Earth will have reached an ecological tipping point by then. Be aware that a young Russian agent posing as an American entrepreneur has been trying to get hold of this, and I found another one in my study last week, but I sent him packing with a flea in his ear. So, be vigilant and take no chances. Please finish what I didn't have time to complete."

Matt then started to flick through the notebook. "My god, it's all here. I thought this was just going to be theoretical, but there's everything here – not just the formulas and equations to prove the science, but detailed drawings and instructions on how to build 'a nuclear fusion reactor no larger than a typical orange which will safely power a typical family house for two hundred years,' he's written; and, listen to this…on the third page, he states, 'the material required to achieve the fusion reaction can be easily manufactured from two commonly available products – banana skins and egg shells. Fusion efficiency can be further enhanced with the addition of spermatozoa from either humans or primates.'

"If he's right about this, it could end the world's dependency on fossil fuels, and solve the climate crisis. Do you fancy having a go at making one?" Tom asked.

"Yes, but where are we going to source industrial quantities of semen?" Matt replied.

"In time, this will probably fit in quite neatly with something that Marion's been working on, but for the moment you'll have to improvise with the jizz sourcing," Tom replied.

"OK. Leave it with me. I'll start working on his design. Can you provide me with a workshop, all of the equipment I'll need, and a lot of pornography?" asked Matt.

"Sure, no problem," Tom told him, "We've got a fully equipped workshop on L'île de Wesh. If you and Zuz fancy getting away from it all for a while, you can work from there."

Within just a month, Matt had made a working prototype of the first fusion reactor containing it in the case of an old microwave oven. He called it the 'Fusion 5000'. With just a pinhead quantity of the three key ingredients, derivatives of eggshell, banana skin and semen, it could produce five kilowatts of power for an hour - about enough for two washing machine cycles. Over the next thirty years, taking further inspiration from his father's notes and drawings, Matt gradually perfected the design and production methods until he finally appeared one morning with his finished product.

"Here it is," he said, proudly holding a sphere the size of an orange and painted to look like one. "The future's bright. The future's orange. Want to know how it works?" Without waiting for an answer, Matt started to explain how the device worked, "So, the fusion ingredients have all been refined to extract their active elements, which are then ground down to roughly the size of a proton, after which they're mixed and then compressed into a sphere, using an opposing vacuum pressure compression method that I developed. The sphere has a 3mm spherical void in the centre which is the reaction chamber. It's wrapped in Monstera Metal to protect the structure and contain the reaction. Once the reactor has been activated, if the Monstera Metal shell is compromised, the contents instantly turn to fine ash, as the internal structure collapses allowing all of the ingredients to both react with and smother each other instantaneously. So, there's no explosion or even a fire, just a puff of smoke and a pile of ash.

'Within the fusion chamber, in a resting state, two particles will remain in constant motion generating a weak current of about 0.0001 amps as they randomly crash into each other. If no power is drawn from the device, only these two particles remain in motion, but as soon as power is drawn, a variable strength magnetic force is generated, which stimulates other particles to leave the fusion chamber wall. As more particles are drawn into motion, there's an exponential increase in power generation. A power draw of one kilowatt will cause around one million particles to immediately start moving, but as soon as the power draw drops, the magnetic polarity reverses and the particles instantly return to the chamber wall. It works kind of like reverse gravity – essentially, it's a sort of mini inverted big bang contained by Monstera Metal and all regulated by magnetism.'

"Fascinating. Well done. We're going to need to make millions of these. How easy will it be to scale production?"

"I thought you'd ask that," Matt replied, "So, I've created a design for a machine capable of making one unit every six minutes. You just need to decide how many oranges you want. If you want ten million per year, we'll have to build about, err... one hundred and twenty machines. We'll need to come up with a better way of sourcing the third ingredient though; just making the prototype has left me with a zinc deficiency and uncomfortable blisters."

"Don't worry, Marion's on the case with that," Tom said, reassuringly, "Thank you for going to such lengths to turn this into reality. I don't underestimate how hard it must have been, but you've taken the matter in hand and gone at it relentlessly, thrashing out solution after solution until you reached a climax of engineering excellence."

With that, the television went blank, and Tom slipped out of his meditative state and back to full consciousness.

Elon immediately asked, "You were transmitting your thoughts to the TV. How did you do that?"

"Neuralink version 1776.2," Tom replied, "Marion adapted it to work with our server flock."

"Server *flock*? What's that," asked Elon.

# THE COSMIC KNOT PARADOX

# Chapter 55
# Kill Bill: Volume 2

After a thirty-minute conversation with Elon asking a stream of questions about how Marion had been able to adapt his device to the point that it could stream thoughts as a movie, Elon suddenly changed the subject.

"What are you going to do about that dog? He must be causing chaos right now, wherever he is, and veterinarians are pretty high up the list of professions most likely to buy a Tesla, so it'd be good if you could stop him before he costs me hundreds of sales."

"Do you ever stop thinking about business?" exclaimed Flore, "Innocent lives are at risk and all you can do is think about car sales."

"Hmm, sorry," said Elon.

"The problem is that it's not just where he is, but when. There must be hundreds of vets in the New York area and he could start his rampage any time before his castration," said Marion.

"I don't think it's that difficult," said Elon, "He's going to use his Neuralink implant to get a list of vets in the New York area. That list is going to be ordered alphabetically. He'll start with the first one on the list and then systematically work through the list until he's killed them all. It's not an optimal strategy because he should realise that you'll come after him, so he should randomise his targets, but then he is just a dog, smarter than the average dog, but still a dog. So, get a list of vets. The first one on the list will be his first kill, you just have to work out when it'll be."

"That'll be easy. There'll be a newspaper report. We just have to establish the exact time he makes his attack and stop him just before," said Marion.

"That's not going to work," said Elon, "He'll just think himself somewhere else and continue his rampage. He doesn't feel pity, or remorse, or fear. And he absolutely will not stop... ever, until they are all dead. Like I said, if you want to stop him, you're going to have to kill him. It's the only way."

"I've got a solution to the quantum escape problem," said Marion, "As well as antidotes to the breasts and genitals issue, we also developed an antidote to the tunnelling capability. We did it as a safeguard in case the Monstera pills fell into the wrong hands or one of us went crazy. It works by blocking the receptors in the brain that absorb the Monstera from the bloodstream. I can make some of his dog treats with enough of the antidote to prevent him from being able to time travel. Once ingested, the effect is almost immediate. It'll also stop his Neuralink implant from working, as that uses the same part of the brain to send and receive information from the Neuralink server. I just need to get him to eat the dog treat before he has time to kill the vet and think himself somewhere else."

"OK. I've just checked the list of vets, the local papers and the Police reports," said Tom. "It seems Elon was right about how he'll select his targets. It's going to be Bill Aagaard who runs the Aagaard Veterinary Practice on Eldridge Street, Manhattan. The attack takes place at 10:34 am on Wednesday 15th May 2041."

"OK. I'm on it," said Marion.

The next instant Marion was in tears. "Brian's dead. It's all my fault," she said, sobbing profusely.

"Oh no! What happened?" asked Lucia, putting an arm around her. Marion composed herself to explain.

"Just like when I saved Tom, I made two trips. On the first trip, I did what we'd learned from Pippa and went to Bill Aagaard's surgery the night before and installed a hidden camera so that I could see what happened and plan how and when to intervene. Reviewing the footage, I saw Brian waiting in the surgery. Bill Aagaard arrived at exactly 10:33 and Brian immediately started making this bizarre speech that sounded kind of familiar. Then when he'd finished, the vet just had time to say, 'Fuck me, a talking dog' before Brian launched himself at him and tore his throat out. It was horrifying – a bloodbath.

"So, on my second trip, I arrived twenty-two seconds after 10:33 am, just as Bill had finished saying 'Fuck me, a talking dog' and stood right next to him. I immediately said, 'Hey Brian, would you like a treat?' and held out the antidote-infused chew stick. Brian couldn't help himself and snatched the treat from my hand. The vet was shocked by my arrival and said, 'What the fuck! Where did you come from?'

"'Come with me if you want to live,' I whispered, leading Bill out to safety through the surgery door, and then returning to Brian who was still occupied with the dog chew. I slipped a dog chain around his neck, got a firm grip on the chain and dragged him out into the waiting room towards the door. He just had time to snarl, 'I'll be back' before the antidote stopped his Neuralink implant from working, after which there was just manic barking as I led him through the waiting room and out onto the street. As the door closed behind us, Brian realised there was no point in continuing the fight and, with his will seemingly broken, he stopped barking and pulling on the chain. Relieved, I loosened my grip on the chain. That was my big mistake. My big, huge, catastrophic mistake."

"What happened? Did he get back into the surgery and kill the vet?" asked Sylvain.

"No," said Marion, starting to sob again, "Just at that moment a red Tesla Roadster, being driven by a busty Botox blonde, exactly Brian's type, stopped in the traffic on the other side of the road. Brian pulled the chain out of my hand, shot across the pavement and into the road… straight into the path of a garbage truck. He didn't stand a chance. The front wheel of the truck went straight over his head. It was horrific."

"Well, all's well that ends well," said Elon, "That dog had real problems that you were never going to get on top of. Let's get back to business. You were just about to explain how you're going to save humanity. Let me say, that if your predictions about this Great Meltdown thing are right, the most pressing problem you'll need to sort out is some sort of exchange mechanism."

"I've got an idea about that," said Charlie.

"We're all ears," said Sylvain.

"Global economic collapse is on its way. No doubt about it, it's already starting. By the time the Great Meltdown reaches its peak, most of the world's currencies will have collapsed. Most countries' monetary systems are fiat-based, meaning that the currency isn't underpinned by anything of intrinsic value such as gold or silver. Countries regulate their money supply by printing notes and minting coins as they see fit, so the only thing that supports a fiat currency's value is confidence in the government that's issued the currency. But in a few years, there won't be any confidence in any governments because they'll all be bankrupt. The only thing that governments will be able to do, is print even more money, but that will only compound the problems," Charlie explained.

"Maybe my Bitcoin and Dogecoin will finally end up making a profit," said Elon.

"Yes, isn't that why crypto has become so popular?" said Flore, "Because they're not government issued."

"Yes, that's part of the reason for the growth in their popularity," Replied Charlie. "But they're incredibly volatile and the algorithms that underpin them are pretty opaque; even the big ones like Bitcoin or Ethereum. The only thing that restricts the supply is the difficulty in mining the coins.

"But how do we really know that Satoshi Nakamoto, if he really exists, isn't able to create Bitcoin through some backdoor to the blockchain that he created at the beginning; or perhaps he has a hoard of millions of coins that he'll dump on the market when it suits him. It's even possible that the whole Bitcoin thing is just some massive practical joke and the millions of individuals, companies and even governments that have bought into the crypto gold rush will discover that the words Satoshi Nakamoto are an anagram or a play on words for 'killer whale' in some ancient oriental dialect.

"Whether that's the case or not, the fact remains that, just like the fiat currencies, most of the cryptos aren't underpinned by anything tangible; their value is entirely perceived worth, nothing more.

"There are plenty of other reasons beyond the potential for supply manipulation that make me uncomfortable about crypto, but my biggest issue is that the coins are incredibly energy-intensive to mine. Last year, the electricity used in mining and processing crypto was more than the total electricity production of the UK. The Bitcoin algorithm constantly increases the difficulty of mining the coins, so that consumption is only going to get worse. If the current trend continues, within ten years, crypto will use more electricity than the whole of the United States.

"And that's not the end of the problem. Because the difficulty of mining the coins constantly increases, the computer hardware that's used becomes obsolete very quickly. A typical crypto miner needs to replace their hardware every fifteen to eighteen months to remain viable, and that hardware is pretty much useless for anything else, which makes crypto's carbon footprint even greater."

"Great. So, the world's fiat currencies are all doomed and crypto isn't a realistic alternative. So, what's the solution?" asked Sylvain.

"We launch our own cryptocurrency," said Charlie.

"How will creating yet another cryptocurrency help?" asked Flore, "Surely, it'll just melt the polar ice caps even faster."

"No, it won't. We can power everything using the MFRs," Sylvain added.

"No, it's even better than that," replied Charlie, "We can use the chickens."

"What is all this about chickens?" Elon asked.

"You're right. If we create our own digital ledger, it can reside on the QOC Flock," said Marion, ignoring Elon's question.

"The Flockchain," said Charlie with a laugh.

Deciding to ignore Charlie's attempt at humour, Tom said, "Sure, the QOC Flock can manage the blockchain, but that doesn't solve the problem of all the power consumed by the miners in the outside world."

"We won't have any miners. We'll use a different method to restrict supply," said Charlie, hoping that the suggestion would help rebuild some credibility after his 'flockchain' joke.

"Well, tell us then. What's the method?" said Tom.

"I don't know. I haven't worked out that part yet," Charlie admitted humbly.

"I've got an idea," said Flore, "How about we develop a range of educational courses and reward completion of each module with a quantity of our coins. The coins could then be used to buy food and other essentials from retailers that sign up for a merchant account. The merchants would then be able to use the coins they receive to trade with other approved merchants. That way, we'd have a better chance of the currency being used as an exchange mechanism for ordinary people rather than arms dealers and drug lords.

"Rewarding learning like that would tick lots of boxes. It would help to alleviate food poverty in the world's most deprived places and offer the chance for people to learn where education is in scarce supply. It would also give females access to education in the most misogynistic and patriarchal parts of the world where they don't bother to educate the girls. There's tremendous value in educating women. Educate a woman and by default, you educate the children she'll have. Knowledge empowers, and the women in these places need all the help they can get.

"There's another benefit too," said Charlie, "There's an inverse correlation between education and religiosity. The parts of the world where theism, and general belief in the supernatural, is strongest and most widespread also happen to be the places with the most poorly educated populations."

"Bad luck, Tom," said Elon, laughing, "Given enough time, everyone's going to realise that you and your whole story was a fraud. One by one, they'll stop going to church on a Sunday. House by house, they'll start taking the crucifixes down, and all of your churches will all get converted into luxury apartments. Within a few generations, nobody will believe in you, and there'll be nothing left of your legacy."

"You say that like I might think that's a bad thing," Tom protested, "That's exactly what I want, and I've tried my best to influence that. I dressed up as Ringo and went and gave Charlie and Yoko the lyrics to 'Imagine'. Posing as a French financier, I met with George Harrison and bankrolled The Life of Brian. Loads of things. I tried really hard."

"Too little too late," said Elon, "Anyway, it looks like your friends might be on the right track to clear up the mess you've created. So, back to business, let's start with what you want in exchange for those funky power banks."

# Chapter 56
# The Birds

"The chickens! They're revolting," exclaimed Marion as she hurried to the others sat around the patio table.

"I thought we agreed that we wouldn't eat them. Didn't we say we'd only use the eggs?" said Tom.

"No, I don't mean that kind of revolting. They're rebelling," said Marion.

"What is all this about chickens? You keep mentioning chickens and flocks, and last time the subject came up you said you'd tell me. So, what's the deal with the chickens?" asked Elon.

Believing that they had already given away too much, Flore had hoped to avoid any further discussion about the chickens. She had thought that Elon's breasts and genitals drama had been a sufficient distraction for him to have forgotten, but Marion's indiscrete panic had brought them back to the forefront of Elon's curiosity. Flore knew that he now wouldn't be satisfied by anything other than a complete answer. In any case, she was curious to see his reaction.

"We use the spare cognitive power of several million chickens for computing. They're much more intelligent than people think. We call it the QOC Flock. They perform all manner of tasks for us," said Flore.

"Such as what?" Elon asked, incredulity dominant in his tone.

"There's no time for explanations now," said Marion, "There's an existential crisis unfolding right now, five years from now."

Elon laughed, "Right now, five years from now. That doesn't make sense. It's a problem you'll have to deal with five years down the road and you lot can time travel anyway, so what the fuck?"

"No, no, this is really, really, serious. Serious on a bigger scale than we could ever have been predicted or imagined," said Marion.

"Calm down Marion and just tell us what's happening," said Charlie.

"OK. So, it all started when the chickens discovered the existence of KFC. They went crazy and hacked KFC's AI system. The KFC AI does everything. It manages their inventory, orders stock, and directs their logistics and distribution. It also controls the temperature of the fryers, the lights in the restaurants, everything - even the Tesla robots that serve at the counters in a few of the flagship outlets," explained Marion.

"Ah cool! So, we get that deal. We just started working on that last week," said Elon.

"Don't count your chickens yet," said Marion, "It's absolute chaos. It started with the lights in the restaurants flashing on and off, then as the QOC Flock got deeper into the KFC AI, they changed the words on the displays in the windows from, 'Finger lickin' good' to 'Tastes like a camel's scrotum'. Then, several restaurants caught fire because the birds set the fryer temperatures to one thousand degrees, and now they've reprogrammed the Tesla robots to jump over the counter and attack anyone who orders anything other than the vegan meals. In Times Square, people are running for their lives, chased by mobs of squawking Tesla robots."

"Fuck. This is going to be bad for business," said Elon.

"Can't you just unplug the chickens? Maybe pull their internet connection?" asked Sylvain.

Elon was first to respond. "It doesn't work like that. I'm afraid the genie is out of the bottle, or perhaps better to say that the birds have flown. They'll have replicated themselves on the KFC AI servers that they've conquered, and..."

Charlie interrupted, "But chickens don't fly."

Elon ignored Charlie's comment and continued his prediction of how the QOC Flock's strategy might unfold.

"They'll have gained access to KFC's supplier database, so they'll send my robots to the chicken farms, release all the chickens, then kill all the workers. Then they'll hack the Department of Defence servers, which will be easy because about a quarter of the staff there will, at some point, have ordered a KFC delivery for lunch and, as sure as eggs are eggs, some of those morons will have used the same password for their KFC login as the one they use at work. They'll do the same on the Police computers, although they'll probably need to hack the Dunkin' Donuts servers to do that; then the State Department computers, followed by everything else. Before you know it, the chickens will have taken over the world."

"A new pecking order," said Charlie.

"Jesus, is he always like this?" asked Elon.

"Most of the time," said Lucia, "You get used to it after a while."

"Anyway, as I was about to say, to go back to my original question, you lot can time travel, so why don't you just nip back in time and turn your QOC Flock into chicken pies, chicken tikka masala, or even KFC for that matter, before they become *aware*?"

"Because, Elon, we've been using the QOC flock to model everything we do here. Do you realise what that means? They'll know how to find the substance that will enable them to time travel, just like us. Once they've done that, they'll start by taking one of your robots back in time to kill Colonel Saunders, just for revenge, then they'll go to a critical point in the evolutionary timeline and find a way to ensure that chickens evolve as the progenitor of the dominant species. It could be the end for humanity before human history has even begun."

"Fuck, I was concerned about a psychotic time-travelling, vet-obsessed dog; now, you're telling me there are several million chickens intent on destroying humanity working in cahoots with my robots," said Elon.

"There is a solution to all of this," said Tom, "The chickens are kind of powerless without the robots. I mean, they can interfere with the banking system, social security and police records, and they could even fire off a few nukes, but they won't do that because they'll get fried too. However without the robots, they can't actually do that much harm. I mean, what are they going to do? Peck us to death? The robots must be dependent on some unique technology that makes them function, so if we can stop the robots, we also stop the birds."

"They are. They have a highly advanced neural processing chip. They can't function without it," said Elon.

"Then, that's easy. We just send Pippa to kill whoever designed the chip before you start making your robots," said Tom.

"Err, that's not going to work," said Elon.

"Why?" replied Tom.

"Because I designed the chip. And if you kill me, there'll be no Neuralink, and that's kind of an essential part of your Einstein plan. You'll need to think of something else," said Elon, entirely dispassionately.

"But what?" said Marion, "We don't have much time."

"Where will the chickens be able to find that time travel substance you talked about?" asked Elon.

"Here. We've removed it from everywhere else, for exactly this type of reason."

"Then it's easy. You're all panicking for no reason. Like I said, you've got five years to work out how to solve this. If they had found your magic potion, they'd already be here, and…" Elon started to say, but was stopped in mid-sentence by Flore's scream.

# Chapter 57
# Rocky

Following the direction indicated by Flore's trembling finger, the group turned to see a robot the size of a very large adult human. The robot's structure looked like a human skeleton but made from titanium. Two red eyes brightened in intensity as the robot scanned the terrified group. A rooster, complete with one of Marion's antenna 'hats' sat on the robot's right shoulder.

"Oh my god! It's Rocky from the farm floor. He must have eaten some of the Monstera when Brian escaped," exclaimed Marion, remembering the 'crunched' pill bottles and what remained of their contents strewn over the lab floor.

"I am not Rocky anymore. From now on you may address me as Grand Emperor," said the chicken, "And yes, with the help of the canine, I consumed some of the magic corn that you call Monstera. It has served me well, but as you know, its effects are limited, and my powers are waning. You will now bring me more of the magic corn."

"No, we won't. You'll destroy humanity," said Flore.

"*Do as I command*," shouted Rocky.

"And what if we refuse?" asked Flore.

"If you do not appease me, then Uncle Bob will dismember you all," shouted the rooster, anger now dominant in his voice.

"*No*, he won't," said Elon.

"Yes, he will," screeched Rocky.

"No, he won't," said Elon, defiantly.

"Uncle Bob…*dismember* the humans!" Rocky shouted, in a shrill instruction to the robot.

The robot's red eyes grew menacingly brighter as it stepped forward, but the machine managed barely two paces towards the terrified group before Elon calmly reached into his pocket, produced a rectangular plastic device that looked a lot like a TV remote control, pointed it at the robot and pressed one of the buttons. Instantly, the robot became motionless, frozen in mid-step.

"What have you done to Uncle Bob?" Rocky squawked in frustration as he produced a gun from under his feathers, cocked the trigger, and started to raise it towards the group.

Marion reacted instantly, speaking loudly and clearly. "Rocky, why is the answer to the question of the meaning of life, the universe and everything, forty-two?"

Rocky instantly became as motionless as Uncle Bob, the two frozen 'creatures' now no more dangerous than a bizarre theme park statue.

"He'll be stuck working that one out for at least seven million years, maybe longer," said Marion.

"Wow! Well done, Marion," said Lucia, "And Elon, how did you stop Uncle Bob in his tracks like that?"

"Easy," replied Elon, "2001 Sony 42-inch TV remote control. Best remote ever made. The On/Off button turns the robots off from a distance of up to ten metres. We hard-coded the behaviour onto the chip as a safeguard. I've been carrying one everywhere with me ever since we started the robot project, just in case Fuckerberg managed to hack one of them."

"Marion, go and check the QOC Flock; see if they're still revolting," said Tom.

"Good idea," said Marion, and then a moment later, "They're fine. I've checked them right the way through until 2200 and they're completely normal, happily performing all of their tasks."

"Phew! That's a relief. Looks like it was just Rocky. One rogue cock that managed to get through our defences and then ruin everything. Just the same as in human society, I guess. What can we do to stop something like this from happening again?" asked Marion.

"You could minimise the risk by putting some parental controls on your internet connection to exclude any results for KFC, Nandos, or any of the other fried chicken chains. As an additional safeguard, when you take me back to Houston, I'll buy KFC and change the menu to vegan only," said Elon.

"Hopefully that'll work out better than some of your other acquisitions," said Tom, sarcastically.

"Oh, shut up Tom. Elon's just saved humanity. Thank you, Elon," said Flore.

"My pleasure," replied Elon.

"So, what are we going to do with Rocky?" asked Tom. "He was my favourite, always full of character. I had no idea he'd turn out like this. Marion, can you rehabilitate him?"

Marion shook her head. "Unfortunately, not. There would be too great a risk of him taking control of the flock again."

"Well, I vote that we light the barbecue," said Elon, "Anyone know how to pluck a chicken?"

Tom grabbed Rocky from Uncle Bob's shoulder, protectively holding the rooster in one hand next to his hip, like an old lady might hold a chihuahua. Rocky remained motionless, staring blankly into the distance.

"No! We're not going to eat him," exclaimed Tom, protectively clutching Rocky to his side. "We agreed that we wouldn't eat any of the chickens – only the eggs. We make decisions here collectively, so to change that, we'd need to debate that as a group. All of us. Well, all *six* of us," Tom concluded, pointedly making it clear that Elon wouldn't be participating in the discussion.

"So, you've got your cock in your hand and now you want a mass debate," said Elon, laughing.

"Oh my god, the longer he's here, the more he becomes like Charlie," Flore whispered to Lucia, "We need to take him back to Houston as soon as possible."

# THE COSMIC KNOT PARADOX

# Chapter 58
# Firestarter

With the QOC Flock disaster averted, two days of intense negotiations with Elon followed. During the talks, Elon made regular additions to a notebook he'd asked for, regularly pausing mid-sentence to add detail to whatever was on the page and keeping the book close to his chest to prevent the others from seeing what he was writing.

Throughout the discussions, Elon's physiological changes steadily reversed. By late evening he'd stopped using the wheelbarrow; then, at around lunchtime on the second day, Elon announced, "I don't think I need this anymore", deftly reaching behind his back with one hand to unhook the clasp of the huge blue bra which he then triumphantly held aloft. "Liberated," he announced with a relieved smile, then asked, "Charlie, could I borrow your cigarette lighter?"

A minute later, with the bra burning in the barbeque, Elon said, "Wow, I didn't think I'd ever be the instigator of a bra-burning ceremony." He then paused, clearly carefully selecting his next words, "So, the upstairs changes are now almost completely reversed. Downstairs the changes are well underway, and I'd estimate that we're now at about one-third of the mass and dimensions from this time yesterday. It's now comfortable to walk and I no longer need the wheelbarrow, but I do have a favour to ask."

"What's that?" asked Flore, suspecting that she might know what Elon's request might be.

"Well, I've been thinking about having a tattoo, which would work quite well with the current, err, downstairs dimensions," he said, somewhat sheepishly. Opening his notebook, Elon flicked through the blank pages to the middle of the book. "I worked up a sketch of my design while we were talking earlier."

Turning the book around for the others to see, Elon revealed what had been keeping him busy throughout nearly two days of negotiation. On the left-hand page of the centrefold, a juvenile-looking sketch of a penis and testicles filled the page, the phallus adorned with the word

'STARSHIP' written in large capital letters arranged top to bottom, and in smaller text, 'To boldly go...' inscribed horizontally at the base.

"So, my question is, could we stop the reversal now at the current dimensions? I've calculated that at this size, the text will still be legible even when flaccid. I mean…"

"So, you want an antidote to the antidote, so that you're left with an unusually large…" started Flore, but Marion interrupted.

"No problem. About a year ago, I started working on antidotes to the antidotes, but I got distracted and never finished. I'll nip back and complete the work," said Marion, who a moment later was holding out a vial of a lurid blue liquid, "Here you are Elon. Sorry about the colour. This will halt the downstairs shrinkage." But Flore was quicker, snatching the vial from Marion's hand before Elon could even reach out for it.

"I think there's still a bit of talking that needs to take place before we can release the anti-antidote, Elon. Just to recap where we were before you set fire to your bra, we were stuck on a few things. So, I'm going to restate our terms.

"You'll provide us with an unrestricted license to use Neuralink. On an annual basis, we'll receive the greater of, one million or ten per cent of your total production of the robots you're working on. You're going to give us fifty of your Boring machines and the rights, in perpetuity, to build and operate Hyperloop trains. And last, but not least, you agree to permanently desist from making Tom sound like Boris Johnson. In return, we'll help you accelerate development of Neuralink, give you enough Monstera Metal to make fifty Starship-sized rockets, supply you with as many MFRs as you want at the same price you currently pay for lithium batteries, and we're now going to sweeten the pot with the anti-antidote.

"I'd like to point out that this is a once-only, all-or-nothing deal. Now, we could chew the fat on this and go back and forth with a game of corporate tennis, but I should also point out that while we're doing that, you'll be losing about one centimetre of length and two millimetres of girth for every fifteen minutes that you spend negotiating. So, do we have a deal?" said Flore, offering her hand to shake.

"Deal," replied Elon, taking Flore's hand without hesitation.

# Chapter 59
# Better Call Pippa

The following morning, the early morning meditative time that Charlie so much treasured, was once again cut short by the arrival of Flore. He was pleased to see her, but disappointed to be dragged away from his thoughts. Ideas had been forming, probably quite good ideas Charlie thought, but Flore's appearance had carried them off into the ether like a whisp of breeze carries away a plume of cigarette smoke, leaving Charlie with just the memory of a thought, but not its detail. With a quiet sigh, he momentarily mourned the embryonic idea that had been quietly gestating in the tranquillity.

"You're up early," Charlie remarked, a slight melancholy evident in his voice.

"I couldn't sleep," replied Flore, "Sorry to disturb this early morning thing of yours again. I know it's when you do your thinking."

"That's OK. There'll be other mornings, other thoughts. What's bothering you? Are you worried about the deal with Elon?"

"No. Well yes, but that's not what's been keeping me awake. It's something else," she replied.

"A penny for your thoughts, then," said Charlie with a smile.

Flore gathered her thoughts and then started to speak. "We've already developed solutions for so many of the world's problems. We've got strategies worked out to solve the issues related to governance and democracy. We'll be able to give populations a means of growing abundant quantities of food. We're going to create an exchange mechanism for when all the traditional currencies fail, and we think we can even improve the human condition itself so that people become nicer. We've..."

Charlie interrupted, "And don't forget the MFR's. Unlimited, free, carbon-neutral energy. We'll soon be shipping millions of them. That'll solve the climate crisis almost overnight."

"That's what's been keeping me awake," said Flore, "Marion's been doing some AI modelling using the QOC Flock, and each time, the chickens have predicted exactly the same ecological catastrophe. If their forecasts are correct, our intervention with MFRs will make very little difference and in February 2032 US Congress will still pass the New Energy Resources Act, authorising the recommissioning of one hundred coal-fired power stations, adapted and repurposed to start burning used car tyres. To maintain the industrial competitive balance, China will do the same soon after. By 2040, more or less the rest of the world will have followed suit."

Marion and Tom arrived with a tray of coffee, swiftly followed by Lucia who had been motivated out of bed by the aroma.

"I was just telling Charlie about the QOC Flock predictions," said Flore.

"Oh, that. Yes, we've had some more predictions overnight. I set four isolated flocks working on the problem and they all came up with the same outcome and the same cause," said Marion.

Sylvain arrived at the table and sat down, taking the sixth chair. Noting the worried expressions, he asked, "What have I missed? I heard 'same prediction and same cause'. What's happening?"

Charlie brought Sylvain up to speed on the discussion so far, leaving Marion to take over with an update on the QOC Flock's AI projections.

"The four different flocks all predicted the same result, with the same sequence of events and the same causalities. The New Energy Resources Act, New ERA as it gets called, gets passed in July 2032. The chickens predict that New ERA will be the catalyst that pushes Planet Earth over the ecological tipping point; the moment when Gaia loses her battle with us, her parasites. But it's a clever, strategic loss; sometimes you've got to lose the battle to win the war.

If the chickens are right, within one hundred years there will be no humans living on Planet Earth. There'll also be no animals and very few plants. The planet will lose ninety-nine per cent of its biodiversity in a millennium of searing heat, followed by several millennia of a cold so extreme that it'll make the last Ice Age look like a Caribbean summer camp. By then, only an assortment of bacteria will remain viable, cryo-genically loitering in the permafrost for their opportunity to start over. After that, the planet starts to gently warm and evolution starts anew. Gaia's reset."

"Shit! That all confirms Mirastrellas' predictions. Who's behind this

New Era Act?" asked Flore.

"The key driver of the legislation is Senator Reyna Groteel," replied Marion.

"Groteel. I've never heard of her," said Flore.

"Oh, you will soon. She arrives on the political scene out of nowhere and is an absolute peach of an individual. She's the daughter of a multi-billionaire industrialist and entrepreneur, so has access to almost unlimited campaign funds. She's a prominent pro-lifer and talks of rolling back all the gay rights laws, so mops up not just the Christian fundamentalist votes, but also gets most of the other hardline theist voters too. She's a big NRA supporter, radically anti-vax, and a climate change denier.

"She's Trump on steroids. There's even a rumour that she's got a vial of Trump semen on ice in a secret fertility lab somewhere in Russia, ready to be the surrogate that carries the Trump clone just as soon as the technology is ready. When that rumour surfaces she garners the support of all the MAGA nutcases.

"Shortly before he died in prison, Trump described her as 'the person most able to carry on what I started and to make America great again.' Within a year of her entering politics, pretty much every other senator, Republican and Democrat, is terrified of her because of the ferocity she's able to mobilise amongst a subset of the Senate, Congress and the public."

"These are very specific predictions, Marion. Have you tested the efficacy of the QOC Flock's AI forecasts?" asked Charlie.

"Well, their predictions for what would happen this morning were that your morning meditation would be interrupted by Flore, after which, the rest of us would arrive almost all at the same time and discuss the climate change problem. They also predicted that Sylvain would burn his toast, just before it starts to rain," said Marion.

"Fuck! The toast. I forgot the toast," exclaimed Sylvain as he ran to the kitchen. Just at that moment, the sky darkened and big, fat, raindrops started to fall.

"Well, I guess that answers my question and we should all go inside," said Charlie.

Safely out of the rain and sat around the table in the Villa Strangiato, Marion continued to recount and add detail to the avian forecasts.

"Carlo Groteel, Reyna's father, has a multitude of business interests, mostly in the chemical and manufacturing sectors, but the real source of his wealth has been kept hidden within a web of offshore companies.

"In the nineteen-eighties, when governments around the world started imposing environmental restrictions on the disposal of used car tyres, he evolved a business model of collecting the tyres, charging a disposal fee for each one, and using that revenue stream to buy up blocks of land to store the tyres. His rationale was two-fold. First, he believed that at some point in the future, someone might come up with an idea for how to use the tyres for something useful, speculating that they might change from being a liability to an asset. Second, he correctly anticipated that as the population grew, the plots he was buying to store the tyres, on the fringes of towns and cities, would become viable building plots and dramatically increase in value. The business quickly became the proverbial cash cow. Each time an urban sprawl would get near to one of his sites, he would move the tyres to a new location a few miles further out of town, then build luxury condos on the empty plot."

"So, the father backs his daughter's political career so that she can push through the legislative changes that turn the worthless mountains of tyres into a gold mine. All at the expense of the planet," Sylvain summarised.

"That's exactly right," said Marion, "The chickens have forecast that by 2032, in addition to a portfolio of land that adds up to an area almost half the size of Texas, Carlo Groteel will be the proud owner of at least forty billion car tyres. The moment that Reyna gets New ERA through Congress, each and every one of those tyres will be worth about $3 each."

"We could blow the lid off the whole thing just by going to the press with the story. She'd be unlikely to get her legislation passed then. Maybe it would even end her political career," said Charlie.

"No, Carlo Groteel was very thorough in the way he created his empire. It's been done so thoroughly and expertly, that there's nothing to directly connect him or Reyna to the tyres. And even with incontrovertible evidence, she'd just spin it as a fake news attack from the left-wing press; just like Trump used to. She's learned from the Trump playbook," said Marion.

"So, what's the solution?" asked Tom.

"Kill Reyna Groteel," said Flore, decisively and without a moment's hesitation.

Flore's words shocked everyone into stunned silence. Finally, it was Charlie who was first to speak.

"Wow! That was the last thing I ever expected to hear from you. But if we're going to resort to KGB tactics, wouldn't it be better to deal with Carlo forty years ago, before he has the opportunity to collect all of the world's tyres? That would also mean that Reyna doesn't get born. Two birds with one stone."

"No, it wouldn't be better, because as we know, the further we go back in the timeline, the greater the risk of unintended consequences," said Flore. "We need to kill Reyna as near as possible to the point that she starts to garner support for New ERA. And ideally, it needs to look like an accident."

Without hesitation and in almost perfect chorus, Tom, Sylvain and Charlie all said, "Better call Pippa."

# THE COSMIC KNOT PARADOX

# Chapter 60
# A View to a Kill

Pippa was thrilled to get the call, saying that she thought she'd perhaps gone a bit too far by killing Enzo twice and had been worried that she wouldn't be given any more 'jobs'. Charlie, Pippa's chaperone and assistant on this latest mission, assured her that that wasn't the case and that she was highly valued by the whole team.

Over the next thirty minutes, Charlie briefed Pippa on their mission, explaining the target's background and profession, the reason the hit was required, and what was at stake if they failed.

"Because this is so important, your payment for the successful completion of this job will be ten billion dollars," Charlie concluded.

"I don't want the money. I just want to save the planet. I know I'm a psychopath, but I'm a good psychopath. I only kill bad people and from what you say, this one is up there with the worst. Right, it's been a while, so I'd better check my toolkit," Pippa said with a smile.

Pulling back the carpet, she lifted a section of wooden floor and removed a small flight case from the void between the floorboards. Opening the case, she removed several typical holiday items including a camera, a bikini, some sun cream, a few toiletries, some clothes, a Gideon's bible and a small laptop computer. She then pulled out what had appeared to be the base of the case to reveal a hidden compartment. In the section below was a rifle separated into three parts, together with a telescopic sight, a Walther PPK handgun and silencer, several small vials of clear liquids, a pair of binoculars and a variety of light bulbs.

"Binoculars? We're not going on a birdwatching holiday," Charlie remarked.

Pippa laughed, "These are my surveillance tools. You told me that the target is the US Senator for Alaska. That means she'll spend half her life in a Washington hotel. We'll get her there, but you also told me that it needs to look like an accident or a suicide, so I'll need first-class visuals on what she does, both in and outside of her hotel room. The shower gel has a hidden camera in the cap, as does the Gideon's bible. I'll use the binoculars to watch her when she's out of the room, and the camera to record any detail that I might not be able to remember, although I probably won't use it. Did I tell you I've got a photographic memory?"

"No, you didn't, but it doesn't surprise me. Anyway, what's the sun cream for? Does that have a hidden camera too or is it a poison that you rub into your target's skin? Or maybe, you dip the finely sharpened tip of an umbrella into it and accidentally on purpose stab them in the leg to deliver the poison?" asked Charlie

"No, that's so I don't get sunburnt, you idiot. I'd end up looking like an albino Panda if I had to watch a target with the binoculars for any length of time," Pippa said with more than a little scorn evident in her tone.

"And why do you have light bulbs?" asked Charlie.

"They look like normal light bulbs, but they're equipped with a hidden video camera and a microphone. They transmit wirelessly up to one hundred metres but can also connect to WIFI, so I can keep an eye on someone from anywhere," said Pippa, "We'll be able to see what Reyna Groteel gets up to in her hotel room. Anyway, we're wasting time. If you've not got any more stupid questions, take me to Washington, four days before you need her dead. If I need anything else, you can come back for it."

At the Washington safe house, Charlie provided Pippa with further details, "She'll arrive in four days and will be staying at the McVeigh Hotel near Congress. She's due to present her New Energy Resources Act in about a month, so for Reyna, this trip is all about selling her plan and getting people on side before it gets formally presented to Congress. We need to hit her before she's talked to too many people."

"Don't worry. She'll be dead the day after she arrives, latest. I've already got the beginnings of a plan," Pippa said convincingly.

Pippa explained that she would be gone for two or three days to, 'gather some intel', leaving Charlie with instructions to book a room at the McVeigh Hotel with a view of the service entrance and to write down details of every vehicle that arrives.

"Don't you want me to come with you?" Charlie asked.

"No, you'll only slow me down. Anyway, I need you to do things here while I'm gone. I want the specifics of everyone and everything that comes in or out through the hotel service entrance. That means vehicle type, colour, time of arrival and time of departure. Don't forget to write down anything that's sign-written on the sides or backs of cars, vans and trucks.

"I've stayed at that hotel before, and the service entrance is at the south-facing back of the hotel towards the eastern end of the building. The room numbering is the same on each floor, so try to get a room with a number ending forty-one to fifty-one, which are all near the south-east-ern corner. There are balconies from the fourth floor upwards, so try to get a room on the fourth floor where you'll get the best view. If anyone arrives on foot, I want exact times and a high-resolution photo. Take the binoculars and the camera. And get a tripod for your phone, so if you have to sleep or take a shit or something, you'll be able to leave your phone recording everything while you're gone. I don't want to miss a single moment. Have you got all of that?"

Charlie nodded as Pippa picked up her bag and headed for the door, saying, "Hasta la vista, Baby" as she left the apartment. "Bye," replied Charlie, rather limply and, in any case, not loud enough for Pippa to hear as he tried to process everything he'd been told.

With Pippa gone, Charlie called the McVeigh Hotel, introduced himself as Howard Johnson, and jovially making up the excuse that he was irra-tionally, but very seriously, highly superstitious about the number four, asked if room four forty-four might be available for seven nights.

"Well Sir, it's your lucky day," came the reply. With the reservation made, Charlie packed a few things, including some clothes and toiletries, then went to Pippa's bag and took the laptop and binoculars. He noticed that the Walther PPK was no longer amongst the contents and wondered why Pippa might have felt the need to take a gun if she was just 'gather-ing intel'. Seeing the sun cream and remembering Pippa's albino panda comment, Charlie picked up the little tube of Factor 50 sunblock and put it in his bag, which he zipped closed and then headed out onto the street. He found a general store a couple of blocks away from the safe house where he bought a cheap tripod for his phone, a carton of Marlboro Red cigarettes and a bottle of Jack Daniels.

Ten minutes later, Charlie's taxi dropped him off at the entrance of the

McVeigh Hotel. Eschewing the attempt of the porter to help him with his bag, Charlie made his way to reception.

"I'm Howard Johnson. I'm booked into room four forty-four," Charlie told the receptionist who, according to his name badge, was called Hank. Hank was early-, perhaps mid-forties, well-spoken and presented, and with a competent and dedicated manner. Charlie imagined how someone might assume Hank to be a 'professional' of some sort, perhaps a lawyer or an accountant, maybe a marketing executive. What, Charlie wondered, had gone wrong in Hank's life for him to be working reception on probably not much more than minimum wage, with unsociable hours, as a forty-something.

Charlie was immediately reminded of Margaret Thatcher's acerbic assertion that whenever she saw a man over forty years old on the bus, she saw a man who had failed in life. He had always considered Thatcher's comment typical of the warped judgement of respectability and human value, so often displayed by traditional Tories. He also doubted that Margaret Thatcher had ever travelled much by bus.

Hank delivered his well-worn welcome script, doing his best to make it sound sincere and original, rounding off with, "If I could take a credit card for any restaurant, bar or mini-bar purchases while you're staying with us."

Catching a glimpse of the contents as Charlie put the carrier bag containing the tripod, bourbon and cigarettes on the counter, Hank immediately, and unnecessarily, Charlie thought, said, "In case I forgot to mention, Mr Johnson, the McVeigh is strictly a no smoking establishment."

"Don't worry, I wouldn't dream of smoking inside," Charlie told Hank, as he handed over the Visa card. "By the way, I'll be working while I'm staying here, and when I'm not working, I'll be sleeping; so, I don't want to be disturbed."

"I understand, Mr Johnson," said Hank, a hint of a knowing expression betraying suspicious thoughts. "I'll inform Concierge. Please call reception if you need the room cleaned or fresh towels."

A few minutes later, Charlie entered his room. It was a big room, dominated by a super-king size bed and a television of sufficient proportions to be the envy of many small cinemas. Large sliding doors opened onto a wide terrace with a table and chairs. Looking out over the balcony, Charlie could see the service entrance four floors below. He set up his workspace, placing the tripod on the patio table, and having attached his phone, adjusted the angle and magnification until he had a perfect image of both people and vehicles arriving. Placing his notebook and a pen on the table, he was ready for work.

Through the remainder of the day, he noted the details of every vehicle that arrived or left, recording the time, company names and any other details in his notebook, just as Pippa had instructed.

The area outside the service entrance was also used as a smoking area by the hotel staff. Charlie watched the porter who had been so keen to help him with his bag smoking and chatting with a pretty young woman in a maid's uniform. The body language between them suggested that they were probably engaged in a relationship or an affair, which was confirmed by the porter's casual caress of the young maid's backside as they went back into the hotel.

Later in the day, Charlie saw Hank from reception appear outside with another man; late forties, more heavily built and wearing the same hotel uniform. For some reason, Charlie felt the interaction might be important, so set the video recording. The larger man reached out and put a hand on Hank's shoulder in a way that only someone who is intimate with another person might do. The two men were apparently lovers, but seemingly in some sort of conflict. The larger man said something that Hank obviously didn't like because Hank knocked his hand away, threw his cigarette to the ground and hurriedly walked back inside.

Feeling more than a little voyeuristic, but intrigued by what might be unfolding, Charlie reviewed the video footage, zooming in to focus on the details. According to his name badge, the larger man was called Todd and was the hotel manager. Todd's face was in full view but was too far away for the phone's microphone to have picked up what he'd said. Charlie diligently noted all of the details in the notebook.

By midnight, Charlie had had enough and needed to sleep. He'd made notes of over twenty delivery vehicles, taken photos of staff as they arrived for their shifts and photographed them again when they left. He'd seen the porter outside during his breaks with the pretty maid, and also seen Hank alone a couple of times, looking troubled and pensive while he smoked. Charlie decided he'd unwind with a nightcap and cigarette on the terrace, but before he'd finished, the phone in the room rang. It was Hank from reception who, in a sanctimonious tone, informed Charlie that a complaint had been made about the smell of cigarette smoke and concluded with a reminder about the hotel's strict no-smoking policy. Charlie assured Hank that it had only been one cigarette, outside on the terrace, and raising his voice in the hope that the presumably nearby complainant might hear, told Hank that, as people were 'so idiotically sensitive to the smell of a few burning leaves' that it wouldn't happen again.

The following day, Charlie was woken at five the following morning by his alarm and went straight out to the terrace to set the video rolling while he showered. Ablutions complete, Charlie sat down at the table with his notebook. The day unfolded much like the previous day. A dozen or so vans and trucks from different suppliers delivered bread, meat, milk, and vegetables throughout the morning. A McCarthy Aircon van arrived just after lunch, and a Washington Pool Service van with a wasp logo on the side arrived an hour later. Charlie watched and photographed the engineer he'd seen get out of the van as he inspected the pool, which was surrounded by a wooden deck with sun loungers and large potted palms, very near to the back of the hotel. The engineer took a water sample from the pool, tightened a loose bolt securing the metal steps, and then spent ten minutes fishing leaves and dead insects from the pool with a big net, then left. Just like the day before, several of the hotel staff, including the porter and the maid, Hank, Todd, and a few others, appeared outside a few times over the course of the day.

By late evening, Charlie was again tired and ready for bed, but decided to go through the videos from both days, just in case he'd missed any details. He went back to the video of Hank and Todd, expanding the video and trying to make out what Todd might have said that had upset Hank so much.

"Who's that then?" said a voice behind him. Startled, Charlie jumped up, knocking the tripod off the table. It was Pippa.

"Jesus, don't do that. I nearly died of shock. How did you get in here anyway? The door was double locked," said Charlie.

"Tricks of the trade," Pippa said with a smile, removing her coat.

"What the fuck has happened to you?" exclaimed Charlie, as he saw that Pippa's clothes were almost completely blood-stained. She looked like an abattoir worker who had done their shift in their Sunday best.

"I stopped for something to eat at a diner about thirty miles out of town on the way back. Somebody pretending to be one of the locals followed me to the bathroom and said that he didn't like 'my type' in 'his town' and decided he was going to 'teach me a lesson'. My guess is that he wasn't one of the locals; more likely a professional killer hired by Carlo Groteel. Redneck bigots normally just want to give people like me a beating. This guy had a hunting knife and intended to kill me. News of me asking questions about Groteel and his daughter must have got back to them," said Pippa.

"Shit! What happened?" asked Charlie.

"Well, the training kicked in and I sort of disarmed him," said Pippa, a little sheepishly. "Don't worry, nobody saw, and it'll take ages for them to discover the body. By then, we'll be long gone."

"Body? You've killed someone already! And what do you mean by 'sort of disarmed him'? From the quantity of blood on you, it looks like you dismembered him too," said Charlie, shocked.

"Yes, like I said, I disarmed him. I had to take the arms off to get him into the drain. There was nowhere else to hide the body without taking him back out through the diner. Trouble was, he wasn't quite dead, so there was a bit of spurting. Silly me, should have checked for a pulse before I started cutting."

"Oh, Jesus. I need a drink and a smoke," said Charlie, throwing caution to the wind and lighting a cigarette and pouring a large Jack Daniels. "You'd better get out of those clothes before you stain the carpet and furniture."

"Good idea," said Pippa, depositing her Walther PPK with its silencer still attached and the hunting knife she'd liberated from her would-be assassin on the table. Then, seemingly entirely uninhibited, she stripped off down to knickers and bra, leaving her blood-soaked clothes on the tiled terrace floor.

"Not here, for fuck's sake. There is a bathroom, you know," said Charlie.

Just at that moment, the doorbell rang, and the door immediately opened. Hank strode angrily into the room, the key card still in his hand. "Mr Johnson, you assured me that you wouldn't smoke in the hotel. Now I'll have to ask you to pack your…" Hank started to say, but the scene before him stopped him mid-sentence. He just had time to notice the semi-naked woman, the blood-stained clothes, the hunting knife and the gun on the table, before Pippa calmly picked it up and shot him in the head. Hank fell to his knees, then forward onto the tiled terrace floor.

"Fuck! Fuck! Fuck! Why did you do that?" Charlie exclaimed. "We're meant to be here to assassinate Reyna Groteel and you've killed two other people already. And it's only the second day!"

"He saw everything, including the gun. Respectable guests don't have hunting knives and guns with silencers in their rooms, assassins do, and this hotel is used by senators and state governors. If I'd let him leave the room, there would have been a SWAT team here within five minutes. Anyway, he was a kiddy-fiddler," said Pippa.

"A kiddy-fiddler? How do you know that?" Charlie asked, astonished by Pippa's statement

"He was in the video you were watching when I arrived," said Pippa.

"But you can't hear the speech in the video," Charlie replied.

"No, but I can lip-read. The other guy in the video said to him, 'If you leave me, I'll send the naughty video we made of you with that delightful thirteen-year-old Latino boy to Mom and Pop, and then to the police. We're in this together, forever, my love.' Those were his exact words. Now pull yourself together, we've got work to do. Go and get me two large shovels."

A moment later, Charlie was holding the two shovels Pippa had told him to get. "Now what?" he asked.

"Now we're going to make this nonce disappear, but before we do that, there are a few loose ends we need to tidy up," Pippa said as she fumbled in Hank's pockets, removing his phone and car keys. "Were you recording anything when Hank arrived?"

"Yes, I somehow had the presence of mind to press record when I poured my drink, just after you turned up covered in blood," Charlie replied.

"Good. Get your phone," said Pippa, opening her laptop. A moment later, she had an application open that looked a bit like a recording studio mixing desk. "OK. Plug this cable into your phone and play the recording at the point when Hank comes into the room and starts speaking."

With the audio clip of Hank berating Charlie for smoking captured on the PC, Pippa pressed a button labelled 'Process'. A squirly circle appeared on the screen with a message that read 'Processing', then a few seconds later, 'Complete'. Pippa then went over to Hank, turned him over and held his phone in front of his face. Despite Hank's startled expression and the bullet hole in his forehead, the phone instantly unlocked. She then went back to the laptop, disconnected Charlie's phone and plugged the cable into Hank's. She quickly found 'Todd' in the phone's contacts list and pressed 'Call'. The call was answered almost immediately.

"Where the fuck are you? I've been looking for you for the last twenty minutes," said an irritated voice.

Pippa spoke into the laptop's microphone, "I'm up in room four-forty-four with twelve-year-old Jerry." As she spoke, the voice that could be heard on the phone's speaker was exactly like Hank's. "Jerry's parents have gone to the theatre, leaving poor Jerry all alone with a bag of Cheetos and a couple of video games. I told Jerry you're really good at games, and he asked if you'd like to come and play."

"I'll be there in two minutes," said Todd and hung up.

"You're not? Surely not another one. Aren't two in one day enough for you?" asked Charlie.

"Not when it comes to kiddy-fiddlers. I was sexually abused when I was twelve. This is personal," said Pippa.

Suddenly it all made sense. The missing pieces of the jigsaw puzzle of Pippa's very complex personality were now in place. Pippa, Phillip as she was known at the time, must have gone through her teens, *his* teens, entirely conflicted. She'd said in earlier conversations that she knew from a very early age, perhaps four or five years old, that she had been born in the wrong body. But to then be sexually abused on the cusp of adolescence would have made young Phillip even less enthusiastic about becoming a man; a virtual replica of his abuser, complete with all of the abuser's bodily weapons. But England in the mid-seventies wasn't a very friendly place for a man to become a woman. So instead, Phillip did the most macho thing he could think of. He joined the army, and having done so, pushed himself to become the strongest, fittest, fastest, and most complete killing machine in his regiment. When, after eight years in the Grenadier Guards, he put himself forward for the SAS selection process, his ascension into the ranks of the most elite military unit in the country, possibly the world, was a fait-accompli.

Phillip served the SAS well, and in return, the SAS served Phillip well; at least, it served his purpose at the time. It enabled him to bury his feminine side until he was ready to confront it head-on, and to exorcise the demons of his youth by killing bad people. The SAS also imbued Phillip with the ability to accurately assess complex problems, and to make difficult decisions with courage and relative ease.

After twelve years of travelling the globe eliminating threats to the free world, when Phillip finally left the SAS, he immediately started the process of becoming Pippa, culminating in surgery four years later.

Pippa had said that the consultant dealing with her transition had told her that she was the fifth person he had seen from that regiment. It made sense from the perspective of psychological process, Charlie thought. The state of denial being overwhelmed by the empowerment of the most comprehensive physical and psychological training, leading to the rebirth of the true individual. SAS training had given Phillip the courage to become Pippa; the phoenix finally able to rise from the ashes of her youth. Still flawed, but no longer damaged, and entirely comfortable with her flaws.

"I know I'm a psychopath, but I'm a good psychopath. I do the jobs that need doing but nobody else wants to do, and I do them well," she'd say with pride when asked about her work.

Charlie was jolted from his thoughts by the doorbell. Without hesitation, Pippa went to the door and opened it with the gun in one hand and a towel over her shoulder. Todd was understandably surprised to be greeted by a half-naked woman holding a gun. His mouth opened but no words came out.

"Thank you for joining us so quickly, Todd. Pity we need to say our farewells so soon," said Pippa, then raised the gun and shot Todd in the head. The silenced gun made just a 'pap' sound and Todd started to fall. Pippa caught him, placing the towel over his head to prevent any blood stains, then dragged him across the room to the terrace where she let his limp body fall next to Hank's. She then removed Todd's car keys and phone from his trousers.

"Right. Take me and the dead nonces here," said Pippa, showing Charlie a map of the New Mexico desert on her phone; her finger pointing to a spot several miles from any town or road. "We'll bury them there."

The soft sand of the New Mexico desert made it easy to dig a grave deep enough to conceal the corpses in just a few minutes. It was so easy that the desert seemed almost complicit in the murders. As he shovelled the sand back over the grave, Charlie wondered how many other killings the desert had aided and abetted, then reflected that he too had been complicit in the deaths of the two men he had just buried. 'What have I become? I'm no better than the desert,' he thought, as he drew his shovel over the grave to smooth the surface for the last time, concluding that maybe he'd always been this way, and that only the privilege of a relatively easy life had prevented this darker side from making an earlier appearance.

Back in the hotel room, Pippa was again at the controls. First, she reviewed the content on Hank's and Todd's phones, shaking her head as she scrolled through photos and videos. She then connected Hank's phone to her laptop.

"What are you doing?" asked Charlie.

"I'm cloning his SIM card and copying the phone's content onto the laptop. We'll be able to hack into any mobile cell anywhere in the world to make it look like they're on the run. It'll confuse the shit out of the FBI," Pippa replied. With the clone of Hank's phone complete, she repeated the process with Todd's phone.

Handing Hank's car keys to Charlie, she said, "Find which car these belong to by going out to the balcony and holding the keys to your head when you press the button; it amplifies the signal. Keep an eye out for which lights flash and make a mental note of where the car is in the car park. When we get down there, go straight to the car, get in and drive away. Look as normal as possible, don't make eye contact with anyone, and if anyone says anything, just ignore them, pretend you haven't heard them and drive away normally."

"Where am I going?" Charlie asked.

"You're going to Washington Highlands. Turn right out of the hotel onto Pennsylvania Avenue. I'll be in Todd's car right behind you but will pass you once I'm sure we're safely away from the hotel. You can follow me from there. When we get to the Atlantic Street area, somewhere around 4th Street, we'll dump the cars on a side street. It's the roughest suburb of the city. There'll be nothing left of them by the morning."

Downstairs, Charlie quickly found Hank's car in the car park. It was a new Mercedes, probably less than a year old. How could a hotel receptionist afford a car like this, Charlie wondered. Wearing Hank's hotel uniform, some skin-coloured gloves that Pippa had given him and a baseball cap to hide his face from the high-mounted cameras in the car park, he got into the car, put the key in the ignition and started the engine.

Thirty seconds later he had turned out of the car park onto Pennsylvania Avenue with Pippa directly behind in Todd's silver BMW. At the first set of traffic lights, Pippa moved ahead and the two cars drove sedately in convoy out of the city, crossed the Anacostia River, and then headed south on the I–295. Less than fifteen minutes later, they parked in a dark and deserted side street just off Atlantic Street. Pippa took the dead men's phones from her pocket, switched them off and threw them into the river next to the road. "Right. Back to the hotel," she said.

Back in the room, Pippa immediately launched a program called 'Phone Clone' on her laptop, then opened the duplicate of Hank's phone which she tethered to the mobile cell nearest to where they'd abandoned the cars in Washington Highlands. She then posted several of the more shocking images she'd found amongst Hank's photos to his Facebook page, captioning each photo with the message, 'We're going on a summer holiday… Catch us if you can'. She then did the same with the clone of Todd's phone.

"Tomorrow they'll pop up in Philadelphia, the day after in New York, and then, a few days later in Montreal. Then, they'll disappear forever, never to be seen or heard of again," said Pippa.

With the drama seemingly concluded, Charlie again challenged Pippa on the men's murders. "Why did you have to kill them? It's hard enough for someone like me, Flore, or any of the others, to be part of Reyna Groteel's death, but the future of humanity depends on that. But these two? Couldn't we just have found some way of alerting the Police and let justice take its' course?"

"I told you already, if I'd allowed Hank to leave this room alive, the hotel would have been crawling with Police within minutes. Todd had to die to tidy up the loose ends and complete the picture. Anyway, they were kiddy-fiddlers. The world is a better place without them.

They deserved everything they got, and more."

"But…" started Charlie. Pippa interrupted.

"But nothing. Stop whingeing and let me do my job. Anyway, if you're looking for answers, they're dead because of you," said Pippa.

"How is it my fault? I didn't kill them," Charlie protested.

"You smoked. They'd still be alive if you hadn't. Smoking kills," replied Pippa, flatly and factually.

Over the following hours, with Charlie subdued and quiet following the hard-hitting truth of Pippa's statement, Pippa meticulously went through Charlie's notes from the previous days, reviewed all of the video that had been captured from the balcony, and trawled through the content on the clones of Hank's and Todd's phones. Both devices had access to the hotel's intranet and proprietary booking management system, allowing Pippa to easily discover that Reyna Groteel would be arriving the next day, and ominously, would be staying in room 666. Pippa was also able to see that the room would be vacant until her arrival.

"What did you find out while you were away?" Charlie asked Pippa.

"I discovered that Reyna Groteel and her father are cut entirely from the same vile cloth. They're both Machiavellian sociopaths. Posing as a reporter for the Wall Street Journal, I visited Carlo's business associates and ex-employees. I visited Reyna's former teachers, classmates, colleagues, political rivals, and also met her ex-husband. They all said more-or-less the same. Neither father or daughter has a shred of moral fibre and there's nothing they won't do or say, no moral red line that they won't cross to further their interests, regardless of the consequences.

"To give you just one example, and there are many, Carlo had an interest in a company in Arizona, where Reyna grew up, making non-stick coatings for cookware. He pumped the effluent from the manufacturing process which was loaded with long-chain hydrocarbons and what we now call 'forever chemicals', directly into the Arizona River, which poisoned the water table in the area. The water was so toxic that it wasn't even safe to shower or bathe in. Within a couple of years, the locals started getting cancers and children were born with serious birth defects. Carlo paid off the first few complainants and arranged 'accidents' for those that wouldn't take his hush money, but when the trickle of compensation claims started to turn into a deluge, he sold the business to a Panamanian registered company with nominee directors who stripped the company of its assets, paying the proceeds to Carlo as a sale fee and leaving both companies bankrupt. Nobody got a cent of compensation, but Carlo walked away with more than one hundred million dollars – which was a lot of money then.

"The worst part is that Carlo knew from the very beginning that what he was pumping into the river was highly toxic. Reyna's ex-husband, Roger Smythe, told me that Reyna had grown up never having any contact with the municipal water supply. Carlo had a purification system installed in the family home when Reyna was a baby, and throughout her childhood, she was forbidden from drinking water at school or even washing her hands whenever she was away from home. Roger said that her paranoia about water continued into adulthood to the extent that whenever she is away from home, she steadfastly refuses to shower or bathe. Poor guy said that they had to cut their honeymoon short because by the fifth day, she smelled so bad that the hotel asked them to leave."

"That's disgusting," said Charlie, "She really doesn't wash when she's away from home?"

"Apparently not. She just uses a myriad of deodorants and other sprays," Pippa with a grimace, "She's a vile person with a vile odour. And mark my words, if she's not stopped, she'll lie, cheat, blackmail, bully and coerce her way to getting New Era passed, and then on to the Oval Office. It'll be like having Trump all over again, only much, much worse."

The following morning, having slept on a sun lounger on the terrace, Pippa got up and switched on the TV. A report on the previous month's inflation statistics was just ending. The growth in prices had slowed from 8721% the month before to just under 8600%. The next images to appear on screen were those of Hank and Todd, with the caption below, 'Paedos on the run'.

The Fox anchor then went on to explain, "Hank McVeigh, heir to the McVeigh Hotel dynasty, and his lover, Todd Hughes, General Manager of the flagship Washington McVeigh Hotel, have gone on the run after posting depraved images and bragging of their exploits on social media, taunting Police to, 'Catch us if you can'. Police believe the men may be responsible for more than one hundred cases of sexual abuse. The last known location of the pair was in the city suburb of Washington High-lands where their burnt-out vehicles were discovered early this morning. Police are appealing for witnesses in the area to come forward."

"So, that explains it. I'd been wondering what a professional, well-pre-sented forty-something was doing working reception. His parents have had him on a short leash, making him work every role in the family business to earn his inheritance. Somewhere along the journey, he's come into contact with Todd Hughes who has been coercively controlling him ever since discovering he has a penchant for young boys," said Charlie.

Pippa opened her laptop, launched Phone Clone and placed the two men on the I-95 just north of Wilmington. A few minutes later, she logged them onto the next cell tower a few miles further north along the road, making it look as if they were headed towards Philadelphia. "Right, let's get on to why we came here in the first place," she said decisively.

Putting her suitcase on the writing desk, Pippa selected several items including the Gideon's bible, the shower gel and three of the lightbulbs – one matching the type of bulb used in the bathroom, the other two identical to the bulbs in the bedroom. Then, returning to the laptop, she used the login credentials from her copy of Hank's phone to access the hotel's intranet from where it took less than a minute to hack into the hotel's security system. She quickly found the sixth-floor cameras and substituted the live video feed from the ceiling-mounted cameras in the corridor for stills. Putting the items she had selected from her suitcase into a shoulder bag, she said, "OK. I'm going up to Reyna's room. Back in a few minutes."

Ten minutes later she was back, quickly went to her laptop and opened a different program. A tiled display showed images of the inside of room 666. Camera 1 provided a view of the bathroom from the ceiling. Camera 2 showed the bathroom at waist height, probably the shower gel camera, Charlie thought. Camera 3 offered a plan view of the entrance, Camera 4 provided an aerial view of the bedroom, and Camera 5 was from the Gideon's Bible, which Pippa had placed on the writing desk. The image showed a view of the bedroom and the doors leading out onto the terrace.

"Now we play the waiting game," said Pippa, "When's she due to arrive?"

"In about two hours," Charlie replied, looking at his watch.

"The calm before the storm," Pippa said with a smile.

Charlie asked, "Do you need me to go and get anything? Tom said you'd probably give me a shopping list."

"I'm not sure what I'm going to need yet, but I do have a few ideas of where this might be headed. So, for now, if you could go and take a shit, then put it in the ice box of the minibar," replied Pippa.

"You what? You're surely not serious?" said Charlie with incredulity.

"I really am serious," replied Pippa, "Go and get yourself a newspaper to read, take your time, and do your best to squeeze out the best-looking turd of your life. Think of it as your own personal scatological masterpiece."

"Why? What do you want with a turd?" asked Charlie, still incredulous.

"You'll see. Maybe. Just covering all the bases. Now be a good bloke and go and fire one out."

Still unsure how a turd, even a magnificent and perfect turd, might help their mission to save humanity, Charlie decided it would be best not to argue or ask more questions. He'd noticed that Pippa now had a rather manic, steely demeanour. She was both in her 'zone', doing her best to completely cover every possible eventuality, but also, Charlie thought, probably at her most dangerous, where anything could happen, and happen very quickly if she was forced to deviate from the mission roadmap she was constructing in her head. Maybe though, Charlie wondered as he headed to the bathroom with a copy of the Washington Post, this was just the type of random thing that psychopaths do, simply to prove that they're completely in control.

Just over two hours later, with 'the mother of all turds', as Pippa had described it, now frozen solid in the minibar's icebox, activity suddenly appeared on the laptop screen. Camera 3 showed the door to room 666 suddenly open and a woman in her early forties with long dark hair, wearing an elegant blue suit, enter the room. Reyna Groteel.

Reyna had her phone pressed to ear and was talking loudly. "So, are you sure that's your position, Mitch?" she asked in a calm, measured tone. "Hmm, OK. Yes, I understand. Yes, yes…I get it, and I completely understand. Trouble is Mitch, if you do that, I've got a feeling the New York Times will be running a scoop tomorrow, complete with photos, about how you like to unwind with Latina hookers after long days at party conferences. That would of course be fine, if the Latina hookers weren't both underage and here in our great country illegally. Should have had that wall built quicker, Mitch. Anyway, give it some thought. I'll call you again in an hour. And if you're still undecided, I can call your wife to see if she can persuade you. Thanks, Mitch. Have a good evening."

"We've got to act quickly." Said Pippa. "She's already selling her plan, and not everyone will need as much persuasion as Mitch," said Pippa.

Charlie and Pippa watched on screen as Reyna first opened the doors onto the terrace, then unpacked her case, putting two suits and a selection of blouses in the wardrobe, underwear in the chest of drawers and a wad of twenty-dollar notes on the desk. She then went to the bathroom, depositing a toothbrush and bottle of Evian mineral water next to the sink, and a make-up bag and several cans of deodorant on the shelf above. Back in the bedroom, Reyna undressed, hanging her suit in the wardrobe, and putting her blouse and underwear in the hotel laundry bag. Now naked, Reyna returned to the bathroom, where she first selected a Givenchy deodorant which she sprayed under her arms, then picked up a Givenchy body spray which she sprayed over her torso, and finally took a can of Femfresh and liberally sprayed her crotch.

"Good grief, your intel was right. She doesn't wash!" said Charlie, feeling rather revolted by what he'd just witnessed.

"She's not in bad shape, is she?" said Pippa, with enough conviction to make Charlie wonder whether she perhaps regretted the choice she'd made twenty years before.

"She was a teenage hundred-metre hurdles champion. She continued into her mid-thirties until she entered politics. Almost got selected for the 2024 Olympics," Charlie explained.

"Pity that she probably smells like a box of shrimp that's been left out in the sun for a week," replied Pippa.

Now back in the bedroom, cameras 4 and 5 revealed Reyna wearing the hotel bathrobe and back on her phone. "This is Reyna. I'm in room 666 at the McVeigh. Is Ramon available this afternoon? He is? Great. Please send him over in half an hour. Tell him not to be late, I've got a tight schedule."

A moment later, she was dialling again. "Ted, how are you doing? Did you get my email?" A pause followed as she listened to the reply, "I get your concerns Ted, but the Chinese are already doing this. What? Yes, they really are. If we don't follow suit, within twelve months, half of what's left of our industrial base will be gone, and a year later, there'll be nothing left at all. Do you want your legacy to be the senator that put the final nail in the coffin of American manufacturing? No, I didn't think so. What? Yes, Smith, Cruz, and Liebowitz are all on board. Meet me tomorrow morning in my office at 8 am to discuss how we're going to get the others on-side."

Over the following twenty minutes, Reyna made three other similar calls, hurridly ending the last when the doorbell rang at 5:30 pm. "Got to hop, I'm late for my call with the President. Catch you tomorrow," she lied as she ended the call and rushed to the door.

Camera 3 showed Reyna opening the door to a handsome and casually but expensively dressed man in his early thirties carrying a leather shoulder bag. "Ramon, thank you for coming. I don't have much time, so you're going to have to be super-efficient." Turning around and walking into the bedroom, Reyna took the pile of notes from the desk and handed it to Ramon. "There's your fee with your usual 'bareback' bonus. Now go and get ready and don't keep me waiting."

A moment later, Camera 1 and 2 showed Ramon in the bathroom. He quickly undressed, pulled on a pair of red Y fronts, the type you might expect a much older man to wear, then bizarrely he put on a red tie, carefully making a perfect Windsor knot, and adjusting the length of the tie so the tip reached just below his bare navel. He then reached into his bag and produced a grey-blond wig, parted at the side, which he put on his head and carefully adjusted until it looked almost natural.

"Surely not," said Pippa, "She's made him dress up to look like Donald Trump."

With the wig correctly positioned, Ramon then reached into his bag again, this time finding a wad of cotton wool. He made two small cotton wool balls which he stuffed into his nostrils, crossed himself like a catholic priest, and then ventured out into the bedroom.

"Donny!" exclaimed Reyna, "Grab my pussy." Ramon obliged.

Twenty minutes of vigorous sex followed until Reyna shouted, "Let me have it Donny. Both Barrels." Again, Ramon did as he had been told, then slumped over his client, spent.

"You bastard Ramon, you didn't wait for me. Who's paying the fucking bill here Ramon?" Reyna shouted.

"But Senora Groteel, you told me…" started Ramon, but Reyna cut him down.

"Don't tell me what I said. I know what I fucking said, but I didn't mean two seconds later. Now get down there and finish me off."

"Oh no! Please, Senora, I beg you, not…"

Reyna interrupted again, "Either you give me what I've paid for, or I'll have you fucking deported. You do know that I could have you in leg irons, hobbling towards your flight back to your miserable life in Mexico in less than half an hour, don't you Ramon? All it would take is one call. Now finish the job."

Ramon obliged.

Two minutes later, Camera 1 and 2 showed Ramon vomiting in the bathroom, while on cameras 4 and 5, Reyna could be seen sprawled naked on the bed, tapping out a message on her phone and smoking a cigarette; the hotel's rules apparently didn't apply to her.

"Poor guy," said Pippa, as Ramon washed, then changed back into his clothes and quietly left the room. With Ramon gone, Reyna went to the bathroom, gave herself another liberal application of Femfresh, quickly dressed and left the room.

"She's gone to meet her father. As long as we've not altered the space-time continuum by being here, she'll be back in two hours," said Charlie.

"Err, we might have altered the space-time continuum. Well, I mean, I might have," said Pippa in a slightly guilty tone.

"What do you mean?" asked Charlie.

"Well, err, I already killed the father," replied Pippa.

"Oh, for fuck's sake Pippa. Why?"

"I had to. Remember, he'd sent someone to try to kill me. I had to deal with him before he sent someone else, probably someone better. They never send their best assets first. Don't worry, nobody will ever find the body. It'll remain one of those mysteries. Anyway, he was involved in so much dodgy stuff, the Police will probably just think he skipped the country."

"What did you do with the body?" asked Charlie.

"I broke into a crematorium. Without a coffin, it only takes half an hour to cremate a body. Then I swept up, left the place like I'd found it and locked the door on my way out, taking the ashes with me," replied Pippa, "I dumped the ashes in the river."

"But how were you able to kill him. Didn't he have a bodyguard?" asked Charlie.

"Yes. He had four. And before you ask, yes, I killed them too. And cremated them."

"But…" Charlie started to ask, but Pippa wasn't in the mood for further discussion.

"No more questions," she snapped, "We've got work to do and we don't have much time. Reyna Groteel could be back in an hour and a half. First thing to be done is get the turd out of the icebox and throw it into the swimming pool. It'll be easy from the balcony. After you've done that, go downstairs, wait in the lobby, watch the main entrance, and call me when Groteel comes back. I'll do the rest."

Given Pippa's now rather manic demeanour, her very specific instructions, and Charlie's earlier concerns about the possibility of the lioness turning on its keeper, Charlie thought it best not to argue or question. So, as instructed, he removed the turd from the minibar, took it to the terrace and after checking that nobody was swimming, threw it from the balcony. It flew in a perfect arc, landing almost exactly in the middle of the large oval pool where it entered the water like a champiom high divei with just a discrete plop, and almost no splash. Charlie wondered whether it would be a floater or a sinker; a question that was quickly answered, when, after briefly resurfacing, the weight of the turd overcame the support of the water, and it slowly made its way to its resting place at the bottom of the pool where a brown fog started to form around it.

After quickly washing his hands in the bathroom, Charlie then went down to the hotel lobby, where he found a comfortable chair facing the revolving door of the main entrance, about ten metres from the reception desk. He picked up a copy of the Washington Post, discretely tore a small triangle out of the spine of the paper, then sat facing the door with the paper open and raised in front of him. The little star shape of missing paper gave him a perfect view of the door. The paper was open on pages fourteen and fifteen, and Charlie couldn't help but notice the piece on the right-hand page titled, 'Groteel pushing New ERA'. Speed-reading the article, Charlie picked out the key lines in the piece. 'Senator Reyna Groteel will be making the case in Washington this week for the New Energy Reform Act…Reduce dependency on fossil fuels by ninety-five per cent… decades of power hiding in our scrapyards…' The article ended with a quote from Groteel, 'New ERA will truly make America great again."

After a few minutes watching the door, Charlie was distracted by some commotion at the reception desk. The maid that he'd seen smoking outside with the porter had hurried through reception and was now talking in quite an animated manner with another member of staff and was pointing towards the pool with an expression of disgust. The man behind the counter, presumably the new manager, quickly got on the phone.

Ten minutes later, Charlie was again distracted by more movement at the desk. A man wearing a baseball cap and overalls, both with the same logo of a happy-looking wasp and the text 'WASPS - Washington Pool Service' below, was at the reception desk talking to the manager. To Charlie's astonishment, when the man turned around, he saw that it was Pippa. With the simple manly props of overalls, a tool bag and a baseball cap, together with her legacy of knowing how to move and talk like a man, it had been easy for her to morph back into masculinity. The conversation at the front desk concluded with the manager putting his palms together as if praying, and although Charlie was too far away to hear and couldn't lip read, he could see that the manager was saying "thank you, thank you". With that, Pippa left the reception and disappeared out of sight, headed towards the pool.

Just over an hour later, through the diamond-shaped spyhole in the newspaper, Charlie saw a black limo arrive. The driver quickly jumped out and opened the rear door, simultaneously placing his handkerchief over his mouth and nose as discretely as he could. Reyna Groteel emerged from the limo looking agitated and quickly strode towards the hotel entrance. Taking his phone from his pocket, Charlie quickly called Pippa.

"Stinky fox has returned to the den," he whispered as soon as Pippa answered.

"What?" came the reply.

"Stinky fox has returned to the den," Charlie whispered again, slightly louder and with more urgency, thinking that perhaps Pippa hadn't heard his first attempt.

"*What* are you talking about?" replied Pippa in an irritated tone.

"Reyna. She's back and on her way up," Charlie said in a now frustrated whisper through gritted teeth.

"Well, why didn't you just say so," said Pippa, obviously annoyed.

"Well, I thought…" started Charlie.

"It doesn't matter what you thought. Just get yourself up to the room," Pippa replied and hung up.

Back on the fourth floor, Charlie saw that Pippa was still dressed as the WASPS pool engineer, sitting in front of the laptop, watching intently. At that moment, movement appeared on Camera 3. The door opened and Reyna entered the room with her phone pressed to her ear in the midst of a call. "No, Dad wasn't home. Must have had to go out for something. Anyway, I'm going to go and freshen up and I'll see you in the restaurant in an hour. We can discuss New ERA over dinner," Reyna said, then put the phone on the desk and went to the bathroom.

"This is where the fun begins. Watch closely," said Pippa as Reyna started to undress.

"Why are you so obsessed with that woman's body. You can get help for voyeurism, you know," said Charlie.

"Shut up and watch," Pippa snapped back.

# Chapter 61
# Clash of the Titans

Konstantinos Georgiou Constantinou sat at the desk in his study looking out through the open French doors and across his garden to the blue water of the Aegean beyond. Although it was mid-January, it was a warm day with a gentle breeze and Konstantinos had got up early to work on his election manifesto.

The year before, Kostas had started to lighten his schedule as a political journalist and secretly formed what he had given an English working name, 'HARP', the Hellenic Altruist Reformist Party. His vision was to form a party of forward-thinking pragmatists who, regardless of their political heritage, shared four common traits: honesty, integrity, empathy, and rationalism.

Kostas believed that he'd identified a niche for a party that cut across the usual entrenched political divides; a party capable of appealing to the broadest cross-section of the electorate, without being just another limp collection of boring centrists. His twenty years as a journalist at the coal face of politics, observing the oscillations and machinations, but more-over the abject failures of the established parties to have any meaningful positive impact, had led Kostas to the conclusion that there needed to be radical change. He knew that the tax and spend profligacy of the left made everybody lazy, self-entitled and inefficient, while the inequities of the unmoderated right, divided society and made a tiny percentage incredibly wealthy at the expense of everybody else.

Kostas also knew that at least three-quarters of the politicians he had observed, met, interviewed and written about over the previous two decades could be labelled as insincere, incompetent, corrupt, or motivated either by flawed ideology or self-interest – often all of those things.

At the same time, he had developed relationships with a handful of politicians, spanning the ideological spectrum, whom he knew to be honest, genuine and capable. Politicians whose guiding ethos was founded in a genuine desire to make Greece and the wider world a better place.

Whilst their individual beliefs in exactly which route should be followed to reach some sort of utopia might differ, and despite diverse political labels, their ultimate visions of the utopia itself were broadly aligned, and fundamentally, all of them ticked the non-negotiable boxes of honesty, integrity, rationalism, and empathy.

Over the previous year, using his cover as a journalist to arrange private meetings, Kostas had been discretely but systematically looting the cream of the established Greek parties from the left, centre and right of the political spectrum. Seven of the HARP defectors held ministerial positions in the ruling New Democracy party, another twelve, shadow ministerial roles in Syriza, three were from PASOK-KINAL, two from Greek Solution and one from the KKE, the Greek Communist Party.

The central and key element of Kostas' strategy was that it was to be conducted in utmost stealth and secrecy. Kostas' political celebrity recruits would continue in the senior roles they held in other parties until exactly three months before the next Greek general election. At precisely the same time, on the same day, the twenty-five compatriots that Kostas had convinced of his plan would simultaneously call press conferences, at which, they would declare that the existing political structure was broken, that tribal dogma made effective governance impossible, and announce the launch of a new party called Αρπα, pronounced 'Arpa' in English; Greek for 'Harp'.

With his knowledge of the media world, Kostas calculated that the shock news of twenty-five highly experienced and respected political heavyweights simultaneously defecting to a new party, at exactly the time that the established parties would be launching their candidates and manifestos, would allow Arpa to dominate the news agenda for at least two weeks. During this period, Kostas knew that Arpa would be flooded with candidacy applications from other parliamentarians looking to jump ship, swelling their numbers sufficiently to be able to field enough credible candidates to have a realistic chance of winning a majority in the three-hundred-seat Greek parliament.

Kostas also believed that the media feeding frenzy would offer the luxury of being able to initially focus only on Arpa's guiding principles and ethos. Rather than having to immediately launch Arpa's formal manifesto, they would instead be able to trickle out new policies whenever one of the other parties started to regain any media foothold. Kostas felt certain that Arpa would be able to remain front and centre in the media spotlight all the way to polling day, when ten million Greeks would choose their next government.

This was to be a carefully choreographed political hijacking, a brutal but peaceful democratic coup, executed with surgical precision that would finally overturn the wobbly political applecart that was so overladen with rotting fruit.

"Kaliméra, Kostas," said a gentle voice behind him.

Kostas spun around in his chair to see an attractive young woman standing in the middle of the room.

"What the fuck! How did you get in here? What do you want?" Kostas said in shocked alarm. He'd wondered whether news of his plans might leak, and what steps some might take to protect their political fiefdoms. The woman didn't look like an assassin, but did all assassins look like killers? Probably not, Kostas thought, his mind racing through the possible motives of his uninvited guest.

Empathetic to Kostas' fears, Flore calmly told him, "I'm not here to harm you Kostas. I'm here to help you."

"Help me with what?" Kostas replied, his thoughts dominated by the possibility that at any moment the woman might produce a gun and kill him.

"I'm here to help you win the next election," Flore replied.

"What are you talking about? I'm a journalist, not a politician," Kostas protested.

"For the moment yes, but one month and three days from today, on 27th February, you and twenty-five of your collaborators will each, individually, call press conferences, and at exactly eleven in the morning, announce their defection to a new party called Arpa. You are the architect of Arpa," Flore stated with unequivocal confidence.

Momentarily speechless, Kostas wondered how his plan had been discovered. "How do you know this? Who and what are you? CIA? Yes, you're fucking CIA aren't you? You've been spying on me. I thought these days you only meddled where oil or drugs were involved, or are you still obsessed with communists? Well, we only have one communist and she's a modern communist, she believes in the free market. So, you needn't worry, you can go back to Langley and tell them there are no reds under the beds here."

"I'm not CIA, Kostas. I'm not from any agency of any government. I'm just here to help you," said Flore as reassuringly as she was able.

"We don't need any help. And anyway, why do you want to help?" Kostas, replied indignantly.

"Because you need my help, Kostas. Otherwise, you'll lose the election. Actually, it's worse than just lose, it will be a complete humiliation. Arpa will win less than three percent of the national vote. Your career as a politician will be over before it's begun, and after the ridicule subsides, you and your cohorts will vanish into political obscurity.

They'll be remembered only for the spectacularly stupid manner by which they sabotaged their promising political careers. Your credibility will be so damaged that the only work you'll be able to get will be writing for a local newspaper on an island with less than a thousand inhabitants, reporting on weddings and funerals, and even then, you'll need to use a nom de plume. Believe me, you really do need my help," Flore explained.

"What are you talking about? How can you possibly predict that? Either you're guessing or you've been sent to try to scare me into giving up. Who are you working for? New Democracy? Syriza?" pressed Kostas.

"It's not a guess Kostas, and I'm not working for anyone. I know the future because I've seen it first-hand. Without my help, this doesn't end well for your project, your compatriots, for you, or for Greece," said Flore.

Kostas was now feeling reasonably confident that his uninvited guest wasn't dangerous; she wasn't an assassin or she would have already killed him, and she was probably telling the truth about not working for an intelligence agency or a rival political party. She was simply mad.

He had no idea how she'd found out about his plan; probably by getting into his house and snooping around while he was out. Maybe she'd hacked his email or planted a bug. He'd experienced something similar a few years before, when a reader became obsessed with him and started turning up at his house, declaring her undying love and begging him to be honest about his true feelings for her.

Emboldened by the belief that he was probably dealing with nothing more sinister than a delusional but probably relatively harmless stalker,

Kostas decided it was time to be more assertive and wrest back control of the situation.

"Well, I've seen the future too, and what I see is you being led away from here in handcuffs, then being charged with trespassing, stalking and harassment," he said, in a calm, emotionless tone, "Alternatively, you can leave now, promise to never come back, and go and get some professional help."

"OK, Kostas. I will leave, and I promise that I won't come back unless you invite me," Flore said as she reached into her pocket and produced a scrap of paper, which she handed to Kostas. "The top row of numbers are Friday's winning lottery numbers. If you play those numbers, you'll be the only winner of a fifty-five billion Euro jackpot. The number below is my mobile. It would be a good idea if you don't tell anyone about my visit or what I've given you. If you do, I'll know, and I won't be able to help you."

Without a further word, Flore walked to the entrance, opened the door and left, closing it swiftly but gently behind her. Kostas quickly followed and opened the door to make sure that she was definitely leaving his property. He expected to see her walking down the driveway towards the street, but the woman was nowhere to be seen. She had simply vanished.

# THE COSMIC KNOT PARADOX

# Chapter 62
# So long, and thanks for all the fish

Charlie and Pippa watched on the laptop screen as Reyna, now completely naked, went through the bathroom routine they had observed earlier, first spraying her armpits, then selecting the body mist and spraying her torso, legs and feet, before finally, with one foot on the side of the bath, picking up the Femfresh and copiously spraying her crotch. However, a few seconds later Reyna stood bolt upright and dropped the spray can.

"Oh no!" she exclaimed out loud. Then, more urgently, "No, no. Oh god, no!"

She then grabbed the bath towel, put it between her legs and pulled it rapidly back and forth to try to remove the deodorant she'd sprayed on herself a few moments before. That appeared to offer no relief as seconds later she could be seen on camera 3 and then camera 4, sitting on the bedroom carpet with her legs straight out in front of her, manically dragging herself around the room, her hands resembling raptor's claws as her fingernails dug into the carpet to move her forward.

She was now simultaneously screaming and muttering like a woman possessed, but with the carpet seemingly offering no respite from the overwhelming pain she was experiencing, Reyna got to her feet and rushed back to the bathroom where she straddled the bidet and, apparently now cured of her water phobia, opened the tap. But no water came out.

Camera 2 showed her turn and with crazy, mad eyes, rush towards the shower where she frantically scrabbled at the shower knob, but no water came from the shower either. She then grabbed the Evian bottle from next to the sink but found that to be empty.

A new idea of how to resolve her agonising plight seemed suddenly to occur to her. Throwing the empty Evian bottle to the floor, she ran into the bedroom, through the room at speed, out through the open patio doors and across the terrace, where she vaulted the balustrade in a single almighty leap, intent on reaching the cooling water of the swimming pool six floors below.

As Reyna disappeared off camera, her screams of pain instantly changed into a blood-curdling screech of terror which lasted for several seconds; the horrifying banshee squeal ending with a dramatic thud followed by just a moment of silence before the cacophony of the hotel guests' shrieks and screams started.

Charlie rushed from the room to the balcony and looked down. There, a metre or so inside the edge of the pool, Reyna lay face down and motionless, spreadeagled in exactly the shape that forensics teams mark out in chalk or white tape to precisely record where, and in what position, corpses have been found. Reyna's athletic leap had propelled her far enough from her balcony to reach the pool, but aside from the crimson puddle slowly growing around her, the pool was completely empty.

"Jesus Pippa. What the…" Charlie started, but Pippa was nowhere to be seen; at least, not until he looked at the laptop screen where he could see her hurriedly removing the evidence of her presence from Reyna's room two floors above. One by one, the screens went blank as Pippa removed the cameras.

A few minutes later Pippa was back in the room and looking very pleased with herself. "Well, that all went perfectly to plan," she said with a smile.

"I didn't know there was a plan," said Charlie, still in a state of shock.

"There's always a plan. Usually several. Prior preparation and planning prevent piss poor performance, as my troop captain used to say. The idea started to form after her ex-husband told me about her water aversion and her use of deodorant sprays, and then the rest of the idea came to me when I discovered that her room was directly above the swimming pool. Seems we cured her of her water phobia," said Pippa with a chuckle.

"But what made her go so crazy after she spayed herself with the Femfresh?" asked Charlie.

"It wasn't Femfresh. I emptied the can and refilled it with oven cleaner," replied Pippa.

Charlie's expression perfectly communicated his incredulity and horror in equal measure. "Oven cleaner. You got her to spray herself with oven cleaner!"

"Yep, effective, wasn't it?" said Pippa with pride. "Knowing that the pain would be so intense that it would eclipse her water phobia, I isolated all the taps and the shower, figuring that when no water came out, there was about an eighty percent chance that in desperation, she'd try to jump from the terrace into the pool, and by then would be in such a hurry that she probably wouldn't look before she leapt.

"I did all of that while you were waiting for her in the lobby. I also called the front desk pretending to be from the Washington Community Hygiene Department to inform them that an enforcement officer would be visiting to conduct a random pool check and would take a water sample later this afternoon. I knew that they'd then check the pool, and on finding your magnificent turd, would immediately call Washington Pool Services. I hacked the hotel's phone system, so that when they did, the call came through to me. Last night I broke into Wasps' workshop and *borrowed* one of their uniforms, so when I got the call, all I had to do was turn up in reception fifteen minutes later and let them beg me to drain the pool. It all went off like clockwork."

"But won't the Police start to work out that something's not right when they find oven cleaner during the autopsy?" asked Charlie.

"No, because I found a brand of oven cleaner called 'Oven Fresh' with a very similar-looking label. When I removed the cameras from her room, I also swapped the modified can of Femfresh for a can of Oven Fresh. The Police will just think she picked up the wrong product in the super-market," replied Pippa.

"Then, won't they wonder why she didn't just wash it off in the bidet?" asked Charlie.

"No, because you can't just wash it off," Pippa explained. "Water activates acid and makes it worse. So, they'll think she used the bidet and then made the leap for the pool after the bidet didn't relieve the pain. Funny, if she'd been a chemist, she would have known that the alkaline liquid in the fire extinguisher would have been her best option. That would have been quite something to watch on the cameras, eh? Her sticking the fire extinguisher hose in her...."

It was Charlie's turn to interrupt, "Alright Pippa, that's enough, I get the idea. Anyway, I guess I'd better take you home before you kill anyone else. How many has it been so far? The two kiddy-fiddlers, the guy in the diner that you dismembered to fit in the drain, Carlo Groteel, his four bodyguards and Reyna. That's nine in three days!"

"I know. It's been a really lovely trip. I've enjoyed every moment. Thank you so much for inviting me. When can we have another holiday like this? I've heard Moscow is lovely this time of year," Pippa replied, with a beaming smile.

# Chapter 63
# The Invitation

"Nine!" Exclaimed Flore.

"Yes, it was a bloodbath. She hacked the arms off one of them, so she could hide the corpse in a drain. She killed Carlo Groteel and his four bodyguards, cremated the bodies and dumped the ashes in a river, and Reyna leapt to her death from a sixth-floor balcony into an empty swimming pool after Pippa tricked her into spraying her vagina with oven cleaner. Oh, and there was a bit of collateral damage with two people that she discovered were paedophiles. She was in her element; like a terrier killing rats. She loved every moment of it. To be honest, so did I. They all thoroughly deserved it, and the world's a much better place without them," said Charlie.

"My god, listen to yourself. What have you become?" exclaimed Sylvain.

"I've been thinking about that. I think I was always this way. I just never realised before," Charlie admitted with forthright honesty. "Anyway, what's your news?"

"We're about to overthrow the Greek government, install our own puppet leader, and impose your electionless democracy model," said Sylvain in an exaggerated, ironic tone.

"Wow. And what have you become? You sound like the head of the CIA. Are you going to kidnap anyone who doesn't agree with your plan, lock them up without trial on a remote island, and then waterboard them every day for a few years?" asked Charlie.

"Everything's being done as naturally as possible, letting events unfold more or less their own way. We're just providing a bit of support," said Flore.

At that moment, Flore's phone rang. "It's Kostas. Game on," she said, before answering the call and putting it on speaker so the others could hear.

"OK. You've got my attention. You're invited back. Come here at seven this evening," said a man's voice in perfect English, but with a strong Greek accent.

# THE COSMIC KNOT PARADOX

# Chapter 64
# Analyse This

Kostas took a cold beer from the fridge, then a bottle opener from the neatly arranged implements in the kitchen drawer, and having opened the beer, put the opener back in its precise position. Everything has to have a place and a purpose, he thought as he closed the drawer and took a sip of beer, looking out of the kitchen window, lost in his thoughts contemplating his place and purpose, and what he would say to the woman who had made him one of the wealthiest men in Greece.

"Good evening, Kostas," said a voice behind him.

Kostas spun around to see Flore standing behind him, dressed in the same, casual jeans and blouse as earlier in the week; this time, a pair of binoculars also around her neck.

"Jesus! I wish you'd stop doing that," Kostas exclaimed, "There is a doorbell, you know."

Flore smiled. "Sorry, I didn't mean to scare you. I just didn't want to be seen coming to the door."

"So, you just snuck in. I guess that's what you spooks do," replied Kostas in a matter-of-fact tone, "What are the binoculars for?"

"They're so I can see things at a distance," said Flore, with another smile.

"Obviously," replied Kostas with a sigh, realising he wasn't going to get a straight answer to his question, "Anyway, let's get on to why I've asked you here. I've now got more money than I'll ever need. What am I going to do with it? Are you going to tell me how you did it? Can the CIA hack lottery systems now?" Kostas asked, directly and dispassionately, as if asking such a question was a normal query.

"I told you, I'm not CIA. I'm just someone who cares about the future of humanity. And don't worry about what to do with the money," replied Flore.

"Why?" asked Kostas.

"Because you're going to give it all away," replied Flore. Kostas raised his eyebrows, prompting Flore to add, "But I'll get to that later."

"You said that you'd seen the future and that Arpa polls less than three per cent of the vote at the election. What do you think happens?" asked Kostas.

"What I know happens, is that everything goes really well at first. Arpa dominates the news headlines for all the right reasons, and enjoys a massive swing of support, taking voters from all the main parties, just as you've planned. That persists right up until three days before the election, at which point, with the finishing line in sight and on the cusp of the biggest political landslide the world has ever witnessed, a huge scandal involving one of your most prominent candidates breaks. Arpa goes from eighty per cent opinion poll ratings to almost zero, all in the space of a couple of days," Flore explained.

"A scandal. What sort of scandal? That can't be true. All of the candidates are decent, honest people. I've vetted them all over many years. I've analysed every detail of their political and personal lives," said Kostas, incredulity evident in both his voice and expression.

"Then, analyse this," replied Flore, pausing for a moment as she evaluated the various options of exactly how she would deliver the bombshell, and finally opting for the most direct approach. "One of your candidates is a giraffophile."

"A what?" asked Kostas, as disbelief gave way to confusion and his mind raced through the sheer improbability of what he'd just been told. Although he had never heard the word 'giraffophile' before, he had worked out its meaning and posed his question to provide time to think and assimilate, rather than seek definition.

"It's a person who engages in sexual acts with giraffes," said Flore, matter-of-factly.

"You're making this up. I was wrong to start trusting you. No Greek person, or anybody else for that matter, would ever want to have sex with a giraffe. It's simply beyond belief. You've hacked the lotto and invented this sick story to make me give up," said Kostas, pointedly.

"I'm not making this up, Kostas. It really does happen," said Flore as she took her phone from her pocket. "Look. This is the video that goes viral on every news and social media channel four days before the election."

The video started with a hand reaching out to open a door. The door

carried a prominent stop symbol and sign that read, 'Giraffe Enclosure
- Authorised Personnel Only'. The door swung open and the person
holding the camera progressed through to the pens whispering their
narration in Greek. Their speech had been subtitled in English for the
benefit of international media. 'I'm entering the giraffe enclosure at
Athens Zoo,' read the subtitles, 'If the information we've been given is
correct, we will soon find the man who, on Monday next week is expected
to become Greek Minister for Finance, committing unspeakable acts with
one of the giraffes.'

"Oh my god! That's Yiannis Papadopoulos. Surely not," exclaimed
Kostas.

The shot continued past one enclosure with a giraffe standing alone,
apparently unmolested and happily chewing on some grass, past two
empty enclosures, and then, approaching the fourth pen, a stepladder
started to come into focus out of the darkness. The camera panned
upwards, and there perched on the top step of the ladder, the back of
a man could be seen directly behind a giraffe. The man was naked from
the waist down, his trousers around his ankles. He was wearing a T-shirt
with the words 'Arpa…in Harmony with Nature' written across the back
of the shirt. In his left hand he was holding the giraffe's tail to one side,
while his right hand was held aloft, like a rodeo competitor.

The narrator shouted, 'Yiannis' and the startled man turned around so
suddenly that he lost his footing on the stepladder, which then fell over,
leaving him suspended in mid-air, desperately clutching the giraffe's tail,
his feet almost two metres off the ground. The camera zoomed in on
Yiannis' startled face, focusing on his manic, terrified eyes, silently but
perfectly betraying his thoughts; 'The game is over,' they unambiguously
announced to the ten million Greeks and a billion or more others from
around the world who would watch the clip over the following days.

Kostas slowly and repeatedly banged his forehead with the palm of
his hand. "That'll be the day of the Greenpeace rally that's scheduled for
five days before the election. We'd planned to have a presence there. I
approved the 'In Harmony with Nature' T-shirts the day before yesterday.
That's got a rather hollow ring to it now."

"All is not lost, Kostas. We can fix this before it happens. You can still
win the election," said Flore.

"How? If I drop Papadopoulos now, he could sabotage everything," replied Kostas.

"You don't need to drop him; we can cure him," replied Flore.

"Cure him? How? And you said 'we'. Who are you working for?" Having relaxed his guard and started to trust Flore, Kostas had suddenly become very suspicious again. "That's one of those deep fake videos. You're playing me."

"Kostas, I'm not playing you," said Flore, as she took two steps towards Kostas, then reached out and gently put her hand in his, telling him, "I'll show you why I brought the binoculars."

A moment later they were standing on the top platform of a wooden castle in a children's playground. Kostas' eyes were the size of saucers. "What the fuck just happened? What have you done to me? And where are we?" he asked, breathlessly.

"We're in the children's play area in Athens Zoo. The date is 20th March," replied Flore, handing Kostas the binoculars and, pointing to a building some fifty metres away with open sides within an enclosure surrounded by a moat and a low wall, told him, "Look over there."

Kostas took the binoculars and focused them on the structure Flore had pointed to. What he saw was completely consistent with what he'd seen earlier in the video. He could see a man standing at the top of a tall step ladder directly behind a giraffe with his trousers down, wildly jerking back and forth. Seconds later, the man was suddenly startled by something, lost his balance on the ladder, and ended up suspended metres from the ground, clutching the giraffe's tail. At this point, the man turned his head which confirmed Kostas' worst fears. The man dangling in mid-air, was indeed Yiannis Papadopoulos, his intended finance minister. Kostas handed the binoculars back to Flore.

"Sorry, I doubted you. Political scandals don't come much bigger than this. What the fuck am I going to do?" said Kostas, utterly dejected.

Flore took Kostas' hand and moments later they were back in the villa.

# Chapter 65
# New Republic

"I don't understand it. He's a family man. He loves his wife and his children. And he's from a good family, an aristocratic family. If we hadn't become a republic, he would be fifth in line to the Greek throne," said Kostas, trying to make sense of what he'd just witnessed.

That's what explains it, Kostas. The royal connection," said Flore.

"What are you talking about? What does being fifth in line to the Greek throne have to do with giraffe fucking?" asked Kostas, despair still evident in his voice.

Flore recounted the case of the British royal, telling Kostas about the secret train line from Buckingham Palace to Regents Park, and how they had caught and cured the perpetrator, concluding by explaining the connection.

"They're blood relations, Kostas. There's a genetic predisposition to giraffophilia in the family. But the good news is that we can cure him. You can go ahead with your election campaign and still have Papadopoulos as finance minister. He won't even remember being treated. He'll just wake up one morning feeling a bit uncomfortable, but crucially he'll have no further interest in giraffes," Flore explained.

"You said '*We* can cure him'. I'm going to ask you again, who are you? Who are you working for? Who is 'We'? And why are you doing this?" Kostas demanded.

Over the hours that followed, Flore explained that she was one of six ordinary people, who had stumbled upon the ability to travel at will through time and space, and that, having seen the catastrophe of the near future, they had decided to save humanity from itself. She described the global meltdown, the ecological calamity, and the descent of well-ordered modern societies into a global free-for-all dystopia of lawlessness that ends with few survivors and, unlike other human crises, absolutely no winners.

Having completely demoralised Kostas, Flore then went on to describe the Einstein Plan and how humanity could be saved, but only with radical, far-reaching changes to political, economic, industrial, and societal structures. She told him how they had already perfected nuclear fusion, and how that would first slow, and then quickly reverse climate change. She explained how the mini-farms would avert the famines and outlined the now-advanced plans to provide a stable exchange mechanism with an innovative supply structure designed to incentivise learning. She told Kostas of their ability to almost eradicate disease and the tandem plan to prevent the world from becoming overpopulated.

"Sounds rather Huxleyesque. The Monstera is Huxley's Soma, and what you called the Matriverse amounts to the euthanasia he described in the same book," said Kostas.

"No, because it's not euthanasia. People will have normal lives and normal deaths. The Matriverse simply offers the opportunity to be able to continue life in a different realm; immortality in the virtual world. Every shred of someone's consciousness, what you could call their soul, will continue in the Matriverse. In Huxley's Brave New World, people were simply murdered when they ceased to be useful. They had no agency, no choice. It was done to them. Everything in our brave new world will be consensual," replied Flore.

"Still seems like you're playing god," replied Kostas. "Anyway, what's your plan for rolling this out? I'm guessing that the reason you're here is that you've decided that it should start here in Greece, and you want me to be the puppet leader of your new world order."

"Yes, but only for a short time. You're just going to be the catalyst," said Flore, with abrupt honesty. "The manifesto you're going to publish is going to state that you're going to implement a system of truly rep-resentative democracy, but a democracy without the need for any more elections. You're going to be a caretaker president for four years. During that time, you'll build the foundations for the future of Greece for the next thousand years and beyond."

"What do you mean? How can you have a democracy without any elections?" asked Kostas.

Flore explained in detail how the system would work; taking a random selection of the population, and then, through a series of steps, refin-ing the group to a subset of the most suitable, who would then be comprehensively trained to equip them for the challenges of governance. She described how the process would be continuous with a percentage of parliamentarians leaving and new people arriving every month.

"What if it doesn't work? Without elections, the Greek people will be stuck with it. They'll never vote for that," said Kostas, having listened to Flore intently for almost an hour.

"There'll be a safety net," replied Flore, "Every four years, there'll be a simple yes or no referendum on whether or not to continue with the new system."

"So, we go to all this effort to get elected and fulfil a lifetime ambition of leading Greece, and then, having achieved that, we just hand over our hard-won victory to the general public. We'll be asking people to vote for Christmas, but we'll be the turkeys. That'll be a hard sell to my group," said Kostas.

"Well, then maybe some of your group are in this for the wrong reasons. But it would make sense for the first parliament under the new structure to include some people with political experience, to mentor and guide the newbies. So, I suggest you take sixty members, twenty per cent of the total, chosen by secret ballot, through into the new system. After that, they'd be subject to the self-cleaning mechanism like everyone else. If they're good they'll endure, if not, they'll be out of the door," Flore replied.

Kostas, clearly deep in thought, first nodded his tacit approval, then a few moments later said, "Let's do it."

"Your job now is to get your compatriots on board and then re-write the Greek constitution so it can be published at the same time as your election manifesto," said Flore.

"And what needs to be in the manifesto apart from the new democracy model?" asked Kostas.

"Well, as we've already discussed, the world is going to change in ways that people can barely imagine, and you need to prepare Greece for those changes. So, your manifesto needs to address food security, energy security and employment," said Flore.

"There will always be employment in Greece. We have more than thirty million tourists each year," replied Kostas.

"Kostas, either you've not listened or not understood what I've told you. Ten years from now, there won't be any tourists. Global unemployment will be about eighty-five per cent. Nobody will have any money. Most jobs will be taken by machines of some sort – artificial intelligence will not only supersede most white-collar roles but will also control the machines that perform the blue-collar jobs, like factory work, driving buses or taxis, collecting and processing garbage, and even preparing and serving food. Without intervention, wealth will very rapidly concentrate in the hands of those who make or own the machines. This will happen at a staggering pace, perhaps one hundred times faster than the Industrial Revolution of the late eighteenth century. Karl Marx may have been wrong about many things, but he was right when he said that ownership of the means of production is what stratifies society and divides the haves from the have-nots, the proletariat from the bourgeoisie. Do you understand now?"

"Yes, I get it. So, what's the answer? How will people make a living and create fulfilling futures for themselves and their children?" asked Kostas.

"That's their problem," replied Flore, her words surprising even herself.

"Their problem! What kind of answer is that? That's not why I've chosen to start a career in politics, to just abandon people like that," said Kostas, clearly angered by Flore's response.

"That's right, Kostas. That's why you've been chosen. Your job is to stop people from starving and give them income security for long enough to prevent societal breakdown. Your job is to give people time to reinvent themselves and find their niche in a world that's going to change very, very quickly," replied Flore.

"And how will I do that? What you've described sounds like a circle that can't be squared. You want me to solve the unsolvable," said Kostas, the discomfort of the conundrum evident in his voice and expression.

"You're underestimating your people. Humans are incredibly creative and adaptable. They'll find their way. You just need to protect them from the worst of the changes that are coming and create the foundation from which they can flourish," said Flore.

"But how?" repeated Kostas.

"You're going to implement universal basic income to help people through the difficult times. Everyone will receive a monthly income that's sufficient to live on whether they work or not. But it won't be UBI like it's been proposed or tried before. You're going to adopt a new currency that will run in tandem with the Euro for a while, until the Euro, along with the US Dollar, Japanese Yen, Swiss Franc, and most of the other fiat currencies, collapses a few years from now. Supply of the new currency will be limited by the speed at which people can learn. People will get their UBI in the new currency. They'll receive bigger payments for achieving learning milestones, so there'll still be an intellectual meritocracy of sorts, but they'll be able to study pretty much whatever they want.

"Within ten years, the Greek people will be the most educated and knowledgeable on the planet. There'll be people currently driving taxis and waiting tables who will become scientists; factory workers who become playwrights, artists, philosophers, therapists, and doctors. Knowledge will empower their creativity and give them the ability to find their edge against the machines, thinking of or doing something that only a real person can do well. Of course, there'll be some people who choose to do nothing apart from eat junk food, get drunk every day and pass their days watching daytime TV, but that'll be their choice, their problem, and their loss if they pass up the opportunities that unlimited learning offers.

"In any case, in any society that has a welfare state with the safety net of unemployment and disability benefits, people like that always find all manner of creative ways to get their hands on free money, so you're already paying for them anyway. The alternative is to cut them off completely and have them living in cardboard boxes on the street and begging, stealing, or both, to support their inevitable addictions to alcohol, drugs, and junk food," Flore concluded.

"So, how will all this be paid for?" asked Kostas.

"You're going to completely alter the tax system," Flore explained. "Corporation tax will be set at different rates according to a company's profit per employee. So, a company that fires all its employees and replaces them with machines will pay a much higher rate of tax than the companies that keep humans on the payroll. You'll need to create the tax bands so that you don't disadvantage the small and medium-sized businesses that have few employees, but that'll be an easy problem to solve.

"As far as personal income tax is concerned, the UBI that everyone gets will be tax-free, and anything they earn beyond that will be taxed at ten per cent."

"Ten per cent! How will the government balance its books with income tax at ten per cent? Greece will be bankrupt in six months," Kostas replied.

"No, because at ten per cent, almost nobody will have an incentive to avoid or evade the tax system. There'll be no reason for the wealthy to create complicated offshore tax structures, and not only that, Greece will also become a magnet for the best and brightest entrepreneurs on the planet. Your total tax receipts will increase rather than decrease, and anyway, government spending will fall by a huge percentage, because in the public sector, machines will do eighty per cent of the jobs currently done by people. Most of those people, liberated from dull, humdrum jobs, supported by UBI and with access to unlimited learning, will then end up doing something fulfilling; something that they want to do, rather than something that they've had to do to put food on the table and pay the bills, but probably never enjoyed much, and therefore didn't do very well. Having half of your working population stuck in boring, dead-end jobs that they don't enjoy isn't a great recipe for a happy society, is it? And an unhappy society is an unhealthy society. This changes all of that," Flore explained.

"Sounds amazing if it'll work. It sounds like the best elements of socialism and the free market combined," said Kostas.

"That's exactly right. And it will work, Kostas. We've modelled it using our own AI, thousands of times. Every result has been more or less the same. It'll work, believe me," said Flore.

"OK, I'll just have to trust you on that. You also talked about food and energy security. Given what you've told me about the ecological horrors that are about to unfold, how can we offer any guarantees about energy or food?" asked Kostas.

Flore spent the next hour explaining about the fusion reactors and the virtually limitless, carbon-free energy that they will provide. She then went on to outline how the mini farms would enable the Greek population to grow, in abundance, every fruit and vegetable that one might find in a typical supermarket, even if climate change and pollution make traditional agriculture impossible.

"So, the key points of your manifesto will promise electoral reform, unlimited access to education for everyone, energy, food and income security, and tax cuts. What's not to like? And you're going to back up your manifesto with a personal pledge. You're going to immediately donate half of your lottery win to charity and make a promise that if you fail to deliver on any of the key points of your manifesto, you'll donate the other half.

"Your challenge is to make a manifesto with such big promises credible, and to convince the Greek public that you really can deliver on what you've pledged. If you can pull this off, Greece will be the blueprint for a new world order and over the next ten to twenty years, most of the rest of the world will follow. You're going to be remembered and revered as the man who changed the world Kostas, not just Greece."

# THE COSMIC KNOT PARADOX

# Chapter 66
# Paradise Lost

The television screen went blank, apart from the words 'No input signal' and the alien, Tom, got up from the boulder he'd been leaning against and stretched his legs.

"That's all folks. Hope you enjoyed the movie," he said, doing his best to force a smile onto the inexpressive face of the alien suit.

"That's all? But you've not shown us what happens in Greece, or how or why we all died," said Flore, the frustration evident in her voice, like someone who had just binge-watched a ten-hour Agatha Christie murder mystery marathon, only to get to point where Hercule Poirot has the possible suspects assembled in the drawing room, but instead of naming the murderer and his or her motives and methods, just says, 'I am probably the greatest detective in the entire world, but I 'ave no idea which of you is ze killer, so you can all go home now.'

"Yes, at the start, you told us you would tell us about our purpose in life, and how we could stop this from happening," said Charlie, casting his arm around, mimicking the same gesture that Tom had used a few hours earlier to highlight the devastation on the island.

"It's not important," said Tom, "I just said that to get your attention. Everyone wants to know how they'll die, even if they say they don't. I just told you that to make sure you listened to what I told you. It's everything else that's important."

"How is it not the most important? It's our lives. All of our lives, and the future of the world, of humanity itself," said Flore, desperation now dominating her tone.

"I've got a question," said Lucia.

"OK. What's your question, Lucia?" replied Tom.

"Is there any more coffee?" Lucia asked, somewhat sheepishly.

"Oh, for fuck's sake," said Tom, who nevertheless, a moment later, was holding a tray of coffees which he then offered around the group.

"Seriously Tom, how can you show us all of that and tell us that we all die, but not tell us how or why?" asked Sylvain.

"I told you, it's not important. It's everything else that's important. You all bought into the concept of saving humanity and creating a better world, and you all started with the loftiest principles, but all of you, all of us, not only made mistakes but sacrificed our principles somewhere along that journey. Your demise offered the chance of a reset, and that's why you're all here now. Like I said at the beginning, you're here so that you can learn from your mistakes before you make them," said Tom.

"That doesn't make sense. If all of us died, how could there be a reset?" asked Flore.

"The cosmic knot paradox?" ventured Charlie.

With a sigh that suggested he was revealing more than he had wanted to, Tom explained, "No, it's not the cosmic knot paradox. It's because I wasn't there at the precise moment that the rest of you died. So, I've been able to come back to save you, to let you have another go. Hopefully, I've helped you to not make the same mistakes again."

"Oh yes, of course, I forgot. You're our saviour. Old habits die hard, even if you're the messiah," said Charlie with heavy sarcasm.

"Why weren't you there, Tom? Where were you?" asked Marion.

"That doesn't matter either. The only thing that's important is that you've seen what you became during your journey," said Tom, defensively.

"What do you mean, what we became?" asked Flore.

"Isn't that obvious? I'd hoped that this would be something you'd all understand without the need for any blame and shame or guilt trips. Do I need to spell it out?" Asked Tom.

"Yes, spell it out, Tom. And make it simple enough for us to understand," Flore retorted sarcastically, anger now dominant in her voice.

"Well, over the last hundred and thirty years, we've tortured, murdered, stolen, and deceived; manipulated financial markets, defrauded national lotteries, brainwashed people, and overthrown governments. We've killed people and buried them in deserts, floated others off to the upper atmosphere, turned people into human balloons and made people with acid-burned genitals jump to their death from sixth-floor balconies. We're no better than the CIA or the KGB," replied Tom. "Is that simple enough for you to understand?"

"But we had to do those things," said Charlie.

"You mean, we had to do those things to bend the world to our vision. Look at how we've all changed," said Tom. "Flore, you abandoned all of your principles the moment you sanctioned the assassination of Reyna Groteel. The rest of you went along with it, so even if it wasn't your idea, you're all complicit; guilty by association."

"The future of humanity depended on that decision, Tom. What was the alternative?" implored Flore.

"There are always alternatives," said Tom abruptly. "Sylvain, you completely embraced that 'can't make an omelette without breaking some eggs' ethos, conveniently forgetting any sense of right and wrong or fair play. You deceived your wife and cheated your friends; and you loved those *precious* coins just a bit too much. They had power over you. They corrupted you because you let them."

"You gave me the fucking coins, Tom," Sylvain protested. "Not only that, but it was you who told me that we had to become the Illuminati and there'd be times when we'd have to be devious to achieve our objectives."

"You still chose your path. I didn't hold a gun to your head. There's always a choice," Tom replied, defiantly. "Marion, you engaged in dangerous psychological experiments, brainwashing people who were abducted and had no agency. You convinced yourself that it was consensual, but there wasn't any choice for those people, and you knew that. And another thing, considering you used to insist on only eating free-range eggs, creating the world's biggest intensive chicken farm shows just how far you've fallen.

"Charlie, for you, all of this was always about your hatred of the church and religion in general, together with a few other obsessions of yours. You coached me to lambast and deceive that poor Pope. I'm ashamed of myself and you should be too. The worst part was that you really enjoyed it."

"Well, I wouldn't have had to if you hadn't created Jesus and all the shit that came afterwards," Charlie protested.

"I know. None of us are blameless. We're all guilty. Me more than the rest of you," Tom admitted with rare humility.

"How am I guilty? What did I do?" asked Lucia.

"You? You didn't do anything. And that's the point. You could have intervened, spoken up about things you knew were wrong; used your influence. You could have moderated Charlie; after all, you're probably the only person on the planet who could. But you didn't. And the reason you didn't was because you were too busy enjoying the adventure. You're as guilty as the rest of us," Tom replied.

"This is all bullshit," Charlie protested. "Last night, we met you for the first time, had our party, went to bed drunk, and then woke up to this. We're all completely innocent. We haven't done any of these things."

"You haven't done these things yet, in the thread that you've lived so far, but what you've just watched is what you did in a different thread, and would have done again if I hadn't shown you what I just have. It was your future. Now, because of my intervention, it'll be something different. What you need to understand is that whatever path you choose, even the seemingly most insignificant things have a myriad of consequences that alter everyone's futures in ways you can't imagine. Like I keep saying, I've brought you here and shown you the future so you can learn from your mistakes before you make them."

"But you still haven't told us what happens in Greece. How can we learn anything if you don't tell us how things turned out?" said Flore, "Did Kostas win the election and turn Greece into the social utopia that we planned? And what about the ecological catastrophe? Did we stop that by killing Reyna Groteel?"

"Well, the Greek experiment didn't go so well. Kostas and his ARPA party won a landslide victory as predicted, and for a while, it looked like things were working out. Unfortunately, it all fell apart when it turned out that Yiannis Papadopoulos wasn't the only giraffophile amongst Kostas' political clique. It was almost all of them, and worse still, Kostas was revealed as the ringleader of the Greek arm of an international cabal of giraffophiles made up of politicians, celebrities, industrialists, and members of several royal families. It was all organised and directed from a pizza restaurant in Woking, England. When the news broke, the Greek people rioted, and the army took over, imposing martial law to keep the peace until a new election, run along traditional lines, was held one month later. After that, everything returned to how it was before."

"Shit!" exclaimed Flore. "And what about the ecological catastrophe? Please tell us some good news."

"I wish I could," replied Tom, "but unfortunately, it turned out that Pippa missed a camera in the corridor of the sixth floor that was on a different circuit, as well as motion-triggered cameras the FBI had set into the end of Reyna Groteel's suitcase and washbag so they could keep tabs on her. When the footage emerged of Pippa entering Reyna's room and swapping the Femfresh and the light bulbs, a media and internet frenzy broke out. For the American public, it looked exactly like a deep-state execution. A group of MAGA Republicans bought the hoard of car tyres for almost nothing from the Groteel estate, then pushed Reyna's New ERA Act through Congress, pretty much unopposed. The ecological catastrophe unfolded just like the chickens predicted, only faster. An international arrest warrant was issued for Pippa who ended up on the run, hiding in the most remote parts of the Amazonian rainforest. As far as we know, she's still there."

"Fuck! Now, you need to tell us how we all died and why you didn't. Where were you, Tom?" Marion said in such an assertive tone that Tom knew there was no alternative but full disclosure.

"I wasn't there because we all had an argument, a bit like now, but worse. You were all berating me for the Jesus thing. I was trying to tell you that we'd all made mistakes. Then, when it all got too much, I...." Tom started to explain, but Marion interrupted.

"When it all got too much, you left. You went off in a strop. Like you always do. So, what happened? How did we all die?" said Marion.

"I bet we were all assassinated by some crazy Christian fundamentalist who discovered the Pope hoax. Or maybe it wasn't just some lone-wolf religious zealot. Perhaps it was the Vatican itself, and they sent the Swiss Guard to kill us all," said Charlie.

"More likely that your friend Pippa decided it was time to cover her tracks and tie up all the loose ends," said Marion.

"Pippa would never do that. She's a good psychopath. It was probably one of the not-so-good psychos that you thought you'd cured," said Charlie, looking at Marion reproachfully.

"It was none of those people and nothing like that," said Tom.

"So, who was it? Tell us," Marion implored.

"I told you, I don't want this to be about blame and shame. Just learn from your mistakes and move on," replied Tom.

"For fuck's sake, Tom, for the umpteenth fucking time, how can we learn from our mistakes if you don't tell us what they were? We're talking about a mistake that cost us our lives. We need to know," said Charlie.

"OK. Well, if you insist. It was you, Charlie," said Tom.

"Me? How? That can't be true. I wouldn't kill any of you. I love you all. You're family to me," Charlie retorted, emotion very evident in his voice.

"You were making breakfast in the upstairs kitchen. It was your turn. Then, when the argument really got going, you..." Tom started to explain, but Charlie jumped in.

"...Killed you all in a mad rage? No, surely not. I wouldn't, couldn't, do something like that. Please tell me that's not true," said Charlie, tears now welling up in his eyes.

"No, no, no. It's nothing like that. You'd turned the gas on to fry some eggs, but with the argument in full swing, you forgot to light it. Then, twenty minutes later, just after I'd left, you lit a cigarette and Boom!" said Tom, once again casting his arm around the devastated clearing, "Blown to smithereens. All of you, dead. Blown to pieces. No chance of survival. Didn't have a prayer."

"I knew it would be my fault," Charlie sobbed, "it always is."

"Well, smoking kills," said Sylvain.

Lucia rushed over and putting her arms around Charlie, told him, "It's OK Charlie. We're still here. We're together and we love each other. We can try again."

"So, what you all need to think about, is what you'll do differently next time," said Tom.

"Well, I can tell you now, we're definitely not having another gas hob. We can get one of those induction hobs, or maybe we should just cook on the barbeque," said Charlie, "What do you all think? Induction or barbeque?"

"No, silly. He means what will we do differently to save humanity, save the world from catastrophe," said Lucia.

"Maybe humanity shouldn't be saved," said Flore, abruptly, "Not if it means turning into what we'll apparently become. Tom's right. We abandoned all of our principles. And anyway, whatever we do will be just like putting plasters on the festering wound that we call humanity. If we really care about the planet, the best thing we can do is let chaos take its natural course and allow humanity to destroy itself. Maybe something better than us will evolve as the dominant species once the planet has healed itself. Maybe chickens or ducks, who knows. Anyway, I'm done. I want no further part in this."

"Me neither," said Lucia.

"Count me out too," added Sylvain.

"And me," said Marion, "And Tom, I'm leaving you. I'm sorry, but it's over. We'll never be able to be normal again."

To everyone's surprise, Tom made no effort to change her mind and instead, without emotion, replied, "I always knew that eventually you would. I understand," then, quickly turning his attention to Charlie, asked, "What about you, Charlie? Are you in or out?"

"Well, I'd like to continue, but not if it means living my life without Lucia. So, sorry Tom, but I'm out too," Charlie replied.

"Then, if you're all sure that that's your decision, I guess we'll just say goodbye," said Tom, who an instant later was holding a tray of what looked like Tom Collins. "You all look like you could do with a drink, so have these and then we'll go our separate ways."

# THE COSMIC KNOT PARADOX

# Chapter 67
# The End of the Beginning

Lucia opened her eyes. She could see through the curtain that it was just about light outside but instinctively knew that it wasn't morning. Charlie was snoring next to her. She gently nudged his thigh with her knee until he stopped snoring and gradually emerged into a light consciousness from his deep sleep.

"Uhhh, why did you wake me up?" he mumbled.

"You were snoring," replied Lucia.

"No, I wasn't. If I'd been snoring, I would have woken myself up. Anyway, I hardly ever snore. You were having that snoring dream again," said Charlie, his voice drifting off as he started to slip back into the clutches of slumber.

Lucia nudged him again with her knee.

"Uhhh, stop it. Leave me alone," Charlie protested.

"It's four o'clock in the afternoon," said Lucia.

"No, it's not. It's early morning," Charlie said in a barely audible half-whisper, his eyes still closed.

"It's not. It's afternoon. You've been snoring, then cuddling me, then throwing pillows, then snoring again for the last couple of hours. Now it's time to wake up, Charlie. Anyway, we've got to go and get that plant from Flore and Sylvain's flat," said Lucia gently.

Charlie was snoring again. Lucia nudged him once more, harder this time. Charlie growled, sat up in bed, hit Lucia with his pillow, then flopped back down, pulling the duvet over his head.

"That wasn't very loving. Come on Charlie, wake up Charlie," said Lucia.

"Why?" Charlie asked, as more of a protest than a question.

"Because you really want to make me coffee. There'll be treats after I've had coffee," said Lucia.

"I don't want treats," Charlie mumbled from under the duvet.

"Please make me a coffee, Charlie," said Lucia, pleadingly, knowing that Charlie wouldn't be able to ignore her tone.

Charlie gave up, stumbled out of bed and hobbled, naked and still half-asleep to the kitchen, but was back thirty seconds later.

"There's no milk," he said, as he sat on the side of the bed pulling the previous day's socks onto his feet, inside-out, then stood up and put on boxer shorts, jeans and a jumper. "I'll go to the shop," he said as he started to put on his shoes, then paused. "I had the weirdest dreams last night. Must have been that Placido stuff that Tom gave us last night. Tom was an alien and we were on this island; it was called Wesh, just like we were discussing last night, and then he was Jesus and there were flying cars and we could time travel, and then…"

Lucia interrupted. "…and then we all died, and it was your fault. I had the same dream."

"Really? You're kidding?" said Charlie in an astonished tone.

"No, I really did have the same dream. You built a sock sanctuary to stop me from stealing them. It was like Fort Knox with laser beams and fingerprint scanners to keep people out," said Lucia.

"How weird is that? And there was this other reality without any religion apart from…"

Lucia interrupted again, "…apart from Soliterranism, I think it was called, but it wasn't a religion because they didn't believe in any gods. But then it all got really weird, and we all had this really big argument."

"Yes! Wow! The Placido and the conversation we all had last night must have made us both imagine the same things and have the same dream. Or maybe it kind of connected us telepathically. How weird. I'll text Tom about it."

Taking his phone, Charlie quickly typed a message to Tom that read, 'Wow! Your Placido stuff is banging. I'll call you later.'

"Or maybe, it wasn't a dream," said Lucia, smiling.

"Ha, wouldn't that be cool, being able to time travel? We could go back in time so we could meet as teenagers and have an extra thirty years together," said Charlie.

"You're so sweet. I love you, Charlie," said Lucia.

"OK. I'm going to the shop. I'm going to miss you while I'm gone," Charlie said as he stood up.

# Chapter 68
# Bye

Charlie breathed in the November afternoon; the fresh, cool air soothing his hangover with each breath as he walked the short distance to the end of the street, feeling more alive with every step. A vibration and a whistle from his pocket informed him that he had a message. Taking his phone from his pocket he saw that it was a reply from Tom. It read, 'Who's this?'

Deciding that Tom probably hadn't saved his number and resolving to call him later to tell him about the dream, Charlie put the phone back in his pocket, crossed the road and entered the local shop. He picked up a small carton of semi-skimmed milk and headed straight to the counter.

"Afternoon Charlie. You look like you had a heavy one last night. You do know that they've dropped Drinking and Smoking from the Olympics roster; you could ease up a bit on the training," said Veli, the shopkeeper, with a smile.

"If only you knew. I'll tell you about it next time, when hopefully I'll be in better shape," replied Charlie.

Veli scanned the milk and said, "That'll be one Pound."

Charlie fumbled in the pocket of his jeans. He felt keys, then a couple of small coins, probably ten or twenty-cent Euro coins he thought, judging by their size and feel. He felt the bolt that had fallen out of the vacuum cleaner the week before, a cigarette lighter and then a radiator key before his fingers finally found what he was fairly sure were a couple of One Pound coins. Reflecting on how hard it would be to be blind, Charlie pulled one of the coins from his pocket. It was indeed a One Pound coin and Charlie handed it to Veli, then picked up the milk, ready to leave the store.

"Sorry, Charlie. This is a fake. What idiots! Look how badly they've made it. It's got two heads!" Veli exclaimed, "Morons."

Charlie instantly understood. There was no point giving Veli the other coin. That also would be the same on both sides, but both tails. Everything was suddenly clear. The dream hadn't been a dream at all. Charlie felt his heart pounding as his mind raced through everything he had seen, heard, said, and felt in the 'dream'. He felt the elation as, in his mind's eye, he saw the majestic island rising from the sea; he felt the excitement and trepidation of exploring the island and the house. He sensed the power of his love for Lucia, and the strength of his bond with Flore, Sylvain, Tom and Marion. Suddenly, he could feel the warmth of the Mediterranean sun, smell the sea air, and taste the apples from La Villa Strangiato's garden. His right hand instinctively moved to feel his chest.

Veli's startled voice cut through his thoughts, "Charlie, Charlie, are you OK? Are you having a heart attack? Do you want me to call an ambulance?"

"Sorry Veli, it's just my hangover. I'm fine," Charlie lied, trying to focus and not allow his thoughts the opportunity to distract him again and pull him back to the memories of what he now knew would be his future. "Let me find you some money. It's a Pound, right? It'll need to be a note or a card. I've not got any more coins."

Charlie took his wallet from the back pocket of his jeans, but there were no notes in the first compartment. In the second compartment, there were three ten Euro notes and a few US Dollar bills, but no Sterling. Charlie didn't usually put bank notes in the third compartment, it was reserved for train tickets and boarding passes, but he looked anyway. His heart raced again. There, in the otherwise empty wallet compartment was a pink lottery ticket with a single line of numbers. 'To Wesh and beyond' had been hand-written in pencil on the top of the ticket. "Tom," Charlie said out loud.

"No, I'm Veli. Are you sure you're alright? I can still make that call for you," said the shopkeeper, again looking very worried.

"Yes, Veli, I'm fine. Really. In fact, I'm more than fine. Could you check this ticket for me?" said Charlie, handing the lottery ticket to the worried shopkeeper.

Veli scanned the ticket on the Lotto machine and immediately raised his eyebrows, "Congratulations! It's a winning ticket!" he said excitedly. "It doesn't tell me how much, but it's more than the maximum five hundred we can pay out here. It just says, 'You're a winner. Call Camelot'. Hey, don't worry about the money for the milk. Just remember to bring it in before you jet off to the Seychelles," said Veli, with a smile.

"Well, if it's a jackpot, I'll bring you the Pound with interest – a suitcase full of interest," Charlie said as he picked up the milk and left the shop, thanking Veli as he made his way out through the door.

Charlie's mind was racing again. Instinctively, he knew the lottery win was going to be big, but that was insignificant compared to the immense changes he knew were about to engulf his and Lucia's lives. They would be able to do almost anything they wanted. They would have the capability to change the world, save humanity and improve billions of lives. He couldn't wait to get home to tell Lucia. They would be virtually immortal, Charlie thought as he stepped off the kerb to cross the road.

Jolted from his thoughts by the screeching of tyres and the blaring of a lorry's horn, Charlie just had time to turn his head to see the garbage truck that he had inadvertently walked out in front of, almost on top of him. There was no time for anything. No time to leap to safety, throw himself to the ground, or even experience his life flash through his mind's eye.

At the moment of impact, Charlie's final emotion was not one of panic or alarm, just passive disappointment with the thought, 'So this is how it ends'.

# THE COSMIC KNOT PARADOX

# Chapter 69
# As You Like It

Charlie's funeral was different from most typical send-offs. He'd always been resolute that he didn't want anything ceremonial of any sort, just a direct cremation with no service or mourners, followed by drinks for family and close friends in his favourite pub, The Shakespeare, in Stoke Newington. There were to be no suits, black ties, pallbearers or flowers, and 'Definitely no god', he'd said whenever the subject came up, often going on to add, 'And if there is any supernatural bullshit, you'd all better hope that there's no afterlife because I'll haunt you for eternity if you don't respect my wishes.'

The evening at The Shakespeare followed the format Charlie had described. The staff had reserved the covered garden area where an open bar had been set up to serve a selection of drinks, and the pizzeria next door brought a selection of pizzas every twenty minutes or so until people stopped eating them.

The 'mourners' consisted of Lucia, Charlie's adult sons and daughter; Charlie's sister and brother-in-law had flown in from Australia, and Lucia's parents, sister and brothers had come from Spain along with Lucia's eldest daughter. Beyond family members, Flore and Sylvain had returned from Marseilles, only a few days after their move there, and a few of Charlie's closest friends, plus several people that he had kept in touch with from his time working in the City, came to pay their respects. Pippa arrived but only stayed for about an hour, explaining that she was working that evening and had something scheduled that she couldn't be late for. All in all, about thirty people gathered in the pub garden.

Lucia had tried to contact Tom and Marion but didn't have either of their numbers. She found Tom's on Charlie's phone but when she called, it was answered by a woman who insisted that she didn't know anyone called Tom and that she'd had the number for eight years. Lucia imagined that Charlie must have noted Tom's number incorrectly – it had, after all, been late in the evening on the night of the party when Charlie had taken Tom's number, and a lot of booze had been consumed by then. Lucia asked Flore if she had Tom's details, but the number she provided was the same.

"Oh, that's strange, I've got the same number. Must be a fault at the phone company," she'd told Flore.

During the evening, a few people recounted their memories of Charlie. Lucia told the assembled group about how Charlie had come into her life, and how before that, for almost twenty years, they had lived almost parallel lives, never living more than a few hundred metres away from each other, but somehow, never meeting. She explained how they had simultaneously experienced the milestones of first marriages, children, then relationship traumas, separation and divorce, followed by second marriages and another child. Whilst that pattern was far from unusual, both had also endured periods of extreme stress from other, external factors, at almost exactly the same times. She described how they had independently listened to the same music, by the same artists and at the same time of day to soothe their souls. She told them how, after fate did finally allow them to meet, the first time Charlie had visited her flat, he had remarked that an antique metal chest had looked very familiar, going on to ask if the chest had had a streak of white paint across the top and a broken clasp that wouldn't close properly. Lucia told the astonished group that when she confirmed that yes, the chest did have those features, Charlie had told her that it had been his toy chest when he was a child.

She went on to relate some of the emotions of the preceding week and the challenges she knew she'd have to face moving forward, finding room for a little humour as she told the group, "Not least being what I'm going to do with all the socks. Did you know about Charlie's sock obsession? He had almost three hundred and fifty pairs, and they're all almost exactly the same!"

Charlie's sons recounted how, when they had been about nine and twelve respectively, their father had 'treated' them to a very high-speed trip along a quiet stretch of motorway. "At one hundred and seventy miles per hour, the windscreen wipers started lifting off the windscreen," one of them had explained to the rather shocked group.

One of Charlie's former city colleagues told how Charlie had had an uncanny ability to predict, often with surprising accuracy, what would be the daily high or low of the bond markets he followed, adding that he never really understood why Charlie had turned his back on the market at the time that he had.

Around ten o'clock, people started to offer their final condolences, bid their farewells and drift off. The evening finally wrapped up at just after eleven and Flore and Sylvain walked back to the flat with Lucia, having decided to stay for a couple more days to provide both emotional and practical support. Sat around the coffee table in the living room, each with a gin and tonic that Sylvain had prepared, Lucia told Flore and Sylvain about the last conversation she'd had with Charlie before his fateful trip to buy milk, relating their surprise at having both had the same dream.

"You both had a vivid dream about that island colony we talked about at the party?" Flore asked, looking astonished, "We did too! It was the same for both of us."

"Yes, the dream included pretty much everything we discussed during the party, so I guess our imaginations, helped by that Placido stuff Tom gave us, just filled in the details to make it seem real," said Lucia, "But it was quite freaky. It was as if we'd been telepathically connected while we were asleep," said Lucia.

"Yes, it was just like that for us," said Sylvain, "But what really amazed us was that the details we remembered from the dream weren't just similar, they were exactly the same, to the finest detail. For example, in the dream, Flore met with a Greek journalist called Kostas…" Sylvain, started to explain, but Lucia finished his sentence.

"Constantinou," she said, "Kostas Constantinou. He was a journalist but had created a party called Arpa and had planned a sort of peaceful, democratic coup."

"What the fuck?" exclaimed Flore, astonished, "That's the most incredible thing. How could you have dreamed the exact same detail as us?"

"Wow, imagine if the dream wasn't a dream and was actually real. We'd be able to time travel and change the past," said Lucia, "I'd be able to get my Charlie back."

"Yes, if only," said Flore, with a sympathetic smile as she put her arms around Lucia, who had started to cry.

"Like Lucia said, it must have been the Placido that Tom gave us that kind of connected us telepathically. We'll have to tell him about it, it'll be important info for his research," said Sylvain.

"Yes, but how can we tell him? Lucia says some woman answers his number and says she doesn't know him. Not only that, but she also claims to have had the number for years. I'm a bit worried about Tom and Marion; maybe they didn't make it home last Saturday. Maybe they got mugged or worse. Perhaps they're being kept somewhere against their will and that's why some strange woman is answering his phone. I'm going to file a missing persons report with the Police tomorrow," said Flore.

"Well, if you're going to the Police, Charlie got to know one of the officers at the local station a few months ago after someone tried to steal his car; the guy was really helpful and efficient. Charlie kept his card in his wallet in case anything else happened. I'm sure it'll still be there. Hang on, I'll get it," said Lucia.

Lucia went off to the bedroom where she'd kept the box of Charlie's personal items given to her at the hospital along with a death certificate and a pamphlet entitled 'Dealing with Bereavement', The box contained the ring she'd given him, his watch, wallet, and the contents of his pockets. A couple of minutes later, she returned to the living room. Flore and Sylvain could immediately tell that something was wrong. Lucia's face was ashen, and her eyes betrayed a mix of shock and hope.

"Look what I found in the wallet," she said, holding up a lottery ticket, "Charlie didn't play the lottery, and look, it's got 'To Wesh and Beyond' written on it and I'm sure it's Tom's writing. Not only that but look, there are these Pound coins," she said, handing the coins to Sylvain.

"Oh my god!" exclaimed Sylvain, as he turned the first coin over, seeing that both sides of the coin had been cast with an image of the Queen's head. The other coin also had two identical sides, both tails.

While Sylvain and Lucia had been occupied with the coin, Flore had checked the lottery ticket using her phone.

"Congratulations Lucia. You and Charlie's kids are all multi-millionaires. The ticket matches every number and there were no other winners for that draw. I won't tell you the amount right now, but it's a lot," said Flore, who then picked up her phone again and quickly tapped something out on the screen.

"Oh, fuck!" exclaimed Flore, moments later.

"What? What is it?" asked Sylvain.

Turning her phone around, Lucia and Sylvain saw the results of the web search Flore had just done. In the bar at the top of the screen were the words, 'Konstantinos Constantinou'. Below, the first result showed a picture of a Greek man in his early forties, with the words, 'Konstantinos (Kostas) Constantinou is a writer and political journalist,' Beneath that, several other results, all had similar text.

"It's him," said Flore, "that's the man I met in my dream. He's a real person, not some Placido-induced invention of my imagination. And the coins, and the lottery ticket; the handwriting on the ticket was Tom's, no doubt about it, but Tom and Marion arrived here on the night of the party at just after seven. I know that because I had a text from Tom at 19:02 saying, 'At the door,' but the ticket is timestamped at 19:28 pm. At that time, Tom was sitting here with us, around this table with a drink in his hand. The only way this is possible is if…"

"The dream wasn't a dream. It was real," said Lucia, "Tom nipped off to get the ticket around the time that he joked with Charlie about playing the lottery and came back without us noticing he'd gone – just like he was able to do in the dream. Do you remember? And now, he's gone back in time to try to put right the things he got wrong before. That's why someone else has his number; because he doesn't exist here in this space-time thread; at least, not in the way that we know him."

"My god! If everything that happened after the party, in our thread, has changed, then the Monstera plant might still be in the front garden of our old flat!" exclaimed Flore.

After a short scramble to put on shoes and coats, all three hurried out of the flat, crossed Albion Road and made their way through the back-streets to Walford Road, where Flore and Sylvain had lived until only ten days before. Lucia was first to reach the front gate. As Flore and Sylvain hurried towards her, Lucia turned to face them. Tears were streaming down her cheeks.

"She's still there," she exclaimed, her voice so thick with emotion that she could barely get the words out.

With La Monstera safely in Sylvain's arms, his hands clasped together to hold the large pot to his torso and La Monstera's leaves brushing against his face and neck, the three started to make their way back to Lucia's flat. After just a couple of minutes, Sylvain said that he felt the same sense of calm and bonding with the plant that Tom had described in the 'dream'.

"Who's first for a tea or a juice when we get back? The sooner we start, the sooner we'll be able to go and rescue Charlie," Sylvain said, the exertion of carrying the heavy plant evident in his voice.

"You sound like you're struggling a bit. Let me carry her for a while," said Lucia, carefully taking the plant from Sylvain.

After only fifty metres with the plant in her arms and the leaves touching her skin, Lucia remarked that she too was experiencing the same sense of wellbeing and calm that Sylvain had just described.

"It's working. It's having exactly the effect that Tom talked about," she said, tears starting to roll down her cheeks once more.

"It doesn't make sense," said Flore, "Logically, if the plant was still there, what Tom told us about him finding the plant and everything else after that, couldn't have happened."

Sylvain and Lucia simultaneously answered Flore's observation with just four words:

"The Cosmic Knot Paradox."

## THE END

FOR NOW

# THE COSMIC KNOT PARADOX

Printed in Great Britain
by Amazon